AF245003

Sweet Rafton Jesus!

This is a work of fiction.
Names, characters, organizations, places, events, and incidents are either
products of the author's imagination or are used fictitiously.
Text copyright © 2020 Camilla Monk
All rights reserved.

No part of this book may be reproduced, or stored in a retrieval system, or
transmitted in any form or by any means, electronic, mechanical, photocopying,
recording, or otherwise, without express written permission of the publisher.

Published by Camilla Monk AKA "Yaypub"
Cover design by Camilla Monk
ISBN: 978-1-64316-080-1

ISLAND CHAPTAL & THE ANCIENT ALIENS' TREASURE

SPOTLESS SERIES #5

CAMILLA MONK

TABLE OF CONTENTS

thank
YOU
SO
much
FOR MAKING
THE SPOTLESS
SERIES HAPPEN,
AND FOR THESE
FIVE AMAZING
YEARS.

This book is dedicated to B. who wasn't allowed to read it, and to you, dear reader: you deserve it.

AUTHOR'S NOTE:

All quotes introducing this book's chapters are—thank God—
fictional. Except for the ones that are legit.

OPENING MONOLOGUE

When they met, it was murder!

Opening monologue to *Hart to Hart*,
seasons 2 to 5. ABC, 1979–198

Okay, so it starts kind of like *Hart to Hart*: he's March November, a self-made millionaire and former legendary hitman who now runs Struthio Security, a wholly legitimate business catering to high-end clients in serious trouble—think being in the crosshairs of a Nigerian warlord or wanting to escape the United Arab Emirates by sea. At night. With your wife, your two kids, and their pet gerbil.

Mr. November works with Mrs. Novemb—I mean with Island Chaptal, his girlfriend and partner, who has a classy gap tooth and fluffy auburn curls like Jennifer Hart. She used to be a computer engineer, but a lot of stuff happened, so now she's his CTO and hacks poorly protected devices and fiber-optic cables for him, which kind of sounds like she slept her way to the top. He swears, though, that her technical skills are second to none, that he would have hired her even if they weren't living together, and it has nothing to do with being able to keep an eye on her 24/7 now that she has an office two doors from his. Love is threaded with little white lies, I guess.

Anyway, they don't have a cool butler named Max, but Struthio has an awesome COO named Phyllis—yeah, everyone got to be chief of something when we reprinted the business cards, except Gerald, March's crabby orange tree, who did nothing to deserve a promotion and just keeps popping greenish and misshapen oranges all over the place.

Together, Island Chaptal and Mr. November fight crime.
With crime.

ONE
THE CREPE PARTY

Rica ran to the airport, tears streaming down the perfect oval of her face. Ricardo had betrayed her, shattered their love like a piñata.

–Kerry-Lee Storm, *The Cost of Rica #5: Blaze of the Phoenix*

Coordinate points are somewhere in the middle of the Gulf of Oman. It is one minute past midnight, Friday, September 20, and therefore officially my twenty-seventh birthday. There's no cake though, not even a candle: just me, wearing black coveralls and pacing in the empty belly of a soviet-era Ekranoplan. Other spoiled little girls might inherit real estate and paintings from their rich biological dad. Mine was a flamboyant supervillain and the former leader of a secret brotherhood of assassins. I *did* inherit properties all over the globe after his death—including a tacky chalet in Gstaad with a spinning bed I am never, *ever* having sex in—but I also became the proud owner of a Russian military hydroplane dating back to the eighties. And tonight, it is coming in handy, or so I pray.

We've gone entirely dark to escape detection, and there are no windows in the main cabin. The only source of light in this nearly three-hundred-feet-long steel grotto is my laptop screen, casting a faint glow on cargo nets hanging from the walls and two rows of spartan seats along the hull. I bite my nails, eyes glued to a map of the gulf onscreen. Still no signal, and my earpiece remains obstinately silent. Earlier today, March managed to extract our client and his family—pet gerbil included—from Abu Dhabi to Sur, a port city on the eastern coast of the Sultanate of Oman. Now all that's left for us is to transport them safely to the only democracy in a thousand-mile radius: India.

Theirs is a classic tale of Emirati sponsorship gone wrong: German robotics tycoon comes to the United Arab Emirates with several million in his pockets, hoping to turn them into billions. Local sheik welcomes him with open arms, and, together, they set up a joint venture to build the next generation of fully automated crepe stands operated by cute robots. Crepes prove disappointing despite extensive R&D investments. Business relationship turns sour. Angry sheik—legally—confiscates the entire family's passports and holds everyone hostage in Abu Dhabi until robot is able to cook a halfway decent banana-Nutella-chantilly (double sprinkles). Engineer ultimately hires a man of the shadows to escape this batter-soaked hell before it is too late.

If everything went according to plan, March sabotaged the fuel tanks of the Omani coastguards' patrol boats after sunset, before he picked up our sorry lot of expatriates in a stealth speedboat. He should have contacted me by now. Scratch that: he should *be* here by now. I shoot yet another anxious glance at the Ekranoplan's rear hatch, which remains shut. I trust him more than anyone else, but that does little to ease the nausea roiling in my stomach.

If March gets caught . . . I don't even want to think about it. Everything we're doing tonight is worth, at the very least, a thousand lashes and life without parole. My stare is threatening to burn a hole into my laptop screen, and I have no nails left to bite when a row of lights starts to blink red on the ceiling. Around me, the Ekranoplan comes alive. Metal creaks and shudders under my feet before a low vibration announces that the eight engines sitting on the wings of the Caspian Sea Monster have been turned up. That will *not* do.

I race to the front of the cabin, where a door leads up a flight of grating stairs to the cockpit. There, an old Lion and his bulldog await in the dark, drooling. I mean the dog, not the man.

"What are you doing?" I hiss. "We can't leave now!"

From the copilot's seat, seventy-pound Andrea dismisses me with a gruff bark, proudly flaunting his brown and white folds in a custom-made leather flight jacket designed to match his master's—soccer patches and all. In the pilot's seat, Jan scratches at the ponytail he never seems to comb, looking away from the dashboard's innumerable buttons, gauges, and switches. His lips are a thin line in his craggy blond beard; the blue in his eyes has turned to a steely gray. "It's past midnight," he reminds me, each syllable made harsher by his faint Flemish accent.

"We wait," I insist.

His carbon prosthetic right hand remains on the yoke, while the blunt and callused fingers of his left one resume flipping up a series of switches. "I have my orders, princess."

"From whom? That's *my* Ekranoplan."

All I get in return is a cool, empty smile. Jan is my friend, and he was my father's friend before that, but I fear I'm wasting my time. March told him to leave at midnight, and Jan will do just that, because they once belonged to the same brotherhood, as did Dries, the father I knew all too briefly. They were—and to some extent remain—*Lions*, a twenty-five-century-old secret society of assassins and mercenaries which has thrived in darkness from the birth of the Roman republic to modern-day South Africa. Theirs is a bond forged in blood, and there's too much respect between them to leave room for any pity.

"Give him ten more minutes," I plead, my voice thick with rising panic. "If you try to leave, I'll have to fight you and Andrea, and I really don't wanna have to do that." Especially since I won't last a second against Jan's ham-sized fists.

A thousand creases carve a wince into the bronze leather of his face. "Island . . ."

"I seriously will."

Jan knows I'm not lying. I've been to space and back with March— literally so. I'd do anything for that man. *Anything*. I'm not leaving until he's safely back here with our client and his freaking gerbil.

"Ten minutes tops," Jan concedes in a grunt. "But I shouldn't listen to you."

"He told you to leave with me, no matter what," I guess softly, even as my heart swells and hammers at the confines of my ribcage. Of course, March would plot something like that behind my back. Protective, pathologically controlling: he can be a tender tyrant, sometimes.

Jan's big frame deflates with a sigh, and he's about to reply when Andrea jerks in his seat, as if stung by a bee. Nature never ceases to amaze: that dog realized my phone was buzzing before I even did. Jan and Andrea study me with unabashed curiosity as I plunge a feverish hand in my front pocket. My fingertips meet cool glass framed in aluminum. It makes no sense that March would call me when my earpiece is connected to an ultra-secure radio frequency, but let it be him, *please . . .*

My pulse peaks and crashes back just as fast when the caller ID is revealed. It's Joy, my ex-roommate, part-time wife, and, incidentally, the other love of my life. She knows I'm supposed to be in the UAE on "business"; she wouldn't call if it weren't important. But I just can't pick up right now, when the clock is ticking and I'm sick with worry for March. My cheeks flush with scathing guilt as I swipe to deny the call.

"It's not him," I inform Jan.

He gives a slow nod and turns back to the dashboard. The final ring and the silence that follows bring me no relief, only another wave of insidious shame as I think of all the lies I've told Joy over the past two years. And yet, she's been patient; she's given me space and pretended to buy my bullshit even when the lawyer in her could see right through me.

It's times like these when I wish she knew everything. I could tell her I'm scared and lost at sea far from home, and she'd tell me not to worry because March can assemble an Ikea bookcase and fire eight shots in under a second. He's the best. But life is a little more complicated than that. There's a knot in my throat that simply won't go away as I pocket my phone. It vibrates again. It's a text this time. I should ignore it and focus, but I can't help it. I take a guilty peek.

> I'm at JFK✈, taking off soon. DEFCON 1 W/ Vince.

Oh God, I'm gonna need sweat pads at this rate. Not this. Not now! DEFCON 1 is imminent total nuclear war, a BFF code reserved for exceptional and catastrophic situations. March dumping me like a rag in Tokyo two years ago because he wasn't ready for a relationship was a messy, tear-soaked DEFCON 2. David-the-clown-dick-accountant catching the bouquet and proposing out of the blue at Joy's cousin's wedding a close brush with DEFCON 1—especially when Joy said no in front of two hundred guests, and he sobbed back that she was the only woman he ever wanted children with.

Bits of data flit around and quickly rearrange themselves in my brain. Joy is at the airport, and to the best of my knowledge, current boyfriend and future ex Vince is in Cancún until Monday, where he's doing a promo shoot for SciFi Unlimited. A tactical airstrike targeting him can mean only one thing. My gaze flits back and forth between Jan, Andrea, and the cockpit's door. "I need a second. Yell or bark if there's anything on the radar."

Jan gives me a thumbs-up with his carbon-fiber hand. "Got it."

Darkness swallows me as I slip out of the cockpit and tap a quick reply.

What's the situation? Can't pick up rn. Calling u back ASAP!

I wait for her answer, but what I get is a picture instead, and well, I guess the proper terminology for what is now gracing my screen is a nude. This tan, anonymous body, however, lacks Joy's lush curves, and the pic is cropped right below a landing strip I can categorically say does not belong to her either—Joy's a blonde.

What—or rather, who—am I looking at? The answer to that comes with Joy's second text.

> Bitch's name is Cachemire.
> He's w/ her in Cancún 4 her shitty alien show.
> He's soooooo fucking dead!!!!!!!! 😬 💣 💣

Oh, Raptor Jesus, who sits in the firmament, save us from Armageddon. I'm not entirely sure what aliens have to do with any of this, but one thing is certain: Vince has been caught red-handed again, and this time I fear he did a lot more than just look. The days are long gone when Joy used to call him Vince-The-Cutest-Photographer-in-The-World. Things have been going downhill between them lately. Kinda like Sisyphus's rock, if said rock kept sending Insta-filtered mirror-selfies and dick pics to doe-eyed twenty-year-olds, and Sisyphus pushed the delinquent boulder back up the hill every time anyway. Not sure I'm making much sense, but Joy is basically Sisyphus, and Vince is simultaneously in a committed relationship and active on Tinder.

I throw another glance at the threatening string of emojis onscreen, my thumb poised on the call icon. March is still out there, and we might have to perform an emergency takeoff any moment. I type "*Full debrief needed!*" and hit *send* just before Andrea's frenzied bark whips me back to the present moment. Vince's case will have to wait. I barge back into the cockpit, my pulse bounding from zero to sixty faster than a McLaren.

"Andrea, zwijg!" *Andrea, be quiet!* Jan shouts, effectively silencing the dog with his own powerful roar.

Silence falls again in the cockpit, and we listen. I can feel sweat beading on my temples as I strain my ears to pick up something over Andrea's relentless panting. Seconds tick on an old analog clock on the dashboard. Five. Ten . . . and then I hear it too. Faint crackling sounds, growing closer. Someone is firing automatic rounds, and they're coming our way.

Jan's head snaps up at me, a voracious grin wiping off his frown. "That's him all right."

I barely notice his hand reaching for the rear hatch switch. I'm already scrambling to the back of the Ekranoplan as fast as my legs will allow. There, a dim silvery thread slashes through the penumbra as the hatch whirrs open. Cool air rushes in, and the steel jaws reveal an inky, oily sea lapping at the cargo ramp under a moonless sky. I grab a pair of night binoculars from a compartment on the wall and focus them on the lights growing on the horizon. The blurry greenish smudge becomes a tall, cleaver-shaped prow before I spot an artillery gun on the bridge. This isn't your average coast guard boat. It's an Arialah patrol ship, complete with 30mm automatic guns and a goddamn Mark missile launcher. Apparently, our client's Emirati sponsor is not just pissed about seeing his business partner abscond, he's also powerful enough to summon a military-class ship over a crepe dispute.

The Arialah is now fully visible, the blinding beams of its searchlights swiping at the calm sea in vain. At this rate, it's *us* that they'll detect, and I still can't see March's boat. Yet the Emirati *did* shoot at something, and they're headed straight our way. A dark blot appears in my binoculars, so faint it might be a wave—or a modified stealth powerboat whose draft is so low the cabin windows sit right above the waterline. Oh, God; it's March.

The ship's guns swivel and boom again in the night, barely missing the black arrow tearing ahead of them. Meanwhile, the low hum of the Ekranoplan's engines amps up to a threatening rumble. We're about to take off, and my heart is drumming all over my body, pounding under my skull all the way to the very tips of my fingers. Jan isn't gaining speed yet. He's giving March time to catch up with us. Another ten seconds pass, and I no longer need the binoculars. I toss them on a nearby seat as the razor-thin black hull closes the distance between us, water misting in its wake.

March's boat veers left, dodging another round of fire in a graceful arc to curb its speed—lest he wants to crash into us. He's still coming on too fast, though. The speedboat drifts to a stop and crashes against the cargo ramp, leaving a deep dent in the fiberglass hull. The moment the boat stops moving, I race down the ramp, waddling ankle-deep in seawater. The cockpit doors slide open, vomiting a panicked troupe. I spot the gray hair and rumpled safari jacket of our client, Mr. Rotwang. Huddled at his side, the dark shape of a woman cloaked in an abaya and hijab, gripping the hands of two brown-haired boys—ten and six, according to their file. All are shepherded by a brawny figure towering over them. Black fatigues. Short chestnut hair that would curl if he only let it grow more than an inch. March made it. Amid the chaos and blinding swipes of the Arialah's searchlights haloing him, our eyes meet, and it's enough. It's all I need. I read his reassurance in those dark-blue depths. *We're gonna be okay.* One breath in, one out, and the moment is gone already.

"Jump!" March thunders to the panicked family when gunfire booms again, ever closer.

Mr. Rotwang reacts first, pulling the older boy with him while March tosses the youngest my way like a football. I intercept the wailing bundle of limbs in a catch worthy of an NFL contract and fall back on my butt, all air knocked out of my lungs. The kid in my arms is screaming for his mama, but she won't move. The Ekranoplan's rear hatch is already starting to rise, but she stands paralyzed on the wrecked speedboat's deck, blinking terror-stricken eyes at the approaching patrol ship—like the proverbial deer caught in headlights. March makes the decision for her, shoving her overboard and into her husband's waiting arms, before sliding down the cargo ramp in the nick of time.

A residual pool of water makes my coveralls stick to my back, and there's something small and incredibly loud fighting my hold as the hatch clanks shut. But everyone's safe. Both the patrol ship and speedboat have now disappeared behind a steel wall several inches thick. I scan my surroundings for March. He's kneeling a few feet away and cradling a pink pet shuttle. I grin in absurd relief; Frederick the gerbil has been successfully extracted from Abu Dhabi.

"Everyone, seat belt on!" March orders as the Ekranoplan stirs at last.

The Emirati are in for the shock of their life when this marvel takes off. I carry the youngest brother to the row of seats lined up against the wall. His big brown eyes widen in fear when he starts to feel the acceleration. The eight turbojets sitting on the craft's short wings roar to full speed above our heads, making the entire cabin rattle. He tries to reach for his father in the seat next to his while I tighten his seat belt. "Papa, werden wir sterben?" *Daddy, are we gonna die?*

March, whose German was always vastly superior to mine, winks at the boy, his expression softening a fraction. "Nein. Dies ist das schnellste Schiff der Welt. In weniger als zwei Stunden sind Sie in Indien." *No. This is the fastest ship in the world. In less than two hours, you'll be in India.*

His brother holds on tight to the thick shoulder straps of his seat belt. "Aber ist das nicht ein Flugzeug?" *But is it not a plane?*

"Weder noch. Das hier ist das Kaspische Seeungeheuer," his father breathes, a trembling smile carving deep lines around his mouth. *Neither. This is the Caspian Sea Monster.*

My lips twitch in response, and my heart goes out to this stranger, this fellow engineer who recognizes two hundred and thirty thousand pounds of thrust when he feels it. I barely have the time to jump in my own seat at March's side before I feel my insides smash against my spine. Jan is hitting the gas hard, and I can't begin to imagine the coast guards' faces while their ship is being whipped and tossed around by the tons of water we're lifting in our wake.

The initial acceleration recedes; at last, I release an exhausted breath. We're gliding thirty feet above the water and under radar detection at over three hundred miles per hour. March lets go of Frederick's shuttle at last and discreetly produces a tiny bottle from his pocket—hand sanitizer, because he made prolonged contact with Frederick's cage, which is full of gerbil germs, poop, and innumerable microorganisms that March must be mentally picturing as he rubs the pads of his fingers insistently. It's his cross to bear: March has been suffering from OCD since adolescence, and while it's gotten better over the past few years and he tries hard to keep it in check most of the time, some triggers simply cannot be ignored—the faint smell of urine surrounding Frederick's pet shuttle being one of those.

Now properly decontaminated, his hand sneaks to graze mine between our seats—he wouldn't indulge in anything more in front of our clients. Our fingertips seek each other in a practiced dance, sparking warmth and electricity everywhere our skin touches. My gaze lingers on his profile: the strong jaw and the aquiline nose I love to kiss, thin lips that rarely smile in public but grin when it's just the two of us. Every line and every crow's foot. Him.

According to my tablet, I've read 2,811 romance books since I open the first one at the age of eighteen—*Slave to The Rich and Sexy Vampire*, memorable sex scene inside a coffin, by the way. None of them prepared me for March, for a happy ending of my own, and the simple certainty that I'm not alone: somewhere on earth, there was a soulmate for me, a man who reads Wikipedia a lot too and doesn't need big words to connect with me. How strange to think that against killer platypuses, supervillains, and every imaginable odd, we found our way to each other.

"Happy birthday, biscuit," he murmurs with that faint British accent he inherited from his father. A better aphrodisiac than Nutella, in my humble opinion.

"What happened? You were late." He knows there's no bite to the question, only the lingering terror of losing him.

"I'm sorry. We ran into some trouble at the Omani border."

I glance at Rotwang, who's busy cooing reassurances to his shell-shocked family. "Did you have to . . . ?" I whisper.

No need to elaborate. My former hitman boyfriend knows exactly what I'm asking. He flashes me a penitent smile as we undo our seat belt and move together toward the cockpit. "No. There were a few scratches, but nothing—"

I slant him a suspicious look. "*Scratches?*"

He clears his throat. "Possibly a few broken bones. Someone crashed a cargo full of watermelons into a control post." When my face starts to pinch, he quickly confesses. "And that someone planted a fragmentation grenade among the crates. I never suspected a flying cucurbit might have such tremendous stopping power."

"Oh my God . . ."

"That's what they all scream," a husky voice remarks as March opens the door to the cockpit.

I glower at Jan, whose hands are barely grazing the yoke while in the copilot's seat, Andrea is munching on what appears to be potato chips, judging by the crumbs clinging to the worn fleece cover he rests on. March's nostrils flare in silent disapproval.

"Will they try to follow us?" I ask Jan.

He shrugs and motions at the cloudy night bleeding into the black line of the horizon ahead. "We'll reach Gujarat long before those guys back there can call for backup. They probably don't even know what they saw."

"What about the Emirati air force? The Indian navy?" I counter.

March bends to me, his warm chuckle raising a trail of pleasurable goosebumps down my nape. "Valuable as he may be to his sponsor,

Mr. Rotwang is no royal princess. I doubt either the UAE or India will get their F-16 off the ground tonight. Not over crepes."

Too true. To the best of my recollection, the last time the UAE and India went through the trouble of a joint operation in international waters, the unfortunate fugitive was the daughter of the prime minister of the UAE himself. *That* was worth an aerial reconnaissance, two warships, and at least fifteen commandos, all of which easily caught up with the princess's chosen means of escape— a sailing yacht that couldn't have cruised at over seven knots. She hasn't been allowed in public on her own since . . .

The Ekranoplan is fifty times faster than that, I remind myself— my father never did things by half. Tension fizzles away in my limbs, and I could almost believe it's over, until a high-pitched scream bursts from the other side of the cockpit door. "Frederick! Frederick!"

Jan watches over his shoulder as March and I rush back to the cabin. The two boys are huddled around the pink pet shuttle March placed on one of the seats earlier, their chubby faces struck with horror. Mrs. Rotwang kneels between her boys and exchanges a saddened glance with her husband. I sit down and hunch over the shuttle to take my first good look at our tiniest passenger. Oh, crap. I don't think it's supposed to lie on its back with its tail all limp and its legs sticking straight up like that . . .

TWO

INTENSIVE CARE

"You and I are spinning around, Cheyenne.
Love is a wheel you can't escape."

—Crystal Viper, *Undercover Shifters #2: Bite of the Billionaire Gerbil*

Maybe it was the acceleration during takeoff. Or the boat chase with the coast guards. In any case, Frederick didn't make it.

Fat tears immediately build in the boys' reddened eyes. "Frederick ist tot!" sobs the youngest. *Frederick is dead!*

His brother remains quiet, but he swallows over and over, his jaw tight from the effort not to bawl in unison.

March clears his throat and darts a look at me. "Perhaps we can check . . ."

We, in this particular case, means *me*, since March only just cleaned his hands, and I don't miss the way his fingertips twitch at the prospect of picking up Frederick. So, I delicately extract the lifeless rodent from its shuttle and bring it closer to my ear, listening for a heartbeat while March wears his best poker face for the sake of his audience.

I glance up at him; his brow furrows in response as he reads the silent message in my eyes: there's no pulse. I never knew Frederick, and I don't particularly like gerbils, but the sight of his closed eyelids and the quiet sobs of the boys make my chest ache in response. I press my forefinger gently to the soft, tiny stomach. It's still warm; Frederick can't have died long ago.

"Let me try something," I mumble, feeling the pressure of everyone's gaze on me. Now I know exactly what it's like to be a doctor in the ER with family members watching as you try to save your patient.

Frederick's body is still lax as I pry open his mouth with infinite care, but it's not easy doing that with only my right hand as the left one serves as Frederick's ER stretcher; I could use a third hand to hold his head in position.

March leans closer. His throat bobs, before he says, "I'll assist you."

Leveling wide eyes at him, I whisper, "Are you sure?"

There's the slightest twitch of his eyelid as he considers Frederick's small body and replies, "Yes."

He'll never know what this single act of valor means to me. I've seen March readily engage in car chases, boat chases, gunfights, or even bloody, bare-knuckled brawls, but he's never been braver in my eyes than right now, steeling his nerves with a slow intake of air as I transfer Frederick onto his upturned palm.

Once our patient in place, I bend down and seal my puckered lips over his, mentally doing some quick math. The average weight of a gerbil is fifty to sixty grams, roughly the same as the hamster I owned for three weeks when I was eight until it escaped its cage and presumably went to forge its own destiny in the streets of Shanghai.

I cried for days until my mom pretended she had seen him in Huangpu Park, where he had a burrow and a girlfriend now. Anyway, if we extrapolate Frederick's biology from that of Don Salluste—that was my hamster's name—we can estimate Frederick's Total Lung Capacity (TLC) at two point five milliliters, to be compared to the average human TLC of . . . six liters.

What I'm saying is anything more than a breeze will blow up my patient's ridiculously small pulmonary alveolae. Think of an elephant farting in the tiniest balloon in the world. I allow a tentative puff to filter through my lips, but dammit, he's so small and fragile that I scarcely dare to exhale at all. I alternate with quick taps on his chest with trembling fingers—I read about that technique in a blog post about avian CPR. Five breaths, ten compressions. Come on, Frederick. Don't give up so close to the finish line. You're probably the first gerbil in history to escape the UAE!

March's palm remains perfectly still through it all, but I can feel his breath on my cheek, just a little faster than it should be. He's rooting for Frederick, too, I can tell. I'm about to give up and call the time of death when something tickles my cheek. Frederick's leg just *twitched.* Two boyish squeals confirm that it's not just my fertile imagination at work. He is risen from the dead! There's more leg kicking against my lips as Frederick regains consciousness and attempts to fight me off. Fire up some epic music in the background: Raptor Jesus and Island Chaptal just performed a miracle!

Meanwhile, Frederick's eyes remain half-closed, but he has unquestionably crossed the Styx back. My eyebrows pinch when I notice a tiny brown speck peeking under his tail. By the time I figure out what's happening, it's too late already: Frederick celebrates his return to life by excreting a single, squishy dropping.

In. March's. *Bare.* Palm.

The kids giggle innocently because pet diarrhea is always funny when you're six, even when you just brushed death. Their parents smile and shake their heads. None of them pays attention to the sudden rigidity in March's posture or the way his throat works silently as he looks straight ahead, his eyes refusing to acknowledge the fecal matter in his hand. I wish I could laugh, too, but I know March isn't okay. I can tell he's already picturing the millions of bacteria transferring to his skin. He's thinking they'll slip through his pores and contaminate him no matter how many times he washes his hand. There's no point in rationalizing, in trying to wrestle his sudden whirlpool of obsessive thoughts back under control. Only a thorough cleaning ritual will relieve him.

"Here," I say quietly, reaching in my front pocket for a small foil packet. Since moving in with March, I've taken to always carrying mini sanitizing wet wipes with me, just like he does.

His jaw clenched so tight I can make out the contraction of his masseters under the skin, March holds out his hand for Mrs. Rotwang to pick up Frederick's quivering body. She smiles down at the little rodent like a benevolent goddess, allowing her sons to caress it shyly. Meanwhile, March has taken my proffered wipe and carefully removed the dropping. He wraps it several times in the soiled wipe. Ignoring the Rotwangs' curious side-eyes, he spins on his heels and heads straight to the Ekranoplan's only lavatory with a muttered, "If you'll excuse me."

I follow him and lean against the wall outside, listening to the sound of water running behind the door, punctuated by telltale splashing. Once, twice, thrice. A bare minimum considering the severity of Frederick's offense. Dammit, I feel so powerless when his OCD takes over and sends him into a tailspin like that. All I can do is sanitize my own hands and lips in solidarity with the remaining wipe: I know the chemical scent will comfort him.

When March comes out after several minutes, he's regained his near-unflappable cool. There's no discernible expression on his features as he motions for me to follow him into the small cabin adjacent to the lavatory. "Miss Chaptal. A word with you if you please."

I don't take offense at the douchebag CEO vibe he exudes in that precise moment. I know he likes to maintain that sort of artificial distance when we're working. I trot after him into the Ekranoplan's only proper sleeping quarter—a tin box with a single window and a narrow cot. Droplets of surf trail across the glass on the other side of the window while March turns to lock the door. At last, we're alone, bathed in the dim glow of a single LED lamp on the ceiling.

March's shoulders slump in a weary exhale. "Biscuit, I'm sorry, I . . ."

"It's okay," I console him. "I'd have freaked out too."

"No. You'd have laughed." There's no reproach in his voice, rather quiet amusement. He knows me too well.

I huddle closer, needing his warmth. My eyes close when his arm reaches around my waist to bring me flush against him. "Don't worry, I cleaned up too," I tell him, before reaching on tiptoe to wrap my arms around his neck.

His head dips: he trusts me without question. March accepts me, gerbil germs and all. Our noses brush tenderly, and our lips part in feverish anticipation. Then it's only the firm curve of his cupid's bow, the sweet tang of mints—he must have munched through his entire tube to calm his nerves when his carefully timed schedule went off the rails earlier. Our mouths press together with deliciously wet noises; I'm desperate for one more taste, one more stroke of his tongue against mine.

When we finally break the kiss, I whisper, "I love you." It's nothing new, but I need to get it out once more, as if my heart might burst if I keep the words in.

"I love you too," he breathes back, before marking a pause. "Island."

"What is it?"

His jaw works silently for a couple seconds, and there's a sudden solemnity in his eyes as he says, "I do have a gift for you. For your birthday."

I shake my head with a smile. "It's okay, I can imagine now's not the best time—"

"It isn't," he confirms, perhaps a little stiffly. "But once we've escorted Rotwang and his family back to Berlin . . ." His voice lowers to a promising purr as he slowly maneuvers my body backward and my calves hit the cot's mattress. "We'll have the rest of the weekend to ourselves."

Oh, yes. I can already picture myself stretched out on super soft sheets in an old European palace, writhing in delight while March catalogs—and kisses—every single mole peppering my body. It's 139, by the way. We've played that game before, and my dermatologist counted, too, because skin cancer.

I'm sold. I shall spend my entire weekend curled in March's arms and squatting his glorious chest hair like a skin mite. But before that . . . "I need a moment to check my messages. Joy texted me earlier, and she wasn't doing great. I think Vince cheated on her with a girl in Cancún."

"Dire news. How many emojis?" March inquires, having become familiar with Joy's quirks over the past months.

"A lot. Also, she was at JFK, and she said she was about to take off. I'm really worried about that part."

He raises an eyebrow at this. "She flew to Mexico to confront him?"

I give an emphatic nod. "He doesn't know it yet, but he's loaded on a Mexican rail gun."

March's eyes take on an icy glint, and there's not a trace of sorrow to be found in his voice as he says, "How unfortunate. Mr. Moravia will be dearly missed."

No, he won't: I can't really expect March to sympathize with a guy who's dubbed him "Alfred" and consistently refuses to wear his mandatory guest slippers in our apartment. As if that wasn't bad enough, Vince—or rather, "Mr. Moravia"— tried to tamper at the deck last time we invited him over for Uno night. Unforgivable. March spent the entire evening staring back and forth between the cards and Vince's feet leaving sweaty prints on the floor, and we had to mop every square inch of the living room afterward. Twice. As a result, Vince's name now sits precariously close to the top of March's hit list.

Secret satisfaction exudes from his every pore as he kisses my forehead. "Very well, Miss Chaptal. I'll go watch over our ungrateful little patient while you monitor the crisis."

"Thank you. I won't be long."

Okay, it's bad. I'd better stock up on a few pints of Chocolate Fudge Brownie B&J when I get back to New York, because the next few weeks are going to be tough. No words could convey the extent of my outrage as I scroll once more through the text novel Joy sent me before boarding.

It goes like this: Cachemire Fazali is a twenty-four-year-old assistant producer for SciFi Unlimited, and Vince is doing a photoshoot on the set of some show she's working on in Cancún. Joy's vibrissae started tingling a few days ago after running into her at a party. Maybe it was the heated look Vince flashed Cachemire, or because she seemed to purposely avoid his gaze in return. One thing is certain, the new girl has perky breasts, she's a brunette, and her pics are all over Vince's iCloud, which Joy hacked last night—and in so became the paranoid girlfriend *GQ* columnists warn you against.

No need to remind her that that part was illegal; she knows it already. As an associate lawyer in a firm that does mostly family law and civil litigation, Joy's days are spent advising cheated parties *not* to hack their spouses' phone. Anyway, after five sleepless hours and an entire morning spent mulling over her options instead of working on her cases, she took the rest of her Friday off, jumped in an Uber, and raced to JFK. There, she bought two bags of M&M's, a cool neck pillow that's shaped like a hotdog, and a ticket to Cancún, where she plans to stage the mother of all breakups.

Hopefully, Vince will choose his security questions more carefully in the future if he survives this.

There's a dull ache in my heart as I read her last message. *He's fucking her. I know he is. I should have cut my losses much earlier, but here we are. I just couldn't accept I had wasted two years on a terminal douche. This time it's over.*

Water is still relentlessly whipping the Ekranoplan's window as we tear toward India in the deep of the night. *It's over.* Just three little words to draw the curtain over two years of emotional acrobatics through turquoise skies and tar-black storms, browsing boho wedding blogs one day, putting together achy-breaky cheating playlists the next. Even though I never liked Vince much—and the feeling was mutual—it feels weird to realize that he's history already.

That things start and end.

I can't help but think of March. Could he ever . . . ? *No.* He'd dump me if he met someone else; he's just too single-minded, too rigid to ever juggle two girls. As if a secret switch flipped up in his brain every time I think of him, I register a soft rap at the door, and, sure enough, March's voice. "Island?"

"Come in."

"We'll rendezvous off the coast of Porbandar in less than an hour. The yacht is there already. Is everything all right?"

I tuck my phone back in my pocket and rise from the cot. "Yeah. It's just . . . a huge mess. He cheated on her, and he kept nudes of the other girl all over his iCloud. Joy found them, and you can imagine how that went down. I hope I can reach her when she lands in Cancún. She's too angry to think straight right now. I don't like this."

March's features freeze into a solemn mask as he verbalizes my worst fear. "Well, I suppose there won't be much left of Yucatan after that breakup."

THREE
THE CAKE PLATE

He swiped his hungry gaze over her golden-brown buns and licked his lips: he couldn't wait to get himself covered in her sweet cream.

–Terry Robs, *Glazed by the Cook #5: Dulce de Leche*

Jan knows a guy who knows some guys in Andaman and Nicobar, a smattering of some five hundred pin-sized islands sprinkled along the seam between the Bay of Bengal and the Andaman sea. He's confident he can hide the Ekranoplan there for a few months because—quoting him—"It's like Tajikistan . . . who the hell even knows where that is?" He should have refueled off the coast of Sri Lanka by now—God knows how he found someone willing to sell him forty thousand gallons of kerosene and look the other way, but he did.

And so, the job is done.

We took off from Porbandar airport five hours ago, exhausted but alive, just before dawn. If no one shoots the plane down above Ukraine, we'll touch ground in Berlin in less than three hours. Standing in the galley of a Paulie Airlines Embraer, March and I are watching the Rotwang family doze, the parents cuddling side by side in their seats while the boys have elected to sleep on the sofa—next to Frederick's shuttle, of course. He looks fine now, by the way. We gave him a handful of Wow Encore! Gourmet Rodent Pellets, which he's happily nibbling on, along with his own poop.

"What a vile little creature," March notes, the faint smile on his lips belying his harsh assessment as he brings a cup of espresso to his lips.

"I prefer to think of him as an Epicurean," I tease, moving closer to rest my head against his arm. Warm muscles cushion my cheek under the fabric of his shirt. We were able to change before boarding, and he's back to his eternal uniform: navy jeans, impeccably pressed white shirt, and since we're working, a holster.

March raises a single eyebrow at the shuttle and toasts it with his espresso. "A modern Diogenes, rather."

I clasp a hand over my mouth to stifle a giggle while he sets the now-empty cup on the counter. His arms encircle me, stroking my back through the worn cotton of my navy hoodie. With every slow glide of his palm, I forget the relentless hum of air rushing along the fuselage, the rustle of Frederick burrowing in his litter. March and I are looking into each other's eyes, like when we fight or when we make love. Like during our very first date in Tokyo.

"Are you happy?" he asks quietly.

I tilt my head at him, unsure whether this is about our daring escape, my upcoming birthday weekend, or maybe some bigger philosophical question. A crease appears on his forehead as he tries to gauge my reaction. I get it; he means now. In this new life, at Struthio Security, with him. I can't stop the grin splitting my face. "Yes. Of course, yes . . . What about you? I'm always scared you'll get bored eventually. I mean, it's not always routine—obviously—but there's also paperwork, crappy meetings with guys who think it's a good idea to deal crude in Yemen right now."

March retired from his former career as a hitman to open Struthio a year and a half ago. It was his decision, taken during the months we spent apart after we met. But I know he ultimately did it for me, so we might have a chance at an almost normal life together: it makes me feel responsible for his happiness, the same way he feels responsible for mine, I guess.

"Reckless oil magnates will make excellent clients once they decide to ignore my recommendations," he replies, his hand rising to comb back auburn curls from my cheek. "But to answer your question, I don't think I've ever been happier. I . . ." His tongue darts to lick his lips. He's looking for his words. "I like going to bed every night knowing I'll wake up at your side in the morning."

March doesn't open up often—at the moment, it could be a lingering effect of the night's rush of adrenaline—but dammit, whenever he does, I can feel myself glowing from the inside out, warm and fuzzy all over. I lean forward, losing myself in the dark waters I know so well. "It's the same for me, and actually I try to keep at least half of my thoughts about you to myself because otherwise, I'm worried you'll think I'm a walking, breathing overly attached girlfriend who's plotting to poke holes in your condoms and customized her video game characters to look like us." When his brow slowly rises, I blurt, "The condom thing was a terrible joke, and I never thought of doing that."

March's lips purse until they all but disappear in an effort to conceal a quivering smile. "I have absolute trust in you."

I'm red. I can tell I am; my ears feel on fire. Did I seriously go there? It's not like I even want kids right away. I do think about it, I guess, in the hazy way of a girl who's been in a committed relationship for almost a year, and who sometimes tries to peer through the fog ahead and get a glimpse of what the future might hold. However, I usually keep my musings to myself, precisely to avoid that kind of Freudian slip. March is seven years older than me—more than old enough to become a father—but he's never broached the topic until now, and that wasn't how I imagined we'd discuss the possibility of passing on our genes to a litter of mini-mes . . .

March's gaze hasn't left me, but his previous amusement has given way to a thoughtful expression. "Have you ever given serious thought to the subject?"

I honestly didn't think he'd pull that particular thread. My cheeks blazing, I scramble for a coherent answer that will convey neither outright dismissal nor creepy eagerness, but the rational take of a mature, well-adjusted young woman on the topic of motherhood. "I don't know. I've investigated it, but all I could realistically picture was the chestburster in Alien."

He blinks once, twice. "Well, I hadn't considered childbirth under that angle." A wrinkle appears between his eyebrows, that only fuels my emotional turmoil. I said the wrong thing. I think I've upset him and now he's seeing the chestburster too.

"But kids are . . . good," I blurt. "I mean, I want to have them at some point, just not tomorrow, I guess. And if *something* happens, I'll manage. I won't let them starve or swallow LEGOs or anything like that. And I'll kid-proof my outlets."

His lips stir. Scratch that, his whole face lights up for a second before his self-contained mask falls back in place. "I'm certain you will. In any case, I want to reassure you that I have a contingency plan ready to address any unforeseen development on that front."

Rotwang rises from his seat and lumbers to the lavatory, but I barely notice him. My eyes are set on March's unblinking ones. *Does he mean . . . ?* "What's in the plan?"

"I'm afraid it's highly classified."

Wait, what? He put together a secret contingency plan in case I get pregnant—which admittedly sounds like him—and my security clearance isn't high enough to know what's in it? "Aw, come on! You can't just drop a bomb like that and prance off!" Throwing apprehensive glances left and right, I ask, "Is it in a PowerPoint?"

"Yes. Fifty-three slides," he confirms in the same secretive tone.

"Show it to me!" I whisper-shout, glancing at the kids over my shoulder.

All I get for my efforts is a stern look. "In due time." But the glint in his eyes doesn't lie. He's loving watching me squirm on white-hot coals. Steering me back toward our seats, he asks, "Speaking of emergency, any update from Joy?"

Dammit, he knows me too well, and his distraction tactic works to perfection. I plop myself in the seat across from his and immediately grab my phone. The last update Joy sent me was a live review of AA's chocolate chip cookies at 6:22 pm local time of arrival, shortly before landing—overall great and just the perfect amount of chewy. Nothing since. She's on voicemail, and it's almost 10:30 in Cancún.

A nagging feeling I'd set aside creeps back up my nape. "She's gone silent," I tell March. "Logically, someone should be swiping off Vince's ashes from the floor by now."

I punch at the screen with my thumb to try another vid call. No answer.

March's eyes meet mine, reading the worry simmering there. "I can think of a thousand reasons why she'd need some time alone . . ."

"Yeah, but it's not like her. Normally, she'd have sent me a complete report by now. Joy isn't the type to bawl in a dark corner and go all emo under her blanket fort. That's *me.*"

"Quite true. I thought you'd never recover from the ending of *Logan*," he recalls.

I smile, but my gaze lingers on my phone's notifications screen. "I don't know. I have a bad feeling about this. Do you think it's creepy if I ping her phone?"

King of control fairies March delivers his verdict without so much as a blink. "Of course not."

Having received the simultaneous blessing of my partner, my

boyfriend, and Struthio's entire chain of command, I raise my phone and bring it a few inches from my face, allowing the iris scan to unlock what I like to call "the dungeon": a suite of obscenely expensive software covering all our illegal needs, from advanced geolocation to access to police databases worldwide.

It feels strange to type in Joy's number, as if I were crossing an unspoken boundary. Over the past year, I've acquired all sorts of skills and equipment that could technically allow me to unearth every last secret of my friends and relatives. Take Vince: I could have found out whether he was cheating much faster than Joy did, but the idea never crossed my mind. I was compartmentalizing, I guess—at least until now.

March leans to peer over my shoulder as the onscreen map zooms in on a pin in the city center, less than a mile away from the shores of Nichupté lagoon. My first thought is that maybe the pin appears to sit in the wrong place because of the zoom level. So, I pinch some more. And more, until I no longer can, and the pin is still sitting in the same place. I can feel the corners of my mouth tugging down. "Her phone is in the Sector 5 police station."

"Do you believe this could be an error?" March asks.

"No. Not in Cancún anyway; there are cell phone towers everywhere for the signal to bounce on. Actually . . ." I load the signal data; blinking green dots pop up all over the map. "There's a tower less than five meters from the station. It doesn't get more precise than that."

He strokes his chin. "Didn't you say she flew there to kill Vince?"

"I didn't mean it like that!" She wouldn't? *Would she?* I massage my temples to soothe the painful drumming there. "Okay, okay . . . I'm calling Vince."

"I doubt he'll be pleased to hear from you, but I agree that it's the next logical step," March concurs, and already there's something a little cold, mechanical to his voice. His mind is switching back to work mode. He compartmentalizes much better than I do, though, and I mean that in the literal sense: he gets up and starts pulling a sliding mahogany door that serves to partition the cabin. "I'll stay with the Rotwangs and give you some privacy," he whispers.

"Thank you . . . I'm *so* sorry," I mouth back, even as I punch Vince's number on my phone and turn on the speaker. One ring, two, three. With every second that passes, I can feel myself become jittery as I mentally rehearse crappy opening lines. At the seventh ring, I'm starting to fear she actually killed him, and his phone is ringing in a dark Cancún alley while he bleeds to death from a fatal testicular wound . . . but the chime is cut short and replaced by a tired male voice.

"Vince here. I was trying to decide if I should call you or her parents. Let's get this shit over with."

"What do you mean? What's going on?"

"I'm in Cancún; she showed up tonight."

"I know. She texted me this afternoon. And I know *why* she flew there." I can feel my nostrils flare as I stress this particular point.

"That's none of your business. I'm not going there with you, Island."

"Fine, I don't care!" I hiss, struggling to keep my voice low. "I've been trying to reach her, but she's gone silent and her phone pings inside a police station."

There's a bitter snort before he says, "You bet it does. She got her ass bagged."

I picture again the pin sitting right on top of the police station on the map, and I so wish I heard that wrong. "I'm sorry, *what*?"

"Joy got arrested here, in Cancún." He marks a pause and seems to check something. "They're keeping her at . . ."

"Sector 5 police station, on Calle Acanceh," I complete.

"Yeah." He sounds a little surprised. "Why did you even need to call me?"

If I grip my phone any tighter, my phalanges are going to snap. "Because I have no idea what the hell happened!"

On the other end of the line Vince, too, sounds shaken. "She tried to fucking kill me with a birthday cake. She missed, but she hit . . . a friend."

"Oh, you mean *Cachemire?*"

"Yes. I was with her at a restaurant. Joy barged in, and she lost her shit."

I draw a slow breath to steady my voice and clear my head. "How bad is it?"

"I'm at the hospital right now. The cake plate broke, and Cachemire's got, like, five stitches on her forehead!"

I hold my breath, unsure whether to give in to relief or renewed alarm. The good: Joy spared Vince's miserable life. The bad: she committed assault with a creamy weapon against his side-chick and got a taste of Mexican Law as a result.

There's a tense pause on the other end of the line, before Vince shouts, "I'm done with that shit! I know I fucked up, okay? But she's *mental.* You wanna hear the best part of this freak show? The cops actually told her she could get out now if she paid them a few hundred bucks. But she had to get on her big lawyer horse in broken Spanish. Good for her. They said she's in there for at least a week with hookers and coke mules!"

This is a complete disaster, and all I manage to stutter is, "But, can't she call another lawyer . . . someone?"

"She told the cops that they have to notify the US consulate or something, but I don't think they're gonna be in any hurry to make that phone call after she tried to bite them."

Indeed. I've never been thrown into a Mexican jail by corrupt cops, and I don't have a law degree either, but even I know that offense isn't always the best defense. A prickling sensation in my cheeks informs me that I'm blanching. "Okay, can you—"

"No, I can't. I told you, I'm done. She's your problem now," he barks before hanging up on me.

Of all Joy's past boyfriends, I'm probably going to miss Vince the least—although it might be a photo finish between him and Clown-dick.

FOUR
THE WILD CARD

The moment Fabio Sanchez laid his eyes on the milky curves barely covered by her torn dress, he knew only the blistering pulse in his aching morcilla. He would have her, no matter what it took or cost.

–Kerry-Lee Storm, *The Cost of Rica #5: Blaze of the Phoenix*

"I expected no less from a man who cheats at Uno," March decrees after I conclude my hushed recap of the phone call. We have three hours of flight left with our clients. I don't want them to overhear the words 'prison' or 'police' and freak out all over again. They've been through enough as it is.

March fishes a promotional mint tin box from his jeans pocket and gobbles a few. We had them printed with Struthio's ostrich logo—March's favorite animal—and clients love them. "Should we call her parents?"

"No, she wouldn't want to get her parents involved unless there's no other choice." At least Vince had that right if nothing else. Sitting in a musty cell with moderately hardened criminals, Joy's probably feeling millimeters away from rock bottom at the moment, and I know she'll want no one's help but mine—a matter of public standing.

Because, to her 73,951 Instagram followers and 1,267 Tinder matches, Joy Richards is *that* girl: a young hot New York family lawyer who always manages to charm her way into the hippest rooftop parties, a notorious femme fatale who's never known a bad hair day or a messy breakup, and who slept with at least one confirmed male model. That's side A, and as Joy's part-time wife, I am one of the select few people privy to side B of this glittery vinyl, where the worst tracks are kept hidden. I won't go into the grisly details of those. Side B is basically a medley of radioactive past relationships, dizzying highs and crushing lows, avant-garde sexual experiments and HPV scares. Also, for the record, she secretly borrows my mafia romances.

Like March, Joy needs her armor and her secrets; they keep her together. There's nothing I can do about Vince's betrayal, but what I *can* and *will* do is help contain the Cancún fiasco and make sure it stays buried under a ten-ton concrete lid with the rest of the nuclear waste. "Okay, I'm gonna look up the consulate's number."

"I doubt anyone will pick up at this hour," March warns me gently. "And they won't move unless charges are pressed or it's a life-and-death situation."

A quick check on the web confirms his gloomy prediction. At almost 11 pm, we're well past office hours. "But she's in *jail*! What if they beat her up or something?"

I'm close to hyperventilating as my brain conjures up a grim scene in which a burly and sweaty cop with an evil mustache taunts Joy until she insults him again, only for him to retaliate with his fists. "It'll take me at least thirteen hours to get there, even if I catch another flight right away in Berlin. What if I call the police station and wire them their bribe?"

March has the good grace to wince. "Island, I believe they favor cash."

"Western Union, then?"

His head lolls in hesitation. "How about a direct intervention?"

A direct intervention? I shrink warily in my seat. "How direct?"

March's chuckle reassures me to some extent. Whatever option he's been contemplating can't be that bad if he retains the ability to smile. "Well, I was thinking that . . ." He frowns. "We could give a call to Antonio. I believe he has the connections to solve this misunderstanding even faster than I can."

I perform a silent fist pump and whisper, "Oh my God, you're right!"

Antonio Romos lives in Mexico—a little all over Mexico, technically, since I know he has a house in San Pancho, near Puerto Vallarta, he also told us his *cuñado*—or rather, brother-in-law—has this massive villa in Cancún where he sometimes stays. Also, he's . . . Well, let's just say the first time I met Antonio, he was in March's trunk, bound, gagged, and scheduled for execution. But he turned out to be a great guy. If I hadn't begged March to let him go, he wouldn't have later returned to save the day with a bazooka.

We saw him with his wife and baby girl when they made a stop in New York back in June, and from what I gathered, he's cleaned up his act a notch. He's now helping the *cuñado* with the family business. We were having a great time over margaritas, so I chose not to spoil the mood and remark that Angel, the aforementioned brother-in-law, is, in fact, an Ecuadorian arms dealer. March claims that 80 percent of his international business is "locally legal," though.

At any rate, I vote Antonio. "Let's call him."

March borrows my phone, and I watch him dial one of Antonio's many numbers, gnashing my teeth tighter with every ring. The moment Antonio picks up, Latino rap blares through the speaker, and he's yelling over the music to greet March.

"Still alive, *Surafricano!*"

"Against all odds," March confirms.

"What's up in New York?" Antonio shouts back, while a young, feminine voice squeals, "Es March?" His wife, Beatriz, and that's a hell of a party around them.

"Yes," March replies to her. "Antonio, we're not in New York, and I'm afraid I'm going to owe you another favor."

"Nothing is impossible for Antonio," comes his reply. Yeah, he's sometimes prone to hubris and loves referring to himself in third person.

"Like getting someone out of jail?" I whisper, eyeing our clients for any sign that they're awake. Thank God, Rotwang has returned to snore in his seat. Frederick is still burrowing with stark dedication, though.

A big laugh bursts in the speaker. "Anything for you, *queridita!*" The moment after, the music in the background dies down, and I register brisk footsteps echoing on a tiled floor. He's leaving the party, and when he speaks again, there's a steely edge to his cheerful tone. "Now, tell me, what kind of shit did you two get yourselves into this time?"

"It's my friend Joy," I explain. "She got arrested in Cancún because she tossed a cake on her ex and his side-chick. She wouldn't grease up the cops, so they won't release her. Do you think you could pull some strings to get her out?"

There's prolonged silence on Antonio's end. I ball my fists, bracing myself for his response. What I get is ten seconds of breathless laughter. March and I share an awkward look and wait for him to be done. He eventually coughs out the last of his hilarity. "No *refresco* for her, uh? Oh man, this is gonna be good. Don't worry about a thing: Antonio is in charge. You let me work my magic, and she's out in sixty minutes tops."

I'm practically jumping in my seat. "Thank you so much! Can you keep us updated?"

"Yes, yes . . ."

I'm about to thank him and hang up when a horrifying thought thunders at the back of my head. "Antonio, one more thing."

"Listening."

"Joy doesn't know. About March and . . . everything."

Pretty vague, but I'm confident Antonio will catch my drift. Joy has no idea what March did before he opened Struthio, and I've remained carefully evasive every time she asked until now. I think her perception is that he's a PI occasionally flirting with the boundaries of the law, possibly even a former spy—a man of the shadows, but not totally because he has a Costco card, and we have a legit office. Like Dog the Bounty Hunter but with better hair and no TV show. Not like him at all, actually.

As if he could hear my thoughts, Antonio gives a gentle chuckle. "Relax, we're all good citizens. No guns, no trouble."

"Thank you . . ."

"No problem. Antonio's got your back, *queridita.*"

In the background, I register Beatriz's frantic whispering in Spanish—presumably inquiring about our conversation. I can't catch the first half of Antonio's reply, but in between muffled snickers, I distinctly hear him tell her, "*Tú vas a amar esto . . .*" You're gonna love this. They sound almost too excited, and I'm starting to entertain doubts about our plan to involve Antonio.

March, on the other hand, doesn't seem to share my misgivings. After he's hung up, he leans down to brush his lips to my temple. "It's going to be all right, Island."

I hope so. I mean, it's not like it could get much worse, right?

Antonio said it'd only take an hour . . . and that was almost three hours ago. Morning rain patters against the floor-to-ceiling windows of Berlin Schönefeld's jet terminal. Everything is gray and sucks, and my soul aches because, six hours behind us, Joy remains presumed dead. Huddled at March's side, I slump in the soft cushions of a leather sofa while we watch a Mercedes van back out of the parking lot. The Rotwangs will have breakfast in their Charlottenburg apartment. Struthio wins again.

"How's the pretzel?" March inquires, glancing at the paper bag I'm still holding. I only took a single bite, and it felt like wood chips in my mouth.

"Okay," I lie. "Has Antonio texted you back?"

"Not yet." He shifts closer, trailing the back of his knuckles in my hair. "Island, I'm sure she's going to be fine. Come now, I hate to admit it, but I really need to sleep a few hours somewhere marginally comfortable. A car seat might even do at this point."

It's not until March says this that I realize he and I have been awake for . . . God, the fact that I'm even struggling to count is a telltale sign of complete exhaustion. I glance down at my Nutella pretzel and remember that the reason I bought it in the first place after we landed was because I needed the sugar rush to even stay on my feet. Momentarily forgoing March's rule that neither Struthio personnel nor any members of our couple may get frisky in public, I crane my head to press a kiss to his jaw. The rasp of newly grown whiskers reminds me he hasn't shaved or had a proper shower either, and it must be nagging at him. "I'm sorry. Let's find a cab and go to the hotel."

"It's all right; I've booked a car."

"Nope. You're not driving right now, and neither am I. I don't want my birthday weekend to start with a crash into a döner st—"

I lose track of my rant midsentence when, at long last, the low buzz of my phone rises from the depths of my black tote. Springing upward like a jack-in-the-box, I plunge a hand in the mysterious abyss March never dares to look into, where keys and tampons float among candy wrappers and receipts. Private number: I pick up anyway.

There's a gasp, a sniff, the hum of an engine in the background—I'm guessing a car—and at last, Joy's brittle voice. "It's me . . . Thank you so fucking much!"

My eyes roll upward in silent thanks to our Lord and Savior. Hallowed be thy name, Raptor Jesus: you bailed Joy out. The lingering headache that was buzzing under my temples seconds ago fizzles out, and I feel a smile tug at the corners of my lips. March sits and flashes me a little wink that seems to say, *see?*

"You're okay now," I reassure her. "It's all that matters. I was already picturing you joining a gang and shanking wardens."

Her giggle is a breeze of fresh air. "Good news is there were no gangs . . . but the cell was so dirty, I think March would have passed out. I saw a roach the size of a van. One of the girls was here for possession, I think, and at some point, she threw up, but she missed the bowl." She goes silent, draws a weary sigh, and adds, "March's friend says Cachemire won't press charges. Honestly, I'm not sure about that. If I were her, I would, and I'd blackmail my ass into settling out of court."

"Maybe she told the cops she wouldn't. I think you can trust his intel. He's well connected," I suggest evasively.

"I kinda figured. He showed up with a whole motorcade. Black limo, sunglasses . . . like in a movie or something."

My jaw hangs limp in silent amazement. I had no idea Antonio was that big a wig. "Where are you now?" I ask, not wanting to dwell too much on topics I'd have to lie about.

"I think we're driving on Tulum Avenue."

"Hotel zone, then. Okay, we'll book you a room in a resort. Can I speak to Antonio for a second? I wanna thank him."

There's a beat of awkward silence before she asks. "Who's Antonio?"

This time it's my turn to pause as last night's tension boomerangs back into my chest. "He's, um . . . he's the guy who picked you up." *Right?*

"No." Joy sounds completely lost. "That's not him." I hear her ask someone in the car. "You're not Antonio, right?" A low, deep voice murmurs something to her that I can't make out in response to her inquiry, and every single finger and toe I possess curls like a goddamn fern when she says, "He's Antonio's brother-in-law, Angel."

FIVE
EL CUÑADO

Quentin tore open his yellow vest and the shirt underneath, revealing the powerful muscles of his ducal chest. "You've tempted the wrong Duke, Josepha!"

–Christina Thorbrad, *The Quavers #1: Taste of a Duke*

"Island, are you still there?"

I am. Sort of. My heart clanked to a stop, but I can already feel it roaring back to full speed. I was so wrong. Things could and did get worse. Antonio stabbed me in the back, and he's never invited to a barbecue on my terrace again.

He rang Angel of all people.

Quick recap: I only met Angel Somoza once, and to his credit, at the time he stepped up to help us save the world from getting nuked by my sketchy uncle. However, Angel is also the very reason Antonio ended up trussed up in March's trunk, as I mentioned earlier. Because, despite his indiscriminately offloading weapons to dictatures and cartels alike, Angel is a devout catholic, and as such, he exploded in just wrath upon discovering that Antonio had gotten his then eighteen-year-old sister pregnant. Outside. Marriage. Angel handled the Lord's trial like any sane, concerned Christian would have; he hired a world-class hitman to eliminate the father of his sister's unborn child. If that doesn't speak to his volatile character, I don't know what does.

And that's the guy who just bailed Joy out of jail. *No guns, no trouble. Right, Antonio?*

Meanwhile, March's eyebrows bounce back down after they took off all the way to his hairline, and he holds out his upturned palm, silently requesting the phone.

"I think March wants to speak to Angel."

"Sure. Are you okay, though?"

I croak out a brittle cheer. "Of course! Putting March through."

"Okay . . ."

March pulls me against his chest and rubs my shoulder with one hand while he takes the phone with the other. "Good evening, Angel. How have you been?"

"Busy," he replies, the single word wrapped in his signature sandpapered Spanish drawl.

March persists, undeterred by this frigid greeting. "Island and I are infinitely grateful that you took the time to personally handle Joy's legal troubles."

"Antonio called from Guayaquil and asked me to cut my business meeting short."

"And you did that?" I gasp, loud enough for him to hear.

"Beatriz insisted it was a matter of life and death."

Figures. Someone could set Antonio on fire before Angel's eyes, and I don't think he'd so much as throw a glass of water to help. More like he'd let the flames reflect in his aviators with some sad guitar playing in the background. Beatriz, on the other hand, is Angel's secret weakness, and she knows it. She'll never hesitate to play the age difference and some waterworks against her big brother, because it works every time—cue to Antonio being alive and partying hard in Ecuador when logic predicts he should be long buried somewhere in the jungle.

After a stifling pause, Angel remarks, "Your friend threw a cake at another girl." Subtext: *I had to interrupt my shady multimillion-dollar deal for this. Someone will have to die.*

"You would have done the same," I blurt out, immediately regretting my candor.

"No." Subtext: *I would have processed the cheating party through an industrial meat grinder. Feet first.*

March clears his throat and raises the phone out of my reach. "Well, thank you again. You can expect Phyllis to send you coupons as a token of our gratitude. May I abuse your kindness and ask you to take Joy to the Nizuc on Kukulcan? I'll have Phyllis book her a—"

"I have fifteen bedrooms," Angel cuts him off icily.

"Really?" Joy cheers in the background. "You've got a pool too?"

"Yes."

Joy goes silent for a couple seconds before I hear her say, "Okay, my post breakup life is looking up."

No, it's not. However, now isn't the best time to tell her about the blind basement where Angel had me handcuffed to a chair and pretended he was going to disfigure me with a straight razor. The whole thing was admittedly a coordinated stunt designed to confuse the enemy, but Angel was amazing in his role. You'd think he'd been doing this all his life. Oh, wait. That's because he *has.*

I wrestle the phone back from March, who admittedly doesn't put up much of a fight. "Are you sure you don't prefer a room in a resort? Or maybe even a suite?" *Anything* but Angel Somoza's bed.

Joy's voice lowers to a conspiring whisper. I gather she took the phone from Angel. "It's okay, no need to spend—"

"It's not about the money," I buzz imperiously.

"I know, but . . . Look, I ditched work today; I'm single and back to square one, except that now I've got my ex on the lease and fifty unanswered emails in my mailbox from middle-aged bankers who just want to skip alimony and start over with their sugar baby. And now I'm here, and March's friend has a villa with a billion bedrooms and a pool, and if I fly back tomorrow all that will be left of the most freaking epic breakup move I ever pulled will be 'I went there, got arrested, and I came back.'" She pauses with a determined huff. "I want to reflect on life and get drunk off my ass on mojitos in that pool."

I gulp, square my shoulders, and shrug on a uniform I haven't worn in a long while: that of Joy's conscience. "Jiminy Cricket says the parties Angel hosts aren't nearly as cool as you think—trust me on that." To be honest, I don't even know if he hosts parties at all, or if he just stays home, binge-watching the *Hostel* franchise in the dark when he wants to unwind.

"But he's March's friend, right?" I sense a vibe of uncertainty. I bet she's gauging her brooding savior as she speaks.

"More like a business acquaintance. March has worked for him a few times." Yes, I'm lying by omission. How many times? How many bodies? March was a contract killer for over ten years, and Angel's weapon of choice against encroaching competitors and slippery business partners. Anyone who had done anything to cross Mr. Somoza was sure to eventually find themselves standing on the wrong end of the "The South African's" suppressor. That's one facet of March's past I usually try not to dwell on: Angel probably got the worst of March more than once, and I'm sure that's exactly what he had paid for.

"Look," Joy begins. "He got me out of jail, and if you and March trust him, that's good enough for me. If he can let me squat at his place over the weekend, awesome. If he can't, that's fine too. I'll just crash at a resort and have a breakup party there."

The worst part about this entire exchange is the knowledge that *he* is sitting in a car with Joy at this very moment, and I'm terrified to imagine what's brewing in Angel's mind as he listens to her casually issuing a challenge. The man's ego is a hydrogen tank that does *not* need a lighter.

The next three seconds feel like a slo-mo crash. Behind her, his husky voice cracks like a whip. "Forty-eight hours. Limited access to some areas of the compound. You don't get drunk in my pool."

Joy's squeal tears through the speaker. "Thank you!"

Abort. Abort, abort, abort! I have a two-second window to avert the apocalypse, so I automatically snap, "I'm coming too. I'll take a flight from Berlin."

"No," Angel decrees.

He can't be serious. Like I'd ever let Joy spend an entire weekend alone with him! I'm jumping in his pool, whether he wants it or not, because I have an ace in the sleeve of my hoodie. I summon my sweetest, meekest voice. "It's okay, Angel; I totally understand. I'll call Beatriz to tell her you were super nice to save Joy. Maybe next time when your house won't be full?"

I mentally picture my arrow covering the five-thousand miles between us to hit him straight between the eyes. Seconds tick and become an ominous pause that has nothing to do with lag as he processes the hidden threat. *Go ahead, say no again. My finger is on your sister's speed dial!*

"Forty-eight hours, same restrictions," he grunts in defeat.

Joy whisper-shouts another exultant "Yes!" but is this truly a victory? It doesn't feel like one. At any rate, I'm not given any time to share my concerns. March, who had taken a backseat to listen to the negotiation until now, delicately pries the phone from my hands. "Thank you again for inviting us to your villa, Angel. It will be a welcome break for Island and me."

I could swear Angel hisses something in Spanish on the other end, but March hangs up too fast for me to ascertain. I can't believe how sanguine he is about this. Am I the only one to see this development for what it is: the eleventh plague of Egypt?

"That was . . ." I begin, regrouping my thoughts after the impact.

"Quite unexpected," March completes. "He was certainly eager to offer Joy his assistance."

I narrow my eyes at him. "He wants to bang her."

March's deadpan face doesn't waver as he says. "The notion has crossed my mind. But—"

"*But?*" I urge him, desperate for one single piece of good news.

"Angel was my second client ever, and always among the most honorable ones—if that makes any sense in the peculiar context of our business. His walls are higher than most, but I don't think Joy is in danger, Island," he says gently, as a teacher would explain to a kid how spiders are our friends because they eat mosquitos. I never fell for that kind of propaganda because even as a kid I knew spiders actually wrap their prey in their web while it's still alive and suck out their insides. My stomach heaves at the mental image etching itself in my mind, involving Joy, Angel, a straw, and . . . oh God.

"She'll be safe," I concur, my jaw tight. "Because I'm going there and dragging her ass back to New York."

March nods tiredly. "All right, biscuit."

My gaze slowly travels from March's conciliatory smile to the greasy Nutella pretzel still waiting in its paper bag on my lap. It is done. We're looking at another nine-hour flight, topped with six more hours of jet lag, all to spend the weekend with Angel Somoza.

Happy birthday, Island.

SIX

A CRIME OF PASSION

The AR15 fired, and immediately, red bloomed all over his shirt.
Falling to his knees, he let go of the shrimp salad bowl and drew
his final breath in a pool of blood and cilantro aïoli.

–Kerry-Lee Storm, *The Cost of Rica #5: Blaze of the Phoenix*

There's a beach somewhere, not in Cancún, hemmed by tall palm trees and a turquoise sea that stretches infinitely. I close my eyes and go there sometimes when the real world becomes a little too much to take.

March's voice permeates the misty boundaries of my dream. I think he's on the phone while I drift back and forth between the downy shelter of my blanket and that quiet, perfect place. My toes sink into sand so white and so fine it's like I'm walking in cornstarch, and I keep wondering if I'll wind up bouncing across a milky expanse of Oobleck if the waves lapping at the shore reach me.

A warm breeze stirs emerald palm leaves, and there's a single table with a white cloth on which sits a basket full of croissants and Nutella cannoli. An antique silver coffeepot is steaming in the hand of a bearded man clad in a classy linen suit. He pours a cup for a waifish woman whose red curls mist together with her muslin summer dress.

My parents are together, at last, having breakfast. She'll never be thirty-nine; he'll never be fifty-five, but that's okay. He's no longer a killer, and she's no longer a spy. All the blood and losses have been washed away by clear waters, and now they're just Dries and Léa. They look happy, chatting . . . fussing as usual. My mother acknowledges me with a tender smile and takes a sip from her cup. My father shakes his head and bites into a cannolo. "I told you that cake was only the beginning, Léa. That girl attracts trouble like a magnet."

At his feet, Bolino, his pet armadillo, is fighting with a red-striped paper bag, curling obstinately around it. Dries bends to his side to take the bag from Bolino before the little freak has a chance to spill its contents. "My popcorn is ready. This is gonna be good."

He raises the bag as if to toast me with it, and a big grin shines through his salt-and-pepper beard, revealing the gap-tooth I inherited from him. "Say hi to March and that putrid clown Angel for me, little Island."

My mother's soft French accent coats her response. "Don't listen to Dries. Joy is going to be fine."

"Wouldn't say the same about the boyfriend," he grumbles in between two mouthfuls of popcorn.

Her lips pinch in comical disdain. "We never liked him much anyway. We prefer March, don't we?"

Dries conceals a frown behind his popcorn bag. "Is this what I get for all my efforts? An eternity of suffering?" His golden hazel eyes narrow at me. "Can't you try Tinder?"

"Joy's boyfriend did that and look where that led him," my mom counters sweetly before laying her minty green gaze on me. "Now go. And don't forget your jelly sandals."

My sandals . . . for Cancún. Joy.

I blink at my mom and Dries, trying to find my voice. I want to move closer and maybe even touch them, hug them. But I never can. Already the beach is fading away, and the dream is smoke in my hands. All I grasp is a firm, cotton-clad forearm. I hold on to March, emerging from under my fleece blanket with a gasp. Reality rushes back to me as the last of my sleep ebbs away. I fell like a log on the sofa nine hours ago, not long after we boarded the Gulfstream that's flying us to Cancún.

March's lips press to my temple. He's showered and shaven already. "Good afternoon, biscuit."

My sleep-numbed neurons attempt to whirr back to life, but it's too early even for time zones and basic calculus. "What time is it?" I croak.

"One-thirty local time. We'll land in an hour."

I emerge slowly, blinking at the black carbon suitcase resting on one of the seats. March's magic suitcase. I hope we won't need any of the stuff he keeps in there this weekend. It's not so much the condoms and clean socks I'm worried about as the guns, mini-grenades, and disassembled rifle resting without a single speck of dust in their bed of urethane foam.

He crouches by the couch and takes my hand, lacing his fingers with mine. "Island, Angel called me. There's been a new development during the night that may complicate Joy's situation."

My surroundings become a blur as I jackknife up. I can't believe we left Joy alone with him for less than *eleven* goddamn hours, and something went wrong already! "What is it? What did he do to her?"

"Nothing; he's actually been quite helpful."

I breathe, but only for a second. The roller coaster in my chest takes me for another loop when March completes his explanation.

"But I'm afraid the police are going to want to speak with Joy again before she returns to the US." His lips thin. "Mr. Moravia was shot in his hotel room during the night, not long after Angel freed Joy."

Oh. Shit.

The cabin is spinning a little, and I'm not sure I'm able to get up yet. "Please tell me you're joking."

"I am not."

"Is he dead?"

"No. Double thoracic wound. According to the police report, Mr. Moravia stumbled into a night visitor around two-thirty upon entering his room. He was subsequently shot, staggered to the balcony, and fell into the hotel's pool from the third floor. He sustained additional minor injuries and developed a Quincke's edema upon landing on a floating salad bar that contained shrimp cocktail—he's apparently allergic. His assailant presumably escaped without leaving any trace, not even on the resort's video surveillance tapes," March recites.

"A pro, then. Burglar?" I ask groggily.

March gives a sharp nod. "His laptop, phone, and iPad were stolen."

"Cachemire . . . Did she see anything?"

"She told the police she was in her own room. She didn't want to spend the night with him after they returned from the hospital."

You bet she needed space after Joy nearly cracked her skull. I rub my eyes with the heel of my palm and fumble for my phone on a nearby table.

Watching me unlock it, March shakes his head. "Joy is on voicemail. It is my understanding that she wasn't yet awake when Angel called me earlier."

This time I spring to my feet, dizziness be damned. "And he didn't think that attempted murder was worth waking her up?"

"I asked him to. I expect to hear back from him shortly."

There's a little voice at the back of my mind susurrating that

Angel is getting way too involved in this mess for it to end well, but I choose to shelve it for now. I can only handle so much before I've even had breakfast. Or lunch. All that jet lag is starting to mess with my sense of time.

I stretch and yawn to tears under March's attentive gaze. "So basically, Vince just became the only guy who'll get mugged in a Cancún resort this year?" No. Even saying it feels off.

His eyes narrow a fraction. "I was similarly surprised. Tourism is the city's golden goose, and these resorts are notoriously safe."

"Yeah, that kind of stuff just doesn't happen. Especially when all you have to do is to wait for tourists to leave their hotel and con them into buying fake tour packages or grab their phone on the street." I shake my head, feeling clear at last. "No self-respecting thug would waste their time dodging resort security for a secondhand Mac. Especially on the third floor. That's way too much work for the payoff."

"Agreed."

"So, it was about him," I conclude. "It was personal."

March sits on the couch next to me, fingers rapping on his knees. "I'm certain the police have already come to a similar conclusion, which will inevitably lead them to suspect Joy."

"But she was with Angel on Isla Mujeres," I reason while dragging myself to the lavatory's tiny shower stall.

March leans against the other side of the frosted glass door and goes on with his debrief while I squeeze the contents of a miniature bottle of shower gel in my palm. "Correct. But a number of witnesses saw Joy threatening and assaulting him and his new conquest earlier. That girl—Cachemire—was questioned a few hours ago. She was adamant that Joy publicly and repeatedly threatened to kill Mr. Moravia."

"Of course, she did," I grunt, "and she probably didn't mean half of the insults she hurled at him yesterday."

"Joy's passport appears to have been flagged already," March adds. "She will need help leaving the country."

And here we are back to that damn cake. Joy was there, knew where Vince was staying, and probably his room number too. Overlooking the burglary part, which could have been staged, one can reasonably conclude that she hired a local gun to exact revenge on her ex. Especially if she happens to hang out with the likes of Angel Somoza. *Oh, God.* What have we done?

I leap out of the shower and grab the towel March hands me. "We're taking the case," I announce, as seriously as one can when making a biased business decision butt naked.

It's only once I'm done drying my face that I realize I'm being subtly, yet efficiently cornered against the sink. March braces his hands on either side of me on the counter and looms—he does love to loom, something made even easier by the fact that I'm barely five feet three, and he has a foot on me. Sweet Jesus, I need to focus on Joy and Vince's attempted murder, but the lower his head dips, the less I remember why I was so concerned with the police report, the shrimp salad, and . . . I release a trembling exhale as March's nose grazes my temple, nuzzling my cheek, the line of my jaw. Then it's a single, burning kiss against my throat, immediately soothed by the touch of his tongue.

"Struthio is, indeed, going to take Joy's case," he whispers huskily.

I clutch my towel tightly against my bare chest and gasp. "I'm on it."

"And once we're done investigating Mr. Moravia's sentimental and culinary woes, we'll cancel all our meetings for, say, the rest of the week."

"Who are you, and what have you done with Mr. November?"

Ignoring my playful jab, he easily lifts me to sit on the narrow sink counter—Hélas, I have no choice but to wrap my legs around his hips to steady myself. "As I said," March resumes, gently prying my fingers away when they attempt to undo the first buttons of his shirt. "We'll cancel our meetings, and I'll confiscate your phone."

That gives me pause. I flatten my palms on his chest. "You won't."

"Very well, I will shoot it first, then I'll take it."

"March!"

His hands cup my cheeks, forcing me to meet his gaze. His pupils are wide, and I read a wistful tenderness in them, a silent plea to let him in. His thumbs massage my temples softly as he says, "There's always a lot going on in that wonderful head of yours, Miss Chaptal. There's room for gerbils, best friends, work, computer science, epistemology, baby octopuses . . ."

"And you," I murmur. "There's a lot of room for you."

"I know. But it's been too long since I've kidnapped you somewhere. I need to have you all to myself for a few days. No interruptions, no cake."

I reach around his neck to hug him. "I'm really sorry about this—"

"Don't be. Just promise me you'll give me your undivided attention once this is over." He raps gently against my skull with his forefinger. "One hundred percent of your brain."

"You'll have it all," I promise.

There's a fleeting intensity, a seriousness that hadn't been there moments ago as he replies, "I do hope so."

I respond with a firm nod and jump into action, hopping down from the counter to go grab some clothes from my suitcase—yet another pit of desolation and chaos whose very existence March strives to ignore for the sake of our love. I wiggle into a T-shirt and a pair of short overalls with a pineapple pattern that I bought at the airport, jump in my sneakers, and I'm ready to roll.

"By the way," I quip in between two sprays of light perfume, "what about my birthday gift? You said you had one, back in the Ekranoplan. I'm kinda curious . . ."

March's previous candor is wiped off by a steel-plated poker smile. "Of course, biscuit. You will receive it as soon as we've dealt with Joy, and you've surrendered your phone and your laptop."

"Aw, come on!"

SEVEN
THE IDOL

"I don't think Atlantis sank. I think Atlantis . . . lifted off."

–Giorgio Tsoukalos, *Ancient Aliens*, season 3.
History Channel, 2011

We're flying over Florida and wasted no time getting to work. Facing each other across a small table, March and I comb through what little Vince has to hide—mostly some credit card debt and a few more racy pics on his iCloud. Except . . .

"Interesting," I announce, looking up from my keyboard.

March's head snaps up from Vince's last bank statement. "What is?"

"His backups; they've been erased. His settings say he's on auto-backup, but his Time Capsule is empty. Since he's supposed to have hourly backups, it could mean his devices are turned off, or maybe they've been destroyed entirely. Either way, they stopped saving data to the cloud."

March's fingers rap on the table's glossy varnish. "I doubt he did that himself."

"But the guy who stole his laptop could have."

"I suppose his cloud's content has been wiped too?"

"No, actually. His stuff is still here," I mumble, checking Vince's calendar and various folders. "But if it were me and I was looking for something very specific, I'd have deleted that file and wiped the backups to make sure it can't be recovered. No need to waste time erasing everything if you know exactly what you're looking for."

"So, we can assume there's nothing of interest in the rest of his files?" March sighs.

"Maybe, maybe not. Won't hurt to check," I reply, before opening Vince's galleries. I'm greeted by his most recent work: a series of Mayan ruins and artsy shots of a movie crew at work, it seems. There are set techs adjusting the light reflectors against a sunset backdrop, more ruins, a guy in an alien costume talking to an old guy . . .

Hold on.

I nearly leap from my seat when I recognize the older man's brown skin, silvery afro, and artfully curled mustache. "Oh, my God! Oh, my God!" I squeak, my hands shaking so badly you'd think I just burned myself trying to grab a searing-hot lasagna dish.

March leans forward in concern. "What is it, biscuit?"

"He was working for Gualtiero Franz!"

His only response is a perplexed blink. "Who?"

"Vince! He was working for *Aliens in Our Past*! I knew his contract was with SciFi U, and Cachemire works for them, but I had no idea . . . *Oh my God*," I gasp again, still balling trembling fists.

March frowns. "Isn't it that show you like?"

I send him a level stare. "It's more than a show. It's a way of life. I've been waiting for Gualtiero Franz to prove that aliens visited Earth since I was seven. I have all his books."

"But they make you angry every time you reread them," March counters, a sly glint in his eyes. "I see you shake your head at your tablet and mumble to yourself."

He may have a point. I deflate in my seat. "Okay . . . It's true that the scientific ground he treads on is shaky, at best, and Franz makes a ton of factual errors, but his point is . . . he's searching for answers that are bigger than us. He's asking why people always look up at the stars when they've run out of explanations. And modern science kind of does the same. We're observing the universe because we believe it'll tell us where we came from."

March leans back and crosses his arms. "And Mr. Moravia worked for his TV show?"

"Yes, the upcoming nineteenth season, apparently. Franz promised new evidence on this huge conspiracy to hide ancient alien spaceships."

He raises an eyebrow but doesn't comment. No need to; it's one of these moments when I can read him like an open book.

"I don't believe in that part," I admit, feeling a tiny speck of my childhood die as I say it out loud for the first time since I started following Gualtiero Franz's international expeditions and somewhat tacky reality dramas. "I think he started doing it for his TV series, the whole story about Illuminati plotting to stop him from uncovering the truth and all." I look up, fighting a blush of mild embarrassment under March's tender gaze. "You know I'm a believer but not a conspiracy theorist."

"I know." March smiles. He isn't a believer—the most I ever heard him admit was that there were perhaps things that were too vast for him to understand—but it's never really been a problem between us. I don't try to convince him, and he refrains from pointing out that the alien onscreen is an extra. His mouth twists as he ponders the news. "However, do you think that—"

"No." I cut him off before he even has a chance to indulge me. "Vince got shot at in the middle of the night in his bedroom in a trashy tourist resort, and as far as we know, he was only in Cancún to take shots for the marketing team and bang Cachemire afterward. I honestly don't think someone tried to get rid of him because he was a truther."

I've barely said this when a bubbling chime and subsequent pop-up on my laptop alert me that our prime suspect is up and kicking. I turn the screen for March to see and accept the call with a rush that's equal parts relief and jitters. The moment after, Joy's mess of sunny curls bounces onscreen, cascading all over the white terry robe she's wearing.

"Before you ask, I should have, but I didn't do it," she states, her voice still husky from sleep.

"I know!"

She leans back in a garden chair, allowing me a glimpse of an azure sky and sapphire sea blending together in the distance. "He hasn't woken up yet, but he should make it. Cops grilled Cachemire, and she basically told them I'm Bellatrix Lestrange with a shitty dye job. And of course, now they're looking for the crazy ex-girlfriend who came back to end it once and for all. Angel says they flagged my passport, so no return ticket for now."

As if on a cue, a tanned forearm with a blue cuff rolled at the elbow moves into view, soon followed by the rest of its owner. Like his hair, Angel's stubble has grown since the last time I saw him. Jet-black curls now lick his neck, and a short beard almost entirely conceals the old acne craters furrowing his cheeks, as well as the deep scar that slices the right half of his face from his cupid's bow to his ear. Everything else conforms to my memories: a hawk of a man, all sinewy muscles and razor-sharp angles, down to his impeccably cut dress shirt—whose top first buttons are open to reveal a tiny golden crucifix nestled in dark chest hair. All he's missing are his aviators— my bad, they're peeking from his breast pocket.

"I can fly her back, but it's already starting to make the news. There's a headline on the Yucatán Times's website," he drawls.

I send March a questioning look. Why would Angel care in the first place? He could just wait for us to land and take over. Maybe it's a matter of pride, like, now that he's started helping Joy—albeit against his will—allowing anyone else to solve her problems would be akin to admitting defeat, letting his enemies know that there are, in fact, situations he can't control.

"Then we need to act fast," March replies, checking his black chronograph. "We should land in half an hour."

"Don't worry," I try to reassure Joy, "March has helped people out of worse countries than Mexico."

She smiles, but I detect something sharp in her attentive gaze. "So Struthio is working for me? Maybe I'll finally have a chance to figure out what it is exactly you guys do."

That sounded very much like a threat. I muster an uneasy chuckle. "I mostly hack crappy surveillance cams and cloud accounts these days."

"You checked Vince's iCloud?" she probes.

"Yep. There was nothing significant. I mean, apart from what you already found."

"Okay. Meanwhile, I think I'm gonna need to find a lawyer pronto."

"I'll take care of that," Angel states, in a tone that doesn't bear any discussion.

But Joy turns in her chair and opens her mouth. Goosebumps bloom on my forearms. She's going to say something, and this time he'll toss her in his basement for sure.

She looks him straight in the eye. "No. It's okay. You've already done so much, and I can't—"

"I will take care of it," Angel repeats, this time more slowly, pinning her with what I've dubbed "the Stare." I don't know if it's his thick eyebrows, his slightly slanted eyes, or because it's impossible to tell if his irises are a dark brown or entirely black, but when Angel Somoza stares you down, it's like your skin is suddenly getting a couple sizes too small.

Yet Joy beams up at him. "Look, I'm gonna email a few colleagues to see if they have someone good to recommend. If I can't find a decent crim lawyer, maybe I'll take you up on the offer."

Angel's eyes widen a fraction, and for a ticking second, he looks almost as shocked as March and me that the Stare unexpectedly failed him. Maybe he didn't aim it right?

"Very well," March interjects before Angel has a chance to reload and give it another try. "We'll start with a visit to Mr. Moravia's hotel when we land."

Having recovered from the previous glitch, Angel fires his glare again, this time at March. "Ernesto will wire you your usual advance. You bill him your expenses when you're done."

March's expression remains courteous, but I sense he's now on guard. "That won't be necessary. Joy is pro bono."

"I'm paying," Angel repeats icily. "That way, we both know you won't fail."

This time Joy studies him in rapt silence while I gulp down a lump of fear. I'm increasingly worried that Angel is somehow making this tale of sordid infidelity and ancient aliens personal. Someone will die for real at this rate.

EIGHT
THE BULL

Rica stood tall, the sumptuous globes of her perfect breasts bouncing proudly. "I killed the last man who tried to enslave me, Fabio!"

– Kerry-Lee Storm, *The Cost of Rica #5: Blaze of the Phoenix*

I say it all the time: we need to pay more attention to global warming and organize inverted curfews for redheads: the moment we step out onto the airstair, a muggy ninety degrees engulfs us as if we'd just opened the door to a dishwasher, and the gusts of hot wind whipping my hair don't really help. I let March proceed first and discreetly spray some more sunblock on my forearms before venturing the tip of my foot down the first step. I'm baking already. I can seriously feel it even through my clothes.

A quick look at the jet terminal's tarmac and there it is: Angel's discreet little retinue. A measly half a dozen Rams and Escalades—all armored, I'm certain, and most of them black to better blend with his men's sunglasses and dark clothes, I assume. There is, however, one car that doesn't belong here—or does it?—a silver Lamborghini whose aggressive profile is the very reflection of its owner: essentially a blade.

The doors flip up like a pair of wings catching the sun, and a pale foot appears, strapped in a coral high-heeled sandal. Joy springs out in a whirl of flowery silk. Dammit, if she weren't my part-time wife, I'd be jealous: *I* turned into a box troll after March dumped me, and she's glowing like a beacon. That sleeveless flare dress clings in all the right places, and she doesn't even have any sunburn, just a smattering of faint freckles on her shoulders and cheeks. Nothing can bring down Joy Richards, not even Mexican law.

Exiting the driver's seat with a tightly set jaw, Angel pretty much looks like the Ramirez to her Rica—and of course, he's put on his aviators. I hurry down the stairs and run to her in slo-mo until we hug on the tarmac like it's the end of the movie already.

"Happy birthday. Sorry for the shitty gift," Joy cries out as I fling my arms around her neck.

I blow aside a blonde coil tickling my nose. "Please tell me nothing worse happened since we spoke."

"Not really. I think . . ." She lowers her voice to whisper in my ear. "I think Angel has one of his beefcakes watching over Vince at the hospital. Someone texted him that he's still in the ICU."

"He's getting super involved in this."

Her only reply is a loaded, "I know . . ." before the culprit pops up behind her and glares me a couple steps away.

"Hey, it's great to see you again. Sorry for, um . . . everything," I say, mustering a cheerful yet suitably apologetic smile.

His face doesn't register any emotion, save for this perpetual air of displeasure, like there's always a raspberry seed stuck between his back molars and he will have to bear with that minor yet infuriating discomfort for the rest his life. It's only when March joins us, that he deigns to tip his chin in greeting. Angel Somoza and I are apparently back to square one: he's going to ignore me because I'm a girl, and he only deals with real men.

"I'm glad you're safe, Joy," March tells her. But he's not looking at her. There's an entire unspoken conversation happening between him and Angel until he simply concludes, "It's been quite a Friday."

Joy wraps her arms around herself, and I notice for the first time a few scrapes and bruises around her wrists—left by handcuffs, no doubt. There's a knot in my throat, but her smile doesn't waver. "So, what do we do, Mr. November? From what I gather, the cops don't have much yet, but if I keep hiding, I'll probably wake up tomorrow with a warrant on my head and my face on CNN's front page."

"Correct. I suggest we let Angel's lawyers take the lead on that. I'm certain they'll do their best to ensure that your involvement in the case remains confidential."

Angel and March exchange a meaningful look, only for Joy to pop their little criminal bubble. "All within the strict boundaries of the law?"

March walls himself in tactful silence.

Joy clasps her hands. "Okay, let's address the elephant in the room before we proceed any further. This isn't *Legally Blonde*, and just because I don't say anything doesn't mean I'm totally blind to whatever's going on around me. You're *shady*," she informs March, emphasizing each syllable for additional damage.

I hold back a gasp as she then whips around and directs her glare at Angel. "And although I am very grateful for everything you did for me—and I love this dress so much, by the way—I asked you three times what you do in life, and three times, you replied, 'business,'" she recounts, deepening her voice to an imitation of his, only to conclude, "You're totally shady too."

The final shuriken hits me square between the eyes as she returns her attention to me. "And *you*, you know all that . . . You know I love you, and I'm cool with not asking about the skeletons in March's closet, although I'm gonna have to at some point. But not now, because this time it's about me, and I don't want anyone intimidating cops or doing illegal shit behind my back."

March appears momentarily at a loss for words while Angel's jaw quivers from an imminent explosion of machismo. Yet before any of us has time to respond, Joy wiggles a pink-nailed forefinger at us and hisses, "So *no one* here does *any* shady stuff before running it by me first."

I stand there dumbly for a couple seconds as the sun above scorches the tarmac and threatens to bake me to a crisp. There it is, Joy's secret power: the ability to lull anyone into thinking she's this happy-go-lucky and somewhat shallow clone of Reese Witherspoon in her worst—or best?—role. Except the act is only skin-deep.

March recovers first, and in his usual straightforward manner, says, "Very well. Do you give Angel's lawyers your consent to bribe or threaten police officers into silence regarding your involvement in Vince's case?"

My jaw hits the ground at the same time that Joy replies, "If they must" with a regal flick of her hand. "Those cops treated me like shit anyway."

Now that he's cooled down, I'm scared to read a new level of appreciation in the way Angel's lips purse and tug at his scar. I step in once more, in an attempt to stop my best friend's rapid descent into the thug life. "Maybe we can try to find out who shot Vince before we start bribing anyone?"

Joy shrugs. "The two aren't mutually exclusive." Her eyes turn to slits. "No one else but me had the right to shoot him. I *want* to know what happened."

"You will," March assures her.

"By the way, you're aware I'm supposed to be behind my desk at eight on Monday?" she muses, like an afterthought.

His mouth quirks. "I'm afraid you're going to have to take a few days off."

"My senior partner is probably gonna fire me if I flake on him."

March checks his watch. "Are you giving me thirty hours to find who shot Mr. Moravia and get you off the no-fly list?"

"Yes," Angel replies. Dammit, I'd almost forgotten he wants to pay us for this.

I square my shoulders and puff up my chest. Just like Joy's truth had to be said, mine shall be heard. "Angel," I snap without meeting his dark gaze—for fear I'll lose my nerve if I make eye contact with the beast. "We already told you we don't want your money. Joy is my best friend, and I'll do everything I can to figure out what happened last night and get her home safely and *legally*. But I have no idea if we can do it over the weekend, and I don't want you breathing down our necks every second of every minute."

He takes a single step forward—a cue for March's stance to shift as he readies to move between us. But Angel doesn't touch me; he just cocks his head with that angry, intense stare of his, as if I'm the weirdest creature he's ever seen, and he's debating whether to crush me under his heel or taxidermize me. "You don't work for me."

Joy flings an arm around my shoulder. "No, we work together. We're our own PI agency now." March raises his palms and opens his mouth with the obvious intent to contradict her, but Joy is a hungry young lawyer. She's used to talking over people to get what she wants. "You go do your own investigating. Island and I will find that snake Cachemire. I've got a few questions—"

"Hold on right there," I warn her, arms akimbo. "I *do* want to hear her side of the story, but given the situation, you need to keep your distance. And same for Vince. You're not going anywhere near Victoria Hospital. Nonnegotiable."

Her nose wrinkles in frustration. "Look, I'm not gonna spend the rest of the day in Angel's spa while she's out there working on getting me framed for attempted murder or something."

"I'd rather you did," I insist. "I swear we'll debrief you on everything we learn. But if you and Cachemire run into each other, it's gonna be—"

"There will be more cake," she predicts, her eyes squinting ominously.

The threat seems to rouse Angel at last, who breaks his self-imposed silence and tells March, "She'll stay with me while you go find the girl."

"Very well," March replies. Again, he does his telepathic thing with Angel, where they keep eye contact just a little too long. I could swear I feel this electric current between them, like they're sealing a deal of their own. My lower lip juts out in suspicion. *Oh, Mr. November, you'd better not be playing wingman here . . .*

"I don't need a chaperone," Joy snaps.

Hélas, Angel's hand is already creeping to her waist to encircle it in a proprietary gesture, and dammit she should slap it away, but she doesn't. Because he's the hero she needs right now, but not the one she deserves—or maybe it's the other way around. At any rate, our Ecuadorian Batman gives his new ward an unforgiving once-over. "With your track record, what you need is a collar and a chain."

The remark immediately conjures up all sorts of ghoulish scenarios in my brain, but Joy doesn't flinch, doesn't even blink. She locks her cornflower gaze straight into Angel's tar-black one and simply says, "Just so you know, I'm not really into that kind of stuff."

Having stated this, she whirls around to face me. "I'm still stalking you, but okay, I won't set foot inside the resort. I'll probably be watching your every move with binoculars from the street."

My shoulders slump. She's gonna be one difficult client. "I can work with that."

"So, we have a plan, we have the car, the aviators . . ." She counts off her fingers. "All we're missing is a theme."

I raise my phone. "*Magnum P.I.?*"

"Yes, perfect!"

Joy then turns to Angel and gives him one of those secret hooded looks she's honed to perfection since high school, at once gamine and expectant—think Eric Cartman asking his mom for KFC—and I think that's when he realizes that what we will soon have are *his* car and *his* sunglasses.

All that's left for me is to look up at the sober rectangular sunglasses sitting on the bridge of March's nose. "Sorry, I'm gonna need yours too."

NINE
THE SPACE RACE

If his sports car is an integral part of who he is, who says you can't love it too?

– Aurelia Nichols & Jillie Beans, *All That Shines: A 21st Century Guide to Inclusive and Responsible Gold Digging*

Apparently, it's not a Lamborghini Aventador but a Veneno—whatever the difference is. When Joy started the engine, it gave out a kind of plaintive whirr that became a steady hum—until her foot grazed the gas pedal. She screamed in delight, and I saw my life flash before my eyes as we nearly crashed into a palm tree driving out of the parking lot.

Our first turn was a close call, too, but I think she's getting the gist of that seven-speed gearbox. We're now lurching up the highway leading to Cancún's Hotel Zone to the roaring guitar of *Miami Vice*. We ultimately voted it a more appropriate theme for us because—quoting Joy here—"You can literally hear your boobs bouncing to those drums."

Well, hers anyway.

I know from looking in the mirror that Angel is driving with March in that black Escalade following us, and I can only imagine the level of stress he's being subjected to, watching his priceless Italian toy jolt and brake over and over along the many shades of green hemming Tulum Avenue. I hold on tight to my seat belt's shoulder straps and mentally picture Angel's tight-fisted grip on his crucifix when Joy swerves to pass a rusty pedo van. I hope Raptor Jesus is on this.

"So, what does he do in life?" Joy's quiet remark snaps me off my thoughts about Vince's predicament as we're driving up around Nichupté Lagoon toward the resort.

"You mean, Angel?"

"Yes."

Vast question. My gaze focused on the specks of blue sea flashing through the bushes and palm trees lining the road, I mentally flip through my options. Lying, dodging . . . those were easier done before Joy got propelled into March's and my world. I slump in my seat like a treacherous slug. "Can we still be friends if I lie?"

She's no longer smiling. "It won't be the same kind of friendship anymore. More like we'll stay in touch."

In other words, it's time to progressively come clean, after months of crafting up excuses and half-assed plots since the day March brought me home after an eight-month-long disappearance last year. Joy knows he found me after I vanished in the explosion of a Polynesian resort, but she doesn't know I was actually held prisoner in Finland by my supervillain uncle, or everything that went down since the day March first broke into our apartment two years ago. She's giving me a chance to lift the veil one corner at a time. I just never expected Angel would be where we started.

When I remain silent, she probes on. "Is it drugs? All of his men . . . they have guns. I saw them. And he didn't buy that seafront villa running churro stands."

"No," I reply, and immediately I feel my world shake and right itself altogether. We can start here. "He's . . ." The next part takes some effort, the words sticking to the back of my throat. "He's an arms dealer. Based in Ecuador, but he sells internationally."

Joy's head lolls back and forth as she takes in the news. "Oh wow . . . Wow."

"But 80 percent of his business is locally legal," I quickly add, spewing March's pitch word for word. I've become a monster.

As expected, she won't take any bullshit. "And the remaining 20 percent?"

I don't want to lose her, and I'm terrified she won't want anything to do with me once she sees me whole, all the strange people I call my friends and owe my life to. But she said it herself, lying is simply off the table at this point. "I don't know the specifics," I admit. "But he has this . . . compound north of the Ecuadorian jungle, close to the Colombian border, and I think he sells to drug cartels. That part is definitively not legal."

Let's stop here for now. Her breathing has gone shallow, and this is not the time to tell her about that time March and Angel had this deep conversation about faith and religion while burying half a dozen bodies in the jungle.

Her fingers quiver as she reaches for the gear paddle on the wheel. We're gonna stall again at this rate. "You said March used to work for him," she notes, her voice even.

I flinch. "He wasn't selling anything . . ."

"Please don't tell me he was working the desk."

"He wasn't." I can feel my nape grow damp with sweat the longer we discuss this. "Look, not everything March ever did in his life was legal, but he's always had a . . . you might call it a *code*. He was never a thug." That's not entirely true either. March was a thug from the age of fourteen to seventeen, breaking into houses and snatching purses until he ended up in a hellish South African jail for almost a year. Freshly out and then eighteen, he met Dries, who made a Lion of him, and gave him the strength to find his own moral compass.

"March wants a new start, and I don't know how to juggle telling you the entire truth and respecting that he wants to move on. I'll do my best," I tell Joy. My voice falters when I add, "I just don't know where to start."

She keeps nodding, her features pinched in concentration. She's filing everything, every single word, nonverbal cue, processing it all. "So, it's not drugs?" she says at last.

"No. It was never about drugs."

"Has anyone ever died?" she goes on coolly.

I grip my knees, staring down at the little pineapples bouncing all over the printed fabric of my overalls. "Yes."

The Veneno vomits a deafening roar and slams us into our seats as Joy's foot accidentally jerks against the gas pedal. She slams the brakes with a gasp before we get a taste of a Honda's bumper. Behind us, March and Angel's SUV plays buffer just in time to prevent a multi on one of Cancún's busiest tourist avenues.

My phone starts buzzing in my tote: March. I quickly text him that we're okay, but I don't pick up.

Meanwhile, Joy's lips move in silence. She shakes her head, and her eyes leave the road a second to meet mine. They're a clear, bright blue, and goddamn wide. She reaches for the touchscreen and replaces the frothy pop coming from my phone with the ominous chorus of Phil Collins's "In The Air Tonight," before lowering Angel's aviators to her eyes.

"Are you scared, pissed, or both?" I ask.

"Both. But mostly scared." She exhales slowly. "Since I know we're only getting started, and I have no idea what you're gonna dump on me next."

I'm grateful for my own sunglasses that I stole from March. My eyes are getting a little hot and glassy, but I don't want her to see the relief and the lingering fear there. "I'm so sorry."

"You fucking should be!" she growls. "I can't believe you set me up with, like . . . Not-El-Chapo."

My lips quiver into an involuntary smile. "It was never a setup, and honestly, you have no idea how I freaked out when we realized Antonio had basically lobbed the ball to Angel of all people."

She shrugs a freckled shoulder as traffic ahead of us slows down to allow a pair of tourist shuttles to merge in. "He's not so bad. Maybe too much into the whole sugar daddy thing, like, '*Chica*, I don't do the talking and dating thing, but here's a Givenchy dress.'"

My eyes pop out as I take a second look at the flowery print. "Seriously?"

"It was in the closet when I woke up, and the lingerie too."

I summon my most sanctimonious tone—which comes out as a horrified gasp. "Joy, he's trying to bang you!"

She bites down on a giggle, her teeth digging into her lower lip in that way men can't resist. "I know. But I told him I wouldn't sleep with him because I respect him too much to use him as a rebound, and it's too early anyway. I mean, Vince and I are over, but it's been what, twenty-four hours, and he managed to get himself shot in that time."

Oh, Lord. I would have wanted to be a fly on the wall—carrying a microscopic camera—to snatch a pic of ticking time bomb Angel Somoza's face when Joy flashed him her secret smile and told him *that.*

She grows quiet as the silhouette of the Tropical Temptation emerges ahead of us, a big concrete pyramid pierced with oval windows and facing the ocean. She chews on the inside of her mouth and eventually asks, "It's not really gold-digging, right?"

The question is an answer in itself, but I'm not sure how to best go about this. "I guess . . . I think it depends on whether the two of you are on the same page. I mean, you told him you wouldn't sleep with him, but are you sure that's what he heard?"

Her eyes narrow at the Escalade, still diligently tailing us in the mirror. "What do you think he heard?"

"That you'd change your mind if he gave you a designer dress and a Lamborghini."

Her nose wrinkles beneath Angel's sunglasses. "The car is just a loan."

"But the dress isn't," I counter.

She nods. "Ergo, if I were to keep the dress and eventually change my mind about sleeping with him, it would become de facto gold-digging. However, if I divest myself of the loaned item and return it prior to—"

"Joy!"

"What? I'm just speculating. I mean, he's cute."

My head slowly rotates left to stare at her now grinning face. Angel is a lot of things. Cute isn't one of them, not even in an alternative universe.

As if she could read my mind, Joy draws a guilty sigh. "I dunno, he's cute like . . . a little pet snake."

I pout so hard my chin threatens to fold over my nose. "I want to judge you right now."

"But you can't. At least not until you've come 100 percent clean about March."

"This isn't a contest of who's got the biggest rap sheet," I groan.

That earns me a suspicious side-eye. "Or is it?"

I ponder this as Joy parks in front of a Starbucks, fifty yards from the twenty-feet-tall golden arch framing the resort's entrance. Is this place for real? When the car's wings unfold and allow a wave of hot air inside the car, I undo my belt and mutter, "March's is bigger. It literally goes all the way to space."

TEN
THE FIRST CONTACT

Tıhk'Tōhk stood in her bedroom, backlit by the glare of his
spaceship's lights. Vaneyssa's secret cove flooded with lust syrup at
the sight of his rippling emerald muscles.

– Charmaine Lorie, *Knock Knock, It's Tıhk'Tōhk*
(Galactical Spacelords #1)

"All the way to space, huh?" Joy sizes March up and down from
behind Angel's sunglasses as he climbs out of the Escalade.

His poker face holds strong, but he's looking at me when he
replies, "I take it you and Island had a little chat."

"Not really," I murmur. There's no accusation in his eyes, but I
feel guilty all the same.

"We've barely scratched the surface," Joy confirms coolly.

He gives a slow nod. "I see. Perhaps later today, Joy and I can sit down together, and I'll try to answer her questions to the best of my abilities."

I shake my head with a pleading grimace even as Joy replies, "Yeah, that'd be nice."

Oh no, it won't be, but she doesn't realize it yet. I haven't forgotten my adoptive father's ghastly pallor the night March gave him "the talk." My dad wanted to know the truth about this elusive savior of mine. He simply couldn't accept March in our lives otherwise. So, March locked himself in a room with him and spilled everything in clinical and explicit detail. How many people. How much money. The bloodstains, sometimes, when the job wasn't clean. Regrets? No, not really regrets, not after the first time. Just a kind of sadness steeping, saturating everything in his life, until he decided to retire . . . for me.

After it was done, my dad asked March to go buy two ounces of weed for him to cope with his new reality. He smoked four joints, scattered the rest on a Parisian sidewalk "for the pigeons," got drunk too, and has been silent on the subject since. And now, my insides are turning into macramé just imagining what will happen if March sits Joy down for the talk. She'll probably find Angel a lot less cute, that much is certain.

Speaking of the devil: he's stepped out of the car in his turn, and I'm almost grateful when he motions to the resort entrance across the street. "Go find me that girl. My men will back you up."

"That shouldn't be necessary," March reassures him. I peer up at the pair of beefcakes guarding the cars. Angel's little task force doesn't exactly blend with Cancún's carefree and colorful crowd. I hope they brought swimming trunks for the job.

"Don't worry, we'll manage," I cheer. To be honest, when his somber gaze briefly deigns to meet mine, the words 'please keep Joy safe' are on the tip of my tongue, but what comes out instead is: "Please don't do anything weird while we're gone."

He torches me with the Stare in response. "You're calling me *weird*?"

Joy pops up at his side and shrugs. "You are. Own it."

I watch with a sort of clinical curiosity as Angel's stony features crack and rearrange into a blend of surprise and indignation that looks totally foreign on him. Have I been reading this guy wrong all along, and maybe all it takes is a brutally honest diss to make him lose his footing?

The answer comes when he diverts his attention from Joy to me, and the Stare immediately takes over, unblinking and ferocious. Nope. Joy's trademark brand of sass will get me nowhere with him, except maybe in a concrete sarcophagus at the bottom of the lagoon.

Their website described the Tropical Temptation as "an over-21 playground offering a whole new level of topless adult vacationing," which sounds like it was built solely for Vince. My first impression of the place as March steers me into the lobby is a whiff of cool, perfumed air. They're blowing something through the aircon, a fruity artificial fragrance with notes of coconut and banana. It's cheap and a little overpowering, like everything else in here: the incurved walls and transparent furniture, or the softcore nudes adorning the ceiling—pictures of bodies enlaced underwater in suggestive poses.

I eye a waiter as he applies a handheld scanner to the fuchsia wristbands around the wrist of a bikini-clad girl—the open-sesame to unlimited booze and access to the resort. "Let's buy day passes," I tell March, while my gaze swipes across the lobby to the egg-shaped alcove housing the desk. Their computers are not entirely concealed under the counter; the top half is within reach, lined with tempting USB ports. I lower my voice. "We'll plug into one of the desk units to access their booking system."

"Excellent," he agrees, shrugging on his most cordial smile as we stride toward the desk.

A tawny receptionist in a tight white dress spots March and immediately flashes him a blinding grin. I can feel my girlfriend claws grow sharper by the second as she drags an appreciative gaze all over my turf. I make sure to retract them and paste an expression of brain-dead candor on my features while March leans against the counter and bullshits her with a smile that could melt tungsten.

I sidle aside and pretend to admire the vase of birds of paradise standing near her computer, my hand discreetly reaching inside my pocket for a USB key that's barely the size of a penny. Once it's in, there'll be nothing but a one-millimeter edge peeking out of the port, nothing anyone will notice until it's way too late to do anything about it.

My hand shoots out to plug in the key while the girl turns to laser print our wristbands and chirps about the resort's ten restaurants and the "house rules."

—No pictures or videos allowed in the topless areas.

—Heavy petting in public is fine; successful intercourse isn't.

—Propositioning other guests is the name of the game, but please don't be clingy.

Also, apparently, we're not allowed to bang any of the in-house strippers, but "feel free to request a list of recommended venues." Sweet Jesus, they really thought of everything.

I tug off the thin plastic tab protecting the USB key—no print or DNA left. By the time the receptionist trots back to the counter with our silicone wristbands, I've already flipped out my phone and logged as an admin into the Temptation's booking system. I hold out my wrist with a happy little smile, as does March, and the moment we're safely away from the desk I tell him, "Cachemire Fazali: she checked in with Vince in room 7307, but it was yellow-taped by the cops last night, and a manager moved her to 7021, ground floor, garden-side. She badged in at 5:12 this morning, ordered room service at 11:47, and hasn't badged out since."

"Then let's go pay her a courtesy visit," he replies.

"Okay." I switch to command prompt on my phone while we hurry across the lobby. "I'm masking the ground floor hallway's surveillance feed with the one from the second floor with a sixty-second delay, just in case. Even if they notice, the guys in the control center will probably think it's a bug at first."

That earns me a wink. "What would I do without you?"

He'd locate all blind spots in a matter of seconds, I guess. Now invisible to security, we make our way around a glass partition printed with a giant picture of a naked, sweaty couple banging against a wall. March and I exchange a pained look, trapped as we are in this strange plastic paradise.

"I don't know how I feel about this place," I admit, staring at my reflection in the pink glass.

The corners of his lips tug downward while he searches his inner pocket for his mini bottle of hand sanitizer. He squeezes a generous dollop in his palm and rubs his hands together before tucking the bottle back where it belongs and swapping it for his black leather gloves. Leather squeaks as he fits them in place. "I wouldn't call it my dream vacation."

"Yeah, I kinda like the idea of the whole tongue-in-cheek softcore imagery, and I low-key hope they have penis-shaped candy in the rooms. But I don't think I could, I mean . . ." I wave my hand at the hallway ahead of us in the guise of an explanation, a labyrinth of purple carpet and white glass walls all topped by a gilded ceiling.

March cocks an eyebrow at the row of doors, several of which bear a doorknob sign informing us not to disturb the guests while they're having a sexy time. "I think I see what you mean."

I bite back a giggle. "Let's go find her."

We hurry toward room 7021. A muffled shriek filters through one of the doors before we've even spotted the number. Bingo.

"Leave me alone, Patrick!" The voice is young, female—Cachemire's, assuredly.

March immediately moves in position near the door, right hand resting inside his jacket on the grip of his gun. He tips his head in a silent order for me to join him against the wall. Inside, our mystery guest is trying to reason with Cachemire. "Once the new season airs —"

"At this rate, we'll all be dead by the time it does! Vince was *literally* shot. I'm not dying for Gualtiero's shit! Now, help me zip it up in the back!" she yells.

March and I exchange a speaking glance. Where's the traumatized side-chica who whined to Mexican cops that Joy was the one who'd threatened Vince? That sounds a lot like suspect talk to me. March motions for me to step back. As soon as I'm a couple feet away from the door, he pulls out his gun with one hand and reaches for the doorknob with the other. Cachemire's probably too busy fighting with "Patrick" to notice the click of the door opening.

There's a sudden splash of light and colors as the door slams open, revealing a room whose walls are covered with a psychedelic rainbow pattern. We barge in, immediately greeted by a shrill scream. That unexpected soprano doesn't belong to Cachemire; she's nowhere in sight. The prey is a guy about my age wearing a white Lacoste polo and impeccably pressed red chinos, whose hands flip up in the air when he sees March's gun.

"Please don't kill me!" begs our college fashion gravure.

I mutter a vague reassurance that we won't while March's icy gaze scans the bedroom in under a second, as does mine. Bed is undone; more naked girls printed on the wall above the headboard; empty suitcase near the bathroom door; open patio door leading to a narrow terrace and a garden beyond. I cast Patrick an accusing glare. "She ran away!"

He whines something about it not being his fault while March and I race to the balcony. He leaps over the garden furniture with feline grace and shouts, "Stay with him!" over his shoulder, before running off across the lawn in search of our suspect.

Maybe we misread Patrick's panicked shrieking and general look of helplessness: the second March is out of sight, I read renewed determination in his saucer-wide eyes. His hands lower cautiously as he gauges me. He's seeing a girl who barely reaches his chin, in pineapple-printed coveralls, and who carries no gun. His eyes dart to the bedroom door, which remains open behind me. Sweat glistens at the roots of his artfully tousled and honey-highlighted hair. I am now the only thing standing between him and freedom.

I can do this—I have to. Breathing out some of the tension humming through my body, I raise my fists in what hope is a proper fighting stance. "Don't move," I warn him. "I know krav maga."

Okay, not really—a little. March gives me basic self-defense lessons in Central Park on Wednesdays and Sundays. Not that Patrick could know about any of this, but he risks it all anyway. He lunges at me with a war cry and the very obvious intent to shove me out of the way. Sudden fear takes over despite my hours of hardcore training on Sheep's Meadow. I stagger back but manage to whirl to his side as he attempts to force his way to the door. I was going for a spinning crescent kick, but I hop on one foot, wobble, and ultimately opt to send my sneaker flying straight to his groin. My aim is mercilessly true, and he's going to feel that one all the way to his kidneys. Patrick collapses with a groan of agony, defeated.

By Randy Couture, I can't believe I took him down! He's the first man I ever neutralized in hand-to-hand combat. He curls up like a salted slug on the pink rug and begs for mercy, shielding his head with his hands.

"Where is she going?" I growl, reaching for the first weapon my hand meets: a pillow on the bed.

"I don't know!"

"Wrong answer!" A whiff of vanilla and flowers tickles my nostrils—Cachemire's perfume—as I hit him with the pillow repeatedly. He coughs a series of moans. I keep hammering, aiming at his head. Thank God he's too shocked and his balls hurt too much for him to realize that, as far as torture instruments go, a pillow deals pretty low damage.

"Stop! Stop! She has a Corolla!"

I pause in my ruthless pummeling. "What?"

"In the parking lot!"

"What color?"

"White!"

That'll do. The clock is ticking fast, and I think I've juiced all I can out of my witness for now. Leaving Patrick to nurse his nut pain, I bolt to the terrace and across the garden. If I remember the floor plan correctly, the parking lot is somewhere to my right on Kukulcan, on the other side of the 'Passion' wing. I pull out my phone and punch March's ostrich icon in the speed dial list as I race through a crowded gym, then a smoothie bar. He picks up immediately, and I yell, "She probably went to the parking lot! Where are you?"

"On the beach. I'll be there in twenty seconds." Trust March to have memorized every detail of the resort's plan and be able to accurately predict how fast he can cover the distance from point A to B, taking into account all potential obstacles in his way.

I hang up and push myself through the lactic acid burn in my calves and the frantic hammering of my heart. Maybe we can still catch her. A flurry of sweaty chests and flashy sarongs flash past me as I barrel through revolving doors and onto the parking lot. My head automatically flips in the direction of the loud, frantic honking coming from across the lot. Twenty yards away, a white Corolla is blaring for a black Dodge SUV to clear the exit. I mentally thank the Dodge's inept driver as I cover the rest of the distance. My feet skid to a halt, mere feet away from the Corolla's driver side.

This is either an optical illusion or the most important moment of my life. Where I expected Cachemire's face, a pair of huge, dark, and almond-shaped eyes reflect the sunlit cars and palm trees around. Behind the wheel, a gray-skinned alien is bobbing its large head at the other driver and furiously hitting the steering wheel to produce the din blasting through my eardrums. My mouth still hangs open in complete stupefaction as the Dodge's passenger door opens, and a blonde girl steps out, looking pissed.

The whole thing hasn't lasted more than a few seconds, and that's all it takes for my mind to adjust to this reality. There was an empty suitcase in Cachemire's bedroom. It's a costume. Our celestial visitor tried to escape under a grotesque disguise, which she probably borrowed on set. Also, the blonde prowling our way is wearing cargo pants, a black tank top, and she's either hitting the gym hard or injecting Synthol in her deltoids. Cachemire stops honking just long enough to look around and notice both the blonde and me.

I don't have time to deal with a case of Mexican 'roid rage on top of everything else. I grab the Corolla's door handle and tug. "Cachemire, get out of the car!" I yell.

She doesn't. And the only good news is that I let go of the locked door just in time not to have my shoulder dislocated when she shifts to reverse and hits the gas. I stumble back with a yelp and watch, helpless, as she rear-rams a tacky turquoise Porsche that was parked nearby. Plastic rains from a shattered light, and the Corolla is now stuck sideways in the aisle. It's over for you, Cachemire.

Meanwhile, the blonde who stepped out of the Dodge just reached behind her back for something. I understand before I can even make out the sharp lines of a gun barrel, the rush of realization turning into a lash of panic that electrifies me. She's aiming at the Corolla, and I don't carry a gun—nor do I wear Kevlar. In the time it takes me to weigh my options, a gunshot cracks to our left, the detonation shaking my frame even as my feet remain wedged in place.

The blonde drops her gun with a shout of pain. She staggers back, holding her now bloody wrist and falls to her knees when a second bullet enters and exits her thigh in a crimson haze. I dart a look in the direction of the resort's entrance, where the shooting came from, and sure enough, March made it in under twenty seconds as promised, semiautomatic in hand. "Island, get down!"

It's the only warning I get before the Dodge's driver jumps out in his turn, an SMG in hand. He raises the submachine gun in March's direction and fires several short rounds of fire, the bullets clanking through the cars around us. I dive to the ground and take cover behind the Corolla as instructed. The blonde girl's moans and Cachemire's screams are a distant racket in my ears as I frantically scan the asphalt under the surrounding cars for a sign of March.

The black-clad legs racing to the Corolla aren't his. Combat boots crush the gravel five feet away from me. I curl into a tight ball and watch the guy's feet stop in front of the driver's door. Then it's a few impatient clicks as he tries the handle in vain. Cachemire has gone ominously quiet, and all I can do is watch, powerless to rescue her— I'm not even sure I'll still be alive a minute from now. I grit my teeth and take slow breaths, even as my mind keeps conjuring images of a flurry of bullets ripping through my limbs and organs in under a second. My muscles coil, anticipating fight, flight, and mostly agony. *March, where the hell are you?*

The shooter takes one step back, right before a shrill scream erupts from inside the Corolla. Cachemire is still alive, and I'm guessing he's now aiming at her. "Get out," barks a gruff voice. There's something familiar about his accent, an anchor for my brain to hold on to in this flood of adrenaline. I screw my eyes shut, mentally replaying the way he hit those T's just a little too hard and diphthongized "out." Dutch, maybe. *Or South African . . .* The sound of the Corolla's door opening breaks through my trance.

A gray three-toed foot peeks out and retreats just as fast when a single gunshot rents the air. The guy gasps a groan, pressing his side. He didn't look behind that red minivan across the lot, and neither did I. His submachine gun clatters to the ground as he lumbers back toward the Dodge. The sight of March leaping over a sedan's hood to go after him is my cue to scramble to my feet. I lunge for the discarded gun still resting on the hot, dusty asphalt, intent on bullying Cachemire out of that goddamn Corolla. Screams are filtering through the glass doors of the resort. We need to get out of here— fast—before the police show up.

Cachemire starts shrieking and shaking her big alien head when she sees me standing by her door, gun in hand, while March wrestles the wounded blonde out of his way to reach the Dodge. The driver's door slams shut; he shifts to reverse. A hissing sound has me swivel my head to the right, toward the entrance of the lot. I glimpse one of Angel's men, a big guy with a ponytail. There's a deceptively short tube propped on his shoulder, and that's the last thing I register before a shock wave sends me flying back to the ground and rattles every bone in my body in the same instant that the Dodge bursts into flames.

"March!" I cry out, only to spot him at once, covering the blonde's body, not even ten feet away from the blazing vehicle. That was the worst possible time to be a gentleman but thank God he's okay. Joined by half a dozen friends, Angel's goon lowers his lovely piece of Russian tech and contemplates the Dodge's smoking carcass while March rushes to my side.

"Are you all right?"

My head bobs in every direction in an attempt at a proper nod. Not the answer he wanted. March's palms quickly skim down my arms and legs, searching for cuts and fractures. When his quick assessment returns only scrapes and dust, his fingers linger in my hair as his frantic gaze searches mine. I'm guessing he's checking my pupils.

"I'm fine," I say, clinging to him to get back to my feet. "We need to get out of here with Cachemire now. This is a disaster."

March glances at the few vacationers cautiously treading toward the crime scene, then at the large glassy eyes of our prime suspect. He nods to himself once, and by the time he opens the Corolla's door, his poker face has slammed in place, at once icy and genial. "Good morning, Miss Fazali. May I ask you to come out?"

Cornered, Cachemire cautiously extracts her costume-clad body from the car—the head is a little big and catches on the roof, but a moment later, she's standing in front of us. The tension in my muscles lessens for all of a second before she steps back and starts yelling at the top of her lungs. "Help me! Somebody help! Security!"

"No, wait—" I try to warn her, but it's too late. A swipe of March's right leg knocks the wind out of her lungs as she loses her footing. He flips her over and controls her fall in one fluid movement until she's facing the ground, pinned by his knee pressing between her shoulder blades. He gives a sharp tug at the foam mask over her head, revealing a tanned face and dark, slanted eyes. Long black tresses spill out that partly conceal a few stitches on the side of her skull—Joy's handiwork.

"Please don't kill me! I don't know anything; I didn't see anything! Somebody help—"

"*Silence,*" March commands, in what has to be the iciest *Scooby-Doo* reveal I've ever witnessed.

Cachemire instantly shuts up. I fight an unbidden pang of guilt when I see her bravely trying to sniff back a silent tear rolling down her cheek: I've once been on the wrong end of March's submission skills, back when the two of us weren't yet passionately in love. All I have to say about it is that while he does make every effort to control his strength, he doesn't always realize that two hundred pounds of muscle are a lot to handle for aliens and short engineers who weigh half of that.

"No one's gonna kill you, but we need you to answer our questions about Vince," I tell her as March hauls her back to her feet and drags her toward a black van in front of which Angel's men await.

She sniffs a few times. "I really don't know anything."

"That remains to be seen," March retorts coolly.

The strange thing about Cancún is that between the thriving sex business, the booze, the drugs, the party scene, and the occasional cartel war leaving a trail of bodies all over a shopping mall, nothing really ever shocks anyone anymore. I mean, we're in the process of smuggling a girl disguised as an alien into a black pedo van, helped by a bunch of threatening gorillas, all while a car is burning on the parking lot and people are screaming and calling the cops inside the resort, but none of that seems to alarm the pair of old dudes who walk by—possibly on their way back to the beach, judging by their matching fluorescent speedos.

They do break their stride to stare at our sad little bunch, but I detect no reprobation in the leathery copper of their features—only amusement. They just stand there on the sidewalk, trailing hooded eyes on Cachemire's costume and the alien mask lying on the ground near the Corolla. A gentle breeze sways the palm trees around us as Cachemire is hauled in the backseat with a terrified whimper, and they're totally okay with all of that.

March and I climb in the back with her, and he's about to shut the doors when one of the two grandpas ventures closer and asks, "Hell of a party, huh?"

"Cancún never disappoints," March concurs, before sliding the door shut.

ELEVEN

THE MEN IN BLACK

"Since the dawn of time, mankind has been looking to the stars for answers. To the gods. But who were these beings said to have descended from the skies, who lived on mountains that exist on no map, who could heal or destroy, ascend to the sun in flying chariots, sow life or death on earth? Were they truly gods? Is it possible that there's another answer? Is it possible that they left clues for us to decipher? Clues to find them?"

– Gualtiero Franz, *Aliens in Our Past: The Book They Don't Want You to Read*

Ours is a short ride in an atmosphere made heavy by the mingled scents of leather and pungent cologne. Walled behind their sunglasses, our brooding colleagues betray nothing of their intentions, but when the van stops and its door slides open, I realize that we've parked alongside Angel's black Escalade, whose door is open as well.

Cachemire's gray three-toed feet drag against the floor mats in a futile effort to stall the inevitable, but she's already being transferred from one vehicle to another, without even touching the pavement. She opens her mouth to scream again, but March hauls her inside the Escalade. Her final call for help is muted when the door slams behind us.

In the opposite seat, Angel awaits in the dark, elbows braced on his knees, bearded chin resting atop his laced fingers. Curled at his side, Joy casts her rival's costume a disdainful glare. Our alien starts hyperventilating and strains against March's hold. "What's she doing here? Who are—"

"Quiet."

Angel's sepulchral growl effectively silences his prey. He leans back into the black leather upholstery as the engine starts and pins her in place with the Stare. A bead of sweat rolls down Cachemire's cheek when he speaks again, this time in a menacing purr. "You've been having problems lately."

She swallows hard but doesn't reply. The silence in that car is so thick I can hear the steady flow of blood pulsing in my eardrums.

"Your lover was shot," Angel goes on, in that same eerily calm tone. "And the men who did it stole his laptop."

His eyes narrow, studying Cachemire's reaction to this bit of news. Her teeth are clenched tight, but she remains perfectly still between us, a mouse frozen before the cobra.

Angel waves a dismissive hand as a soulless smile bares his incisors. "It's all right. Forget all that. The cops, those men . . . they're not your problem anymore."

Cachemire's shoulders slump in premature relief before he concludes, "Now, I'm your biggest problem."

Well, that's one way to put it, and not entirely inaccurate, I suppose: trapped in the inky depths of Angel's stare, Cachemire comes apart like a dandelion. Her face scrunches up as her frame is shaken by loud sobs. "Please don't kill me! P-please! I don't know anything!"

"She's lying. She believes that what happened to Mr. Moravia is related to the archeology show they were both working on. She was about to leave the resort in disguise when we intercepted her," March informs Angel, while I search my dusty tote for tissues and give them to Cachemire. She dabs at the trails of mascara on her cheeks and blows her nose loudly, much to March's chagrin—he discreetly inches away from her.

Angel watches with a glum, bored expression, but Joy fidgets in the seat, clasping her hands on her lap with a frown that does little to hide the spark of empathy in her eyes. Maybe because she's been there, and twenty-four hours ago, she was the one blowing her nose— all thanks to Cachemire, I remind myself.

Angel sighs impatiently, shakes his head at our prisoner. "Are you done crying?"

She takes a series of gasping breaths and manages a trembling nod.

"Now you're going to tell me everything you know. If you lie again, my men will break your legs. First."

Seeing Joy blanch and Cachemire threaten to lose it again, I quickly tell the latter, "He's joking, he's joking! He's just trying to scare you."

Angel's glare knifes me, but only for a second, before Joy roars, "She's my problem, and we do things *my* way! So, don't you *dare* threaten her. What the fuck is wrong with you?"

The entire car holds its breath, including the driver hiding behind the partition, I'm certain. Angel's eyes screw shut; his nostrils flare as he slowly inhales and exhales, reining in whatever furious beast lurks inside him. "Then question her," he orders Joy.

A silent observer of whatever-the-hell just happened, March

ducks his chin, encouraging Joy to lead the interrogation.

Joy leans forward and searches Cachemire's shifty gaze. "We've been through the police report. You told them I threatened to kill Vince, and during yesterday's incident, you quoted me as telling him—" She takes a tablet resting on the seat at her side. Her fingers skim across the glass; she clears her throat. "*You steaming can of ass-Ebola. I will curb-stomp your balls. I will throw all your shit out the window and you with it.*"

Cachemire stares down at the three-toed feet of her costume. "It's true," she mumbles. "You really said that." Her fingers reach for the stitches on her scalp and graze them, perhaps to emphasize her point that Joy could definitively have ended Vince after finding them together.

Joy's pink nails rap on the tablet's screen. She scoffs. "And you took off in your Roswell costume because you were scared of *me*, right?"

Cachemire swallows, but no sound comes out.

"You told your colleague that you believed the entire crew would die," March reminds her.

She inches away from him in response—understandable. "I really don't know anything. It was Vince: he took a pic with his phone. I told him to delete it!"

"A pic of what, Cachemire?" I encourage.

"Gualtiero found something under the golf course at El Rey. Some kind of tomb, I think. He had the coffin shut before guys moved it, and no one was allowed to take any picture. But I think Vince slipped into the truck and took one."

A shiver of curiosity runs down my spine. "Have you seen it?"

Her gaze turns shifty. "Just for a second. I didn't care."

"And what was on it?" I insist. Dammit, what kind of girl isn't interested in stolen pics of mysterious alien tombs?

"It was just a dried-up dead guy, I think," she mumbles. "Not even an alien or anything. It was gross, but Vince thought it was cool and mysterious or whatever."

March's eyes narrow in interest. "And you think that whoever shot Mr. Moravia was looking for that picture?"

"I don't know, okay?" Her breathing grows frantic. "I just know Gualtiero thinks they're after him, and he was like, 'No one must know. These people won't hesitate to kill us.' And everyone thought he was just being his usual insane self. I mean . . ." She rolls her eyes. "He thinks Jesus was an alien."

Angel's chest heaves in silent indignation, while March drags a hand across his mouth, perhaps to conceal any sign of disbelief. I'm willing to admit that the Jesus thing isn't Franz's most convincing theory, and his only support is Raël, the French guru of a UFO cult who claims to have been personally visited by aliens in 1973. But back to our current extraterrestrial detainee. "Do you know who he was talking about? Who is Franz afraid of?" I ask Cachemire.

Her next word comes in a terrified whisper. "The Collegium."

I barely have the time to glimpse March's eyes grow wider than I've ever seen them before his poker face takes over.

Meanwhile, my mouth hangs half-open in shock. "You mean like in the show? I think they were mentioned a few times, right?"

March turns to me, and I think I glimpse a tic in his jaw. "Oh, is that so?"

"Yeah. He says they're this evil secret society paid by governments to hide the truth from the public about ancient astronauts," I explain. "But, um . . ." I give Cachemire an apologetic wince. "I think he made them up. It's a classic case of circular reference. When you look it up, Gualtiero Franz's stuff comes up, and he cites works by other ancient alien specialists, but these guys actually base their theory about the Collegium on his own early episodes and books. There's no academic work credibly expanding on his initial claims. I spent a lot of time researching it back when I was in college."

March seems pleased with my explanation, and I can even see the hint of a dimple, but everyone else is judging. I can feel it in the beat of stunned silence that stretches in the car. Joy won't speak, but I can read it all in her eyes, hear her chastening in my head. *You always said you had "work to do" every time I wanted to take you to parties. Were you seriously looking up ancient alien shit on Wikipedia while I tried everything in my power to get you laid? How could you do this to me?*

Her eyes laser me apart from the opposite seat before she gives a shrug. "Maybe someone's really after the show, and your boss wants to believe it's that Collegium thing. What are they like, anyway?"

"Let me show you," Cachemire pleads, reaching into the neck of her costume with a shaky hand.

March's shoulders tense in readiness, but all she pulls out is her iPhone. She starts scrolling and tapping under four pairs of attentive eyes. "These are roughs we shot in Rome about a year ago. They've never been aired."

I chew on my lower lip in anticipation when the show's logo spins into view against a star-studded cosmos. The screen fades to black and cuts to a night scene. The camera pans over ancient ruins, archways, and brick walls illuminated by the glare of flashlights. Footsteps hurry on the gravel; the focus shakes and threatens to make me seasick.

"They were at the Baths of Caracalla," Cachemire comments. "Gualtiero wanted to explore the tunnels underneath. He thought there was a secret passage leading to some temple." She fast-forwards the video to a part where sixty-something Gualtiero Franz and his trademark gray 'fro and twitching mustache pop up in front of the camera.

He whispers in a headset with his distinctive German-Swiss accent. "Dear friends, I don't think we've ever taken that level of risk before." He freezes without warning. "Did anyone hear *that*?"

Clanking echoes in the dark off camera, followed by a gurgling growl. Chills cascade down my back as the camera and flashlights swipe around the ruins and focus on a moving shape. The camera zooms, and someone lets out an audible "*fuck*" of relief in the background. Spoiler alert: Gualtiero Franz didn't find an alien this time either.

March raises an amused eyebrow at me while onscreen a young bum with a mess of sandy-blond curls and a craggy beard raises his can at the cameraman and belches again. He looks so drunk even his gnarled wooden cane isn't of much use to support him when he takes a few hesitant steps before lumbering back in the night.

Cachemire huffs and fast-forwards. "Sorry, it was after that part."

When the video resumes playing, Franz and his crew appear to have descended underground. He can be heard panting loudly as he motions to the entrance to a dark corridor. The camera zooms in, lingering on columns of inscriptions engraved in the walls—Latin and cuneiform. "Behind me is the only access left to a secret temple dedicated to the Mesopotamian god Nergal, solar deity and harbinger of war and destruction."

My ears perk up. *Hang on, Nergal?* As in, Nergal, the lion-shaped god who, according to ancient Mesopotamian tablets, "paralyzes with fear" those who behold him, and incidentally serves as the symbol of an ancient society of assassins who're best left in the shadows they favor? My muscles tense so hard you could pluck a C-sharp from me as the crew progresses down a dank tunnel. The glare of their flashlights reveals a rusty armored door barring the way.

"This," he announces in a febrile voice, "is what the Collegium doesn't want you to see: the definitive proof that they—"

His tirade is cut short by a crashing sound as the camera is sent flying to the ground. A crewman picks it up just in time for it to record a beefy shadow in cargo pants. A male voice barks in a thick Italian accent, "Visits are closed; you're trespassing!" Franz attempts to argue, but that same shadow lunges to charge the cameraman and head-butts him before smashing the camera too. The screen goes black and cuts to Franz sitting in an old library with bandage strips all over his face.

"They don't want you to know," he announces solemnly. "The Collegium is funded by some of this world's darkest powers to hide the truth about ancient astronauts from the public. I've been fighting them for thirty years, and, as you've seen, our crew risked their lives to pierce their secrets. But I won't give up. You deserve to know; mankind has a right to know where we came from."

It's only after I stop the video that I notice the way March's hands are clasping his knees in an uncharacteristic display of emotion. His grip eventually loosens, and it takes him a couple more seconds to find his words—or rather one single word. "Regrettable."

Joy considers the tablet with a thoughtful pout and asks him, "Have you ever heard of these guys?"

He doesn't miss a beat. "No, but they do seem quite violent."

I know that absent look and vaguely compassionate tone; he's lying his ass off, like when I asked him if there was a reason he never wore the pairs of funny boxer briefs I kept buying for him. He said no, really, maybe he just hadn't gotten around to wearing them yet . . . until I discovered his underwear was color-coded for each day of the week, and there was no slot allotted in his schedule for platypus-printed boxer briefs. He's made one since: last Saturday of the month.

But this isn't about March's neurotic underwear routine, and if those "quite violent" guys from the Collegium are who I think they are, I can see a very good reason why Vince would have been casually shot and thrown out the window directly into a salad bar for the sole crime of having taken a pic of a dead guy.

In the opposite seat, Angel has reclined and is staring at us in silence, each menacing angle of his face sculpted by the shadows. Goosebumps bloom on my nape when his gaze meets March's—probing, drilling. His eyes narrow a fraction. "You and I are going to have a—"

"Hold on, what's that noise?" Joy cuts him off, her chin jerking up at the SUV's roof.

I strain my ears and see March's pensive expression become a cool glare. *That* . . . is the growing hum of a rotor right above the car.

TWELVE
THE BIKINI PARTY

"I don't believe you people. You haul my butt outta bed at
midnight, you fly me off to only God knows where to see some
lousy helicopter, and there's not even any cream cheese!"

– *Airwolf*, "Shadow of The Hawke: Part 1," January 22, 1984.

Joy and Cachemire don't react as fast as March, Angel and I do,
probably because it takes a Tiger firing a pair of Hellfire IIs at your
house for you to learn how close is too close when it comes to
choppers—which is exactly what happened to March's crib the last
time he got dragged into Lions' business.

As the droning engulfs us, Angel lunges at the tinted window
with a muttered curse. "¡Chucha!" *Fuck!*

I do the same and see a shadow stretching along the road. "It's right above us!"

Joy, too, leans to her window and cranes her neck. "What's going on? Is there a helicopter?"

"I'm afraid so," March tells her, just as the partition goes down and Angel barks to his driver, a big guy with a jet-black ponytail, "¡Más rápido!". *Faster!*

And faster he goes. That guy hits the gas pedal like a sledgehammer. There's a roar so loud I feel my ribs rattle before my back gets slammed into the leather upholstery along with the rest of my organs as we career right to climb on the sidewalk and pass several cars. Joy wasn't wearing her seat belt, and her body jerks forward from the sudden momentum. I reach out to catch her, but Angel is faster and clamps his arms around her waist to stop her from flying my way—and possibly through the open partition.

Through it all, Cachemire keeps sobbing and screeching hysterically, shielding her face with her arms like it's gonna help. Was I ever that loud in my humble beginnings? For March's sake, I hope not.

March, who, by the way, is . . . *Sweet Raptor Jesus in a quesadilla!* "What are you doing?" I yell, a gust of wind whipping my hair in my eyes as he lowers his window. Who am I kidding? I know exactly what he's doing, and at this rate, I'll be single by nightfall. He risks an arm outside to grip the SUV's roof and hauls his upper body out of the vehicle to take a better look at our assailants.

My heart skips a beat when his grip goes white-knuckled on the windowsill. I lean, contort, and it only takes a second for me to see what he's seeing: we're racing in the massive shadow of an Osprey— two rotors, elongated body, dark paint. That, at least, is a danger I can identify. What I'm much more worried about is the dark circular plate hanging from a steel cable and being reeled down toward us. *Hold on, is that a . . . ?*

March shouts, "Everyone put on your seat belts!"

I vaguely register Angel asking him, "What is it?" before

something hits the roof with a deafening clang. A hum immediately follows, whose potent vibrations reverberate through the car's body—and mine. The tablet that was still sitting next to Joy quivers and freaking flies to the car's roof, to stay stuck up there, along with Angel's sunglasses—that were sitting unsecured in Joy's hair—and Cachemire's phone. My seat belt comes to life and floats like seaweed before I'm able to fasten it. You gotta be kidding me . . . An electromagnet?

March manages to secure a wailing Cachemire with an arm and leans across her lap to check on me.

"Please tell me this isn't what I think it is," I gasp.

He gives my arm a squeeze. "It's going to be all right."

No, it's not, because we're going up. I take in a deep breath and hold on to his gaze just half a second longer. It's my shelter, my center. There I can forget the wild pounding in my chest and focus.

Joy is staring at me in incomprehension, paralyzed in her seat. "W-What . . ." She fumbles to hold on to something and grips Angel's shirt, then his arm as we gain speed. Faster, faster, until the wheels are barely touching the ground. And we are weightless, rising above the roofs and palm trees of the Hotel Zone. Fifty feet below a few cars spin out of control, as if sucked into the wind of the rotor—the reality is that those drivers just freaked out of their mind and let go of the wheel in the middle of the avenue.

"They're hauling us up!" Angel barks, looking through his window at the ground below while in the front, his henchman slowly lifts his hands from the wheel, in a state of sideration. In the backseat, too, there's this beat of stunned silence, and even Cachemire's screaming dials down to quiet moans as we fly several hundred feet over Cancún.

I won't lie: the smaller the resorts and the beach get, the worse my stomach is lurching, and I wish I had the luxury to shriek my eyeballs out that we were just snatched by a giant electromagnet dangling from a goddamn helicopter—which is a first even for me.

But there's no room for one more hysterical passenger in this vehicle. Joy is gasping for air and gripping Angel's forearm so hard she's gonna give him new scars to add to his legend, and the strangled sounds escaping Cachemire are rapidly rising in intensity again.

I grab her hand in a bid to keep her sane and turn to March. "What do we do now?"

"Too high to jump safely," Angel notes after a glance through the window. "We need to go down."

"Yes! I want to go down!" Joy howls. "Please!"

Gripping my belt like a lifeline, I try to feign the composure I lack. "We're gonna be fine, I promise." Truth is, I have no idea what's going to happen. Especially if those guys up there are Lions.

"They're taking us south," March grits out. He's right. Upon risking a peek outside, I spot the Tropical Temptation's roof and a large splash of turquoise—the ocean.

Angel's eyes turn to slits. "Make them lose altitude. I'll take care of the rest."

What's the rest—*us*? What kind of plan are these two telepathically cooking up this time? Apparently yet another one where March dies. My pulse revs dangerously close to heart attack speed when he hoists his body out the window again, jacket flapping in the wind against an impossibly blue sky. One last look for me, like a crack through the ice freezing his features into a scowl. "Trust Angel," he shouts. And the rest he just mouths, so fast I'm probably the only one to catch it. *I love you.*

The second after, he grips the roof and climbs out of the car. A series of thumps above our heads—his footsteps—and nothing. I fear he's trying to climb that steel line, which is marginally worse than that time he did the same with one of the Roosevelt Tram's cars and broke the whole thing, cable included. Scratch that. It's much worse, and my stomach is leaping up my throat so badly I think I'm gonna be sick.

Meanwhile, Angel has managed to pry Joy's fingers off his arm to reach under the seat. Never mind, she's got his thigh now.

"Breathe!" I yell. "We're gonna make it!" I think. I hope.

Angel opens a compartment and retrieves two round, flat, and silvery packages the size of large pizzas. He tosses one to me. It's made of supple silicone and looks like some kind of vacuum-sealed inflatable pool toy, with a small cord dangling from the side and a thick red nylon handle in the middle. Before I can figure out whether we're looking at a base jump down to the solid ground in a life raft, the car lurches and sends us flying to the side. My cheeks get squished against a window while Cachemire clings to me with a shrill cry that obliterates what's left of my right eardrum. "Stop! Stop it! Take me down! Please! *Please!*"

Joy's skin has turned a pasty white; her head is lolling against Angel's shoulder as if her neck were made of jelly. *Dammit,* I think she's passing out. Over the rotor's continuous roar and the wind rushing through the open window, I register the faint crack of gunshots. Blood hammering in my temples, I strain to peek outside as we swing in all directions in the worst ride Cancún has to offer. March is doing something up there, and it's sort of working: we're swaying down, and I glimpse the mottled blue of the ocean and the resort's colorful roofs and terraces, way too far—or much too close.

Angel seizes the opportunity of a brutal swing left to gather Joy in his arms, and I try to do the same with a shaking and sobbing Cachemire. He brings the mysterious plastic package to his chest with a white-knuckled grip on its nylon handle. "Island!" he calls, and I shudder when I realize he just called my *name.* Our situation must be desperate. "You grip the handle, and you tug at the cord. *Nothing else!*"

"Now?" I yell, panic squeezing my throat and threatening to take over rational thought.

"Twenty seconds!" he shouts back.

I look out the window: we're already circling away from the shore above the ocean. But even if we manage to jump in the water, we're still way too high. A fall from this height is guaranteed to shatter every bone in our bodies unless we're Olympic divers. Spoiler alert: I mostly know how to do bombs.

"It's too high!" I cry out. "And March is still up there. I'm not jumping without him!"

"He knows what he's doing!"

Does he? I brave the wind whipping my hair in my eyes and stick my head out the window to get a glimpse of the steel line, knowing all along that it's useless: I can't see him, only the sapphire mirror of the ocean below, stretching all the way to the green shores of Isla Mujeres.

Angel opens his door and bellows, "Jump!"

This is going too fast. My head is spinning in tune with the car, Cachemire is going to break my arm soon if she keeps crushing it, and I have a millisecond window to make a decision. I can't get to March, and we're going down one way or another. Everywhere I look, I see the shimmering blue closing in on us.

It's the water or nothing; the water or we all die, so I squeeze my eyes shut and put every fiber of faith and hope I possess in March. Dragging a frenzied Cachemire with me, I tug at the door handle. My door slams open and . . . *Oh, God.* Angel freaking jumped with Joy! Something dark is moving at the edge of my vision. His driver is about to dive too. My hair is whipping my face; I can't see them, and the car is tilting again. I see the waves below as if through a kaleidoscope and feel myself spiral down toward their white crest.

I need to breathe, but my lungs are frantically pumping in vain. *Take the jump, my rational brain screams.* And I do. Or rather, Cachemire and I are catapulted out by yet another swing of the car. She's gripping my neck—strangling me—and her yowl is a siren ringing in my skull as we tumble down. Gasping for air that won't come, I grip the precious red nylon handle and strain to tug at the cord, once, twice. There's not enough strength in my wrist; colorful spots blur my vision, and I have this remote, cottony thought that I'm gonna die before I even hit the water. I tug once more with all I have.

Something clicks, sighs, and it's not a silvery raft inflating, but round, transparent walls. A protective shell pops around Cachemire and me lightning fast to cocoons us.

It's a ball.

It's a fricking ball. Angel keeps *inflatable balls* in his car in case he has to jump out. Honestly, who does that? I can't see the sea anymore; I just know the fall is coming. I register a splash somewhere outside this terrifying silicone bubble. The moment after, my body jerks and violently collides with Cachemire's, and I think I black out for a few seconds. We bounce hard, and at last comes the blessed sound of water sloshing around the ball's walls. Blowing hair that's not mine from my face, I squint and see blurred azure all around me, dark shapes shivering beyond the walls of our silicone bubble. The few functional neurons I have left conclude that we somehow made it. We're alive.

A rotor throbs softly, slowly at the edge of my consciousness. The helicopter . . . March. My body jerks. "March, March! Where are you!"

My screams are muted by an earsplitting crash and a sudden shock wave that sends our bubble underwater, drowned by a powerful roll before it bounces back to the surface. I know that plaintive whirring sound as the rotors sputter and die, the charred smell that goes with it. I blink the shock off and shove Cachemire off my chest. March! Did he jump? *Oh no, no . . .* My eyes watering fast, I punch the ball's walls desperately until my fist meets a slit in the doughy surface. Cool water laps at my hand, then my arm as I try to birth myself from that bizarre plastic womb.

The air is fogged by a cloud of vaporized droplets—probably the result of the blades whipping the surface upon impact. It's the car I see first, or rather glimpse before churning water engulfs it. Then the Osprey's shattered carcass, floating belly up and rapidly sinking, too, as water rushes inside with the same ominous bubbling noises. The steel cable snapped during the crash, and the three-foot-wide electromagnet that lifted us off Kukulcan Avenue is no doubt fast on its way to the bottom of the Atlantic.

I free my legs from the silicone bubble and paddle my way closer to what's left of the aircraft—a rapidly disappearing metal islet. I can't see March. I sputter salty water, take a gasping breath and swim underwater, but there's nothing, just a shroud of floating parts and foam clouding my vision. I reach out in vain, will my legs to propel myself toward the wreck, only to be brutally hauled back.

I squirm around with a gurgling scream and choke on a gulp of water that burns down my throat. My hands claw at the arm locked around my torso until they meet a drenched indigo shirt and hard, wiry muscles. It takes another half-second for my brain to register the second bubble floating in my peripheral vision and a lump of flowery silk inside. Thank God, Angel and Joy landed safely.

"Let me go!" I yell at him. "We have to find March! We—"

"He's here," Angel snaps back.

"Where?" I scan the surf frantically and spot a patch of stark white—his shirt. My heart rams against my rib cage as if to fly to him. He's on the other side of the helicopter's wreck, maneuvering something—someone—out of the water. A man, but not Angel's driver, whose ponytail and black leather jacket I just spotted, and who's holding on to the second bubble where Joy lies. I can't believe we all survived this.

March swims toward us, dragging a listless body clad in dark fatigues. I immediately slip out of Angel's loosening grip to crawl to him.

I am aware, to some degree, that the moment calls for a clear mind and efficient use of what little energy we have left, but as soon as he relinquishes his catch to Angel, I grab his shoulders and crush my mouth to his, licking salty water off his lips. He returns the favor, but our kiss is little more than a brief and desperate taste before I press my forehead to his, panting. "Are you okay?"

It takes March a few husky intakes of air before he replies. "Assuredly in better shape than our friend over here."

I sneak a better look at the brown-haired guy Angel is now keeping afloat, whose Kevlar bears several bullet holes—even a military-grade vest would have stood no chance against March's tungsten bullets at close range. "Is he . . ."

"He's dead," March confirms.

"Then why did you—"

"I want to check his back."

To see if he's a Lion. All members of the brotherhood receive a ritual scarification piece in the shape of a lion head on their back upon joining the ranks. Having seen and touched March's more than once, I know there's no way you can hide that: even a medical procedure to erase it would leave a scar of its own. One wears their oath to the Lions on their skin until the day one dies.

I'm left little time to ponder this, however, as a new hum in the distance makes my stress levels skyrocket all over again. A white arrow is flying our way, raising a cloud of water in its wake.

March eyes Angel. "Yours?"

I tether at the very top of a roller coaster of panic until Angel gives a single nod. Thank you, Raptor Jesus, for always keeping an eye out for me. Indeed, soon enough, a long white and black catamaran draws a graceful arc around us, like an eagle feather that's barely touching the waves. No need to ask what kind of horsepower this thing packs; its glossy hull is sharp as a knife, and the engine sounds like there's an entire nuclear plant crammed inside. I bet my scalp is going to come off once we reach cruising speed.

March steers me toward the boat where two guys who have 'bruiser' written all over their dark shirts and somber expressions await. "Excellent timing. Let's leave before the coast guards arrive."

There's some sloshing, paddling—and yes, more soul-shattering screams—as we push the silicone bubbles closer to the catamaran, so Joy and Cachemire can be safely extracted to the eight-seat cockpit. They both look completely shell-shocked, but otherwise okay—not even drenched like the rest of us. Once we're all onboard the sea monster, Cachemire curls up into a tight fetal ball in the crimson leather of a bucket seat, while Joy brushes her hair from her eyes with shaking hands. Renewed fear licks at my spine at the thought that she might have a bad concussion, but she eventually manages to gasp out a coherent sentence. "W-What the fuck was that?"

"A helicopter," Angel supplies, slicking his hair back before rubbing his jaw with a scowl. Come to think of it, he's been doing that sporadically since we got out of the water. I suspect a dental implant, and my molars hurt for him. That magnet must have drilled it out of his bone or something nasty like that. Ouch.

"No . . ." Joy waves a trembling hand at the devastation surrounding us. "All of that!"

"I'm not sure," I admit, shooting a glance at Cachemire. If I were to venture a guess, I'd say the same Lions who shot Vince because he had been a direct witness to Franz's mystery finding took an interest in Cachemire because she too worked for Franz, and she had been sharing Vince's hotel room—until Joy tried to kill her with a cake plate.

March's hand reaches around my shoulder, pulling me close to him. We're both dripping, but I don't mind the cool contact of his damp shirt. I squeeze his hand tightly to say all the things I can't say out loud, and he returns the favor with a gentle rub of his thumb across my palm. After that, he goes to the front of the cockpit to help Angel's men haul our final guest onboard. The unfortunate young pilot's body tumbles at our feet, a pool of rosy water rapidly spreading around him on the smooth white deck.

Joy's eyes go wide and glassy, and she huddles closer to me. "Oh my God, is he . . . dead?"

I squeeze her hand tight. "Yes."

Her breath hitches in her throat. "Oh my . . . Oh *shit*. What are we gonna do?"

Get rid of the body and try to close our eyes at night when the memory invites itself at the back of our mind—*is what I don't say. "I think March and Angel will handle that part."*

Joy shakes her head like something just won't compute and she's seeing me for the first time. "What do you mean, *handle*? And what is he—" She turns in the seat, and her voice turns shrill when March pulls out the small carbon knife he always keeps strapped around his ankle. "What is he gonna do with that?"

"March," I call softly. My head hurts, my throat is knotted tightly, and I don't know how to tell him out loud that I don't want more blood in front of my best friend. "Maybe . . . not now."

He looks up from the body, guilt deepening the thin lines around his mouth, but Angel casually flips the cadaver on its face and holds out his hand for the knife. "Do it, or I will," he says, back to his usual frosty tone.

March gives a sharp nod and unfastens the guy's Kevlar, before ripping his black jacket open with the blade. Joy clasps a hand over her mouth, her eyes begging me to say or do something.

I can't. I've gone still, even as shivers course across my skin. The scars start right above the gunshot wound that took the man's life. They form a disc, made of dots etched deeply into his flesh: an intricate pattern of curves and chevrons, the mane and the fangs, all carved across his left shoulder. A lion head.

I can practically feel the knots and dents in the scarred flesh, just like as I do when March and I make love, and I caress that same lion on his back. I don't like to imagine the hands that carved it into his skin sixteen years ago, the blood seeping from each new cut and March's agony. It was the price an eighteen-year-old boy paid to join a brotherhood of fellow assassins, a family to make up for the one he had lost too soon: the birthmark of a Lion.

Underneath the seat, the low hum of the catamaran's engine becomes a steady purr whose vibrations I feel in my very bones. Angel stares down at the scarification, his stony gaze letting nothing through. "We're going to return to the villa," he says with that icy quietude I know promises a cyclone. "We're going to dry ourselves and change." He marks a pause and looks up at March while the boat gains speed toward the south point of Isla Mujeres. "But before that, you're going to explain to me why Lions just dropped my car in the middle of the Cancún bay."

THIRTEEN
NAÏVE ART

"I do recall wondering if I would get lasting PTSD over this."

– Manila Clonk, *Clean Shot: A Hitman Romance*

The words Angel just spoke remain suspended above the blue for a short eternity as the wind whips our hair. Then they hit home. Blinking her stupor off, Joy takes a circular look at the dead body, March, and eventually me. "What's that . . . a *Lion*? What is he talking about?" she calls over the mingled roar of the engine and the tons of water we're lifting in our wake.

An excellent—and crucial—question—but not one I want to answer while I'm sitting shivering in Angel's catamaran. We're now gliding along a dock touching a stripe of pristine sand; beyond, a modern hacienda overlooks the private beach, its traditional white concrete walls and tiled roofs encasing immense windows. Joy's accusing gaze is still boring into my avoidant one. She's waiting for an answer.

When March drags a hand over his chin but doesn't offer to enlighten her, Angel moves closer, offering a hand to help her up. "Don't worry about it."

She gives an irritated snort. "Allow me to be the judge of what I worry about."

I'm bracing myself for his inevitable stare of death, followed by some bold social commentary about women's place. What I wasn't counting on is the way his features relax, allowing a flicker of warmth in his eyes. I don't dare to use the word, but I'd almost say he looks . . . gentle. He tips his head to the villa. "Go rest in your room. Abelardo will bring you new dresses." He shoots a dark look at one of his goons, the ponytailed giant with a leather jacket, whose imposing mustache and grim expression remind me of the titular character of *Machete*. "*A toda prisa.*" As fast as possible.

Let's give credit where it's due; Angel tried to be nice. He catastrophically misjudged the gravity of our quandary—as well as Joy's character—but he tried.

She takes a shuddering breath through her nostrils and shrugs off his hand from her shoulder. From the corner of my eye, I notice that Cachemire's head is shrinking into her shoulders as she leans on the aforementioned Abelardo for support—she knows what's coming.

"I don't want any dresses," Joy clips. "Especially not ones you'll buy with . . . with cartel money or whatever. What I *want* is to understand what the fuck just happened here!"

March's expression hardens, and he casually steps over the dead Lion to tower over her. Joy is three inches taller than me but leave it to March to dwarf anyone with a stare cold enough to shatter you like a liquid nitrogen shower. "I'm afraid Island is right; we can't involve you any further. I apologize for the inconvenience you experienced. He and I will arrange your return to New York under escort as soon as possible."

I'm 100 percent behind March on this, but his personal brand of threatening courtesy won't do it either. Joy's chest swells with another wave of outrage, her jaw trembling as she prepares to lash back. I step between the two of them before she can open her mouth. "Look, I'm not even entirely sure what's going on, but one thing I'm sure is we'll put you in danger if we drag you into this."

"I think that's already done," she snaps before shaking her head as if to wrestle her anger away. When she looks at me again, her eyes are the clear aquamarine I know, transparent waters that won't lie. "I can risk my life for my best friend. You know I already did—"

"You have no idea how freaking sorry I am for all of this," I murmur.

Actually, sorry doesn't even begin to describe how shitty I feel at the moment. I'm standing at the top of the mountain of my lies, and under my feet, the ground is quaking, cracking fast. We're past making up clunky scenarios, slapping some glue here and duct tape there to make it all hold together just a little longer. Joy could have seriously died.

Yet her mouth quirks. "I was talking about that time when our old self-cleaning oven caught fire, and I put it out with a Coke bottle because you just panicked and stood there."

"That was epic," I concede, while behind her Angel's chin ducks in evident approval.

She sighs. "What I'm trying to say is that I won't shake any Coke bottles for someone who keeps lying to me."

I take the ultimatum with a straight face, but that sinking feeling in my stomach feels like I'm seconds away from being served divorce papers by my best friend. The catamaran sways gently against the dock, bouncing against a row of fenders. I look past her, at March. His chest heaves, conflict etched in every tired line of his face. "I won't ask you to choose," he says softly.

The tension in my limbs ebbs. This is certainly not an

encouragement to air every last one of our secrets, but rather a compromise. Enough truth for Joy to understand what I need to hide. Enough truth for us to stay friends. I mouth a silent thank-you. He'll never know how much I love him for giving me this and how tight my chest is right now.

I lock eyes with Joy. "Anything I tell you, you can never repeat to anyone. We can't even discuss it again when we return to New York, not over the phone, not by chat, not in public, *nowhere* except my apartment and Struthio's office," I say, watching March nod at these strict terms.

"Deal," Joy replies, her jaw set.

As soon as she's said this, Angel snaps his finger at two of his goons, who've been silently standing guard on the dock until now. "*Limpia eso y prepara la meeting room.*" Clean that up and prepare the meeting room.

One guy immediately leaps back onboard and flips up a seat to retrieve a body bag from the storage compartment underneath. Ignoring the hand Angel holds out to help her off the boat, Joy watches with grim fascination as the man unfolds the bag, made of black plastic . . . printed with a pattern of little llamas, palm trees, and bananas—equally cute and inappropriate.

March catches me as I slip off the deck, his eyes never leaving the bag. "Charming design," he notes as Angel's men work on wrapping the Lion's body.

"Heavy-duty, biodegradable plastic, five colors. You can buy them from my website," Angel replies.

Upon her landing on the dock's sun-washed boards, Joy's next question is one I've heard before. "You have a website?"

He does, and I shudder at the idea of what Joy will find if she connects to Yaythug's notorious "turnpike": a directory hidden on the dark web and listing all sorts of IPs no one should ever connect to, from

Angel's online shop to drug supermarkets, and quite a few hitman boutiques—one of which used to be March's before he deleted it.

"It's a nice villa," I remark, in a bid to lighten the mood as Angel's goons lead the way across the cool concrete floor of the lobby. The sparse designer furniture and mile-high diaphanous white curtains partitioning the living room and den remind me of his Refugio in Ecuador. I recognize Angel's touch—specifically, his pronounced taste for pricey minimalism and dark wood.

He doesn't bother with an answer, but Joy jumps on the occasion. "Wait until you've seen the pool; it's half-indoor in the living room, and it flows under a glass floor."

"I don't remember seeing it the last time I was here. Robust year, I assume?" March remarks with a wry smile Angel doesn't return.

"Guns are the only product no one will ever stop buying."

His comment chills the mood like no freezer ever could, and by the time our guides open the reinforced steel doors to a vast, windowless conference room, Joy has gone quiet. I shift closer and brush my fingers to hers to offer what little comfort I can. She responds with a fleeting smile before sitting at a long stone table at the center of the room. Its rugged edge and dark veins are a stark contrast to the otherwise sleek white walls and polished surfaces of the room. Already my eyes are glued to the main course: a fifteen-foot-wide incurved tactile screen taking most of the opposite wall. Next to four water bottles and glasses, I notice the same number of plastic pens thoughtfully lined up on the table: Angel's goons work fast. My fingers are itching to grab one and just test this beauty.

Angel sits at the center of the table in a black president chair that seems to have been carefully handpicked for its villainous edge, and we gather on each side of him. One of his men turns the screen on and displays a few icons on an otherwise empty desktop whose background is a snowcapped mountain. "Bring her up to speed. You have five minutes," he announces, looking at me.

I'm practically drooling on the table as my fingers reach for a tactile pen. I trot to the screen, tap my fingers to the whiteboard icon, crack my knuckles, and here it goes, my improvised keynote.

"What are the Lions of Nergal?" I ask—rather rhetorically—to my audience. I notice March lacing his fingers with an expression of intense concentration and press my lips tight to conceal a secret smile. "You could call them a secret society of assassins," I explain, doodling a schematic on that oh-so-smooth, oh-so-bright screen. "They're mercenaries, hitmen, operating as a brotherhood. Super well-trained and characterized by their ritualistic practices and command structure—such as their name, which was inspired by an ancient Mesopotamian god, or the scarification you saw on the guy from the helicopter. It's like a narrative that brings them together."

Joy's head bobs as she watches me draw. "What do they have to do with Gualtiero Franz's Collegium thing? Are they the same thing?"

I pause, considering the point. "I'm not sure. I sort of assumed . . ."

March's gaze flits to meet mine, before lowering, as if he's pondering what to say—or not. His old tether to the brotherhood is stretched so thin that if you blink, you could almost believe it's entirely gone, but the truth is that March remains bound by the Lions' secrets, and we're about to spill quite a few. Releasing a quiet sigh, he eventually says, "The Collegium is one of their subdivisions. They collect archeological pieces tied to the brotherhood's history. They do conservation work, negotiate with museums and governments behind the scenes, and steal pieces sometimes . . . usually with minimal violence."

Except for today, I mentally complete.

"Is that why the one in the back is cosplaying as a gladiator?" Joy inquires.

"Yeah," I reply. "It's because they've been around for over two thousand years. A small group of them followed the Boer migration during the eighteenth century, while the others disbanded during the French Revolution and subsequent wars, so today they're 80% South African," I explain, regurgitating stories March told me.

I know what's coming next before I'm even done talking. She casts March a suspicious look. "And how exactly do you know these guys?"

"We will get to that part," I interrupt, "but first, I think you should know they were the ones who kidnapped me a year and a half ago."

She jumps from her seat, slamming her palms to the meeting table. "Holy fuck! I knew that hospital story was bullshit!"

It was. I disappeared for eight months, presumably dead in the bombing of the Poseidon, a glass dome enclosing a giant underwater vacation resort in French Polynesia. The official version everyone saw on TV, from my grandparents to my ob-gyn, is that I was stuck in a French hospital with complete retrograde amnesia and no ID—which sounds better than: *My supervillain uncle kidnapped me to Finland and tried to fire nuclear missiles from space to blow up the free world.*

"But . . . you faked your amnesia?" Joy asks, a scowl chasing her previous shock.

"No. They did something to me." I avert my eyes. I still don't like rehashing these memories. "I couldn't even recognize March's face when he came to save me."

"So that part was true." She covers her mouth with a reverent hand, eyeing him with a whole new level of uncertainty and, I think, respect.

"Yes."

She nods again. "But why did these Lions guys kidnap you?"

"It was . . . very personal." I stare at the virtual whiteboard, wondering where to start. "A long time ago, two brothers who were Lions were in love with the same woman," I begin. "But she chose one, and when she became pregnant with his child, the other brother couldn't stand it. It drove him nuts, and he held on to that grudge for decades."

As I draw and Joy's eyes widen more and more with each swipe of my pen, I remember Angel's silent presence. He'll know every secret we bury in this room, and I don't know how I feel about that, or rather, to what extent I can trust him not to one day use those against March. But I've said too much already anyway. There's no backpedaling.

Joy stares at this new doodle, her brow furrowed. "That potato with the bucktooth . . ."

"Is a lovely tuber," March retorts.

She eyes me expectantly. "Yeah, but isn't that Island?"

There's a growing ache in my chest as I take the pen again, a ghost that sometimes still returns to haunt me at night on the rare occasions when March isn't home and I sleep alone. "His name was Dries," I say quietly. "My mom later met Simon, and he became my dad, but he wasn't my biological father." I swallow. "That was Dries, and together with his brother Anies, he commanded the Lions for decades."

"You're shitting me. How the hell did your mom end up with that guy?"

Despite all the grief and the void their absence left in my life, the thought manages to bring a timid smile to my lips. "They were meant for each other. All my life I thought she was a diplomat, and she was actually this incredible thief, like Catwoman, or maybe Karen McCoy."

"Okay . . ." I can almost hear the gears whirr fast in Joy's brain to figure out the bigger picture. Call it a lawyer's intuition when she asks, "She died in a car accident, right?"

"It wasn't an accident. I thought it was, but the truth is Anies had her executed by one of his men. She got herself tangled in a nasty affair involving the Lions. Anies thought that she threatened his grandiose plans and that Dries, my father, would eventually betray him for my mother. So Anies killed her. He had one of his men shoot her in Tokyo. She was driving, and I was in the passenger's seat."

My hand is shaking, but I keep drawing because Angel's screen is really cool and it's kind of funny, all those stickmen. It's a good way to resurrect the past, even as I can feel something hot roll down my cheek and taste salt at the corner of my mouth.

A shadow moves at the edge of my field of vision. I didn't hear

March rise from the meeting table. His hand strokes my back in slow circles. "Biscuit, do you want to take a break?"

Shaking my head, I wipe my eyes with the back of my hand. "I'm good."

When she sees this, Joy gets up from her chair and joins us to pull me into a tight hug. "Why didn't you tell me?" she asks in a sorrowful whisper.

I swallow back a stupid sob. "Because I didn't know until a year and a half ago."

Composing myself with a few deep breaths, I start another doodle. "It ends well: Dries's favorite disciple saved me from my mom's burning car. He was a dashing young Lion, but I honestly was too out of it to notice back then." My smile returns, as does March's when I draw a handsome potato rescuing me from the flames. "That's when I went to live with my dad—Simon—in New York."

I didn't explicitly state who the disciple was, but Joy knows me too well. She shakes her head slowly, looking March up and down like he just grew a second head. "Oh my God . . . You're one of them? But—"

"I left the brotherhood after the murder of Island's mother," March explains, his poker face firmly in place. "What little values I had at the time were incompatible with the demands of the position."

Joy's features soften as she looks past him, at the tearful stick figures now populating the screen. I think she's starting to understand the depth of March's and my bond. She turns to me. "So, you've known him since you were fifteen? You never mentioned him when we were in college."

"No, I had no idea who he was until I met him again years later. It's another pretty complicated story, but my mom had left loose ends with the Lions and a bunch of evil doucheb—" I notice embers reignite in Angel's dark gaze at my clumsy evocation of The Board, the criminal organization *he* is part of. Its leader, the Queen, used to be another of March's regulars, and Angel's business is only allowed to thrive because it is part of the greater criminal ecosystem the Queen rules over.

I gulp; March shakes his head to signal me not to go there. "My mom had a misunderstanding with a powerful client, but it turned out it was mostly the Lions' fault. They used her to betray that client. Anyway, it all came back to bite me in the ass because some people thought I knew some stuff."

"That's incredibly vague," Joy notes with a doubtful pout. "But basically, March popped back in your life?"

"In short, yes." I exhale a discreet sigh of relief. The Board is a stone I prefer not to turn with Angel sitting ten feet away and dissecting me with that inscrutable glare of his.

After a few seconds of pensive silence, Joy takes a pen from the table and walks up to the screen with the apparent intent to add a doodle of her own. "Was that around the time I caught the two of you in the middle of a BDSM scene in your bedroom?"

Mr. Big

"I can't think of a worse scenario for a first time."

– Manila Clonk, *Clean Shot: A Hitman Romance*

Is it me, or did it just get way hotter in this room? Blood is hammering in my ears, and I can tell I'm flushing all shades of red, a nice scarlet here, a touch of cherry there.

Joy's drawing skills may be far superior to mine, but March's erasing ones are on par. He lunges at the screen to wipe it with his palm almost as soon as she's lifted the pen. "That's a largely fictionalized account of the events which took place that day," he mutters, and I could swear his neck and cheeks are slightly pink—I didn't even think that was physiologically possible for him outside of, say, private moments during which he flushes like the rest of mankind.

Meanwhile, I register some sort of asthmatic rasp coming from the meeting table, a foreign sound that lasts only a couple seconds. I spin around just in time to see Angel's hand move to conceal his mouth. By all the bananas in Ecuador—which is the largest exporter in the world and grows a quarter of earth's production, by the way—I think I just saw Angel Somoza laugh.

I glare at Joy. "The nipple clamps were really unnecessary."

She gives a shrug, complete with a foxy smile. "That's how I remember it. Anyway, what about the guy who had your mom killed? And your father, Dries? Where are they now?"

"Okay, back to my story: After my mother's death, Dries had no idea Anies was the one responsible, and they kept leading the Lions together for another decade.

"Is that a glass in Anies's hand?"

"Yeah. He drank absinthe all the time to numb himself because he had terminal cancer."

She shrugs. "Not sorry for him."

"Me neither." *Definitively not.* "At any rate, they were co-leading, but Anies was plotting stuff behind Dries's back, and when the time came to get rid of him, it wasn't enough for Anies that he had killed my mom; he needed to destroy Dries, so he framed him for the bombing of flight DL504."

Something clicks. Joy's eyes widen so much I fear they might pop out. "Holy fucking shit! He was the guy on TV, the terrorist! His face was everywhere!"

I confirm with another doodle. "Exactly. In a way, it was the worst thing Anies could have done to him. Dries had lived all his life in the shadows, and Anies totally exposed him."

"No," March says quietly, looking at me. "It wasn't the worst thing Anies did to him."

I close my eyes briefly, feeling an old fear creep back, a nightmare that still clings to my skin even after months of recovery. "Anies also tried to eliminate all of Dries's disciples, so no Lion would be left who might support him. They came for March and blew up his house in Cape Saint-Francis," I explain.

Joy tilts her head at this new drawing. "Someone shot dicks at his house?"

"No, they're missiles!"

Her hands fly to her mouth as the full implications of my crude schematics dawn on her. "Oh my God, and you were there?"

"Yes, and it was only the beginning. Some psycho who worked for Anies blew up the Poseidon dome a few days later. We tried to stop him, but we failed," I recount bitterly.

It was all over the news at the time: the complete destruction of the Poseidon vacation resort in the Pacific and its glass dome, the largest ever built. Anies enlisted the help of a psychotic engineer who had a score to settle against the dome's builder. That guy—who went down in history as the Crystal Whisperer—knew that there was a flaw in the chemical structure of the dome's Plexiglas compound. Armed with that, he used an ultrasound weapon to make fireworks of twelve hundred-tons of glass and unstable crystals.

"And that's when Anies took you," Joy guesses.

I fight a shudder in my stomach as memories resurface. Hours spent screaming alone, strapped to a hospital bed, and later, endless months spent trapped in the golden cage of Anies's Finnish castle. "Yes."

"That was his kick. I think he wanted to show to the Lions that he had erased Dries, taken everything back from him. He hired a Norwegian neurosurgeon who had lost her license to basically rewire my brain." I brush the scar hidden in my hair on my nape. "She jammed an implant in my head. Anies kept me with him for almost a year, drugged to my eyeballs, and he made me believe he was my father."

I stare at the drawing I just finished and picture his face again, the false kindness radiating from his smile every time he returned from a "business trip" to find me listless, barely able to hold a glass of water without dropping it. It was my mother he saw then. In his mind, it was her in the cage.

I clear my throat and go on. "He rewrote my entire life, stole it, and I think it's the happiest he ever was," I say, each word a bitter pill melting at the back of my mouth.

Joy shakes her head slowly. For the first time since I started my presentation, I see her cheeks pale from genuine horror. "You're joking. Please tell me you're making at least half of that shit up."

March grazes my hand in a discreet caress before he takes the pen from my hand. "I'm afraid she's not. Dries and I were reported dead after the incident, which suited us well since we spent the next eight months looking for Island."

She flashes him a weird look. "Do I want to ask why there's a reindeer and an ice cream truck involved?"

"They found me in Finland," I clarify. "And the ice-cream truck . . ." March and I exchange a sad smile.

"Dries was fearless in everything he did," March recalls. "And he was also hopelessly addicted to sugar."

Sadness clouds the blue in Joy's eyes. "Was?"

The wound is still fresh, and the pang in my chest just as intense. "Anies killed him," I confirm quietly.

She shakes her head slowly, her lips working as if to summon words that won't come, until she says, "Oh God, I had no idea . . . I'm so sorry. What happened?"

I resume my explanations, but my hand moves more slowly,

weighed down by regrets. "A lot. But the bottom line is that Anies took me to this secret base in the Ecuadorian jungle. March and Dries fought against the other Lions to get me back, and," I pause in my drawing to smile at our host even though I know he couldn't care less. "Angel helped."

"Why the hell did they take you to Ecuador in the first place?"

I almost reply: *Because Anies was hiding a stolen US spaceship there* . . . but I decide to keep aside the part where March and I went to space for now—Joy's mind appears sufficiently blown as it is. "Let's just say the Lions had some business there that conflicted with Angel's, so he helped us raid their compound," I summarize, eyeing March and Angel to check whether my version passes muster. One won't stop glowering at me, while the other gives a faint smile of approval. I'm gonna take that as a collective yes.

Meanwhile, Joy twirls her fingers as if she's spinning wool—Oh God, she's combing through everything I just said. Her eyes turn to slits. "Helped *us?* I thought you were a prisoner there?"

My pulse revs, no doubt turning my cheeks a guilty crimson. *Shit.* She truly misses nothing, not even the slightest pronoun. Thank God Angel gets up and prowls to the screen to rescue me. "Details are classified," he tells Joy, with an obvious effort to modulate his gruff tone into an almost urbane one—by his standards anyway.

He glowers at my doodle and takes the pen from my hand. "Draw me bigger."

THE LAMENTATION

Fabio was an artist, drawing all over her sublime curves
with the potent heat of his massive paintbrush, soaked with
the varnish of love.

— Kerry-Lee Storm, *The Cost of Rica #5: Blaze of the Phoenix*

A reverent silence follows the last swipe of Angel's pen across the screen.

Joy blinks. "Wow. Did you go to art school?"

"No."

March strokes his chin in genuine admiration. "A masterpiece."

Leaning against him with a tired sigh and a heavy heart, I conclude my keynote, since Angel gives no sign that he's going to give me the pen back. "Anyway, we kicked Anies's rotten ass, but

Dries was killed." By Alex, my ex, to whom Joy used to offer coffee and bagels when he came home, but that's a story for another day.

Angel resumes sketching while I'm speaking and eventually drops the pen back on the table, taking a few steps back to assess his rendition of Dries's final moments.

Once again, his artistic skills command total silence in the meeting room. The longer I gaze at his drawing, the more I'm filled with overwhelming, physical sorrow—a raw emotion that drains me to the bone. A rational part of me knows this is probably a belated backlash from the stress we experienced earlier, but if this is grief, I accept it.

Dries doesn't have an actual grave. The CIA wouldn't give me his body back after they raided Anies's lair. His and Anies's names are inscribed on marble tombstones standing above empty graves next to their mother's, but those date back from 1986—the year they faked their death in order to join the Lions. Because the first thing a Lion must give up is his very name, the same way March did sixteen years ago.

Maybe Angel's art and this soothing beat of silence are the closest thing to a ceremony we'll ever have. I blink back new tears that blur the whiteboard's chaotic horde of stickmen. March's hand finds mine and squeezes it as we say goodbye one last time. "Thank you," I eventually tell Angel. "He looks good; I think he'd have approved."

Joy trails a melancholy gaze across the canvas of my life and moves closer to hug me. We stay like this for a minute or so, until she moves away and collapses in Angel's villain chair, looking completely drained. "I'll be honest . . . If you had tried to tell me any of this a week ago, I'd have called your dad and possibly the psych ward."

I give a tired shrug. "Hence the secrecy. I just didn't know how to tell you any of this. I didn't want to put your life in danger, and I wasn't sure you'd believe me anyway."

She slumps in Angel's chair, eyeing March speculatively. "I still have one question. What the hell do you do? Is Struthio a front for, I don't know, being James Bond?"

He shakes his head. "Absolutely not, and I can direct you to our brochure which—"

"I read the brochure," she shoots back. "I can sum it up for you: 'We're people who solve problems police won't solve.'"

"Accurate," he concurs, letting go of me to plant himself across the table from her.

She straightens and crosses her legs with regal grace. Angel's eyes may be void of any warmth, but they are *glued* to those legs. I suspect by now he's figured he won't meet two women like Joy in his lifetime and wish he wouldn't look at her this way. "You've killed people," she states with almost perfect control of her voice, save for a telltale tremor.

March treats her to the cool stare usually reserved for clients. "I have."

I study the two of them anxiously—Joy's sharp exhale and March's cool façade. Will she ever return for Uno night after this?

She glances again at my doodles—specifically at my artist representation of March killing a bunch of stickmen at Anies's evil lair, then at Angel. And she asks March, "Have you ever been paid for that?"

She's guessed. I chose to carefully censor any reference to March's line of work from my presentation, and I honestly hoped we'd save that part for another day, but Joy guessed anyway—a practical reminder to never lie to your lawyer. I've made my peace with March's past a long time ago, but only because I got to know the gentle soul under the legendary bogeyman. I've seen what he's capable of: the good, the bad, the worst, and I take it all. Joy, however, knows only the somewhat cold and secretive front March presents to the world. I don't know if she's ready for "the talk," but it's too late to back out anyway.

My armpits turn clammy when March replies, "I executed contracts for ten years. The last one was twenty-one months ago. I retired and created Struthio Security a month later."

Joy seems to take this new hit without flinching. Instead, she counts on her fingers. "Last contract in December, the year I first met you, and Struthio in January of last year . . . not long before you popped back and replaced Alex."

The tendons in March's neck briefly strain at her evocation of his old nemesis. I, on the other hand, have no anger left. Not even after Alex slit Dries's throat before my eyes. Anies killed him a minute later, and I see now that Alex was broken in a million pieces that could never be glued back together. Not by me or anyone else. Had my life turned out differently, I too might have winded up consumed by the same hate that gangrened him.

Joy gives a cautious nod and asks March, "Why did you stop with that . . . the *contracts*?"

I think she already knows the answer to that. Her gaze drifts to me as March replies, "I wanted a different life."

My chest goes a little tight at his quiet words, this understated reminder of how far he's come from being a solitary hitman whose roommate and confidant was a sociopathic orange tree, to Mr. November, owner of Struthio Security, legit boyfriend, Uno legend.

Joy peruses him from under her lashes, like she would a big cat prowling behind rust-bitten bars that could shatter any second. She springs from Angel's chair. "What if what happened with the helicopter has to do with someone you killed in the past? I mean, after all I've heard and seen today, I honestly have a hard time believing that this, this . . . *apocalypse* was all about an ancient alien show!"

"And yet Mr. Moravia was shot," March reminds her. "And this admittedly extreme attempt at kidnapping occurred minutes after we intercepted Cachemire."

Joy motions to the drawings on the whiteboard, glaring at him. "Look. At. Yourself. In. A. Mirror. The worst shit Vince ever did in his life was showing his ass to a deputy in Indiana when he was in college."

"Joy," I warn her. I may not be the loud and angry type, but I don't like the way she's talking to March. "Let's keep our heads cool. One thing I can tell you for sure is that the Lions wanted something on Vince's iCloud, and I don't think this was personal. I think the only reason they shot him is that he found them in his room when he got back from the hospital."

She breathes her temper out. "Okay, say I believe you. What about Cachemire?"

"She shared Vince's room, and she had a copy of Franz's top-secret episode. They probably thought she knew something about his latest finding."

"And then March showed up at the Temptation: that probably solidified their hunch that the girl was worth taking," Angel supplies. Dammit, he has this way of going silent until you could almost forget he's in the room, and then he speaks with that deep, bad-guy voice that makes me jump out of my skin.

Joy flips the pen nonchalantly. "A real celebrity, uh?"

Angel's scarred lips stretch into a smile—not a smirk, an actual, decent *smile.* "Everybody knows the South African. This man"—he points to March—"I've known him for over a decade. He's always had issues. He's a bit crazy." He spins his finger against his temple. "But back in the day, he was the best money could buy." He crosses his arms with a disdainful frown. "Now he's just a shell of his former self. No edge left."

"He singlehandedly took down a helicopter and killed at least two guys an hour ago," Joy notes sharply.

Angel shrugs. "He can do better. He knows it."

March welcomes this backhanded compliment with a humble bow, but this time it's my turn to fire the best glare I have at Angel—which amounts to an angry Powerpuff girl on the best of days. "Stop it," I grit out. "Stop goading him into . . . you know. You know what you're doing."

He gives a snort but doesn't bother contradicting me.

"In any case," March resumes, "let's not forget that *you* were also in the car," he tells Angel. "Given last year's incident, I'd say going after you was uncharacteristically brazen on their part."

"They're desperate," Angel suggests. "They're looking for something, and the clock is ticking fast for them."

"Maybe they want to make sure that episode about them doesn't air," Joy suggests.

I tap my nose thoughtfully. "But in that case, all they needed to do was to kill Gualtiero Franz."

"Yet they didn't. They want something else," March concludes, "and only Gualtiero Franz knows what it is."

"Then you're going to find him for me," Angel clips.

March tilts his head at him. "Do you truly want to get involved in Lions' business?"

"They got involved in mine when they attacked me," Angel replies. He locks his tar-black gaze with March's. "I want to know what they want from Franz, and when they come to take it, they'll find me waiting for them."

"I can only discourage you, and you know that."

Unexpectedly, Angel's lips quirk in his beard. "I remember texting you something to that effect two years ago. You replied that my concerns were being taken into consideration. A middle finger emoji would have sufficed."

March's eyebrows draw together as he combs through his memory, then jolt in reminiscence. The lines of tension bracketing his mouth soften. "I did."

Angel tips his head in the ghost of a bow. "And you were apparently right to want to die on that hill. So, you let me choose mine."

My head swivels back and forth between the two like I'm watching a tennis game; Joy appears similarly puzzled. "I don't get it. What did you text him?" I ask Angel.

He crosses his arms, allowing a beat of silence to stretch in the room. Rolls surge and ebb with distant whispers on the beach outside before Angel eventually says, "He told me he was pulling out of our contract—for the first time in ten years—to take care of personal business. I told him nothing personal was worth losing my trust."

And March replied with the equivalent of a middle finger, on the day he chose to spare Antonio because I begged him to. A stupid, emotional grin tugs at the corners of my lips as I see him again on that airport tarmac in Massachusetts, calling Phyllis and instructing her to give his apologies to Angel and send chocolates to his mom. That simple, decent decision set in motion a chain of events that eventually saw Angel's baby niece being born fourteen months later—tiny Isla is named after me, and she's a fierce little bundle with a mop of curly dark hair and a big, toothless grin.

Talk of a butterfly effect.

"Did she like the chocolates?" I ask quietly, smiling at Angel under Joy's curious scrutiny.

He doesn't reply—I didn't expect him to share anything about his mom—but I catch a faint quirk of his lips before he flips out his phone from his pocket, taps to make a call, and snaps, "Tráela aquí." *Bring her here.*

SIXTEEN
THE REBOUND

"I'll make you forget every other guy you've ever known,
Jessebelle. You'd better write down your door code, 'cause I'm
gonna fuck you amnesiac!"

– Queen Goldstorm, *Under His Wheels: An MC Romance*

I suspect the participant we're now waiting for is Cachemire, but there seems to be a minor setback. Whoever is on the phone with Angel offers several seconds of apparently convoluted explanations, until he barks, "¿Por qué la está cocinando llapingachos?" *Why is he cooking potato patties?*

More buzzing explanations on the other end of the line, which Angel cuts off. "No, desecha el aji criollo y ven aquí." *No, ditch the hot sauce and come here.*

Less than a minute after he hangs up, the doors to the meeting room part to reveal Cachemire, now wearing the yellow romper she had under her alien costume. She's framed by two men—one of whom I recognize as Abelardo, with his ponytail, a double holster over his maroon shirt, and a large belt buckle where under the Ecuadorian flag, a golden tag proudly proclaims: "Ecuador mi amor."

Cachemire flinches the moment her gaze meets Angel's punishing one, but she actually looked fine when she walked in five seconds ago; they gave her pancakes, after all. My stomach growls in envy. Maybe I was quick to judge Abelardo and the others. Or maybe I'm just hungry, and I'll befriend anyone who feeds me at this point.

When Angel bombards her with the Stare, I lunge forward to play good cop before he once more reduces her to a puddle of tears. "We need your help. No one is going to hurt you."

"You're going to introduce us to Mr. Franz," March announces in a tone that bears no discussion.

"I-I can't!" she whimpers, retreating behind Abelardo, who delicately seizes the shoulder of her romper to steer her back to the front like he's maneuvering the wing of a frail canary.

"Don't you work on set?" Joy counters.

Cachemire flits back behind Abelardo. "Gualtiero hasn't been on set for two days. He's staying in a villa near Puerto Morelos, but he's never gonna want to see you. He's getting ready for his party tonight, and with what happened to Vince . . . It's crazy down there; he's tripled security."

My mouth twists in disbelief. "Franz is throwing a party when one of his crew members got nearly killed last night?"

Her posture slumps at my evocation of Vince's predicament. "He wants the cash."

My invisible antennae spring up upon hearing the C-word. Maybe we're getting somewhere.

"What money are we talking about, and why?" March probes with the same sort of icy kidnapper expression he practices when trying to assemble Ikea shelves.

"It's because of the tomb," Cachemire explains, risking her head out of the safe haven of Abelardo's shadow. "We were supposed to wrap season nineteen here in Cancún—we've already shot the finale. But after they found the tomb, Gualtiero was all over the place, and he said he wanted to do a huge two-hour special. He called the execs, and he's like 'I need ten million additional budget for on-location shooting and special effects.' They said they wouldn't fork out the cash unless he could show them something worth that much money."

"Fairly reasonable," March notes.

Joy moves to sit on the meeting table, closer to her unfortunate rival. Cachemire eyeballs her warily, but Abelardo steps aside, leaving her alone in the arena.

"And what's the party got to do with any of that?" Joy asks tartly.

Cachemire creeps sideways toward her second choice of shield: me. "Gualtiero is throwing this big party at the villa with some local jet-set and B-list celebs. But the party is just a front. The whole point for him is to gather his producers and have this private conference where he's gonna show them what he dug up, and he thinks they'll write him a check on the spot."

March's eyes narrow in interest. "You mean the dead man you told us about earlier?"

"Yes, maybe . . . Look, I don't know. No one saw what was really inside the box except Gualtiero and Vince, I think. Gualtiero had it screwed shut, and his personal security took it away immediately." Her face scrunches up. Dammit, she's gonna cry again.

Angel returns to life, cracking his neck. "Now at least we know what's the hurry, they probably want to get their hands on that box before Franz shows it to his producers."

"Agreed," I say. "Once it's out in the open, even with the best security protocol, someone will take pics just like Vince did, make copies, share those online, and it'll be too late to hide whatever's inside that tomb."

March acquiesces, his gaze drifting to the misshapen Lions I drew earlier on the whiteboard. "In other words, they probably have no choice left but to invite themselves to the reveal."

"And so must we," I conclude. "You're going to get us into that party," I order Cachemire, pumping my nonexistent pectorals to give myself an air of authority. No point in trying March's looming technique. The damn girl has a solid inch on me.

Her eyes pop wide. "Are you kidding me?"

Taking a single step toward Cachemire—who tries to back away but bumps against Abelardo's massive chest—Angel sends a smartphone spinning her way across the concrete meeting table. "You call Gualtiero Franz, and you tell him Ecuapasión wants to co-produce and distribute his special. Ten million dollars cash, but only if it's worth it."

She cringes. "Ecua . . . um, what's that?"

"A TV channel," Angel states, without the slightest hint of a smile. He's dead serious about this—like about everything he does, really.

March raises an eyebrow. "Oh, you still own it?"

"Yes," Angel confirms before narrowing his eyes at Cachemire. "Now, make that call."

"He prefers texts," she whines.

He looks up to the ceiling in an obvious bid to stay calm. "Then. Text."

I stand tethering on the thin edge between dismay and shock while Cachemire's thumbs hammer at the screen. Angel owns a TV channel.

March bends to whisper in my ear. "His mother was terribly upset when Ecuapasión decided to end her favorite telenovela. Angel acquired a majority share in the channel and issued a firm encouragement for them to keep the series running. I think it's called—"

"*Hechizado por amor*," a deep baritone murmurs above us, like the low hum of a didgeridoo. March and I turn around at the same time to find Abelardo huddled with us.

Joy scuttles close and lowers her voice to join our little side-meeting. "He seriously bought his mom an entire TV channel?"

"For her sixtieth birthday," March recounts.

Her face falls. "I got mine a ravioli attachment for her Kitchen Aid."

"I took mine to see Leo Rojas in concert," Abelardo shares.

The three of us stare up at him. Yes, even March; this guy is that tall.

"What?"

March waves it off. "Nothing. Excellent choice."

Cachemire's whine to Angel pops our bubble. "He's asking what's your name and how much money you have."

"Tell him to contact Ecuapasión directly for financial statements. And tell him I'm Mr. Somoza, and he's wasting my time."

Cachemire hesitates, then types dutifully—such is the power of firm and confident management, I guess. She seems to have almost entirely forgotten that she's his hostage, not his assistant. After the message has been sent, tense seconds tick by in the meeting room. Cachemire looks up from the phone and studies our little group with an expression that's now down to fifty percent fear and fifty percent curiosity.

Her gaze bounces back and forth between Joy and Angel, again and again, until it seems she can't take the suspense anymore and she asks Joy, "Is he, like . . . your rebound?"

I could swear I hear invisible crickets chirping as the room goes deadly quiet again. Joy clears her throat, while March discreetly raises his hand to conceal his mouth—dammit, I can see the outline of a dimple poking his cheek; he's trying not to laugh.

Angel crosses his arms and waits, his head tilted at Joy.

She stands a little straighter, and with an understated hair flip, replies, "No, he's just a friend."

Next to me, Abelardo exhales a low whistle, and March's brow creases in a quasi-cringe. She whooped Angel straight into the friend zone. No airbag, no mercy.

I think he took it well. I mean, his face is set in its usual permanent scowl; he must be fine. I can't thank his phone enough for distracting us with a welcome chime, immediately followed by Cachemire saying, "He wants to know if you have a security detail."

"Twelve men, four vehicles," Angel replies.

Cachemire types the reply, and the phone chimes almost immediately again. "They'll need to coordinate with the guys who protect the villa. No weapons allowed inside."

"No problem," he snaps.

Obviously not, since one of Angel's bestsellers is a disassembled polymer 9mm 1911 with ceramic bullets that would be TSA's nightmare if they only knew it's out there, joyfully breezing through airport security across the globe.

When Gualtiero Franz's—or more likely his assistant's—final text chimes in, Cachemire winces at Joy and Angel. "Will you be bringing a plus one?" she asks him.

His expected answer flies in the direction of the interested party, delivered with a smoldering glare. "I'll bring a friend."

SEVENTEEN
TWO BOYS

The boiling batter of his passion poured into her like a torrent,
glazing her ovaries like mirror cakes.

– Terry Robs, *Glazed by the Cook #6: His Bun in Her Oven*

After the stickman meeting was over, Angel barged out of the room with an order for us to stay out of his sight for the next two hours or else he'll shoot us—although I'm pretty sure he'll make an exception for Joy.

Abelardo escorted Cachemire back to her room, and now it's just the three of us, standing in the middle of the villa's living room under the discreet surveillance of three of Angel's men strategically positioned near the bar and exits. I remove my sneakers and take a few steps on the long section of glass tiling under which turquoise water flows from the pool outside and separates the room in half. March watches me, his mouth a tight line.

"You disapprove," I state quietly.

Joy turns to him. "Of what?"

"Of Angel's plan." He sighs. "I already made it clear I don't think you should get involved any further, and by now, you should understand why."

Joy goes to stand near the open windows, her heels teasing the edge of the tiling. A gentle breeze fluffs her curls around her face. She crosses her arms with a defiant glare. "Except you're working for Angel, and he's the one who calls the shots."

March treats her to a wry, unkind smile that barely dents his dimples. "Are you playing him against me? How unwise."

"Is that a threat?"

I rub my eyeballs tiredly. "Stop it, both of you. Joy, March is right. We have no idea what could happen tonight, and you're placing us in a position where we're gonna have to worry about your safety on top of everything else."

She shrugs. "Right back at you. I don't see myself spending the next few days with my fingers grafted to my phone, checking every five minutes if you're still alive or something just exploded again."

Touché. I stare at my toes against the undulating blue underneath. "You know I had that exact conversation with March a year and a half ago, on a yacht, between Italy and Croatia." She leans forward in curiosity. I keep going. "I told him these things—that to me the Lions were a personal matter, that I didn't want to watch from the sidelines. I wanted the truth about my parents, and, honestly, I wanted to be a part of this." I fling my hand in a vague, all-encompassing gesture. "The thrill, the secrets . . ."

"But you regretted it once they caught you, and it nearly cost you everything," Joy completes.

"No. I never regretted it," I say, noticing with a kind of dark satisfaction the way her eyebrows jolt in surprise. "Back when Anies had me locked up, there was nothing to remember or regret; I was mostly empty on a good day, and absent the rest of the time." I sense March shifting closer to me as I say this. I know it's twisting him from the inside to listen and remember the way it was when he found me, all my frayed edges he was desperately trying to mend. I soldier on because I think Joy needs to hear it. "And after I recovered, I didn't regret anything. I took risks, I paid the price, but I couldn't have stayed away." I shrug. "Kind of like my mom, I guess."

Joy draws a shivering sigh and takes a few steps toward me. "I'm not gonna die, you know," she says softly.

I muster a smile. "We're gonna try to avoid that."

"Don't worry, I'll stay away from the guns, and I think I can actually be useful."

"In what capacity?" March asks, perhaps a little curtly.

"Diversion." She moves to stand with her back directly to the afternoon sun, her tangle of blonde curls gleaming like a golden halo behind her. "Trust me. I'll make sure to be the only thing Gualtiero Franz's guests notice."

"And that's basically where we're at," I finish summing up for Phyllis, who's grinning on my phone's screen. I'm lying sprawled on the silky white sheets of a bed that was apparently designed to accommodate entire families, gazing dourly out the windows at the kind of sea view Cancún-goers sell their firstborn for.

"It's typical," Chief Operations Officer and Struthio resident love columnist Phyllis replies, tucking back a red lock in her loose bun. "She's trying to get over a bad breakup with a worse rebound."

"I know! She always does that!" I whine under March's commiserating gaze.

"And it won't help that he saved her life with his giant balls," Phyllis adds. I know which balls she's referring too, but the evocation makes me cringe nonetheless, summoning a visual I wish I could scrub off my brain forever. "I'm sure she's rationalizing the hell out of everything she's learned about him as we speak."

"She called him a cute pet snake," I recount dolefully while March plops himself at my side on the bed.

"She's in too deep already," Phyllis rules. "Do you want me to arrange a flight back for her? She's still on the no-flight list, but Paulie can probably come up with something . . ." You bet he can: Paulie, one of March's oldest friends, operates the eponymous Paulie Airlines, a private aviation company that basically provides private jets to people with fake passports and real rap sheets.

March rubs a hand over his jaw while I hand him the phone. "If only she would let us."

Phyllis shrugs. "That's what propofol is for, just saying."

"Hey!" I spring up and lean over March's lap, frowning at the screen.

She raises her palms in surrender. "I'm kidding. Now the two of you relax. Fresh luggage is on its way across the bay." Because our suitcases now rest at the bottom of the Atlantic . . .

"Thank you, Phyllis," March says, echoed by my own goodbye before he hangs up.

I get to my feet and pull my dress over my head, fold the wrinkled garment, and place it delicately on the bed—one of the many habits I picked up living with March. "I suggest we factorize our shower time. In the name of water saving and efficiency, of course," I say casually, fighting the old instinct to blush. It won't be our first shower together, and hopefully not the last, but there's a carnal appeal to it I'll never tire of—I think it has to do with the idea of rubbing conditioner in his chest hair.

My gaze zeroes on his fingers as he starts unbuttoning his shirt. "Very well, Miss Chaptal," he says, all business.

The white cotton parts to reveal the divine fleece, a rug of silky, springy chestnut hair covering his pecs all the way up to his clavicles and cascading down his abs to disappear under the waist of his jeans. Novices might call it a happy trail, but to me, the term conjures up the kind of sparse, pencil-thin line guys flaunt in cologne ads. March never wears any cologne, never trims a single hair below his neck, and that, right here, is a goddamn interstate leading down to paradise.

My body is ready. It's all I can think about, watching the muscles ripple in his shoulders as he carefully folds each item of his clothes on the back of a chair. It's not fair: my own limbs are a tangle of noodles because the elliptical comes to life and tries to kill me the moment I get near it, but March somehow finds the time for daily workouts, and his muscles have muscles.

Trying for a bit striptease, I slip through the misty curtains leading to the bathroom and unclasp my bra before tossing it with a regal flick of my wrist into a palm laundry basket. I never quite manage to look sexy while taking off my panties, though: I always end up hopping on one foot while pulling them down my other leg. March's warm chuckle is my only warning before he effortlessly lifts me bridal-style and maneuvers us under the showerhead. He reaches to turn the brass knob sticking out the wall, prompting a waterfall to pour from the ceiling in glossy ribbons. "See," I stretch my arms to catch the stream of water. "there's our dream weekend, after all."

I meant that comment to lighten the mood, but unexpected sadness weighs on March's features as he carefully lowers me until my toes touch the shower tiling. "I had hoped our Saturday would go differently. Island, you could have died back there," he says, his voice a little hoarse as he reaches for a pair of bottles sitting on a recessed shelf in the wall and pours some shower gel in his palm.

"Says the guy who climbed out of a car and onto a helicopter," I retort in a sigh that gets cut short when his head dips and his lips crash against mine. My tongue swipes in response to catch the droplets clinging to his cupid's bow: it's the only way I know how to make him feel that I don't care that my birthday weekend blew up and sunk in the Atlantic. I need nothing but this wordless connection between us, the breath we share, and his fingertips roaming all over my body under the guise of meticulous washing. I return the favor eagerly, scrubbing him to a steady purr as the water washes our stress away.

Too busy pawing at March's wet chest hair and kissing his clavicles, I'm barely aware of the shower being turned off. "Do you think we have a little time?" I plead as he grabs one of the towels stacked in the vanity and runs it up and down my back.

His hands pause in their task as he presses my body subtly to his to let me know he's in a similar mood. I step on tiptoes to kiss him a little harder, flinging my arms around his neck awkwardly.

March sucks on a sensitive spot under my ear. "Biscuit, we don't have any condoms."

And we never skip the condoms. I bite back a groan of disappointment. Contraception is one of the few aspects of our relationship I know I should get more involved with, but I get off easy because March never—*ever*—forgets the condom. Part of it is obviously making sure to avoid a surprise pregnancy plot, but there's something else left unsaid between us, a boundary of his that I've never dared to question, and that I suspect has something to do with his OCD. March is uncomfortable with the reproductive fluid which shall not be named.

He won't allow a single drop to come in contact with any part of me and doesn't want it anywhere on the sheets either, of course. From tentative caresses to strategic retreats, I've learned to accept the occasional frustration of feeling his hands guide mine away when we're making love, but I remain desperately curious about the physical properties of the mystery potion. He's my first sexual partner, after all, and hopefully the last. Yet semen—let us be daring and call it by its name—remains off-limits.

"Okay," I mutter, stealing one last taste of his jawline before taking the towel from him to wrap myself in it.

March's hand steals around my waist to stop me, his voice

dropping a velvety octave. "But that doesn't preclude all forms of entertainment." He bunches up the terry cloth as he says this, his fingertips skating up my thighs, my hips. And, sweet raptor Jesus, he gets on one knee.

My pulse revs up feverishly at the idea of taking what he's offering, and my mind toys with the absurd concern that maybe Angel has cameras hidden in here and his mustached bruisers will see everything if March . . . My knees nearly buckle when his lips brush my inner thigh. A hot exhale fans against my skin, higher and higher; his palms slide upward to cup my backside and steady me against his mouth.

And it takes every ounce of will I possess to kneel in my turn, so I can be at eye-level with him and say, "No."

His brow wrinkles in surprise, and I suspect, some amount of frustration. "Not in the mood?"

"It's not that." I press my forehead to his and kiss the tip of his nose softly. "I know it would feel great, but I don't like that it would be just for me."

His lips seek mine, a seductive smile in his voice. "That's the whole point."

"But you won't let me touch you afterward." And I can't bring myself to tell him that it's all I want. I just want to touch him, explore him as completely as he does me, feel that final wall between us fall. Just once.

I feel his shoulders tense under my fingertips, even as his touch remains nothing but gentle. "Biscuit, it's not . . . It's not the best time."

Not here, in Angel's home, where he doesn't feel safe enough to relinquish even a single thread of control. Not when there're too many unknown factors about tonight's expedition at Franz's house. Not without a condom. I place a rueful kiss at the corner of his mouth. "I get it, but mark my words, Mr. November: I'll celebrate my birthday in your chest hair before this weekend is over."

That earns me a slow blink.

"Figurately speaking."

March shakes his head with a smile that vanishes just as fast when the door to our room clicks open. I let go of him while he rises to check the intruder's reflection in the vanity mirror—whose perfect angle simultaneously preserves our privacy and allows us to see a maid carefully placing two suitcases and garment bags on the ottoman standing at the foot of our bed. I wonder if someone briefed her; she tugs out a wipe from a pocket in her blue uniform and uses it to dust our luggage before slipping away with the discretion of a mouse.

The corners of his eyes crinkle in approval as he wraps a towel around his waist. "Excellent timing."

I follow him back to the bedroom as he retrieves a flawlessly pressed white shirt and black tux from their bag and inspects them. I check my own delivery with giddy curiosity. Phyllis usually has impeccable taste, a fact that's once again confirmed when the plastic zips apart to reveal a sleeveless, teal cocktail dress. Chic and totally unremarkable in a crowd: perfect.

I plop myself on the bed while, in the bathroom, March retrieves a brand-new safety razor from his shaving kit and swirls his shaving brush over the soap—it's silly, but I just love his old-fashioned soap thing. "By the way, there's something I wanted to ask you." I muse, watching him drag the razor up in the closest shave a man can get save for getting his throat sliced. "Back in the meeting room, Angel said he's known you for over a decade. So, you met him around what, twenty-two?"

"Yes, shortly after I left the Lions." He angles his chin to finish a spot there. "We were *both* quite young. He was still a student at the time."

I nearly drop the underwear I just took from my suitcase. "Angel has a degree?"

"In Classical Studies and Biblical Archeology ... from the

Pontifical University of Salamanca if memory serves."

I stand dumbly in the middle of the room, bra in one hand, panties in the other, mouth hanging open. "Get out."

"Did you perhaps imagine there was a mold all crime lords came from?" March chuckles, making quick work of the buttons of his dress shirt.

"I dunno . . . maybe. I guess it's just strange he chose that life after doing Biblical studies. What happened?"

"His father was murdered, and his mother begged him to return to Ecuador to take over the family business before someone else did," he explains, watching me wiggle into my dress with a tender smile. "He had to shed his old skin and learn on the field. Fast."

"So, he wasn't always Mr. Somoza?" I ask, pondering all that's left unspoken in March's story, the choices and trauma that no doubt shaped Angel's path.

"You have no idea. The first time I met him, it was in El Sagrario church. It was right after he received his scar—a welcome present from one of his father's competitors."

I wince at his mention of the old gash that's now half-hidden in Angel's newly grown beard. I saw it last winter, and it wasn't pretty. Even back then, I suspected that such a deep and straight cut had been no accident. I join March on the bed as he goes through his memories. "I'll never forget it: he wore a John Paul II T-shirt, and he made me sit down and pray with him because together, we were going to do things our Lord and Savior wouldn't approve of."

"Ambiguous, much?"

"I actually asked him to clarify the purpose of our meeting," he recalls, two dimples creasing his cheeks.

"I wish I'd been there to see it: a newly-minted arms lord and his hitman, plotting murder right under Jesus's nose." I can't suppress a smile, picturing the two of them praying side by side . . . Whenever I looked at him until now, I sort of assumed Angel was born that way, that he came out of his mom's womb with his scar and his aviators, and immediately started selling ammo to the other babies in the maternity ward. But just like being a hitman never fully defined March, I see now that Angel is a lot more than whatever stiff persona he chooses to cloak himself in. And maybe Joy gets under his skin because she figured that out much faster than I did.

March shakes his head in mock-sorrow. "We were two boys."

I picture the two of them, back on the boat: Angel pitching his llama-printed body bags to March, who could hardly conceal his interest. A smile touches my lips as I reply, "You still are."

THE CUTTLEFISH

"Vous avez l'air contracté. Je vous intimide ?"

Le grand blond avec une chaussure noire, Yves Robert, 1972

"Is she always late like this?"

Angel checks his watch, a tic in his jaw. The sun is setting over Cancún bay, and the three of us stand in the lobby, waiting for Joy. March's lips part, but he seems to think better of what he was about to say and, instead, remains a silent witness to Angel's rising aggravation.

Yes, Joy is always late, and March is probably thinking of the last time the three of us went to see a movie together. He sent us an email insisting that "every participant" be present thirty minutes before the movie starts—with a valid ticket—because that's what he always does, but Joy barged in during the ads with a bucket of popcorn in hand, and she spilled some on his lap. I thought he was going to walk out of *Smurfs 4: Apocalypse.*

"Give her a little more time," I suggest, considering the satin tips of my high-heeled pumps. God, I love being tall, even for an evening. "She's probably still sorting through all those dresses you gave her." Because Angel had an entire rack of dresses delivered directly to her bedroom, and when I went to check on her half-an-hour ago, Joy stood in her underwear amid a sea of colorful silk and sequins, looking like a cat in a catnip warehouse.

Angel shanks me the Stare, one hand fidgeting with the snakeskin lapel of his tux jacket—the villain touch to his otherwise conventional evening dress. He takes a threatening step toward the stairs, apparently intent on hauling her downstairs himself, but comes to a stop when the clatter of heels echoes atop the staircase. Joy makes her entrance, looking angelic in a figure-hugging, black sheath dress whose long sleeves and turtleneck are an unexpectedly conservative choice for her. She fluffs her golden curls and sirens down the marble stairs, stretching out her arms to strike a pose on the bottom step. "What do you think?"

March and I purse our lips in approval, while Angel gives her a hooded once-over that lingers just a second too long on the voluptuous flare of her hips. "Good," is all he condescends to say.

She notices his gaze caressing her and responds with the little sideways smile of a favorite who knows the king only has eyes for her tonight. You can practically taste the electricity arcing in the air between them as she tucks back a wayward coil behind her ear and crosses the lobby. "Look at us. It's like a group date about to go horribly wrong."

"Let's make sure it doesn't," I retort, once more mentally cursing Antonio for the mother of all accidental setups.

"Everyone here will act according to plan," March reminds her with a pointed look. "You and Angel will front our operation while

Island and I locate Franz's finding before the private reveal." *And before the Lions strike*, I mentally complete.

"I'll map out the villa and access their security system to clear the way for March," I explain, taking out my phone from a silk clutch that's crammed with all the wonderful toys Santa delivered this afternoon: universal keys, sedative spray because I'll never be a gun person, and a Mui-Bon chocolate bar in case I get hungry on the field.

Meanwhile, Angel searches his inside pocket and retrieves four miniature earpieces and mics that he drops in each of our upturned palms.

Joy watches us stick the pea-sized devices in our ears and eventually does the same with a wince. "Won't it stay stuck?"

"It's meant to," I explain, helping her fasten a mic smaller than a watch battery to the inside of her dress collar. "We'll use an elongated magnet to retrieve it. Don't worry, it's too big to get to your eardrum or anything. You'll get used to it fast," I reassure her.

"It records and transmits," Angel tells her, his eyes narrowing. "I'll be able to locate you as long as it's in place."

She mock-glowers at him. "You remind me of one of my exes right now."

I know which one, and let's just say we're lucky Angel will never know she just compared him to the overbearing Clown-dick.

"Very well," March concludes. "Cachemire will come with us and ensure we get inside without arousing suspicion. Once we're in, we'll release her."

Joy frowns. "What if she tries to go to the cops?"

Angel's scar stirs upward. "No one will stop her if she does." His smirk darkens. "She can go to the police, sit down and tell them she wants to press charges against Angel Somoza."

And they'll show her out with a pat on the back, I mentally complete. I just hope she won't remain durably traumatized by this episode. One thing is certain: I doubt she'll ever try to steal another girl's man ever again.

"Okay, let's roll," Joy cheers, carrying a whiff of vanilla and flowers as she breezes past me.

The moment they catch a look at her departing figure, March and Angel stand frozen in place, their eyebrows shooting up in sync. March wrestles his features back into a neutral mask almost right away, but Angel remains stricken, his scar quivering from a complicated mix of emotions I can't quite decipher. Shock. Anger—no, not anger, more like frustration, like she's done something just to provoke him, and it worked.

"You guys coming?" Joy calls.

I send March a querulous look before turning around to follow Joy. That's when my eyebrows hit my hairline. There's *nothing* in the back of that dress. The front looked pretty understated, but as she stands in the villa's monumental doorway, the smooth slope of Joy's back is entirely bare, save for a gold chain holding the dress together at her waist. The backline actually dips so low that I can see—Sweet raptor Jesus, that's at least an inch of her butt-crack, and the dress's stretchy material betrays no underwear lines, which could mean that . . .

Her earlier pledge rings back in my ears as I trot across the lobby after her. Trust me. I'll make sure to be the only thing Gualtiero Franz's guests notice.

"Jiminy cricket has a question for you," I whisper. "Are you wearing, like . . . something underneath?"

She turns her head with feline grace to look back at Angel, who has yet to move. He stands petrified in contemplation of her naked back, like that little crab I saw on TV who gets hypnotized by the changing colors of a merciless cuttlefish before she snatches and eats him. A slow smile stirs the red-lacquered lips of ground predator Joy Richards, and she gives the slightest shrug.

Without answering my question.

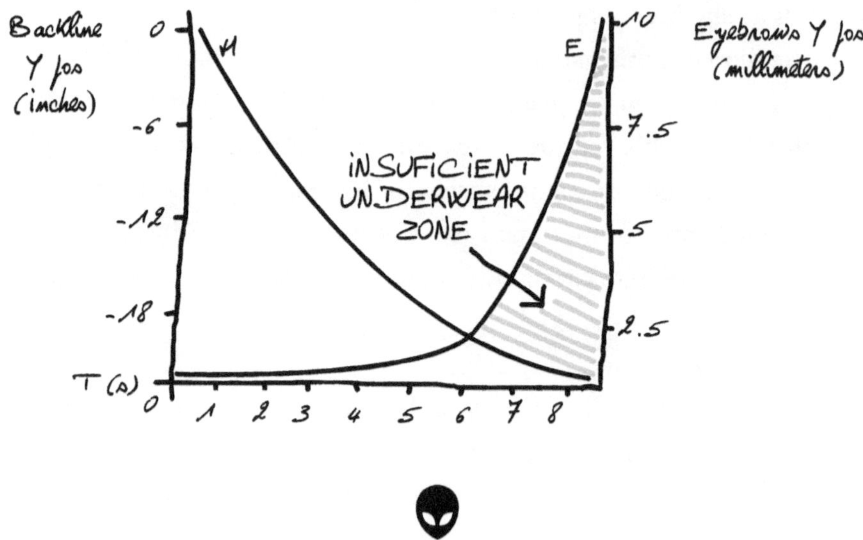

Along Cancún's busy coastal roads, a car might have taken up to an hour to take us to Puerto Morelos: Angel's catamaran covered the distance in less than fifteen minutes, tearing at 130 mph between the star-studded sky and inky sea. The coast stretches to our right, speckled with the gold, reds, and purples of a thousand lights and windows. I wonder what the night looked like fifty years ago when Cancún was still a deserted vein of sand emerging from the blue—a point of grass, as the Mayas called it.

Puerto Morelos's *faro inclinado* comes in sight a minute later, standing right by the dock we're sailing to; I read it's an old lighthouse that was nearly toppled by a hurricane in '67 and now stands tilted at an angle of approximately 16.3 degrees, according to my protractor app—March convinced me to install that tool he sometimes uses to stealthily double-check my parking jobs. I've since been struggling with a case of mild addiction. There's no end to the fun one can have with angles.

Meanwhile, Abelardo has moored us against the dock at the end of which two Rezvani tanks await. Technically, they're just armored SUVs, but their sharp angles and low, bulletproof windows do warrant the appellation, in my humble opinion. Parked right behind them is the dreaded Veneno. Apparently, Angel intends to make a memorable impression on our host.

Joy's stainless-steel spirits have returned, and she takes conquering strides toward the sports car, only to be stopped inches away from the driver door by Angel's sour bark. "You're not driving."

The curve of her bare spine is sculpted by the faro's lights as she spins around with a fierce glare. "Okay, I get what this is about. You're friend-zoning me back."

Angel presses his key fob to unfold the passenger door but doesn't otherwise deny her claim.

"He totally is," Cachemire whispers, while Abelardo looms over our shoulders and gives a low grunt of agreement.

March draws a weary sigh. "Let's go. They're adults and will sort their issues as such."

No, they won't. I narrow worried eyes at the two of them as the car's doors slowly fold shut. The way this is going, either they'll have a savage tryst behind the wheel, or we'll find Joy's dismembered body on the beach by dawn. Possibly both. I climb in the minivan's backseat opposite Cachemire and Abelardo to the sound of the Veneno roaring away angrily.

With no time to linger, little I see of Puerto Morelos feels like a postcard—a few white houses and thatched roofs, some shops, a garage, and we're already driving into the backcountry, straight through thick greenery. Cachemire leans her forehead to her window, watching palm trees flash by in the dark. "It's all so weird. Like, yesterday, I was doing spreadsheets for our editing schedule, and now I got caught in a spy adventure or something." She sighs. "And you know what's the funniest part?"

I shake my head slowly. March apparently won't indulge our temptress-in-chief.

"I didn't even sleep with him."

I feel my jaw unhook and roll at my feet at the same time that

Abelardo brings a big hand to his mouth.

"Wait—what?" I murmur. "Joy showed me—"

Her face bunches in sudden anger. "Like you've never sent nudes? Just because we traded pics doesn't mean we fucked!"

I, indeed, have never sent nudes—not even to March. His brow wrinkles in distress. I think he'd prefer to be anywhere but trapped in a car with a near-stranger discussing the deeper ramifications of her Tinder woes.

"Look," I mutter, "you've probably noticed we're having bigger problems right now, and honestly, I don't want to get into what happened or didn't."

She points to the stitches above her temple. "Hey, she nearly killed me over something I didn't even do. I think I deserve to give my version of events." Abelardo nods along as she makes her case. "Maybe I was going to sleep with him, but I didn't. So there."

March's lips pinch as the car slows down on a sandy trail snaking toward distant lights. "This is one of the rare situations where I would rule that intent supersedes results."

Meanwhile, we've stopped in front of a pair of high metal gates, ahead of the Veneno and the rest of Angel's escort. The whole place is enclosed inside a fifteen-foot wall. Cachemire wasn't joking when she mentioned that Franz wanted to properly secure his discovery.

She's still glaring at March in the opposite seat, but all it takes is the slightest hardening of his gaze for her to relent. "Please do the introductions," he orders coolly, eyeing the pair of bodyguards in tuxedos ostensibly talking in their earpieces and barring access to the residence.

Abelardo's leather jacket squeaks as he gives Cachemire an unexpected thumbs-up before her door unlocks. She responds with a reluctant smile before climbing out. March and I watch her walk up to Franz's bodyguards and engage in a brief explanation, pointing at the sports car. One of the men slides open the doors to each van, asks everyone to step out, and halfheartedly waggles a metal detector at us.

In a pattern typical of private security hired at the last minute, the wand he's holding keeps blinking red in a sense of general indifference. Maybe it's watches, belt buckles, phones . . . or maybe it's the knives and guns we were forbidden to carry. *Who knows? Who cares?* seems to say the guard's apathetic brown gaze. That, or he just doesn't realize this model has a silent mode, which is currently switched on. They move on to the Veneno. Angel lowers his window with his most convincing don't-waste-my-time-you-insignificant-maggot face. This time the guard doesn't even try to ask him to step out. He glances inside the car and waves his hand for his buddy to open the gates. I climb back in and lean back in my seat with a sharp exhale. That was step one.

I pick up a deep electro bass that grows louder as our motorcade resumes its slow progress up the alley. A brightly lit Mayan-style villa comes into view that's literally sitting in the middle of the ridiculously big pool encircling it. The traditional hay roofing and exposed beams are the only discernable trace of sobriety in what's otherwise an extravaganza of garden torches and flowers everywhere—among which sashays a roster of tanned guests who all look like they were featured on TV at least once in their life—and I'm not talking about being interviewed in Sonic's parking lot about their new pancake on a stick. That doesn't count.

Ahead of us, I notice a bunch of heads turn when Joy and Angel step out of his car. At least she looks okay—better than okay, actually. She's strutting at his arm and drawing every pair of eyes to her naked back like she was born for this. I'm ready to step out with the rest of his goons when a mint-green polo flashes by and catches my eye. March reaches for the door handle; I stop him, searching the crowd for the quasi-fluorescent garment's lanky wearer.

Crap.

"Wait, it's the guy from this morning," I warn, pointing at the honey-haired guy I kicked in the nuts at the resort when we kidnapped Cachemire.

She scoots over to my window, grimaces. "Oh, that's Patrick."

"What is he doing here?" March asks curtly.

She shrugs. "He's Gualtiero's PA. He buys his sushi, takes care of dry cleaning, that kind of stuff. He thinks it's gonna help his acting career."

March gives a faint huff that's clearly meant for Abelardo. "You let him go?"

"Yes. We told Sonny and Francis to drop him after we returned to the villa," he explains, leaning to scan the guests. "Mr. Somoza said he was useless now."

"But he *saw* us," I grit out. "He didn't see Angel and Joy, but he could recognize March and me and go warn security."

Cachemire curls away from the window and won't meet my eyes. "I can't do anything about that . . ."

March crosses his arms, considering the young assistant running around the garden, arranging champagne bottles in their ice bucket, buzzing among VIPs who won't even spare him a glance. "Franz's security team might notice his disappearance if we subtract him."

Who knew Abelardo could move his massive body with such ease? He's out of the car and drawing a beeline toward young Patrick before I've even had the time to voice my disapproval.

March observes him, brow furrowed. "His hunting skills are impeccable," he casually remarks when Abelardo waits for Patrick to walk by a bush.

Bursts of ear-grating laughter ricochet in the muggy night air; booze flows like the Niagara falls; a pair of girls plunge in the pool, splashing water all over the terrace, and through it all, no one notices a lowly assistant being swiftly grabbed by the collar and wrestled behind a shrub—not even the two bodyguards covering the sector.

Cachemire cringes at Abelardo's prowling figure, reemerging from the dark . . . alone. "Oh my God, did he kill him?"

"More likely knocked him out," March reassures her.

Cachemire nods to herself. "Of course. Abelardo isn't like that."

March and I exchange a look of understanding. No need to burst her bubble and remind her that he packs a double holster, like the rest of Angel's personnel tonight.

"Very well." March adjusts his cuffs. "Cachemire, thank you for your help in these exceptional circumstances; I'm certain Angel's driver won't mind calling a taxi for you. I wish you and Mr. Moravia the best in your future . . . amours."

She gives him a puzzled look, and, as if it could explain countless undisclosed developments and PhD-level sentimental equations, says, "But Abelardo is following me on Instagram now."

THE MARZIPAN

His hands were roaring quads speeding down the smooth valley of her back and up the hills of her perfect ass.

— Crystal Bluebonnet, *Mowed Down by the Texan ATV Dealer*

No need to look for Joy: I just have to follow the direction of half of the gazes around us. I spot her and Angel on the other side of the bridge crossing the pool and leading to the villa. Feminine eyebrows rise in sartorial curiosity and masculine heads turn or perform discreet double takes in her wake. *Was that . . . ? Yes sir, you just glimpsed my best friend's butt crack. Have another rum horchata to go with that.*

"I see you. What was the holdup?" Joy's voice whispers in my earpiece.

March shields me from a wobbly tray of mojitos as the waiter carrying it races past us, then murmurs back: "We had a witness to eliminate, Abelardo took care of it."

"Holy sh—Did he kill a guy?"

"No, he kind of tossed him into a bush," I recount. "Have you spotted Franz yet?"

"Not yet . . . I was told I'd be introduced later tonight," Angel replies.

I spot the two of them in the living room. Joy is inspecting a Mayan stela representing either a god or a king, while Angel stands by, tracking every move of a forty-something guy sniffing around her, and whose transparent plastic tux jacket and Hawaii print cummerbund alone should constitute major red flags.

Angel's voice echoes again in our ears. "Check the basement. Pool windows."

My gaze cuts to the underwater windows lining the pool's walls and looking into the house's basement. Three of them have their blinds shut. Moving shapes streak the rays of light filtering through. Someone in there isn't just here to admire aspiring actresses in bikinis.

"Let's see if we're welcome downstairs," March decides.

We make our way among the hubbub of flamboyant guests Franz invited to front his secret reveal. I'm pretty sure I recognize B-list faces I've seen on the Internet; my fingers itch with the need to take just one pic, so I can later tell my grandkids that it really happened, March and I were there, and—oh my God, I think that grandpa with the Santa beard was Russell Crowe! I heard he spotted a UFO once, but I had no idea he was tight with Gualtiero Franz.

At the other end of the mile-wide semicircular living room, a tangle of sculpted driftwood half-conceals a flight of stairs leading down to the basement. Standing in front of it, a pair of somber beefcakes guard the access. "Bingo," I say quietly, taking my phone out.

March leans closer and tips his chin at the camera on the wall above their heads. "Can you cut that one?"

"Yeah. Their server is completely out of date; I just need to . . ." Infect the router with one of the many hacking frameworks readily available on the darknet and which I modified for my personal needs. *Et voilà*, I'm basically riding their data packets like ponies to get inside their server.

I chew the inside of my cheek, typing fast on my phone to access the interface of their surveillance software. "So, we have these two guys on the first floor, guarding the stairs leading down to some kind of den. I can't see what's downstairs: the cameras are offline, and I can't reactivate them: I'm guessing they've been unplugged because Franz didn't want anyone to watch his meeting. I can delay and cut the feed to give us a short window to slip downstairs. Angel?"

"Yes."

"Can you send us two goons over here?" I shoot a discreet glance across the room at the pair of guards down the hallway. "Short hair, no ponytail, white shirt."

March's eyes narrow in interest, while in my earpiece, the runner-up for *Best Place to Work in South America* hisses, "They're *employees*."

"Sorry." He's right, and Abelardo's friendly manners have certainly uprooted my prejudice against men who channel early 2000s Steven Seagal while choosing to embrace a life of crime—but I'll return to self-flagellating later.

"Here's what I suggest," I tell March. "We try to create a diversion and turn off the cameras just long enough for you to deal with the two guys over there, and by the time the cameras go back, it's Angel's *employees* guarding that door. They have the same kind of dark costume. If the camera's feed is low-res, we'll have at least a few minutes before anyone notices the switch."

A dimple dents the corner of his mouth. "All right. And our diversion . . ."

We both glance in Joy's direction, who's still entertaining Franz's guests at Angel's arm. "Joy," I murmur. "Do you think you can give those guys near the stairs a little show? Something to catch their attention just a few seconds?"

"Gotcha," her voice buzzes back.

I tap to cut the camera feed as she leads Angel across the room toward us. She stops near the screen of driftwood, a few feet away from the pair of guards, and spins around, giving them a perfect view of her glorious backside. Their chins snap up in readiness, a second before she grabs Angel's head. And. Kisses. Him.

My mouth pinches in outrage as she all but devours him alive, threading her fingers in his dark locks while his hands steal around her bare waist. A shared sigh reaches us through their mic, followed by a medley of wet sounds I'd rather forget. But it works: the two guards exchange a secret smile at the telenovela unfolding before their eyes; they pay no heed to March's approach until he's standing right in front of them.

"Private area. *Zona Privada*," one of them grumbles before March's fist flies straight in his face and knocks him out. He smoothly clamps a hand around the second man's throat and presses just long enough for his victim to pass out. Seconds later, Angel's perfectly disciplined Cerberuses pop up to replace their counterparts. I look back at Joy and Angel to find that they've thankfully parted. His hand lingers on the small of her back though, and they're looking at each other like the squirrels who bang each other on my grandpa's patio in spring.

"Thanks. I think that's enough . . ." I hiss quietly.

Joy appears too busy contemplating whatever just transpired between her and Angel to reply. His ominous drawl echoes in my ear as he steers her back toward the pool. "You're welcome."

The whole thing went too fast for any of the guards to even scream. Angel's men drag the two bodies and toss them in a cramped service room next to the stairs. One of our victims stirs upon hitting the floor: I wince as March casually maces him with the sedative spray I keep in my clutch—a lovely golden bottle that could be any perfume. "Phyllis was right to recommend it," he remarks. "It's an excellent product."

Next, Angel's employees flip out two of his bestsellers on Yaythug:

—*The band-aid gag*: 3"x3.7", 2 mm-thin packets you can slip in any pocket. Rip open and peel off a pre-cut piece of duct-tape, ready to apply on any surface. Choose between over twenty novelty patterns!

—*High-grade stainless-steel zip ties.* Fasten anything, anyone, everywhere, all the time! Comes in silver or hypoallergenic black coating.

They do a quick job of restraining the unconscious guards while I fiddle with my phone to re-sync the surveillance feed. Angel's henchmen appear on camera seventeen, looking even better on video than the originals.

March moves to the stairs but holds up a finger when I follow him. "I'll give you my go."

I nod and hunch behind a thick wooden beam to monitor his progress down the stairs. I'm always amazed at how quiet he is—mostly thanks to self-stick pads under his shoe soles. He disappears behind a turn and I don't hear a single sound until his voice echoes simultaneously in my earpiece and in the den, cold and courteous. "Good evening sir, could you please direct me to the nearest restroom—"

A gruff voice cuts him off to ask what he's doing here, followed by the dull thud of a punch that will keep local dentists busy. My head shrinks into my shoulders in empathy for the unknown guard. To be fair though, March used to handle these matters with hollow points, so it's sort of an improvement that he's broken countless jaws, incisors, and a number of unexpectedly fragile body parts over the past year.

"The den is clear," he whispers in my ear, prompting me to come out of my hiding spot and trot downstairs. A bluish hue streaks the room through the pool window's lowered blinds, enveloping us in a shivering penumbra. Muted splashing sounds echo from the other side of the Plexiglas. The water casts turquoise swirls on a pair of designer sofas and a stone coffee table. On a wall, a flat-screen the size of Manhattan is paused on Netflix: I feel a pang of guilt that we knocked out a guy who was just chilling and watching *Madagascar 3* on the job—while eating peanut marzipan, judging by the crumbs and wrappers scattered on the table.

By the time I spot him in the dark, March is laying the third bodyguard's body under the counter of a wet bar occupying a corner of the den. He zip-ties, duct-tapes, and sprays him like his colleagues and emerges from the shadows, readjusting his right cuff with a huff.

"Not killing people is a lot of work," I whisper, shuffling closer.

"A full-time job," he agrees, his eyes flashing with irritation as he spots the marzipan crumbs. I sense the moment when he's about to make a move for them, but he pauses when the faint echo of hushed voices catches our attention. Across the room, a trickle of golden light filters through a set of sliding doors. Someone laughs before a shrill male voice with a familiar German accent silences the ruckus. "Your attention, please! Everyone! We're about to start."

I bite back an excited squeal when I recognize Gualtiero Franz's voice. There it is, the secret alien meeting. March's hand takes mine, guiding me as we dash in perfect silence across a faux-fur rug and flatten our bodies to the wall, mere inches from the door. On the other side, there's some shuffling while Franz's voice grows frantic. "Patrick—where is Patrick? I need Patrick for the slides!"

My toes curl when a younger voice with a Spanish accent offers to go get the assistant Abelardo tossed in a bush twenty minutes ago. I release a trembling breath as Franz replies, "No, it's too late now. He missed the train of history. Jaime, take care of the slides, please."

"Of course," the young guy mumbles.

As expected, Franz's presentation still isn't starting: his aide now appears to be fumbling with connecting his laptop to a TV. An elderly male voice suggests he try the other cable, while another commands Cortana to make the cable work—a feminine voice objects that the laptop is evidently a MacBook. That's going to take a while . . .

"We need eyes inside," I whisper to March, pulling out my phone. "I think I have an idea."

If Franz's minion is currently struggling to connect his computer to a smart TV, it means said TV is probably also connected to the Wi-Fi signal I currently have control of. I open the admin console to the villa's router, checking all connected devices. I'm going to venture a guess that "SamsungSotano2" is what I'm looking for.

Now, here's the bad news: in Soviet Russia and pretty much everywhere else in the world these days, your smart TV is watching you—through the built-in camera you use to vidcall grandma and film your cat licking its butthole. In this case, all it takes is a payload I'm injecting into the meeting room's grossly unprotected TV via the villa's router. Footprint in the infected system is minimal: communications are encrypted and I'm not creating any new files that might trigger the antivirus. All I'm doing is turning the webcam on.

March hunches to look over my shoulder as a bright meeting room appears on the screen of my phone. "Management will approve your request to have a soft-serve machine installed in the break room," he whispers.

My lifelong dream come true, I ball my left fist in silent victory while studying Gualtiero Franz's special guests: six people await the show on a long sofa curving around a cluster of glass coffee tables. Four men in their mid-forties to late sixties, who all opted to wear anything but a pressed shirt under their tux—I spot two polos, a camo T-shirt, and . . . Okay, maybe that scoop-neck tank top would have worked on Sonny Crockett thirty years ago, but not on a grandpa with an orange tan and a food baby. Among them sits a blonde woman with a gauzy blue gown and a lot of Restylane in her high, puffy cheeks. Last is a black guy in a suit. Classically good looking, well-built with short dreads: that one could be either an actor or another bodyguard.

Franz's eternal safari shirt and khakis move into view: he's ready to start. At one end of the sofa, a young Hispanic guy with messy hair balances a laptop on his knees, his gaze shifting anxiously between the TV screen and his own device. I'm guessing that's Jaime and that he'd better not screw up the slideshow if he wants to keep his job. When Franz clears his throat, his aide disappears from the camera's view and returns wheeling a steel cart atop which rests a long plastic crate. As Jaime works on unlocking the crate's lid, Franz turns to his audience, who have set their glasses down to watch the container with a sort of cautious curiosity. "Are you ready for this?" he asks them, rubbing his hands in anticipation.

I am. Mouth slightly parted, I hold my breath for each endless second it takes Jaime to raise the lid. The first thing the TV camera captures is a reflection: the crate's content is protected by a second transparent lid—most likely Plexiglas. Underneath lies a brownish mass my 4K phone does little justice to. I pinch the screen to zoom, feeling March leaning closer over my shoulder.

I see the skull at the same time that Gualtiero Franz's guests shoot up from the sofa to look at it. Soon it becomes clear that we're looking at a badly damaged mummy. A few locks of dried-up hair still cling to the dead body's skull, but the skin appears to have been extensively damaged to the point of being missing on most of the torso and part of the right arm. I squint my eyes in the dark at the elongated shape lying next to the body.

"It's a sword," March breathes in my ear.

He's right; I can make out a dusty hilt, peeking from the piece of black fabric the blade has been wrapped into. My heart drums fast in my ears, almost covering the noises reaching us through the door. I am living an episode of *Aliens in Our Past* and there's an actual top-secret mummy. I feel March's palm slide up my rib cage, his fingers splaying over my heart in a calming gesture: I didn't realize I was hyperventilating.

The blonde woman bends to look at the excavated body and clasps a hand over her painted red lips. "Gualt, that is absolutely gross!"

"Viewers are gonna love it," rasps the faux Sonny Crockett. "But watcha gonna do with it? What's your narrative?"

Franz runs a shaking hand in his hair like he sometimes does in his show when he's presenting an archeological site he's certain aliens visited in the past. He motions to the remains in the crate. "This man . . . was an adventurer, a warrior, a scholar, a visionary. He laid the ground for our entire knowledge about ancient astronauts."

The guy with a camo T-shirt under his white tux shrugs. "Who is he? A conquistador?"

Franz coughs a near-hysterical laugh, a strident sound that's like the last string of his sanity vibrating right before it snaps. "You want to know who he is?"

Oh, yes, I want to know. I grip my phone tighter as he reaches for the Plexiglas lid covering the remains, only to be stopped by Jaime, who produces latex gloves from a box and gives them to him. Franz gives an impatient snort but consents to slip on the gloves and, at last, removes the final wall separating him from his discovery. With excruciating care, he nudges the sword aside to take a second object in the crate: a two-foot-long smoked glass tube containing a thick, misshapen parchment roll.

"The sword is a two-handed blade of Dutch facture. Exceptional piece. But that's not what we're interested in tonight," Franz notes.

He unscrews the tube's lid and pulls out the parchment, his afro quivering in boyish excitement. Next to him, Jaime slides the Plexiglas lid back in place to act as a makeshift desk. Careful not to damage it, Franz unrolls the document slowly, marking suspenseful pauses every few inches or so.

Once he's done and the parchment comes into view between him and Jaime, I don't need to zoom anymore. Before I can even fully process what I'm seeing, March inhales sharply at the sight of the expanse of tan leather, mottled brown by centuries spent underground. Most of the surface is inked with indecipherable texts and symbols, by there's one thing I recognize in a heartbeat, even stained, battered, and darkened.

Carved in the top left corner is a lion head encased in a circle. My stomach heaves from the sickening realization that this vaguely rectangular hide didn't come from a cow or even a pig.

That's a Lion's skin.

THE HIDE

Evil is there, at the gate, against the skin.

– Marguerite Duras, *The Lover*

There's a gory visual in my mind that I wish I could erase, and my temples are growing damp from a sudden sheen of sweat. "He was flayed, and someone turned his skin into a hide?"

March's eyes narrow at the scene. "It would seem so. I'm afraid I know who Franz thinks this is."

His cryptic response does little to alleviate my concern. Franz's fervent yell booms through the door, answering my next question before I can even ask. "Tonight, after years of research, I can announce with absolute certainty that I have found the body and legendary hide of Alonso de Cornellà, the forefather of ancient astronaut theories, and founder of the Collegium!"

Some would say the profound silence that follows is one of shocked reverence, but all I read on the faces of Franz's guests is a sense of perplexity. At my side, March slowly massages the bridge of his nose and mutters, "You have to be kidding me."

"Do you know him?" I whisper.

"I'll tell you about it later, but he's essentially a Lion with a taste for archaeology who devoted the latter half of his life to cataloging their ancient history and reviving their creeds. The brotherhood won't turn a blind eye on this discovery, even knowing it could be a hoax. They'll do anything to recover that mummy."

Like shooting Vince or trying to snatch an entire car with a giant magnet.

Meanwhile, the grilling is still going strong on the other side of the door. "Do you have hard evidence for any of these claims?" the blonde probes, eyeing the hide with blatant disgust. She waves her hands as she goes on. "I can create a moment, get the press on this to promote a special, but they're gonna try to fact-check us. We need a solid story; otherwise all we'll get is alternative media as usual." The air quotes accompanying this comment speak for themselves: the only big newspaper that ever wrote about Franz's work is *The Sun*, and they're also the ones who came up with that headline about UFOs hitting windmills.

"What's so special about this guy anyway?" Faux Sonny Crockett asks.

Franz slams his palms on either side of the hide, causing Jaime to shrink away. "For God's sake, that's his skin!" he yells as the group recoils in horror. "There's a lion carved into his skin right *here*. Symbol of Nergal, like in their secret temple! Have *any* of you paid the slightest amount of attention to the keynote I sent you?"

"All right, cool down, Gualt." The old man chuckles. "What I'm asking is where you're going with this. You wrapped a solid nineteenth season already, and your budget is spent, so what does this"—he points at the hide— "bring to the table that we don't have yet?"

Franz looks like he's about to explode, but Jaime creeps back toward the crate to intervene in an unsteady voice. "I'm not gonna try to sum up my entire thesis, but here's what you need to know: Cornellà was a mercenary serving the Spanish crown in the first half of the sixteenth century. He was a bodyguard for Queen Joanna the mad, until 1521 when her son, the future king Charles V, had her imprisoned in a convent. It's not clear what Cornellà did after that: we know he traveled the world for two decades as an adventurer with a clear penchant for alchemy and relic hunting, and he also seems to have been involved in several political assassinations."

I wince. That last part definitely sounds like Lion business.

"And what's that story about his skin? Who cut it off?" the blonde inquires.

"Good question," Jaime says, resuming his debrief. "He died around 1545, after joining a Spanish expedition to Yucatán. According to legend, he had gone mad and he died trying to flay himself. Whether there's any truth to that, whoever buried him thought that his skin was valuable enough to turn it into a hide." He draws an excited breath before adding, "Our current theory is that Cornellà himself meant to turn it into a map. We dug up some traces of his correspondence to Queen Joanna in the Vatican Secret Archives, and he told her—"

"He told her about an alien tomb!" Franz interjects.

March utters a quiet, "No, he did not."

Unfazed by the lack of enthusiasm of his audience on either side of the door, Franz draws a deep breath and starts declaiming a few lines he must have memorized by heart. "Those who first came to guide us were no men but born from the blood of the god of war and descended from His burning star. They know not death, for their bones rest amidst the sands of the old kingdom, where the deathless are born and reborn."

"Is it gonna be about Atlantis again?" the guy with the camo T-shirt inquires. "We already did an episode about Atlantis last year."

Franz exults. "Did you hear a word of what I just said? *Born from the god of war and descended from His burning star*! It's Nergal again! He means Nergal, and the burning star is Mars! The ancients believed Mars was, in fact, Nergal sitting in the night sky. But Cornellà *explicitly* tells us that those who first came to guide us *descended* from Mars and that their bones lie in the sands of the old kingdom: *Egypt*, where we have previously discovered unquestionable evidence of extraterrestrial presence! Who helped build the pyramids? Who engineered our species and transmitted their knowledge to us? Who are those travelers from Mars whose secrets the members of the Collegium have tried to protect for centuries? There is only one possible answer: *ancient astronauts*."

Under normal circumstances it'd take a ride in a wind tunnel to so much as wrinkle March's composure, but I think he wasn't ready for Gualtiero Franz. His mouth hanging open in consternation, he won't stop blinking at the train wreck unfolding simultaneously on my phone's screen and on the other side of the door. "That's not how it works," he murmurs. "That's not how any of this works. I have no idea how he even managed to uncover so much about Cornellà, but these things he quotes . . . they're metaphors for strength and endurance, romanticized accounts. Aliens have nothing to do with it."

"Cornellà was talking about the first Lions, the ones from antiquity, right?"

March gives a sharp nod.

A sympathetic cringe tugs at my maxillaries, but before I can say more, Jaime tentatively corrects his boss. "Actually, Cornellà never used the term ancient astronauts, and he only left scant written traces about that. But there's a certain ambiguity in his—"

"It's enough for me if he wrote down that they came from Mars," the blonde remarks with a dismissive flick of her wrist.

Jaime grimaces. "It's . . . more complicated than that."

You bet it is, since a guy from the sixteenth century probably didn't even have the words to conceptualize aliens, let alone space travel. But I'm starting to see how Franz ended up conflating his own beliefs with Cornellà's opaque mysticism. Franz has always been a strong supporter of the theory that ancient pagan gods were actually clumsy human representations of ancient aliens—think Apollo in his sun chariot wearing a gold leotard and flying the *Millennium Falcon.* And here comes this Cornellà guy, weaving cryptic metaphors from the threads of the Lions' ancient history, inking mysterious symbols all over his skin. Then today's Lions beat him up and broke his camera when he tried to unveil their secrets: a match made in conspiracy heaven.

While Franz resumes his bickering with Jaime and his producers in the meeting room, March drags a hand over his face and murmurs, "These people have lost their mind. If the remains are truly Cornellà's, Mr. Franz will be dead by morning. We need to confiscate that crate and surrender it to the Lions to end this madness right now."

"Agreed." I glance down at the heated business negotiations still unfolding onscreen. "I can trigger the fire sprinklers to clear the room for you, but the crate is probably at least two hundred pounds, and we need to move it upstairs."

He frowns at the screen. "The fire alarm will force them to move the crate quickly. Once it's upstairs, Angel and his men can help us extract it."

"They'll be waiting for your signal," a husky voice confirms in our earpieces—a reminder that Angel has been following each new development since Joy officially made him her rebound half an hour ago.

"And Joy?" I whisper back.

"She's with me. Offline. I'm sending her back to the cars."

Or at least he's going to try, I think with a grimace. "Okay, do what you can to get her out of the way," I plead before swiping across my screen to open the interface to the villa's security system.

While I type away to override the smoke detectors manually and set off the fire alarm, March checks his ammo with swift, practiced gestures. I release a deep breath when the magazine clicks back in place, and he racks the gun. We're ready—or not. In any case, we need that crate, and for someone who cherishes order so much in his personal life, chaos has always proven to be the strategy that works best for March.

He reaches to stroke my cheek with the tip of his fingers, just a tender second between us in the dark. "It's going to be all right," he says—as much to reassure himself as me, I suspect.

I respond with a fleeting smile before his features harden and he nods for me to proceed. I tap to confirm that yes, I want to launch every alarm and sprinkler in the villa's nineteen rooms.

A weak blipping sound above our heads announces the apocalypse to come, followed by a flash of red light. Then the howl of the alarm tears through my eardrums, sudden and loud to the very point of pain. Droplets start raining in my hair barely a second later. And it works: panicked calls erupt through the meeting room's doors. Voices ask what's happening, only to get covered by Franz's orders to reseal the crate.

When the doors slide open with a bang and vomit a splash of light and Gualtiero Franz's drenched guests, my first impulse is to hide, but March tucks his gun inside his jacket and instead jumps into view, his damp tuxedo mottled turquoise by the pool lights and blood-red by the alarm LEDs flashing above our heads.

In the meeting room, Jaime's hands freeze on the cart's handle. Gualtiero Franz glares at March, scanning the den for an explanation to his presence—and mine, when I take an uncertain step into the light as well. I keep blinking water out of my eyes, the blare of the alarm is shattering my skull, and I still can't believe I'm now standing mere feet away from my idol.

March, on the other hand, remains perfectly composed as he greets the two of them under the sprinklers' relentless shower. "We're part of Mr. Somoza's security detail. I'm afraid there's been a serious incident involving a garden torch: you need to evacuate, sir."

Franz's wrinkled brow curves upward in shock, only to collapse in suspicion just as fast. "What are you talking about? Patrick would have called! Where the hell is he?"

I step in without thinking, dazed by this surreal moment. And the first words I speak to Gualtiero Franz are: "Patrick *is* the incident. It was horrible; it smelled like tandoori chicken up there."

Franz mouths a silent scream of horror before his voice returns in a gasp. "Then where's security? I have . . . There's supposed to be people everywhere—"

"They'll be here in a second," March assures him, uttering a quiet order for Angel's men to come downstairs.

Because any beefcake will do when you need to save your life's work, Franz welcomes the dark and glistening silhouettes stomping down the stairs with an expression of genuine relief. He doesn't notice the switch—probably didn't care much about the original guys in the first place. Our esteemed colleagues grab a handle on each side of the crate, and when a tall silhouette moves out of the shadows to assist them, I realize that the black guy who kinda looked like a model didn't leave with the rest of Franz's producers: he was still in the meeting room. He joins us in silence and grabs a handle at the front of the crate, apparently to help guide our soaked procession toward the stairs.

Franz's afro bobs in acknowledgment. "Thank you, uh . . ." He waves an evasive hand to signify he's forgotten the guy's name— bodyguard, then?

March and I exchange a look. Something's off: if he's part of the villa's security crew, then by now he should have noticed the absence of his teammate who was watching *Madagascar* in the den—and who's still happily snoozing behind the bar as all hell breaks loose. But our handsome bodyguard didn't react when Gualtiero started freaking out that the den was empty . . .

His gaze finds March's in the darkness, flashes of blue and red light outlining their features. Two ice-cold and determined stares mirror each other. The stranger's elegant eyebrows furrow ever so slightly, and his grip tightens around the crate's handle. The only sign that he recognizes March.

What Lion wouldn't?

It goes fast, and I'm petrified, as if the droplets raining from the sprinklers had stilled in the air. The intruder reaches inside his jacket at the same time March does. I catch the glint of his gun, the outline of March's suppressor.

But March doesn't fire. "Take the remains," he urges. "Take them and *go!*"

Surprise registers on the young Lion's face, right before Franz lunges at the cart to protect it with his body. His drenched palms produce a squeaky sound as he drags them over the Plexiglas lid. "Never!"

The Lion's aim lowers to Franz, who lets go of the crate and staggers backward with his hands up. "I'm taking him too," he grits out, the words coated in a distinctive South African accent.

That sends my adrenaline spiking, and I pop from behind March, brushing dripping curls away from my eyes. "Just the crate," I say. "Only the crate. No one touches Franz!"

I sort of thought this was a negotiation. It isn't. The Lion casually angles his gun at me and fires.

TWENTY-ONE
QUICKENING

"Oh, dear Josette, I have already lost my mind over you; I'm not
afraid of losing my head too!"

— Henriette Wildrose, A Heart on the Scaffold
(Revolutionary Passions #2)

"Island!"

March's hand clamps around my shoulder and he whirls me out
of the way a millisecond before two shots hiss past my ear in rapid
succession. Angel's men collapse, killed with absolute precision. The
room becomes a dark blur but the raw fear prickling through my
veins triggers my survival instinct: I crouch and scramble on all fours
to take cover behind the sofa with Franz and Jaime as March and the
Lion lunge to opposite sides. They fire at the same time in a perfectly

coordinated choreography that speaks of the same training, probably a decade apart.

Bullets crash into the doors and shatter the TV screen in a bright web of abstract pixels. Between Franz and Jaime, it's a concert of panicked screams in the dark as March shoves the cart toward his adversary. The young Lion slams against a wall, recovers fast, and shoots again. This time he hits the crate twice when March takes cover behind it.

That sends Gualtiero Franz into a frenzy. He jumps to his feet and lunges to protect his precious crate with a war cry. Between two desperate pants, I grab his leg, but all I get for my efforts to save him is white-hot pain crackling under my ribs. Goddammit, my favorite host is actually a manic douche who just tried to kick me out of the way! Spurred by pure adrenaline, I get up on one knee and launch myself at his midsection to shove him away from the crate—and mostly out of the crossfire before *Aliens in Our Past* gets canceled for good.

The young Lion raises his gun again but never pulls the trigger: March leaps atop the crate and rams into him. I'm having a hard time keeping track of their struggle in this semi-obscurity streaked by changing lights. The vaporized water saturating the air shrouds them in glimmering chaos. I recognize March's short, drenched hair; his hand wrestles the gun out of the Lion's hand right before a bone-rattling punch sends him flying back into the cart.

March's low grunt of pain is swallowed by Gualtiero Franz's inhuman howl when the cart topples. The crate's lid snaps off, and Cornellà's remains spill all over the glistening floor.

Franz crawls toward the crate with incoherent gasps. "Please stop! Stop this!"

Meanwhile, March has pounced back on the Lion and managed to get his hands around his neck, tightening his hold with a snarl that bares his clenched teeth. The guy writhes and tries to claw at March's carotid to escape the slow crushing of his windpipe. When that fails, he contorts his body to the side, fighting March's weight on his torso.

The Lion's suit molds to his powerful frame as he pushes every muscle, every joint to its tearing point, all to reach for a dark shape lying on the floor a couple feet away.

I recognize the suppressor of March's gun. The Lion's fingers hook around the barrel, dragging it closer, and all I can think is that I need to do something *now*. I make a lightning-fast decision and scramble to the toppled crate on all fours. I'm barely aware of my own shaking hands as I unclasp the wet Plexiglas lid protecting the tomb's contents. My stomach heaves in visceral horror when my fingertips meet dried-up bones and leathery skin. I can't see anything and I have less than a second to act: I grope the skeleton frantically until I feel damp fabric and cool metal.

The sword is much heavier than I expected. I release a gasping breath, my wrist bending at an awkward angle from the effort to extract the weapon from its bed. Then I send it spinning toward March. Five-hundred-year-old steel clanks against ceramic tiles, only to be picked up immediately. The blade rises in March's hand in the same instant that the Lion gets a firm hold on the gun. There's a single gunshot. A silvery thread swiping down.

The first thing I know for sure is that March is kneeling by the Lion's prone body, drawing ragged breaths. Pink and red stain his shirt, but as I crawl toward him, I can see no entry wound and relief bubbles in my chest. The Lion, though . . . Okay, *that* is a serious entry wound—one he won't recover from. I get to my feet and close the distance to wrap my arms around March's torso. My palms find the reassuring warmth of his skin seeping through drenched cotton, the steady rise and fall of his chest. "Are you okay?"

He releases a hoarse sigh. "Yes. I suppose there can only be one."

I know I shouldn't laugh because he just seriously decapitated a guy with an antique sword, but I can't stop the nervous chuckle shaking my frame. "No quickening please, I just want to leave this place alive."

A wheezing moan pops our bubble. "What . . . what have you done?"

March and I direct our attention to the open crate at the same time. I had almost forgotten about Franz and Jaime—the latter is checking on Cornellà's remains with trembling hands.

"The hide is intact," Jaime whimpers. "We need to save it."

Franz grips the crate. "We can't leave him!"

"It's too heavy." Jaime tries to reason with him.

March gets to his feet with a grunt. "Mr. Franz, we are not taking it. Let the Collegium have it and worry about your immediate future instead."

Franz's afro quivers in indignation. "Is that a threat? Who are you, people? CIA? MI6?"

"Uh, no." I raise my palms in a pacifying gesture. "We're here to help you. We just want to make sure the Collegium doesn't kill you."

"But you want to give them the hide!" he squeaks. That roll of human leather and the tattoos covering it are all that matter to him: he said himself that he didn't care about the sword that much despite its archeological value . . .

"You'll be in danger as long as you have it," I plead.

March takes a threatening step toward Franz and cracks his neck to indicate that we're done mediating. Jaime's arms look like they're made of the same flan as mine and according to Wikipedia Franz is sixty-seven: if March wants them to leave that den without Cornellà's hide, they *will*.

"Angel," he whispers, "the den is clear, but I'm going to need—"

He pauses as an all too familiar din breaks out on the floor above and filters through the pool's windows: shrill screams, water splashing, and the rattling of automatic rifles. Oh, God . . . our headless Lion didn't show up alone; he brought friends.

"What's going on?" Franz clambers to the window and the dark blinds shielding it. March barks for him to stay back and dashes across the room to haul him to the relative safety of a corner of the room. But it's too late; by the time March hooks his arm around Franz's torso and starts to drag him away, the old man has already pressed the button on the wall that commands the blinds.

Turquoise slowly illuminates the den, stained by crimson ribbons swirling around a body I recognize as one of Angel's men—maybe Sonny, or was it Francis?

"Angel?" March hisses for the second time, even as bubbly trails tear through the pool's blue. Bullets.

Sudden panic curdles in my stomach: Angel said he'd take Joy back to the cars, but did he have enough time to? "Joy? Joy? Where are you?" I whisper-shout, only to be greeted by a silent feed.

The fire sprinklers are still going strong above our head, splashing droplets all over my screen, but I just realized all the lights have gone out in the meeting room at some point. I pull out my phone from my clutch with shaking hands. "All connections are out. Someone cut the power," I tell March.

"They planned a complete takeover," March concludes.

"We need to find Joy," I urge him. Goosebumps pop all over my body where my dress's damp material clings to my skin. She's up there, somewhere—wounded . . . or worse. I force the thought at the back of my mind. We need to focus on getting out of here alive, ideally with Franz and his research assistant, but mostly with Joy and Angel.

March swipes a hard look at Franz and Jaime, who are now kneeling against the wall and busy trying to wrap Cornellà's hide in the piece of linen in which the sword was wrapped. "Stay here with them. I'll find Joy."

I want to tell him to be careful, that we have no idea what happened on the first floor and how many Lions have entered the compound: I'm given no time to. A new series of gunshots in the garden become a multitude of bullet trails streaking the pool's water, reddening it further as they shred the body floating there. Each impact spiders the laminated glass with terrifying cracks, but the surface seems to resist . . . For now.

Crap. Last time something like that happened to me, I was

crawling across a glass mezzanine in Tokyo and it didn't end well. "They're trying to force us out!"

And it's working. "Stairs!" March shouts, dragging me so fast my feet skid on the blood-and-water soaked tiling. Franz and Jaime follow us, one of them accidentally tripping on the dead Lion's head in his escape. The vocalization that follows is a five-octave auditory experience, a supernatural hoot that would make Russian pop sensation Vitas proud. I'm pretty sure I feel dreadlocks graze my foot too as the head rolls across the floor—I bite back a yelp of my own. But I need to focus on running, on not spraining my ankles or letting go of March's hand as we climb the stairs.

I register another round of fire that turns the pool window into a shivering web. The shooting stops and the silence barely lasts a second. First comes the ear-splitting crash of glass giving way, then a sudden drift of cool air as tons of water rush and roar into the den. We're almost halfway up, but the water keeps rising fast on our heels. I smell chlorine and realize I'm wading ankle-deep while behind me, Franz and Jaime scramble with panicked gasps, their pants drenched all the way up to their knees.

Light pours from the first floor. We made it. March hoists me atop the final step, and I look back at the seething tide, which is now receding to leave a foot of water in the basement. I try to catch my breath; we're only getting started.

The screaming has stopped, as if the guests were never there. The doors leading to the staircase are wide open. March motions for me to stay back and raises his gun at the empty spot Angel's men were supposed to guard. He lowers it almost as soon: the welcome committee is here already. Chills run up and down my soaked limbs at the sight of a cluster of dark silhouettes waiting for us atop the stairs: five men wearing black fatigues and their most welcoming frown, their eyes hidden under lightweight, state-of-the-art night goggles. I count three assault rifles and seven guns in total: that's up to 400 bullets ready to shred us to smithereens.

March darts a look back at me. He's done the math too. He slowly holsters his gun. "We did not come here to fight, only to ensure Mr. Franz's safety. What you're looking for is downstairs, likely damaged by the water."

"Your weapon," one of the Lions demands, ignoring the proffered olive branch.

All barrels, long and short, follow March's moves as he slowly reaches inside his jacket and kneels to place his gun on the floor before kicking it their way. "I want to speak to your commander, so we can clear up this misunderstanding."

I draw slow, controlled breaths while Franz and Jaime shake in silent terror behind me. They wanted the "Collegium": here it is in all its glory. As for their commander, the new supreme leader of this quietly demented horde . . . of course, he's behind all this. The helicopter, an operation of this size: none of this could have happened without the green light of the ever-lovable Mr. Stiles.

Memories flash behind my eyelids, of his gentle, almost handsome features. Baby blue eyes so kind I found it in me twice to save his miserable ass. I should have let Dries shoot him in that church in Venice. I should have let March beat his face to an unrecognizable pulp in the woods in Finland. But I didn't, and that allowed him to betray Anies and take over the Lions. To his credit, Stiles did ultimately arrange for Anies's mad doctor to remove the implant she'd stuck in my brain, but that didn't raise his overall standing much in my and March's eyes.

I step forward to stand at March's side. "Is he here?" I ask, my voice so cold I don't recognize it. "I want to speak to him. He knows me very well."

After all, he and I lived almost an entire year together. I know which one of his cats is his favorite—Ron—which pancakes he prefers—raisins, of course—and I know how it felt to have him pin me down with his full weight and stab my arm with a needle full of sedative.

When one of the Lions focuses his goggles on me and his lips part to speak, what comes out is like an echo of the past. "You're Dries's daughter." There's the slightest hint of curiosity, perhaps even respect. I sometimes forget that my father's legacy follows me everywhere I go.

I give a single nod.

"Follow us," the Lion says.

TWENTY-TWO
THE COST OF RICA

The guard rattled his baton against the iron bars of Rica's cell. His peaked cap shadowed most of his face, but his mustache . . . even in her worst nightmares, she could never forget that jet-black curtain. "Did you think I was dead, Rica?"

– Kerry-Lee Storm, *The Cost of Rica #5: Blaze of the Phoenix*

The torches are still burning and bathing the empty garden in an eerie orange hue, but the party is over. The group of Lions escorts us across the deserted living room where shattered drinks and petit fours scattered on the floor are the only traces left of Franz's exclusive guests. As we make our way to the garden, I spot the bodies of three of Angel's men, lying lifeless near a fourth man I recognize as one of Franz's guards.

"Where's everyone else?" I rasp, my back growing clammy at the idea that they might have . . .

"In the guest house," the Lion who spoke to me earlier deigns to reply.

March and I glance at the oval Mayan-style house tucked away from the villa among palm trees and guarded by heavily armed Lions. I experience some infinitesimal amount of relief upon seeing shapes move in the dark through the windows. There must have been thirty guests: if the Lions crammed them in there when they took over, Joy might be with them. And Angel too? I can't imagine him letting anyone pen him without a gory fight.

Any hope I had entertained dies the moment we step out on the bridge crossing the now reddened pool. Her black dress is the first thing I see. Joy is sitting at a table, rigid and pale next to a guy in a dark leather jacket who's definitely not Stiles. More like . . . Sheikh Auda Abu Tayi from *Lawrence of Arabia*. Okay, Anthony Quinn is actually dead, but there's a resemblance. The same strong, hooked nose and coppery tan, thick wavy black hair streaked with silver, and a carefully trimmed goatee that's just long enough to evoke vague discomfort, with a single patch of gray-white right under the lower lip. He's eating from a tiny glass of ceviche in front of him, as if his colleagues hadn't just attacked and taken hostage an entire villa full of innocent celebrities.

Every hair on my body rises on end when I realize that one of the Lions is aiming a bulky gun at Joy—integrated suppressor, I'm guessing. Beyond a second defense line, I spot Angel, Abelardo, and a third man whose sleeve is stained red from a bullet wound. Angel stands still, alight with a quiet, devastating rage I can feel rippling to me in dark waves. Even so, he won't move as long as that Lion near the table is holding his gun inches from Joy's disheveled curls.

March's gaze meets mine for a second. He knows exactly how I feel: that I'd give anything to be in Joy's place. Her features light up in equal fear and relief when she sees us, but she presses her lips together tight and stays silent. The man at her side raises his head from the ceviche and holds up the half-finished glass, studying it with dark eyes. Once we're mere feet away from the table, he motions for us to sit across from him and Joy. There're only three chairs: March and I take our place around the table with slow, controlled movements, as does Gualtiero Franz, but one of the Lions holds Jaime back when he tries to join Franz. He's not invited to the party, and honestly, I'd skip it too if I could.

Our mystery villain reaches for a bottle of white Casa Madero and pours some into three glasses. "Be my guests." He chuckles, the words rolling off his tongue with a husky Hispanic drawl.

Franz shakes his head and glares at the man, while March adjusts the cuffs of his drenched tux jacket with an icy expression. "I'm afraid we must decline, Mr..." He tilts his head, waiting for the introduction to be made.

Our host gives a superior snort. "People call me Ramirez."

I wish I could welcome the news with the same cool as March, but I can no more stop the unhinging of my jaw than Joy can: she's read *Cost of Rica* too. She knows this is bad news. If this guy is only half as evil as his fictional alter ego, someone will get fed alive to alligators tonight. Her eyes widen, meet mine, and she mouths a silent, *Fucking really?*

Franz grips the edge of the table to stop the shaking of his hands. "Are you from the Collegium?"

Ramirez responds with a snarl I believe he meant to be a smile. "Yes. You've found us at last." Ignoring the horror disintegrating Franz's features, he turns to me. "And you are Island. Dries's daughter... I knew your father very well—admired him, in fact. He funded us generously and understood the importance of our work. Please accept my deepest condolences."

Joy's gaze flits between the two of us. If she needed any more proof that all I told her was true, there it is. The lines of dismay forming between her eyebrows tell me she's wishing hard she could undo the past twenty-four hours right now.

Meanwhile, Ramirez's unkind stare lands on March. "And here's the infamous *Mr. November* . . . I presume our brother Oliver didn't survive his encounter with you?"

March returns Ramirez's wry smile. "You'll find both halves of him downstairs. Hopefully, we can end the hostilities here."

"Hopefully," Ramirez drawls, stroking the curly tip of his mustache.

"Where's Stiles?" I snap. "We want to sort this out with him."

Ramirez marks a tense pause. His nostrils flare, the only warning before his palms slam the table hard enough to crack the smooth teak boards and shatter the ceviche glass. I jump and recoil against the back of my chair as he leans forward, his features twisted in raw hate. "You are talking to *me*. And you will sort things out with *me*."

Joy inches away from him and toward the gun aimed at her, her chest heaving in silent panic. I ball my fists, trying desperately to anchor her gaze to mine. March is my rock when life shakes me too hard; right now, I have to find the strength to be hers. She swallows hard and gives a small nod when our eyes meet. *It's gonna be okay. We're gonna find a way out of this.*

I glare at Ramirez. "What do you want? March already told your men you can have Cornellà's remains. We're not here to fight; we just want to end this ridiculous crusade."

My anger reignites Joy's wavering inner flame. "You shot my ex, asshole!"

He indulges in a hoarse laugh. "A tragedy, especially since he knew so little he was barely worth killing. But I want to reassure you, ladies, that we're solving this tonight."

"Agreed," March acquiesces. "Please take the hide, the bones, and *leave*."

"Oh, I am taking the hide," Ramirez hisses. He snaps his fingers at the men encircling us; one of them leaves the group to stand right behind Franz. The latter blanches and inches away from the beefcake towering over him, but the Lion clamps a strong hand around his shoulder and casually plunges the other in Franz's shirt to retrieve the tube containing Cornellà's hide. That's a new level of determination I didn't expect from him: he somehow found the time to tuck it in there during our escape from the basement while people were shooting at him!

Franz lets out a quasi-wail as his precious find is torn from him and presented to Ramirez. The old Lion unseals the hide, but he doesn't unroll it; he just caresses the thick parchment slowly, almost like he would a lover, before delicately slipping it back in the tube.

Once the hide is safe in its case, he leans back and raps long nails on the table he cracked earlier. "Thank you. However, I'm afraid we're not quite done with Mr. Franz. He'll come with us as well."

"Never!" Franz shouts. The Lion behind him whips out a semi-automatic, and the steel muzzle pressing against the back of his skull immediately dampens Franz's ardor.

I nearly jump from my seat. "Wait a min—"

"Out of the question," March states. "The hide, the bones, the sword. Nothing more."

Franz lets out a brittle plea. "Don't let him take the hide! He'll—" The Lion aiming at him hits him hard with the gun to shut him up.

"Hey!" I scream, leaning to my side to check on Franz. No blood, but he looks a little dizzy and completely desperate. Joy watches me hold his hand, powerless under the threat of her own warden.

Next to her, Ramirez's mocking smile peels off at last, and what's underneath is a mask of pure contempt. He exhales a mock-dramatic sigh. "Mr. November, I don't think you understand the magnitude of what's at stake here."

"Then, by all means, enlighten me," March replies. "Why do you need Franz? If you need reassurance he'll stop chasing after the Collegium, then you have my guarantee that I'll handle him personally."

Ramirez waves the offer off. "The Collegium doesn't need your help, Mr. November. What it needs is Mr. Franz's expertise."

Recalling Franz's exalted rant back in the basement, I venture. "Is it about that secret tomb in Egypt?"

Ramirez leans forward to rest his elbows on the table and locks his obsidian gaze with mine. "What did your father tell you about the first brothers?"

"Nothing. I didn't even know the Collegium existed until I watched the episode Franz shot in Rome. It was you guys, right? You found him sniffing around one of your temples, and you beat him up."

His mouth pinches like a butthole tucked under his mustache. "I see," he drawls. "You should have taught her to lie more convincingly, Mr. November."

I know that tic in March's jaw. Ramirez is getting on his last nerve. "Every single word she spoke is the truth. Cut to the chase. Why do you need Franz?"

Our dollar-store Scar rises from the table, the row of flaming garden torches a perfect background for his little show. "What does every man want? Answers." His blazing gaze cuts to me. "Tell me, Island, what do you think Cornellà found in Egypt? What kind of discovery could have been so momentous that he had to keep it even from his brothers, and that he lost his mind after he witnessed it?"

"Bones," I venture warily.

All I get in return is a slow cackle that grows in intensity and becomes more awkward with every second that passes. That man isn't just a sinister douche apparatus: he's also seconds away from a complete meltdown.

Joy sends me a distraught look before boldly asking Ramirez, "Are you high?"

He gives the briefest eye roll. "No. Please keep quiet. You're too beautiful to waste that gift by opening your mouth." Following this grotesque burst of machismo, his attention returns to me. "Bones! Yes, indeed. But the true question is, were those *human* bones?"

March's mouth tightens in aggravation while I take a circular look at Ramirez's men. Surely someone in here is going to realize that this has nothing to do with either contract killing or proper archeology. My eyes stop on Franz, who's rolling terrified eyes at Ramirez and squeezing my hand so hard it's starting to hurt. *Sweet Raptor Jesus in a spacesuit.* I shake my head at Ramirez. "Please don't tell me you think the First Lions were aliens. This is serious; people are *dead*!"

Joy shakes her head, her eyes wide. "Hold on. *Alien mummies*? Is that why you're doing all this shit?"

Our worst fears appear to be confirmed when Franz yells, "I will never help you find that tomb!" with the same determination, the same passion I've always admired so much in his show. When everything else abandons him, even his own courage, he still has that inner flame that keeps him going.

"Somehow, I doubt Mr. Stiles condones this scientific quest," March warns Ramirez.

Indeed: to the best of my knowledge, Stiles has never expressed any interest in ancient astronauts, and back in the meeting room, March said Collegium members usually kept violence to a minimum anyway.

Interestingly, like my earlier request to talk to the big boss, March's comment seems to agitate our psycho-in-chief. He paces along the pool with nervous strides. "*Stiles!* Too busy pasting kitten pictures in his motivational newsletters to see the truth!" He drags a hand over his face and walks back to the table. "Never mind. Mr. November, Island, let's end this now. Franz is coming with us. Once we've safely left the premises with him and the hide, I'm pleased to say you and I will never meet again."

When more of Ramirez's Lions move to seize Franz, he ignores the gun pointed at him and tries to spring from his chair, raising jittery palms to keep them at a distance. "I will never collaborate! You're not worthy of piercing the secrets ancient astronauts left for us!"

March jackknifes up to shield Franz as they close in on the three of us, but it's no use; two Lions move from behind and hook their arms with Franz's to restrain him while the rest of them never stop aiming at March and me. It's been a long time since I've felt so helpless. Franz and Jaime are about to get taken away, Joy still held at gunpoint by her captor. For a complete madman, Ramirez has learned from his predecessors: he's leaving us no escape, not a single opening.

He moves to stand face to face with Franz and grabs his cheeks between his long, tanned fingers, digging nails like claws into his beard. "You will *bend.* Or I'll have every inch of your skin flayed from your body like Cornellà ripped his own when his mind deserted him." Turning to his men, he bellows, "Someone bring me Logan!"

TWENTY-THREE

THE ROAR OF THE TIGER

Our hero had no choice but to surrender his defenseless butthole
to the prehistorical billionaire's vilest urges: a single swipe of the
roaring beast's claws would tear him apart like toilet paper.

– Tuck Chingle, *Pounded in the Butt by the Handsome
Megatherium*

I don't know who that Logan person is, but after Ramirez's order
echoes through the silent compound, a few Lions bustle around three
armored 6x6 trucks parked near the villa's gates—whose bent iron
bars suggest that they were rammed through, by the way. Now at
least we know how they got in here.

One of them opens a truck to retrieve a small brown object from
the backseat. *No . . . wait a minute.* I squint my eyes as the soldier

walks toward us, only for them to pop wide open when I recognized the strange cargo that's now latched to his tactical vest.

Joy darts a discomfited look at March and me. "What the . . . ?"

March and Franz's eyebrows rise in sync, my mouth falls open, and there's something weird hanging in the air, a sense of complete disbelief as this Lion in full black military gear returns with . . . a sloth. Short brown fur, nerdy bowl cut, and vaguely threatening black markings around his eyes, like really angry, scheming eyebrows: that is without any possible doubt a three-toed sloth, clad in a tiny black tactical vest—I wonder if you can order those online or if Ramirez had it custom-made. Standing fifty feet away from us and encircled by a group of Lions, Angel recognizes it too. A quivering snarl tugs at his scar. He has a problem with sloths because they keep breaking into his secret lair in Ecuador and he thinks they're after him personally. I have no idea what happened for him to develop this severe case of misofolivory, but according to Beatriz, his trauma and hatred run deep.

At any rate, that guy is bringing a sloth, and I don't think my evening could get any weirder until I notice the way the torches' flames are reflecting off its claws. Gleaming.

I don't even find it in me to be scared; I'm just physically gob-smacked. Ramirez owns a pet sloth whose long and sharp claws are coated—or fitted—with some sort of golden metal. And he named it Logan. Because, well . . . I guess it works?

He takes a step back to welcome the furry creature in his arms. His lips stir malevolently through his goatee as the sloth latches onto his leather jacket.

March blinks twice and shakes his head. "I'm terribly confused."

Ramirez turns to Franz with a dark chuckle. "Do you understand the true meaning of agony?"

When Franz remains speechless, Ramirez walks up to Joy, who's still sitting at the table in a state of equal sideration. I don't like that at all: the shitty smirk tugging at the corner of his lips seems mirrored by Logan's expression of detached cruelty.

"Then I'll show you," Ramirez says at last.

I feel the muscles in my legs detonate the very second his hand moves to fist Joy's hair and twist it to expose her throat. She groans from the sudden pain, and I leap forward, only to be immediately stopped by a Lion who clamps his elbow around my neck. March lunges at him but freezes when my captor presses his gun to my temple. March watches me, teeth gritted tight, nostrils flaring with every breath as the Lion tightens his grip and forces me to arch my back in order not to suffocate. My spine hurts so badly I feel it's gonna snap, but the worst part is hearing Joy's whimper of terror just a few feet away.

Ramirez bends down, allowing Logan to transfer to her chest and rest his golden claws inches from her carotid. Tremors course through her body in response, but I can tell she's doing everything to keep still as the cluster of incurved blades caress her sweat-soaked skin.

"Stop! Stop that!" I shriek when Logan starts applying pressure above her clavicle, drawing a single pearl of blood there.

"Ramirez!" Angel barks helplessly, restrained by Lions as I am.

Ramirez pays him no heed, a sneer nested in his beard as the puncture on Joy's neck threatens to become a gash. Her chest heaves and dips to the rhythm of her frantic panting, but she doesn't scream. She stares up at Ramirez's demonic features, tears brimming at the corner of her eyes.

"Logan loves to take his time," he purrs. "He can spend hours tearing her to ribbons, and it'll never be enough for him."

As if he understood, the sloth plunges its claws a fraction deeper, drawing a gasp from Joy.

I struggle against the muscular arm keeping me in a chokehold. "Take it off! Don't touch her!"

"You're a monster!" Franz sobs.

Ramirez slams his fist on the table. "Tell me where's the tomb or you'll be next!"

"Tell him!" I urge in my turn when I see a trickle of blood run down's Joy's neck.

"I can't! But her sacrifice won't be in vain," Franz whines while the sloth never pauses in its abominable task.

He can't be serious. I've never missed a single episode of this man's show; I bought every single book he's ever written, and he's gonna let Logan flay my best friend for a bunch of nonexistent alien bones?

"Ramirez!" Angel bellows again, this time loud enough to catch the Lion in chief's attention. His voice echoes across the garden like a cannon. "You enter my territory. You kill my men . . . You torture my *friend!*"

Ramirez chuckles as Angel marks a pause. What is he trying to achieve? Get Ramirez to unleash Logan on him instead to save Joy? The silence stretches in the night, pounds in my eardrums like a muted beat as my captor keeps slowly crushing my throat. I try to focus on March, the tumultuous blue in his eyes, and I can tell every single neuron he possesses is trying to find a safe opening, a way out of this mess.

Meanwhile, Angel stretches out his arms to the sky and simply concludes with a thunderous, "I have helicopters too."

Confusion registers on Ramirez's features, which only grows as we pick up a hissing sound coming from above. Logan raises his head slowly to look up at his master. Reflected like shooting stars in his beady eyes, two fiery trails light up the sky of Puerto Morelos. *Sweet. Jesus.* I suck in a strangled breath, but the shock wave hits before I can even exhale. Disjointed thoughts flash in quick succession in my brain. The air around me feels blistering hot, and I can tell the Lion's gun is no longer against my temple. I'm flying forward, and Joy is falling backward, her eyes impossibly wide.

My face meets something hard yet soft that stops my body before it hits the table. March has lunged at me and shields me as half of Gualtiero's Franz's villa is instantly reduced to ground zero by a pair of missiles. Everything goes white, and my ears are ringing so loud; I don't know anything anymore except the agony in my skull.

I blink around, searching for Joy, but all my gaze finds are flames engulfing pale walls and wooden beams, greedily licking the villa's straw roof. It's not just my eardrums thrumming from the shock: at last, the hum of a rotor is growing louder and louder above us. I release the breath I've been holding for three seconds that felt like an eternity. March's body is pressed to mine; his hand darts to pick up something from the grass, then comes the inevitable bang of a gun firing. That was the Lion who tried to strangle me: he should never have let go of his weapon, explosion or not.

March rolls away from me and, without even getting to his feet, takes out a second guy who had the misfortune to fall to his knees right next to us. Two shots in the face that shatter his night-vision goggles and stain them with a splatter of fresh blood. I register more gunfire crackling across the lawn: Angel and Abelardo must have seized their chance to retaliate as well. I raise a shaking hand to shield my eyes when the droning in the sky becomes harsh gusts lashing at my face, blinding lights, and the unmistakable emerald filament of a laser-guided aim.

Sparks crackle in the dark; I press my hands to block the sudden, painful din of a pair of gun turrets showering black-clad silhouettes with 30mm caliber. A part of my brain that still works notices the characteristically sharp angles of the cockpit's windows and diagnoses a Tiger. *Well-played, Angel.* Running among the rows of torches and yelling commands to fall back to their armored trucks, the Lions are retreating. Franz and his assistant are huddled against each other behind a toppled dessert cart, covered in frosting and fruit, but alive. I blink unfocused eyes but can't see Ramirez and his evil sloth anywhere, just a prone figure on the lawn.

Rumpled black silk gapes to reveal the smooth, pale hill of a naked back. *Joy.*

I scramble toward her, only to realize that she's moving away from me. *No.* She's being *dragged away,* half-conscious, by Ramirez.

My thoughts collide and coalesce like lightning balls: that turd pudding couldn't get to Franz when everything blew up, and now March stands between them, so he's trying to take off with a hostage instead. Ahead of us, one of his men has picked up Logan, and they're racing toward the armored trucks that brought them here.

"March; he's got Joy!" I howl, even as the brief rattle of an assault rifle is soon silenced by another single gunshot. March never wastes bullets.

He shoves aside a disoriented Lion to run in pursuit of Ramirez and Joy with powerful strides, like a juggernaut barreling through the flames. As if this were a football game and Joy were the ball, March bellows Angel's name. He's seen Joy too and detonates across the ravaged lawn in a blur of black linen and sinewy limbs. *He can make it*, I think over the blood pounding in my ears. He's closer than us, and his lighter build grants him unexpected velocity.

"Get her!" I wail, my voice breaking from exhaustion. I can't keep up with either of them: my legs are shaking so much that I'm not entirely sure I'm running. Hindered by my heels, I hobble among burning debris as March and Angel gain ground on Ramirez and a now struggling Joy. She's shrieking and contorting in his grip, her pale fingers digging into the arm wrapped around her throat. She's slowing him down, but he's already mere steps away from the trucks. March raises his gun as Ramirez wrestles Joy in one of the trucks, but he can't pull the trigger and neither dares Angel. They don't have a clear shot.

I see, hear the door slam shut through a haze of smoke, powerless to stop Ramirez. He's taken her. He's taken her and I can't breathe. A scream builds at the back of my throat, only to be silenced by the sound of gunshots. March is emptying the rest of his magazine in the truck's bulletproof windshield. The top layer of glass instantly shatters, but the polycarbonate underneath resists as the truck backs away, crushing what's left of Franz's fence under its massive honeycomb tires. Those too are bulletproof, a distant part of me notes.

Ramirez has truly learned from the failures of his predecessors.

Angel's bark rips through my daze. "To the cars!"

My head whips right to the blinding lights barreling our way in a cloud of dust: Angel's surviving men made it to the SUVs that drove us here. I wobble backward, only to find March's solid warmth against my shoulder blades. "Biscuit, can you walk?"

My mouth opens, but the whole second it takes me to form a positive answer is time we don't have. Air whizzes out of my lungs as March picks me up bridal-style and covers the distance toward the cars in a few dizzying strides. By the time I manage to breathe and blink, I've been tossed and buckled up in the back of an SUV, and March has jumped in the passenger seat. I glimpse Abelardo's ponytail and register the rumble of the engine before a mad acceleration pins me to the backseat.

We tear through dense, dark vegetation and careen onto a straight band of asphalt where Ramirez's motorcade of three armored trucks is racing into the night ahead of us.

"Where—where are they going?" I manage to gasp. "Where is he taking her?"

"West," March replies, eying a tactile screen sitting at the center of the dashboard.

I take in the map onscreen; they're headed straight to the backcountry with nothing but brambly plains for miles and miles until the next town, Leona Vicario. "There's nothing there. Unless he's got backup?"

March's tense gaze meets mine in the mirror. "Possible."

"Then, we have to get Joy back before more Lions show up!" I urge.

The Veneno's headlights flash in March's mirror. A roar coming from our right is our only warning before Angel passes us in a flash of silver and pure, undiluted rage.

"I doubt Ramirez will make it far," March predicts, watching the Veneno gain on the trucks ahead. "But we need to extract her safely."

An ominous droning above us signals that the Tiger is back,

probably to tail Ramirez's convoy. It's all it can do for now: even Angel is sane enough to realize that shooting them up is out of the question as long as Joy is in the car.

"¡Cuidado!" *Watch out!* Abelardo's sudden bark has me jerking forward to see what caused him to raise his voice for the first time since we've met.

Sweet Raptor Jesus. In a move that seems borrowed directly from March's gentleman handbook, one of Ramirez's Lions just popped out the rear window of the truck closest to Angel with a grenade launcher in hand. I register a loud crack, a flash of light renting the night, and it begins. Two sizzling arcs target the Veneno right before it veers left to avoid them. The projectiles explode on the road, flames licking the bolide as it drifts, spins, and resumes its pursuit with a vengeance. Angel Somoza isn't just single-minded; apparently, he also knows how to drive.

"We have to stop them! Joy's gonna get killed at this rate!"

Well aware of the fact, March has lowered his window and leans outside, barely hindered by the wind whipping us as he takes aim for the douche with the grenade launcher. "A tad to the left, please," he asks Abelardo, who complies dutifully.

It's a millisecond window, but that's all March needs. He presses the trigger once, and I glimpse a dark shape slinking back inside the truck, either dead or otherwise incapacitated. March's second shot makes it through the open window an instant later: the truck starts zigzagging erratically before it launches off the road in a crash of metal—I think he killed the driver.

I grip March's headrest to get a better look at the road. "Okay, that's one down; we need—" My imprecation is cut short by a sudden hiss above our heads, followed by a bone-rattling explosion. In front of us, one of the trucks bursts into flames and flips off the road, only to crash into the surrounding trees. You've got to be kidding me: Angel's Tiger just fired.

"I thought they wouldn't risk it!" I shriek. I'm pretty sure that wasn't Joy and Ramirez's truck, but "pretty sure" isn't good enough when someone is firing missiles at your BFF.

"But now there's only one left to take out," Abelardo notes, all the while swerving to avoid flaming debris.

As he says this, I notice for the first time a new dot on the dashboard's screen, approaching fast . . . behind us? March and I exchange a tense look before our eyes flit in sync to the mirror. Nothing. I turn to check the rear window, a knot in my throat.

"It's higher," March says, a crease between his eyebrows. He's *worried*.

At last, I pick up a growing hum, half a second before something hisses above our car. I don't see the explosion, but I feel it rattling the SUV's solid frame. Ominous sparks light up the sky around us and rain down, along with a dark carcass that crashes between us and Ramirez's convoy. A bent steel blade and a shattered rotor come flying at us, scraping against March's door with a chilling groan. Something above us shot Angel's Tiger down.

"Island, down!" March shouts.

I frantically fold over and cradle my head between my knees, just before Abelardo hits the brakes so hard I can almost hear my internal organs splatter against my ribcage. Right ahead, the Veneno spins through a curtain of fire while a looming shadow soon stretches and roars above our heads. The need to know is stronger than the fear singing in my bones: I peer out my window to see what the hell is going on, and when I do, my hands freeze inches from my head, shaking.

Raptor Jesus and all his saints save us: Ramirez brought a bomber to a helicopter fight. A humongous silhouette storms over the motorcade, engulfing us in the shade of its wings as it descends toward the road. Once it's ahead of us, the dark mouth of a rear hatch parts open. Ramirez's truck races toward it with Joy in tow.

"March, they're going to . . ."

My shout gets lost in the sound of tires screeching against the asphalt as Abelardo hits the gas. To my right, a flash of silver tears through flaming debris in the same instant: Angel managed to regain control of his monster. But Ramirez's bomber is licking the markings already, the yellow ribbon disappearing under its massive frame. Dammit, we've lost too much ground. So much *goddamn* ground. I grit my teeth as the Veneno passes us with a feral blast, and there's this split second when I feel in my marrow that Angel is going to make it. He's right behind, *right . . .*

Ramirez's truck jolts as its wheels bite the ledge of the hatch. Everything goes quiet in my head as I watch the darkness swallow Joy, powerless to save her while the hatch slowly rises. The Veneno attempts to catch up one last time, even as the plane starts to lift from the ground.

Ramirez has learned every last trick in his adversaries' book, and I can't yet process that he's taken Joy. I'm barely aware of our car slowing down, then stopping. I can't blink, can't close my eyes: the bomber's crimson taillights are imprinting themselves in my retinae like a trio of burning stars.

"Biscuit, are you all right?"

March's soft call tears through my stupefaction. He's turned around; his hand reaches for mine between the seats, stroking my fingers with his thumb. As if an invisible pair of scissors had cut the strings that were dragging us, we've stopped on that road in the middle of nowhere, under the crushing beauty of the Milky Way. Abelardo releases the wheel with a low growl while Angel steps out from the Veneno, his fists clenched so hard the tendons under his skin seem about to snap.

Ramirez has taken Joy.

DANCING WITH A STAR

Ramirez stroked a vile, criminal finger along the perfect oval
of Rica's tear-streaked cheek. He chuckled evilly. "And so,
you are now Sanchez's mistress. He always had impeccable taste,
but so do I, Rica!"

— Kerry-Lee Storm, *The Cost of Rica #5: Blaze of the Phoenix*

It takes me one breath, then another, before thoughts and blood rush back to my brain. "Holy sh . . . We have to save her!" I implore March, undoing my belt with shaking hands. We climb out at the same time, joined by Abelardo. Behind us, Angel's second SUV has drifted to a halt.

He walks to us, his eyes blazing with the kind of rage that gives you goosebumps even in the heat of Cancún. "Wherever he lands, he'll find me waiting," he promises, checking his watch's dial.

As the glass turns into a GPS tracking screen, I remember that March actually buys his chronographs from him: Angel cut a deal with a discreet Swiss watchmaker and helped them turn their understated models into a fashion accessory anyone about to commit multiple felonies needs at their wrist. On the watch's sleek screen, a 3D map of the coast zooms on a red dot. A modicum of relief surges in my veins: Joy is still wearing her earpiece.

"They're leaving the Mexican airspace," I say, my gaze glued to that tiny, tiny dot, the only proof that Joy might still be okay. "We'll lose her over the Atlantic, but we might be able to pick up the signal again depending on where and when they'll land. The miniaturized battery won't last long though, and if they land in a dead zone, there will be no network for her earpiece to latch onto." I search March's steady gaze. "Do you think Ramirez might . . ."

"He won't touch a hair on her head," he reassures me before I even try to verbalize the unthinkable. If anything happens to Joy . . .

In a rare display of humanity, Angel nods to this, his hard gaze softening a fraction. "He knows what he took, and who he took it from."

"He thinks Joy is your girlfriend," I translate with a grimace. "He probably figures we're going to bring him Gualtiero Franz in exchange for her."

"A bold strategy," March notes dryly.

A snarl twists Angel's scar under his beard. "*No one* blackmails Angel Somoza." His tar-black gaze locks with March's. "You bring me that TV *payaso* tonight. If Ramirez wants to play with me, we're going to play."

I don't like the way he stresses out that final verb and I fear no one is going to have fun, least of all Joy. "Maybe there's another way," I venture.

The subtle stiffening of March's posture doesn't escape me, but he knows it's time to address the elephant in the room, so I press on.

"I don't think Stiles gave Ramirez his orders: back there, he sounded like he was on a personal quest or something. We need to contact Stiles. Maybe he can put the leash back on his Lions and help us recover Joy safely." *For a price*, I mentally complete. But I don't want to say it out loud: March knows exactly how Stiles functions: he's a complete sociopath who sees nothing but assets and liabilities, profit and losses.

March's chest heaves. "I'd much rather you don't."

"I don't have a choice." My fingers twitch out of habit, seeking my clutch and the phone inside, but I realize with rising panic that my hands are empty. "Crap. I lost my phone at the villa." I send March a pleading look. "You still have yours?"

"Yes."

"Can you wipe mine?"

The Mexican police will probably search the ruins of Franz's villa for clues as to what went down. I trust Angel to distribute copious amounts of "*refrescos*" and possibly have his employees shove those bribes down the throat of the most recalcitrant cops—I cringe at the thought, a comforting reminder that I'm not yet morally bankrupt. March unlocks a remote-control app on his phone with a quick scan of his iris. By the time Puerto Morelos's finest arrive, there'll be nothing left but a dead device, void of a single bit of data.

"Okay, now . . ." I begin, before noticing that March has already tucked his phone back in his pocket. Safely out my reach.

"I messaged Jan," he says flatly, with a glance in Angel's direction. "He's kept closer ties with the Lions than I have; he'll find me a secure channel to contact Mr. Stiles."

I narrow my eyes at March, fighting a surge of aggravation. Joy's been taken, and I'm in no mood to deal with his goddamn controlling streak. "Look, I don't need intermediates. I need to speak to Stiles directly and—"

"Sir, I am warning you; do not touch me! Mankind has a right to know!"

All three of our heads flip in sync to the direction of the outraged male voice that just burst from Angel's second SUV that was following us. His men are apparently wrestling with a passenger in the backseat, no, hang on, I see two figures as the rear doors open. Even the crickets in the surrounding thicket stop chirping as Gualtiero Franz and his assistant Jaime tumble out of the vehicle, disheveled and out of breath.

My eyebrows perform a somersault while March remains perfectly composed at my side. To Angel's credit, his face barely registers any emotion save for his usual cold, angry mask #1—or it could be #3 since his helicopter got blown up. "You took him," he states, addressing his goons.

A lean guy with some blood on the side of his face and cracked sunglasses comes forward—I gather he had a close brush with a couple bullets earlier tonight. He rubs the back of his neck, his mouth twisting in apology. "*Saltó con su asistente.*" He jumped in with his assistant.

This is unreal: no earthly force can stop Gualtiero Franz. No Lion, no Ecuadorian mobster, no missile. As if to confirm my omen, Franz aims a phone at us that gets ripped from his hand by Angel's goon. "No filming!" he barks with a strong Spanish accent.

Franz's afro gives a defiant shake. He extends a hand to his trembling assistant. "Jaime, your phone."

"But he just said . . ."

Seeing Franz try to search's Jaime's sweater pockets, I step in. "Sir, I wouldn't do that. You really can't film any of this."

His face prunes up, solemn and determined. "It is too late for secrets, Miss. Who do you work for?"

My mouth opens to deny it all and closes just as fast when I notice the blue logo on his phone that still rests in the hand of Angel's bruiser. I lunge to take it and hastily close the window. *Holy shit.* "Where you *live streaming* all of this?"

"That would be a terrible mistake," March warns silkily.

Unaware that his life hangs in the balance, Franz doesn't flinch. "Our viewers deserve the truth. Now they understand the threat the Collegium poses."

You bet they do: they just watched two trucks and an attack helicopter get blown up in a car chase. Worst of all, they saw *us*. It might have been only a second, but he aimed the screen at us when he got out of the car and I'm pretty sure he got a clean shot of March and me. Angel was behind us; it's possible Franz didn't get him in the frame. Still, this is a disaster: Joy got kidnapped, and we've committed several life terms worth of felonies tonight for the entire fricking world to see.

"Show me the phone."

Angel's icy drawl freezes my spine, but Franz only stands straighter as I turn the screen for March and Angel to see and skim through the live stream. Franz took out his phone shortly after we left the flaming ruins of his villa. The frame is shaking too badly to make out the features of Angel's men: it's mostly Franz and Jaime shrieking and holding each other in the backseat, sounds of explosions and flames licking the car's windows. My skin prickles as, onscreen, Franz yells that Ramirez took a hostage. He managed to film the bomber when it picked up the truck. The last trace of Joy.

I fast forward to the moment when Angel's men started dragging him out of the car, my muscles taut with stress and anger. I'm the only one he clearly caught onscreen. Franz focused on my face, and since March is a head taller than me, he's been mostly cut from the frame except for a brief peek at his chin. As for Angel, he was backlit by the Veneno's headlights: the only trace of him is a menacing silhouette behind us.

"He got me," I announce, backed by the choir of crickets shaking their tegmina in the dark. I raise my palm to my forehead, forcefully massaging it against an incipient headache. We need to get Joy back and, in the midst of it, I'm about to become famous for all the wrong reasons.

March's gaze drops to the post stats tucked under the video. "Two thousand shares and counting."

His jaw tics as if he were in desperate need for a mint to grind between his molars. He may not be a computer whiz, but he knows that at every second, millions of bots are crawling trending Internet content and replicating it across servers all over the world. It's only a matter of minutes—perhaps even seconds—until someone runs a screengrab of my face against a matching algorithm: they'll find me in old news about the Poseidon dome, in Columbia's alumni; they'll find my father, my connection to Joy, then Vince, whose murder attempt made the news. All of that means that in the upcoming hours, we're going to need to rescue Joy *and* cover up this whole mess under worldwide scrutiny.

I screw my eyes shut. My head is pounding harder and harder, and I just don't know how we're going to shoot our way out of that one and recover Joy alive.

"The truth can never be erased," Franz asserts, combing a dramatic hand in his hair.

Angel carpet-bombs him with the Stare. "You'd be surprised what I can erase."

March has the good grace to clear his throat with an air of boyish innocence. *He* would know: over the course of his career as a hitman, he has more than once rewritten history with the tip of a suppressor.

Franz puffs up his chest at Angel. "But are you willing to silence me at the cost of your friend's life?"

His mention of Joy electrifies me as if I'd just been whipped with live wires. "What do you mean?"

"Look for yourself," Franz says. Pointing to the phone in my hand. "Top comment."

I return to his regrettable Facebook contribution and scroll down. My heart skips a beat and revs back to life with renewed fury when I see a picture of a gagged Joy at the top of the comments; her face is pixelated, but her black dress is unmistakable; she's strapped in what appears to be the backseat of Ramirez's truck. Above it, a user named "Logan y su papi" wrote:

The next episode will take place in Cairo. You have sixteen hours. Wait for my instructions.

I do the math in my head, trying to focus on the numbers instead of the throbbing pain around my eye sockets. That's barely three hours more than it'll take a long-range jet to cross the Atlantic and make it to Cairo. We need to find a plane, fast, and catch up with our psycho sloth daddy before he kills Joy over a chase for ancient alien Lions. Under Ramirez's message, likes and comments tick up uncontrollably as thousands of excited fans speculate over whether *Aliens in Our Past* is experimenting with a new, live social media format. This is a nightmare.

Angel's right hand is shaking, tightening harder and harder until I fear his knuckles are going to crack through his skin. "*Hijo de puta de peresozo.* I almost had him," he seethes. "If Ramirez hadn't picked him up in the garden . . ."

I sigh. Angel Somoza's boundless anger and secret obsession have a new face, a new name, that of a "son of a bitch sloth."

March drags a hand over his jaw, his eyes set on Ramirez's social media offering. "That man has completely lost his mind."

Meanwhile, Franz turns to Jaime, whose limp bangs fall over a mask of quiet terror. He applies a manly pat to the young researcher's shoulder. "We've never been so close; this will be our best episode yet."

"Certainly not," March warns. "Mr. Franz, I'm afraid the Collegium is a plotline you're going to have to cut."

"No." Angel steps closer, appraising Franz and Jaime like his next meal. "I can use him."

March shifts to shielding Franz. Lowering his voice, he tells Angel, "I can only advise you not to involve yourself any further in this fiasco. I will handle things from this point on and recover Joy without starting a full-blown war."

"Have you lost all respect for me?" Angel hisses back, reaching for the gun in his jacket.

A shadow passes over March's features, sadness tempered by fleeting warmth. "You know there are few men I respect more in this business. However, pandering to Ramirez's psychosis is *not* the way."

My body goes rigid as Angel draws, the car lights outlining a semiautomatic's muzzle. "Your brothers have *defied* me."

I'm ready to interpose myself between them, but in the millisecond it takes for my neurons to fire the command for my legs to move, March grabs the gun's barrel. He locks eyes with Angel while the men around us all reach behind their backs or inside their jackets, to the notable exception of Abelardo, who towers over the showdown in statuary silence. "Then let me be your arm," March urges.

The gun's muzzle is pointing straight at his stomach, and the sight of his white-knuckled grip on the glinting steel raises my adrenaline level through the roof. This time, I don't hesitate: I slip between the two of them, forcing myself to meet Angel's irate gaze.

"Island, don't . . ." There's a steely edge to March's low warning, but I stand my ground.

"We don't have time for this. He has Joy and—" I motion to the gleaming embers of helicopter debris scattered further down the road. "The cops will be here soon."

"You listen to your man and stay out of this," Angel growls, his finger still curled perilously tight around the trigger.

"No. *You* listen to me, because I really don't have time to deal with a goddamn testosterone tantrum right now! You're both right," I grind out.

My conciliatory words produce the desired effect: Angel lowers his gun, and March lets go of the barrel as the masculine tension saturating the air becomes wary curiosity on either side. I take it as a green light to plead my case, lowering my voice. "Angel is right: we *need* Franz. We have sixteen hours to deal with Ramirez, and if we don't at least pretend to deliver Franz to him, he's gonna kill Joy."

"What do you suggest?" March asks, glancing over my head at

Franz and Jaime, who stand huddled together in watchful silence near the cars. Franz's avid gaze is set on the gun still resting in Angel's hand: he's probably trying to file every detail of this showdown for a future episode.

If I'm being entirely honest with myself, all I wanted was to prevent Angel from shooting March on top of everything else. My thoughts are still coalescing in the fog of a headache that threatens to turn into a full-blown migraine any moment. As I mentally leaf through a limited list of options, it dawns on me then that we've just lost the only person who would know what to do in this situation. Joy, with all her friends and followers, who always knows how to take advantage of a public debacle and land back on her stilettos. Joy would know how to reclaim the narrative, spin it by its tail and . . . *Yes. I think I know what to do.*

"Okay," I say, tapping my nose to think faster. "Franz wants a good story. Ramirez wants Franz. We want to save Joy, and we're gonna have to do that with millions of netizens who saw her getting kidnapped and are watching Franz's next move."

March and Angel nod at my recap.

"Then let's use him. Let's go to Egypt and have Ecuapasión produce Franz's episode on our terms. That way, we can dangle him in front of Ramirez to get Joy back, but we decide what makes it to the final cut." Yep, that's *exactly* what Joy would do. If the train can no longer be stopped, she'd take control of the tracks.

March exhales slowly before fishing for his tube of mints in his inner pocket. He gobbles half a dozen, the sound of his molars grinding the candy covering the relentless chanting of the crickets. I ball my fists tighter and tighter, waiting until he delivers his verdict in a minty breath. "Inconceivable."

"We've done worse," I defend, wounded.

Angel strokes his bearded chin, sizing up March, "You think you're not up to the job?"

"No. I *refuse* to do the job surrounded by cameras," March clips.

"My cameras, operated by my people," Angel counters.

"We can clean up the files afterward," I insist, trying to keep the plea out of my voice. "And with all the attention on Franz's special, I don't think Ramirez will be able to resist the bait: he's a narcissistic showman."

March considers my point, dark-blue eyes assessing me without blinking. "Three conditions."

I hold my breath as he raises his hand and counts off his fingers. "One: I decide what's safe or not. If I say filming is over, it's over. Two: *no one* films me. Three . . ." He locks eyes with the generous sponsor of our new production. "We're bringing *all* of the toys."

"You're speaking to my heart," Angel replies.

Turning to face Gualtiero Franz, I stand as tall as my heels will allow. Here we go. This one's for Joy and for science. "Mr. Franz, people call me Island Chaptal, and I have an offer for you."

Franz's afro bobs in anticipation before I've even begun to explain. "I'm ready. I have been ready for this all my life."

THE FACEBOOK FRIEND

The Illuminati sects operating in the occult and sexual magick [sic]
circles unite people ranging from the ex-terrorist to the
fundamentalist Catholic.

– Leo Lyon Zagami, *Confessions of an Illuminati, Volume I: The
Whole Truth About the Illuminati and the New World Order*

"No. This way. What's his name? Wilmer? Yes, Wilmer: I need you to direct the spotlight at us. Higher . . . but not too high. There. Perfect."

Standing near the car, March and I watch Wilmer, a tattooed guy with Charles Manson's mug and an M-16 strapped over his black T-shirt, aim his LED torch at a gesticulating Gualtiero Franz. Once a heartless German mercenary, Wilmer has been promoted to lighting tech as per the terms of the contract Franz, Angel, and I digi-signed moments ago—special thanks to Angel's lawyer, who was rung out of bed and given fifteen minutes to draft and send a copy. Angel used his Bond villain voice, and the guy did it in fourteen.

It's almost eleven pm The wind is rising, stirring sheets of dust across the deserted tarmac of a dismal aerodrome west of Puerto Morelos. Gualtiero Franz is a man on a mission. He no longer cares that his villa got razed by a pair of Hellfire II missiles barely ninety minutes ago, nor is he overly concerned that we're waiting for the jet that will smuggle him out of Mexico, along with a band of big-league thugs, armed to the teeth and riding in bullet-hole-studded SUVs.

No, the only thing Franz cares about is the contract which states that I agreed to appear in a live, worldwide battle against the Collegium, a race for the truth about ancient astronauts, generously funded by Angel's inexhaustible well of cash and fury, and supervised by March. The whole idea was admittedly mine, but now that Franz has agreed and we'll be taking off for Cairo soon, I'm getting a little dizzy: everything has been going too fast for the past couple hours, and I'm shivering in the cool night as I try to process it all.

Unconsciously leaning against March's body, I startle when a warm weight drops on my shoulders. I sigh, welcoming his bulletproof jacket and his scent as he discreetly draws me to his chest. His palm reaches under the jacket, carefully brushing a fresh bruise on my arm.

"I don't like these . . ." March murmurs, low enough that Angel's goons won't pry on this stolen moment of solace: they're busy pandering to Franz's every whim while simultaneously unloading a number of crates from two trucks that just stopped on the tarmac: Angel's "toys" mostly, but also filming equipment that Franz demanded—I don't want to know how many laws were broken to procure a full portable filming set, a makeup case, and an alien costume on such short notice.

I press my cheek to his shirt, sighing at the feeling of his chest hair crimpling underneath and the quietude I find only in his arms.

"I'm okay. I can do this," I whisper back. I can keep going, and going, and going until we've found Joy and saved her from that psychotic dirtbag Ramirez.

"You'll be able to get some sleep in Angel's jet," March says softly, taking one of my hands to stroke my knuckles with his thumb. I try to relax, draw what little strength I can from his touch.

"I messed up so bad. I let her down," I rasp, only for him to hear.

"You didn't. She was my responsibility as well, and I underestimated Ramirez." There's an icy edge to March's voice as he adds, "It won't happen twice."

"I know." I check the brand-new phone Angel's men brought me. That's it. We lost her signal over Nassau, either because her earpiece battery gave out, someone took it from her, or they've begun the long cross over the Atlantic, and there's no longer any unprotected network for the device to latch onto. I have no way to know, and it's the wait, the uncertainty that's eating at my nerves like acid. As I mull over the abominations Ramirez and Logan might inflict on Joy if we don't get to her on time, a sudden glare splashes us. Wilmer's goddamn torch.

I raise a palm to shield my eyes. Haloed in blinding white light, Franz is waving his arms at me, surrounded by the bulky silhouettes of Angel's men.

"Miss Chaptal? Are you ready?" he calls, a thread of irritation in his voice.

"Ready? Uh . . . Are you filming us right now?"

"No. We can't film the South African: it's in the contract," Abelardo's deep bass reassures me, as he walks up to us.

The reminder is a subtle jab at Franz, who fusses under his mustache at his new production assistant. "I know what's in the contract, but you people understand nothing about good television." He tweaks his hair and presses anxious fingers to his forehead. "My forehead is getting shiny. I can't work like this. Towel! Powder!"

Abelardo—who also doubles as our makeup artist—bends down

to pat Franz's forehead with a fluffy towel, then a makeup sponge, produced from the makeup case sitting at his feet.

March has retreated into the shadows but I don't miss the question in the slight tilt of his head. *Do you want me to step in?*

"I'm good," I tell him with a confidence I don't yet feel.

If we can survive Ramirez and Logan and save Joy, I'll have the rest of my life to worry about my online reputation: I brave the spotlight and go join Franz in front of Sonny, who's carrying a big camcorder on his shoulder—he's our new cameraman because he did a semester of film school in Quito when he was nineteen and Angel's clauses specified that no one but his personal crew could participate in the filming.

"Silence on set, please! We're rolling!" Franz announces, before launching into an introductory monologue about how years of research and risk-taking are about to come to fruition: tonight, with the support of his viewers—who can purchase their ΛΙΘΡ merchandise in his online store—he's about to make history.

He steps closer, rolling wide eyes at the camera. "Tonight, the world has seen the true face of the Collegium. Murder, destruction, kidnapping: they stop at *nothing* to keep us from revealing the truth. But as I progress in my investigation, new forces have revealed themselves, men and women who fight the Collegium so that the truth of the ancient astronauts may one day be revealed. Island Chaptal is one of them."

That's when he turns to me, and I stand there, waving awkwardly at the camera lens with a grimacing smile. Sonny is zooming in on my face; I can hear the lens whirring. "I, uh . . ."

Franz drops a clammy hand on my shoulder. "Miss Chaptal, can you tell us more about the organization you work for?"

"No, sorry," I croak.

His face prunes up. "What can you tell us about the man who attacked us tonight, Mr. Ramirez?"

I was wrong: I'm not ready for this.

As I shake my head helplessly, Franz extends his arm to take a notepad Jaime hands him. "Allow me to refresh your memory: I distinctly heard Mr. Ramirez say that he 'knew your father very well' and 'admired him.' *'He funded us generously, and understood the importance of our work,'*" he quotes from Jaime's notes.

I search the dark angles of March's and Angel's faces through the flare of Wilmer's torch. What the hell? When did Franz even find the time to take notes? Weren't we supposed to greenlight a script or something?

Meanwhile, our host plows on. "Was your father's name Dries Chaptal?"

I remember with horror that Ramirez did mention Dries by name back at the villa, but that initial shock is soon washed away by something deeper, a tidal wave of grief and regret. My chest tightens painfully upon hearing my mom's last name appended to Dries's for the very first time, as if our shattered family had once truly existed whole.

March emerges from the shadows right behind Sonny, wearing his best 'it's no' expression. "That question will be cut. Miss Chaptal's personal ties are off-limits."

Franz's shoulders roll back as he pushes himself to his full—medium—height and stalks to March. "Do you expect me to censor the truth from my show?"

"Yes," March replies steadily.

"Do you even realize what's at stake?" Franz erupts.

"Miss Chaptal's safety," March retorts with the same stony gaze.

Sensing he's hit a literal six feet three wall Franz relents with a frustrated sigh. "I understand. Not everyone is willing to take the kind of risks we take."

March, who killed at least half-a-dozen Lions tonight in the name of *Aliens in Our Past*, raises a caustic eyebrow. "Evidently."

"Look," I tell Franz. "Maybe you could write a backstory without mentioning my family?"

He huffs. "What do you suggest?"

"I don't know. Can't I be, like . . ."

"Indiana Jones," a gruff voice with a German accent supplies from behind me. I whirl around to discover that it belongs to Wilmer.

"But Indiana Jones has a dad," Sonny counters.

Abelardo buzzes in. "Not in the first movie."

"A female adventurer . . ." Franz strokes his chin. "I like that narrative: a young, female adventurer, teaming up with the legendary Gualtiero Franz to uncover the secret of mankind's origins. Alberto!"

Abelardo shuffles closer, unfazed by the blatant misnaming—neither the first nor the last, I suspect. "We'll need a hat and a whip ready for Miss Chaptal when we land in Cairo."

Our production assistant, makeup artist, and now costume designer nods to this, taking notes with an old Ikea mini pencil on a crumpled paper sheet. I catch him doodling a stick figure of me with Indiana Jones's hat and a long whip in my hand.

Fine, whatever. On any other day, this would be the pinnacle of my twenty-seven years on earth, but at the moment, I just want for us to be done, and for that plane to arrive so we can get to Cairo yesterday. "I can work with that. I have cargo shorts in my suitcase."

I'm ready to resume Franz's interview and face the blinding glare of Wilmer's torch when I feel a single buzz in my bra, where my phone is safely tucked. I take it out, give a passing glance at the new Facebook notification that pops in my navigation bar . . . and nearly drop my phone.

Joshua Stiles wants to be friends on Facebook.

March is at my side in an instant, his hands sliding to support my elbows as I fumble to regain my grip on the damn phone. "What is it?"

I tilt the screen for him to see. "I think he knows."

It's one of the many things I hate to say amaze me about Stiles: unlike most Lions, he's not even really hiding. He's out there, in the open, and no one cares because everything about him is so damn friendly and banal. Type in "Josh's Cats" in the search bar, and you'll find his official page, a compilation of his YouTube Roomba cat videos, interspersed with occasional posts about Southern cooking and ammo tests. A page liked by millions of people who have no idea the faceless gentleman in a gray suit holding a kitten in the header is one of the most dangerous sociopaths on earth.

That's how it began for me too, eighteen months ago, back when he was still infiltrated in the CIA: I met this debonair, fortyish agent who gave me a link to his page and sent me a friend request. Needless to say, I came to dearly regret it. After it was all over, I blocked him and even reported his page and account to Facebook several times, but they didn't do anything because Mark Zuckerberg only cares about nipples and ad money.

And now I'm back to square one, my nape clammy from a cold sweat as I offer Franz an apologetic wince. "I have to take care of something. Just give me a moment."

"Decline and let me contact him," March clips as we walk away on the darkened tarmac.

I steel myself against the chills slithering under my skin as good and terrible times flash in my mind, bland softness weaved with absolute terror: the essence of my relationship with Stiles. Never again. "I'll call him. And we're gonna sort this out."

I expected a battle of wills, but March ducks his chin in surrender. "Very well."

His relinquishing that particular bit of control to me is more symbolic than practical though: I feel his arm stealing protectively around my waist as I tap to accept Stiles's friend request. Immediately, a new message chimes in: a phone number with a Western Samoa code. I doubt Stiles is vacationing there; that number will have been erased by the time we're done talking. I make the call, an undefinable sense of dread licking up my spine at the first ring. That asshole waits five rings to pick up. I guess it's the closest I'll ever get to seeing Stiles exert petty retribution.

The Southern drawls he's never bothered to disguise greets me, making my scalp prickle. "Island, it's been a while. How have you been?"

Standing this close, March can hear every word. His jaw works in silence from the supreme effort not to intervene. I suspect every fiber of him wants to rip the phone from my hands and toss a death threat or two in the mic.

"Spare me your bullshit. What do you know about Ramirez?"

"Oh? You've seen him? Actually, we've been looking for him everywhere."

"He's here in Cancún; I think you already know that. And don't tell me you haven't noticed that he's. Lost. His. Goddamn. *Mind,*" I snap back.

"Oh, yes, I know that." I can almost picture his saddened pout. "Island, I wish I could help but I'm afraid Ramirez is no longer a part of our family. He's chosen to leave us."

I freeze and look up at March, my mouth half-parted in a dumbstruck "o." He gives a slow shake of his head that would translate as the F-word if he were in the habit of using it. This is much worse than I imagined. Ramirez isn't just a grandiloquent fruitcake. He's a *Renegade.*

"Let me guess," I tell Stiles. "You brushed him off when he told you the Lions had been founded by aliens?"

"I didn't brush him off. He wanted to assemble a team to kidnap Gualtiero Franz and steal his . . . research." That last word, he speaks with a hint of reluctance.

"What did you say?"

"I asked him for a PowerPoint to walk me through his plan."

"And?"

"I told him I'd be in touch."

"*And?*"

"Apparently, he couldn't wait that long, so he raised his little fan club against me. He took off a week ago with thirty exalted idiots and a lot of costly equipment."

Perfect, Joy is risking her life over a case of catty office politics between Lions. I can't tune out the rising anger in my voice as I reply, "Just so you know, your Osprey is at the bottom of the Cancún bay."

"Damn . . . What about the Antonov? It cost us an arm and a leg to fit it with missile launchers." Knowing Stiles, he could mean it in the literal sense.

"Oh, they work great. They blew up one of Angel Somoza's Tigers an hour ago. Just before Ramirez kidnapped my best friend!"

There's a bit of silence, during which I can feel March lean closer to better listen. Stiles lets out a low sigh. "Yes, I've seen the live stream. Pass my regards to Somoza and tell him we'll compensate him for the Tiger: it's the least a friend can do."

"I honestly don't think he's your friend."

"But I'm his, as I'm yours, and I want you to know that Joy's safe return is my highest priority at the moment: we all love her Instagram."

I swallow back the urge to gag at this unnecessary piece of intel. I'll worry later about the fact that Stiles and an unspecified number of Lions creep on Joy's yoga poses or bikini vacation pics. Stiles's help is the last thing I want, but he could be our safest bet: he has more than enough reach to crush Ramirez like a fortune cookie if he decides to. "Okay, so what are you gonna do?"

"Well, not much for now, I suppose. Let Franz be our bait. If Ramirez truly needs him, he'll make his move."

"You're joking, right?"

"Island, I wish I could do more to help—"

"Then, fricking do it!" I'm about to yell a few choice words into the upturned phone when March's fingers brush mine in silent entreaty. I let him take the phone: it wouldn't do any good to go off at Stiles anyway.

"Good evening, Mr. Stiles," he says, his tone smooth as polished ice.

"Dis net 'n plesier om van jou te hoor, broer," Stiles replies in Afrikaans, with an impeccable accent. *It's a pleasure to hear from you, brother.*

It was one of the tiny things I noticed back during my captivity in Finland, he'd occasionally speak a few words in Finnish to the staff, always with an indetectable accent. Once again, I'm queasy from the realization of how much every particle of this man is manufactured. His attempt at fraternity falls flat, however, as March all but ignores it.

"I assume you already know what Ramirez was looking for in Cancún?" he asks.

"I've heard rumors . . ." Stiles drawls, almost too low for me to hear.

"Consider those rumors confirmed. The remains were significantly damaged during the skirmish at Franz's villa, but Ramirez has escaped with a piece I'm certain the brotherhood will find to be of inestimable value."

I listen, aghast, as he blatantly baits Stiles with Cornellà's hide to force the Lions to back us up. March can be smooth when he wants to, but he's not fond of manipulation and negotiation tactics: I honestly didn't expect him to play with Stiles's favorite weapons.

"I know," Stiles retorts, dropping the Pee-wee act at last. When he resumes speaking, his voice sounds frosted over. "Gualtiero Franz tweeted about Cornellà's hide minutes ago. I'd have preferred the brotherhood be left out of that particular plotline, but it looks like Island made that decision for us."

Shivers dance up and down my spine as I process the subtle accusation, the razorblades lining each word. I had forgotten. After Finland, I healed, wrestled my life back together, and month after month, I forgot what it was to be truly scared of Stiles.

March brushes back an errant curl behind my ear with his free hand—I'm blanching, and he detected it, even in the tarmac's penumbra. "Isn't hiding in plain sight your favorite strategy? Ramirez is the one who took the risk to expose all of us. You own, in fact, a debt of gratitude to Mr. Somoza for taking it upon himself to produce Mr. Franz's latest episode under my supervision."

"And so, we must trust your and Somoza's editing skills, for the good of all the brotherhood," Stiles infers wryly.

"I'm afraid so. Please let your best elements know that we will land in Cairo in less than six hours," March says tersely, before hanging up on the commander of the Lions.

I frown up at him. "Six hours? Are you sure you got that number right? Cairo is seven thousand miles away, so we'd need . . ."

A distant rumble has me trailing off and staring up at a triangular set of trailing orbs in the night sky. If we'd come here for a bout of UFO sighting, I'd be wetting myself about right now, but the law of Occam's razor predicts that this is, in fact, the plane we've been waiting for. *What* plane remains to be seen though: the noise is growing so loud and its vibration so intense that I can feel it buzzing all over my body, and I can already pick up the stench of jet fuel even from a distance.

Across the tarmac, I spot Angel's men shepherding Franz and Jaime away from the runway while Franz yells for Sonny to film the fast-approaching monster. I remain frozen in fascination, my hand unconsciously gripping March's as a long, arrow-shaped jet decelerates gracefully, its four rear burners blazing bright as stars in the darkness.

Cairo is seven thousand miles away. We will, indeed, need a supersonic airliner to make it there before Ramirez.

THE TACO

"Do not think I exaggerate when I say that Concorde is the single most important piece of design in my long lifetime. Will we see anything quite so elegant, beautiful, and optimistic again? (. . .)
Can you make us dream like that again?
Can you show us the future?"

– Sir Terence Conran

"Oh my God, you stole a Concorde?"

I ran to Angel's side the moment the monster's wheels touched the ground. The pencil-thin fuselage, the drooping stork nose, and single-wing design with four rectangular burners tucked underneath, combining a face-melting 144,000 horsepower: *this* is, unquestionably, a Franco-British supersonic jet that was supposedly retired nearly twenty years ago and now resides only in aviation museums and research facilities. I await Angel's explanations, my hands balled into fists as I teeter on a fine line between outrage and gratitude. Mach 2 at cruising speed: nothing will get us faster to Cairo.

"I bought it from a museum in Barbados," he states, his mouth thinning in distaste, it seems, at the implication that he might have done something so low as stealing that plane.

And he got it off the ground in record time, for Joy. "Thank you," I say quietly.

"Don't thank me until we've recovered her," he replies, while an airstair is wheeled in position by a dusty truck. At the other end of the tarmac, a pair of silhouettes have jumped into action at the top of a control tower that's little more than a glorified toy model.

I square my shoulders. "We're getting her back." When he slants me a look that could almost be construed as one of begrudging respect, I lower my voice and add: "Don't get me wrong: this is a temporary alliance. I'm never letting you bang her."

His chin ducks in a slow nod as he takes his aviators from his inner pocket and puts them on, the Concorde's sleek line reflected in their dark lenses. "Have you ever tried roasted crickets?"

My eyes nearly pop out of their sockets. Joy told him about our roleplay thing! Or maybe he overheard? My pulse racing, I leap back and meet the solid wall of March's body.

"Are you ready to go, biscuit?"

"Uh . . . yeah." I dart a wary look at Angel's impenetrable expression.

He starts walking toward the airstair with a final warning for me. "They have a particular crunch to them. Like taco shells."

March's gaze shuttles between the two of us and settles on me, filled with curiosity. "Culinary debate?"

"He said he's going to crush me like a taco shell," I reply earnestly.

I kinda hoped he'd take my side and promise to shoot Angel for me, but instead, he glances at his departing back over my head and says, "He's warming up to you."

I barely had the time to take a tour of the Concorde's narrow cabin before the engines started. While the airframe is built for speed rather than luxury, the interior looks pretty much like your average private jet with its ten pairs of luxurious black seats, a small meeting room, partitioned with glass, and at the rear, a single door I gather leads to a bedroom.

Seated across from March, I watch the tarmac and control flash by and disappear in the night, through a window half the size of a regular airliner's—to limit depressurization in the event that it'd pop out while we'll be cruising at a whopping 60,000 feet, at the edge of the atmosphere. A female pilot's voice crackles from the cabin speaker, announcing in Spanish that we're clear for takeoff. At the front of the cabin, Sonny is filming Franz from his seat; he pans briefly to the wall separating the cockpit from the cabin, where a digital speedometer is now rapidly ticking up. When the engine's low rumble becomes a roll of thunder, March's eyes meet mine, the reassurance in their dark-blue depth quieting the storm in my mind.

A dizzying thrust pins me to my seat, followed by a glorious pull upward. I grip the soft leather armrests through the second-fastest takeoff of my life. Fifteen seconds after we've left the ground, we're already climbing at three hundred miles per hour. The numbers on the speedometer keep ticking up madly as we approach Mach 1—by now, the pilots are probably raising the plane's long mobile nose to streamline it for supersonic flight. I hold my breath as we smoothly reach and break the sound barrier. Here, inside the cabin, speed is only a number: we're flying too fast to hear the sonic boom that will echo miles and miles over the Cancún bay in the night.

My eyes never leave the speedometer and altimeter as we climb higher and higher, faster and faster. 1.21 . . . 1.47 . . . 1.89. This might be the last time in my life I'm flying at Mach 2, and in spite of all the stress, the lingering fear, the corners of my lips quiver up. We're coming for you, Joy.

TWENTY-SEVEN
THE LEO

Watching his powerful muscles flex as he turned the pages of the
book, Stiffany knew, down to her soaked core, that he wouldn't
conquer her with his strength, but his mind.

– Gilda Sapphire, *When She Kissed the Teacher*

"Ramirez should land in Cairo around 5 pm local time. He'll probably
send us his instructions then," March says, motioning to the digital
map displayed under the glass top of the meeting room's table.

He, Angel, and I have isolated ourselves there, the milky
electronic glass affording us some privacy to discuss our next move.
Franz is thankfully out of my hair for now: he commandeered a laptop
from Abelardo and downloaded scans he'd made of Cornellà's hide.
He and Jaime are studying the images for more clues about the resting

place of long-dead Lions who may or may not have been Martians—no need to say Sonny is filming that too: he's really getting into this.

I rap my fingers against the glass surface. "We can set up satellite surveillance of the airports he's most likely to land at, but . . ." I frown at the potential targets we've identified.

"He's already proven his pilot is capable of a successful touch and go, even in adverse conditions," March completes, reading my mind.

I massage my tired eyeballs with the heels of my hands. "So, we can add pretty much any freeway within a hundred miles radius from Cairo to our list."

"No," Angel clips. "We need to bait him somewhere remote, with limited accessways."

March eyes the map, crossing his arms. "Are you suggesting we drive Franz in the middle of the desert?"

A sinister smirk cracks through Angel's beard. "Perfect backdrop for his documentary."

"However, that might put us at a disadvantage: if he's confident that we're out of reach from law enforcement, Ramirez won't bother with subtlety," March warns him.

"I won't either. I'm going to nuke that *bobo peruano* and his sloth."

I raise my palms to halt the crazy train: no nuke within a thousand-mile radius of my best friend. "Hang on, are we packing that kind of heat in the hold? Also, how do you know Ramirez is Peruvian?"

Decades of border disputes and soccer rivalry infuse Angel's voice as he grits out: "I *feel* it."

March's chest heaves in silent dismay. "I'd rather we leave the tank busters in their crates and avoid straining the Egyptian authorities' hospitality if possible . . ." Seeing Angel's eyes smolder with raw hate, he adds, "until Joy is safe in our keep. Anything that happens after that is between you and Ramirez, I suppose."

A soft rap against the meeting room's opacified glass wall intrudes on our palavers. I get up to slide the door open and find myself staring at Abelardo's maroon shirt. I have to crane my neck to look him in the eye as he quietly motions to the front of the cabin, where Franz and Jaime are still gathered around their scan of Cornellà's hide.

Franz waves an impatient hand at me. "Come join us, Miss Chaptal. I want to show you something."

I get to my feet, glancing back at March and Angel. I'd rather be plotting Joy's rescue right now, but Franz is our bait: I owe him to at least pretend to play my part in his documentary. The folding table between his and Jaime's seats is covered in hastily scribbled post-it notes: Greek letters and hieroglyphic symbols, linked together by arrows and illegible comments full of exclamation marks. I lean on Franz's headrest and gaze down at the screen of the laptop he ~~stole~~ borrowed from Angel's men. He's already changed the desktop wallpaper to his show's logo: I think Angel is never getting that computer back.

Franz enlarges a hi-res image of Cornellà's hide. His afro bobs twice before he clears his throat and begins. "We had a scan done immediately after we found it because we were worried it might be unstable and degrade fast. But it was in a jar, so the dry soil protected it well."

Jaime takes over with a shaky breath—I think it's the first time I hear him say a word since he survived the villa's destruction. "We were filming in the archeological zone across the road, and when I heard they had found the tomb of a conquistador under the golf's parking lot, I just knew this was it: I was sure that Cornellà had died in the area. The last record of his presence in Yucatán was in 1544 by Franciscan friars who had just arrived after the Montejo family conquered the peninsula. One of the Franciscans mentions in his letters the case of a heretic Spanish soldier who took part in Mayan rituals and lived among the locals in an important port where one of their ancient kings was buried. It was obvious to me that the letter referred to the pyramidal remains of structure number 2 in El Rey."

I give a noncommittal nod. "Okay. How come local museums didn't try to take it from you, though?"

His eyes meet Franz's before he looks away, barely concealing a cringe. "It's our curse and our blessing. Dig something up anywhere in the world, and you'll have local authorities on your back in a matter of days. Tell them you think it's about ancient astronauts, and they won't even take a look: they'll automatically assume it's a fake you planted there, or that you mistook a jerrycan for a five-hundred-year-old Mayan jar. The guy they sent from the museum of archeology turned around right after he saw the show's logo on our trucks."

"Well, the loss of mainstream archeologists is our gain," Franz concludes gravely.

Transfixed by Cornellà's hide onscreen, I barely notice March and Angel as they join us, settling on a narrow sofa facing Franz and Jaime's seats. Even in its degraded state, there's something poignant about that expanse of ravaged skin, made of tattoos and brownish scars. It's not just the mangled Lion roaring in the top left where Cornellà's shoulder once was; there's pain etched in every square inch, gripping me with unexpected intensity as I try to decipher the jumble of Greek and Latin words he recorded in his flesh throughout his life. A few compact sentences stand out, tattooed on his side, but I can only decipher one word clearly among the warped clusters of letters. Χάος.

"Chaos," I read out loud.

To my complete astonishment, the husky voice that comes next and easily transcribes the other sentences I could barely decipher is . . . Angel's. "*Verily at the first Chaos came to be, but next wide-bosomed Earth, the ever-sure foundations of all the deathless ones who hold the peaks of snowy Olympus.* It's Hesiod's Theogony."

"A fellow Hellenist!" Franz chirps, unaware that pretty much everyone else on that plane is staring at Angel Somoza, international arms dealer, licensed supervillain, telenovela sponsor, and . . . well, Hellenist.

March's mouth purses in sober admiration for his ex-client's erudition. I did believe him when he told me about Angel's degree, but it's even stranger to witness the evidence in action.

Unfazed, Franz resumes his commentary. "But surely you've noticed something odd in Cornellà's transcription."

Jaime points to one word in the verse. "Here."

"He made an error," Angel clips. "It should read *édos*, for 'foundations,' not *pigés*."

"What does *pigés* mean?" I ask.

There's a gleam of boyish excitement in Franz's eyes as he says, "It means *the sources*, and I doubt that was a mistake on Cornellà's part. Jaime, can you show us the lower section of the front half?"

Jaime complies and zooms on an area below a horribly wrinkled and tattooed navel. There, amid another tangle of Greek words, a mountain is drawn.

"What's that?" Unexpectedly, this came from March, who's leaning forward to better see the hide. He's doing a good job of concealing it behind a perfectly deadpan face, but I can detect the faintest glint of curiosity in his eyes. No one can resist Gualtiero Franz, even at a time like this.

Franz points triumphantly at a delicate lace of Arabic calligraphy below the mountain. "This reads *Ain El Sohkna.*"

"The hot sources," Jaime translates.

"Okay, but which ones?" I ask automatically.

"It's obvious," Franz exults. "We know from Cornellà's correspondence to Joanna of Spain that he visited Egypt between 1542 and 1543, shortly before his mental health started to deteriorate. And what hot sources are more famous than the ones sitting at the foot of mount Ataqah, and which quite simply gave their name to a town people still call *Ain Sokhna,* even today!"

Meanwhile, Jaime has opened a map of Egypt that he centers on a small coastal town sitting on the Western shore of the Gulf of Suez, seventy miles south of Cairo. Franz's afro quivers in anticipation.

"The *source* of our origins . . . the resting place of those mysterious 'deathless' visitors 'who first came to guide us' and descended from the burning star of Mars!"

I don't miss March's fleeting wince as Franz repeats Cornellà's words, twisted to fit into his theories about ancient astronauts. I almost wish Franz were right, though: if the mystical rants and clues Cornellà inked into his skin do lead us to a tomb where the First Lions were buried . . . then it'd be the perfect bait for Ramirez. We wouldn't even need Franz anymore: we'd have the ultimate bargaining chip in our hands.

Franz draws a wistful breath. "All the answers are there; I can feel it. Jaime, show them the rest."

Jaime loads a map of the various archeological sites in the mountains encircling the port of Ain El Sokhna, over which they've superposed schematics of the many tattoos and scarifications of Cornellà's hide.

"The French and the Egyptians have been episodically digging around the resort since 2001," Franz explains. "There are traces of Egyptian occupation from the old to the new kingdom. Galleries were found, where boats were stored to be later put afloat in the port." He waves his forefinger at a spot where the Ataqah Mountains seem to dive into the Suez Gulf, and several rectangular caves are indicated on the map. "Now, Miss Chaptal, I want your opinion on this."

Jaime gives a fleeting eye roll—whatever Franz's theory is, he disagrees with it—before dragging a semi-transparent image of Cornellà's hide over the map of the caves. "It doesn't match," he mumbles.

Franz's nostrils flare obstinately. "I can clearly see it! Just look at it!"

"What are we supposed to see?" I ask.

"These scars." Franz's finger lands atop a brownish dent in the hide, in the lower portion of the torso. Then another to the left, and a third one.

"They could be anything." Jaime sulks.

"But they perfectly align with the entrance of each cave!"

March's lips pinch in a frown that's part disagreement, part reprobation at the fingerprints now marring the screen. "They do not. You have six caves along the coast, and only three scars barely aligning with their entrances. Look at the other marks; that triangle on the left clearly doesn't match any . . ." His voice trails off as his eyes narrow on the cluster of deep dents carved into Cornellà's skin.

Realization dawns on his face moments before I see it too. I honestly didn't pay attention until he mentioned those three dents forming a triangle. An inch to the right, another group of six scars draw a shape that could be a mirrored question mark.

"Can I?"

I lean between Franz and Jaime and open the picture editing tools. Using the touchpad, I draw a wobbly red line, linking the scars, one after another.

March, king of all skeptics, indulges in an incredulous smile as a familiar shape appears onscreen. "That's the Leo constellation."

TWENTY-EIGHT
THE WAR STAR WANDERER

You can parse and use those ascii JPL ephemeris files.
Warning: This is an exercise for people who like to torture themselves.

— David Hammen (2015/10/30). Re: "What is the exact format of the JPL ephemeris files?" Retrieved from Space Exploration StackExchange

"Sweet Raptor Jes . . ." I squeak and stop short of desecrating our Lord's name when I catch Angel's incinerating glare on me.

Now I know how Franz felt in that episode when he stepped into Hathor's Temple and swiped his flashlight at the legendary bas-relief of the Dendera lamp, convinced that in this particular carving—which looks suspiciously like a lightbulb—he had found definitive proof that aliens not only used electricity, but they taught ancient Egyptians how to harness it as well. And now it's my turn. I've joined the club, pierced a centuries-old mystery of my own. Hand over your Mickey Mouse watch, Robert Langdon!

My hand tingling from trepidation, I link another series of three dents, higher up. "That one's the Leo Minor, and that line here, that's the three leaps of the gazelle," I say, bringing the cursor to a cluster of six scars gathered in pairs above the Leo Minor—this is the best connect-the-dots game I've ever done since I was five. "I don't know them all, but this one on the left, it's probably Alula Borealis, and on the right, Tania Borealis. And, above them, the Big Dipper." I draw a straight vertical line to a lone scar that was probably resting between Cornellà's clavicles. "And all the way up, Polaris, the North Star."

March tilts his head at the constellations I drew and gets up from the sofa. Bending to the laptop, he silently asks for my permission to take over. After I've relinquished control of the touchpad to him, he places the cursor on Polaris and uses the geometry tool to draw a vertical line that smoothly links Dubhe in the Big Dipper, then Zosma, and Chort in the Leo.

He pauses above the hide's shriveled navel. There, a blotched symbol is surrounded by a ring of flames: the sun, I gather. March nods to himself and resumes tracing his red line, all the way down to the tattoo that led us to Egypt in the first place—Mount Ataqah and the Arabic words for "hot sources" underneath. The result is a straight vertical line from the North Star to the top of the mountain. You gotta be kidding me: what Cornellà carved and inked in his skin is a perfect stellar alignment.

At last, March lays down the pen, a smug smile etching his dimples. "There it is; your map."

Franz joins his hands, his breathing coming in fast pants. "They were space travelers, so they gave him instructions using the most universal language: the position of the stars. It's the same with the Ancient Egyptians, the Mayans. It's always the stars. How could I miss this!"

Angel's eyes screw shut in quiet dismay, mirrored by March's and my embarrassed miens.

"While the intent in this design is quite clear, I don't know that we can make anything of it," March ventures.

But Gualtiero Franz couldn't care less. Ancient astronauts just sent him an actual sign. "How do we use it?" he asks me.

"Well, let's say we follow your logic of taking whatever Cornellà marked on his skin at face value without looking for any symbolic meaning—"

"Yes, yes! We follow the clues!"

"Um, so we have a map of the sky with the position of several major constellations, the sun, and a specific stellar alignment, and we also have a vague reference point on earth. Which could be Mount Ataquah or any of the mountains surrounding it. Supposing Cornellà's rendition is reliable, and that the alignment did actually occur as described—and these are big ifs, by the way."

I frown, raking my brain for a solution. "Since the night sky changes all the time due to the earth's rotation and a ton of other factors, we'd need to have a precise date and time to infer the coordinates of the point of observation. Except we don't have those, and I'm not sure what to make of the sun in all this. I'd expect the moon instead in a sky map."

Jaime gives me a pleading look. "But can't you narrow a guess since you already know the approximate area and the window of time he was in Egypt?"

"Isn't there software for that?" Franz insists.

This is the part I hate: having to remind people that just because I can competently change an ink cartridge and hack a router doesn't mean I can make Kool-Aid rain from the sky with a computer. "All we know is that we're possibly looking for something near Mount Ataqah north of the 29th parallel, and since you said Cornellà started tattooing his crazy rants after he visited Egypt, and he arrived in Yucatán in January 1544, we can infer that he was here in the years before."

"Very likely in 1543. Before that, I think he was in Rome," Jaime supplies.

"To be honest, that's still totally vague. However, there *is* software that can do the calculation you want, provided you feed it an exact date and time, and that you have a database of astronomical events going back all the way to the Renaissance."

"Where do we procure it?" Franz asks, sweat beading along his hairline.

"I, well, I worked on something like that as a course project back when I was in engineering school, but . . ."

Unexpectedly, it's meek, quiet Jaime who shoots up from his seat and grabs my shoulders. "Then do it again!"

March lunges to pry him off me in the blink of an eye, but I wriggle free before Jaime can get punched in the face. "It's not that simple: without a date of observation, it'd be like looking for a needle in a haystack. We'd need a program that would test all possible combinations of coordinates and timestamps and render a sky map for each of those until we find the right alignment: it'd take time and server resources we don't have, and it might not even work: maybe Cornellà never observed the alignment he tattooed on his body. It could just be symbolic, I don't know—"

"That planet above the navel isn't the sun."

All eyes whip to Angel, who's leaned forward in his seat, his elbows braced on his thighs, his chin supported by his clenched fist as he stares at the hide's scan as if he meant to set the laptop on fire.

I follow the direction of his gaze. "Why do you say that?"

"Take a better look. The symbol tattooed at the center is Jupiter's."

Sweet Jesus, he's right. It's barely decipherable, but now that he's pointed it out to me, I can recognize the curious intersection of lines which I've always thought looked like a badly written '21'. "But the circle of flames around it really looks like the sun," I muse. "Jupiter was never represented like that in ancient times."

"Then it's both," Angel concludes, emotionless.

It's both Jupiter and the sun, I mentally rehash, blinking at the dark smudges of ink. "I think it's Jupiter at opposition with the sun."

March squints his eyes at the hide. "Do you mean they were aligned too?"

"Maybe. It's actually a recurring and easily observable event. It happens every year when Jupiter, the Sun, and the Earth line up. You can see it at sunset when the sun goes under the horizon with Jupiter sitting right above it."

The fleeting crease of a dimple appears at the corner of his mouth. "Doesn't that mean astronomical ephemerides would have a date and time for that in 1543?"

"Some models go back to -3000 BC, so yeah, I guess." My heart drums a little faster as I say this. What are the chances that something could come of the obscure sky map a mad Lion tattooed on himself five hundred years ago?

Franz balls victorious fists, while Jaime collapses in his seat and releases a trembling sigh. Meanwhile, Angel leans back regally in the sofa and directs the Stare at me. "That means you have a precise date. Get to work."

The more time I spend time with Franz, the more I realize that celebrities are better admired from afar. I had to go hide in the meeting room with my laptop because he kept looking over my shoulder. I couldn't concentrate with him breathing heavily like that every time I pressed enter or typed a line of code—with Sonny filming it all.

For now, we're sailing above a sea of ink-black clouds toward sunrise while I'm trying to resurrect a long-forgotten college project that's been sleeping in an online repository for the past six years. A faint click has me looking up from the screen to the meeting room door as it comes ajar. March comes in, a steaming cup in hand. My nostrils quiver at the titillating scent of cocoa filling the air: he knows me far too well.

"I thought you might need a refuel," he says softly, setting the hot drink and a wrapped dulce de leche cake roll on the table. "How is it going?"

I take a blissful sip of hot cocoa while he sits at my side in front of the laptop screen. "I'm almost done. According to NASA's ephemerides, Jupiter was at opposition with the sun on March 10th, 1543, at or around 5:53 pm—basically at sunset. Of course, that's assuming Cornellà had a crystal-clear sky, a working sextant to ascertain the alignment, and that he waited until the sunlight had dimmed enough that Jupiter started to be visible."

March nods, studying the black and white sky map that's being rendered over and over on my screen in a separate window. "So now you're trying to find the coordinates from which the alignment could be observed at that time."

"Yeah. That's what takes time and resources: we're going to need to test all possible coordinates within a reasonable range of mount Ataqah and compare each render to our reference alignment. I've tried to optimize my algorithm to quickly decrease our search radius, but that's still going to take a while," I explain, dipping my dulce de leche roll in the little cloud of foam sitting atop my hot cocoa.

"How long?" March inquires, his brows knotting briefly: the only sign that he's a yawn away from complete exhaustion.

"Hopefully no more than a couple hours. You should try to get some shut-eye until then," I coax, motioning to the electronic glass partition separating us from the rest of the cabin. "No one will know if you take a nap in here."

His eyelids droop like those of a lazy feline but don't close. "There'll be time to rest after we've recovered Joy."

"We will," I say, renewed determination spiking in my veins as I gaze at the ever-morphing sky map on my screen. "Once I get the coordinates, we'll have the upper hand on Ramirez."

"What do you want to do?"

"We set up a rendezvous point and trade him the coordinates for Joy." The corners of my mouth swing downward until I'm pretty sure I look like Grumpy Cat. "Then we give the coordinates to Stiles too, and we let God sort the rest out."

"You've never scared me until tonight, Miss Chaptal."

"I'm done playing nice. Also, I'm starting to get why Angel doesn't like sloths."

"Their beatific smile is only skin-deep," he agrees. "In any case, I vote for your plan. We'll put Joy safely on a flight back to New York while Ramirez and the brotherhood sort out their ideological differences. I wish them much fun doing so."

I gobble up the last of my roll, careful to wipe the crumbs with my napkin before March is tempted to do it for me. As I toss it all in a little trashcan compartment tucked in the wall, my laptop emits a low ding that I've come to associate with impending doom and stomach aches. I have a new Facebook message from Stiles. Dammit, I should have never accepted that friend invite.

March's jaw works in aggravation, all levity gone from his until-now relaxed posture. "Speaking of the devil . . ."

"We'll have to talk to him soon anyway," I rationalize. There's a one-line message in my inbox with a PDF file in attachment. My mouth falls open at the same time that my forefinger hits the touchpad to open it.

Hello, friend. I think you'll be interested in this. Maybe Mr. November too needs to refresh his memory.

"The course material has changed," March comments soberly.

You bet it has: I can't imagine cold-war era supervillain Anies ever condoning that kind of presentation—and of course, Stiles uses Comic Sans MS in internal communications. This man is a monster. I shake my head at this corporate abomination, skimming through pages and pages of horribly crowded layout, colorful arrows, and kitten pics. He did it himself; I can tell. I recognize some clip art illustrations he stole from the Internet and also uses in his Roomba cat videos on YouTube. "Do you think aspiring Lions get shot if they fail the quiz?"

"Presumably. The carving is . . . a physical test to reflect a mental commitment. It's difficult to describe the sort of awe it can inspire in the minds of malleable young recruits," he says, his voice softening as he contemplates memories he's never shared with me until now. He was once such a young, 'malleable' cub in Dries's hands, and the scarification on his back determined the rest of his life. With it, he chose to lose his name, shed everything he had ever been, to become Dries's creature, a Lion.

"But what does Cornellà have to do with it? You said you'd tell me about him, back at the villa, but . . . we've been busy since."

"That we have." March reaches an arm around me, stroking my shoulder absently as he unwinds with a low sigh. "Would you like to go through this fascinating document?" he says, eyeing Stile's file on my laptop.

Kinda. Maybe. The Lions aren't something March and I discuss often. He means to leave them to rest in the fog of his past where they belong, since nothing about them makes for good dinner conversation anyway. Nevertheless, I can already tell that trudging through Stiles's horribly designed PowerPoint will do little to keep my anxiety levels in check, so I say: "Not really. I'd like to hear what *you* think and what you know."

"Very well. The short answer to your question is that the brotherhood's old rites were discontinued through the Dark Ages, and Cornellà resuscitated those."

"Among which the carving," I infer.

"Yes. Most of the brotherhood's rituals were a direct heritage of the antiquity, that progressively got lost throughout the dark age. The empires the Lions used to serve had collapsed one after another, and that reflected on their command structure and their mindset: by the time Cornellà joined the brotherhood, the Lions had become your average band of sixteenth-century mercenaries, rounding up untrained boys to die on Charles V's battlefields."

March shakes his head in quiet disapproval at this less than glorious episode, and in this tiny gesture, I see that he'll never really stop being a Lion—even if he'd rather lick sink mold than accept Stiles's gift of a shitty presentation. "Back then," he goes on, "the carving had been abandoned in favor of a mere tattoo: the times were hard, and too many brothers would die from sepsis during the healing process. Since the ties of the brotherhood were getting loose, they no longer understood the deeper meaning of the ritual or the point of going through it."

"But Cornellà did?"

"Certainly. Jaime's research is fortunately incomplete, but mostly correct: Cornellà was the prototype of a Renaissance man, obsessed with knowledge and determined to dig up all that lay in the ruins of the past. He spent the second half of his life trying to catalog the brotherhood's most ancient traces and revive the roots of their credo. The Lions would probably have disappeared within a generation or two if he hadn't brought back this sense of being not one but part of something greater, of having a purpose that transcends time."

My cheek pressed to March's chest, I listen, feel the calm tiding and ebbing of his breathing, but it's not him I hear. If I close my eyes, the voice caressing my forehead is Dries's. That passion, that sense of purpose were *his*, and I don't need to ask to know that March is unconsciously reciting the lessons Dries taught him when he was barely out of boyhood.

"Cornellà revived the carving to give the Lions their past back," I reflect, my gaze lost in the dark clouds stretching along an incurved streak of silver: the very edge of the earth, and beyond, higher, space.

March acquiesces, resuming his exposé. "The Lions keep letters and notes from him at the Rome temple, and they're essentially a treaty on the virtues of suffering, endurance, obedience, and surrendering your sense of self to the group."

I swallow softly, my heart tight as I look up at March's tranquil profile. Centuries later, he came awfully close to being Cornellà's perfect creation: a man who was nearly rendered incapable of feeling anything, no remorse, no sense of self, neither fear nor regrets. If he had stayed, if he hadn't chosen to save my fifteen-year-old self the day Anies's men killed my mother, that kind of life might have taken anything he'd left deep inside him, that soft center he tried to protect in spite of it all. "Lovely . . ." I mutter. "The name thing—having to lose your name: it was his idea too?"

"He didn't create that aspect of the ritual, but he did resuscitate it as well. He carved his first two disciples around 1540, and he had one of them carve him. They vowed to give up their name and, for one of them, his title. They gave themselves arbitrary code numbers, based on Cornellà's calculations. The rest of the brotherhood saw them as complete fanatics at the time." He gives a quasi-shrug. "But they were bringing strength and purpose when the rest of their brothers no longer knew how to, so the trend caught on fast with young recruits. Fifty years later, the carving was back for everyone's enjoyment, and every brother wore a single name, a number, and no other title of any kind."

"Strength and purpose . . . " I repeat, trying to remember where I've heard those words before.

"Anies's favorite motto," March says quietly.

"You're right . . . What about the whole mystic phase and the self-flaying? Were you taught anything about that?"

Under me, his chest heaves from a rueful sigh. "To some extent. That's the part Lions usually prefer to skip, for fear it might put the rest of Cornellà's contributions in perspective, I suppose. His driving force was pathologic hyperreligiosity: he started out a fervent catholic; then he became a fanatic Lion . . . I suppose it was only a matter of time before he went mad."

"So, you don't think Franz is right about the tomb of the first Lions?"

"Do you mean whether they came down from Mars?"

I mock-punch his chest. "About everything else. Do you think that's what Cornellà was looking for in Egypt?"

"It would fit what we know of him, but I'd be wary of any . . ."

A sudden chime coming from my laptop interrupts March before he can finish trashing Franz's theories. I leave the comfort of his arms to go check my script that was still running in the background.

I can barely believe the words even as I say, "There's a match."

TWENTY-NINE
DO UT DES

Fabio raised his machine gun to the ashen sky, heedless of the rain that soaked his shirt and made the fabric cling to his muscular frame. "I'll raze Peru to save you if I must, Rica!"

– Kerry-Lee Storm, *Cost of Rica #5: Blaze of the Phoenix*

It's been a solid five seconds, and I still have both my hands clasped over my mouth while I gape at my laptop screen. Cornellà's stellar alignment did actually occur on the day Jupiter was at opposition with the sun, and my algorithm has narrowed down the possible points of observation to a handful of neighboring coordinates. Two hours ago, I feared I might be grasping at straws, hoping to actually locate the first brothers' tomb and make it my bargaining chip to rescue Joy. But . . . it's real.

March, too, sounds like someone just bashed him on the skull. "Can you locate it on a map?"

"Yeah . . . just a sec." I load our coordinates on a satellite map of the area of Ain Sokhna. Twenty miles north of the city, in the Ataqah chain, a cluster of several pins all sit in the same spot, a gorge barely a hundred feet wide snaking through the desert. I zoom in on the desolate terrain.

"There are building structures," March comments as the screen pans over a half-shattered dome of mud brick. A few rectangular outlines in the ground suggest the rest of a now-destroyed building that must have leaned against the gorge's walls.

Fingers hammering at the keyboard, I run a quick online search to identify the ruins. "The dome and the ruins around it are a Coptic burial ground from the seventh century."

"Too recent, then," March says with a rueful shake of his head. The first brothers banded together around the time the Roman republic was founded in the fifth century BC.

"That doesn't mean there isn't something older underneath. It's not unusual for a monument to be layered atop another on consecrated ground," I remark.

A crease forms between March's eyebrows as he stares at the ruins' pictures, unblinking. I can tell he's envisioning the same possibility I am: that there might be something there, still waiting to be discovered. Blood is pounding so fast in my temples, that I can sense an oncoming headache from the sudden rush of excitement.

March raps his thumb against the mirror-like table-top, eying the opaque glass partition beyond which our star awaits the news that might overturn centuries of scientific certainties. "We can't let Franz know about this."

Lowering my voice to a guilty whisper, I say, "I could give him different coordinates."

"And send him to film barren rocks in the middle of the desert while we deal with Ramirez. How devious . . . The management approves of this plan of action."

I switch between the open windows to open Facebook. "Okay, so now we need to message 'Logan y su papi' and let him know we have something he desperately wants." Let's hope he treats Joy like a jewel the moment he realizes what his hostage is truly worth.

I'm about to add yet another disreputable name to my contact list when the meeting room's door slides open, revealing Angel's wiry form. My finger freezes above the touchpad as he swipes a hawkish look at March and me, his mouth a grim line in the ebony nest of his beard. "This is my meeting room," he informs us as the door closes behind him, the air between us thick with warning. "I know everything that happens inside it."

Great. The smurfs were having a party without him, and Gargamel is pissed.

March levels a frosty look at Angel. "Spying on us? I thought we were past that point."

Ignoring the jab, our overbearing employer leans over my shoulder to check the laptop screen. I flinch, mentally picturing a plate of roasted crickets who all look like me as he swipes across the touchpad to open my sky map simulation then the satellite view of the ruins.

"You're going to trade the coordinates for her," he states, not looking at us.

March acquiesces. "That is the plan. We were getting ready to contact Ramirez."

"Go ahead," Angel snaps. He has this irritating way of always taking charge of things even when they're running smoothly without him.

I comply anyway, sending Ramirez a curt missive.

We've located the tomb. Send proof of life and we can talk.

Thirty seconds later, my message is accepted. A picture is sent in response. My first reaction is a rush of panic at the sight of Joy's prone form and closed eyes, lying under Logan as he smiles evilly at the camera.

Hammering at the keyboard, I type a one-word reply: *Asleep? For now . . .*

That does little to slow down my heart rate. I zoom in on her: there's no blood: she's likely asleep across a row of seats under a military blanket. Okay. She's alive and in one piece: it's enough for now.

A cracking sound alerts me to the fact that, next to me, Angel has just crushed my empty plastic cup in his fist, his features taut with fury. I really wish I knew what sloths ever did to him.

"We'll bring her back," March says, as much to reassure me as to defuse Angel's temper.

As soon as he's spoken, a new message pops under the picture.

Saint Simon cave church at sunset. One vehicle, no escort. If I see anyone with you, Logan will slit her lovely throat.

A vision of his claws on her chest flashes in my mind. The scene is the same as the one I witnessed back at Franz's villa, but this time, the single drop of blood is a crimson ribbon. Ramirez won't hesitate: he's already killed countless people to find that tomb. "I'm going alone," I snap automatically.

"He has no intention to release her. He's going to kill you both," Angel states.

March's gaze turns the darkest shade of ice. "Indeed."

"But he doesn't know we'll get there six hours before he does. I'll have a welcome party ready for him," Angel adds.

March's gaze narrows at the milky glass door separating us from the cabin. "Does he? I believe there's something else we need to discuss before we inform Mr. Franz of our momentous discovery . . . "

"Holy Mother of God, it matches!"

A scowl of disapproval tugs at Angel's scar as Franz crosses himself for the third consecutive time in front of my laptop.

"You were right all along," I tell Franz with a wooden smile. "It was those galleries on the coast. That's where Cornellà observed the alignment from."

Are my ears getting red already? I can feel them heat up. I hate lying, especially to Franz, who spent so much time and energy gathering each clue leading to Cornellà's hide until he did find it. This truth, this secret should be his, but it can't be: I need him out of our way while we're facing Ramirez.

March gazes at me steadily from across the meeting table. We agreed to give Franz fake coordinates: he'll be safe filming rocks and chasing aliens thirty miles away from the actual location of the ruins Cornellà's hide led us to. I avert my eyes, so I won't have to see the emotion in Franz's . . . or the doubt in Jaime's.

"The French never found anything there." He mutters, running a shaky hand in his dark locks to comb them away from his eyes.

"But one of their papers did mention an unexplored cavity," Franz counters. He inhales deeply, pressing a hand over his heart. "We're getting close."

"That could be the entrance to the tomb," I try to cheer, well aware that I sound like I'm trying to sell spray-on hair in an 'As Seen on TV' commercial.

"One of the expedition reports mentions sulfur water infiltrations around a rectangular structure inside one of the galleries," Franz stresses. "It could be a hidden chamber. We're going there!"

March gives him his most soulless smile. "I certainly hope so. Miss Chaptal and I have some business to attend today; we'll leave you in the capable hands of Mr. Somoza's production team and will join you in Ain Sokhna tomorrow morning."

As expected, his announcement is welcomed with a beat of leery silence, then knitted brows.

Franz scowls. "But that means she'll miss an entire day of shooting. I need her there. We have several scenes written for her, and the weather forecast for tonight is—"

"Then I'll be on set tomorrow at dawn, but not today," I cut him off, trying to keep my voice pleasant even as my skin prickles with irritation. He can't expect me to deliver any sort of performance until I've recovered Joy.

Franz's face prunes up as understanding dawns at last. "This is about Ramirez and your blonde friend. Are you going to rescue her?"

"This conversation is over," March says flatly.

"What about you?" Franz asks him. "Would you be willing to wear a GoPro during the faceoff?"

"No."

"It will be attached to your forehead: you'll barely notice it."

"Oh, for God's sake . . . *No!*"

He did it. The legendary Gualtiero Franz has managed to step on March's last nerve. A muscle twitching in his jaw, March performs a smooth 180-degree turn and strides back to his seat. I follow him as he all but collapses in the soft black leather, searching the empty gaze of a pair of air vents above our heads. He takes out his mints from his pocket, and as he tosses a few in his palm, murmurs words I have, never, ever heard him utter since we've known each other. "I think I need a drink."

I consider the galley fridge longingly. So do I.

THIRTY
THE CHURCH

"This ain't holy water, but it's gonna get you wet all the same, Shelly!"

– Gem Windcrest, *Her Biker Priest*

"I'm ready," I announce, adjusting the straps of a Kevlar over my linen shirt and cargo shorts—a rare occurrence for me, but then again, we're up against a different kind of evil. Reflected in the brass-framed, floor-to-ceiling windows of Cairo's Four Seasons, my features are taut from worry and lack of sleep. I did try to lie down after raiding a plate of mezza and fruit, but I kept thinking of Joy. I ended up reviewing every detail of our plan and making a flow diagram of everything that could possibly go wrong . . . and I couldn't close my eyes.

Thirty floors below, the Nile is turning pink as it mirrors a blushing sky. It's almost six-thirty. The sun will set in half-an-hour, and if all goes as planned, Ramirez will be awaiting us with Joy in Saint-Simon the Tanner, a giant, open-air church carved directly into the side of the Mokattam mountain in the impoverished garbage district. You'd think that diabolical asswipe tried to come up with the one thing that was sure to trigger March.

Speaking of the devil, he's already wearing his black gloves. His reflection smiles at me in the glass before I turn around to face him. His hand rises to cup my cheek and stroke the dark circles that are probably forming under my eyes. "I wish there had been more time for you to rest."

"That's my line," I say, smoothing a hand down the front of his white pressed shirt. He dozed in an armchair for all of fifty minutes after a quick shower, and I heard the frantic squeaking of a squeegee after he was done. I didn't dare to comment on it: it's his way to cope under pressure.

"Don't worry. I've known worse."

I sigh and rub my eyes forcefully with the heels of my palms. "I just want to get her back and be done with this crap weekend."

"She'll be all right," he says softly.

"Yep." I give a martial nod. "One hour from now, I'll be with her, and Ramirez will be on his way to get shredded by Stiles's kittens."

We gave Stiles the coordinates of the ruins and an outline of our plan of action: that gave his "boys" five hours to organize a welcome party for Ramirez. Turns out he has Lions on duty in Egypt at the moment, and, from what I gather, he's going to fly in reinforcements. I wonder if he'll come in person . . . The idea of finding myself standing in front of him again makes my skin crawl as if I'd plunged my whole arm in a jar of live botflies—yes, the ones that lay their eggs under your skin and then the larva pops out horribly like bad acne. I fight a bone-rattling shudder at the mental image of a botfly larva with Stiles's head piercing through my skin, and yelling "Damn!" in its tiny Southern fly voice.

"Biscuit, are you sure you're all right?" March insists, his brow creasing in concern as he watches me zone out.

"Yeah . . ." I rub residual chills off my arm while he shrugs on his bulletproof jacket. Double holster underneath: Christmas is coming early for Ramirez. "I don't like to ask, but maybe I should take a gun too?"

"No," he replies. "The first things his men will do is scan and frisk you. Ramirez is unhinged enough as it is, I don't want to risk riling him any further. Angel and I will cover you from each side of the bleachers. We won't intervene unless something goes off-script."

"Okay. Let's do this."

Over a century ago, thousands of destitute Coptic farmers migrated north from Upper Egypt to find better fortune in Cairo. That did not go as planned. They ended up being ostracized and settled in a shantytown in the hills of southeastern Cairo, where they've been making a living collecting and recycling garbage since, from father to son. Their kingdom is Zabbaleen, the garbage city, whose decrepit brick buildings glide by, reflected in the windows of the drab, gray Corolla I'm driving. Anything else would be ostentatious in those muddy streets littered with bursting trash bags. They pile up on balconies, up cracked walls, in the beds of small, rusty three-wheelers that seem to lean under the weight of mankind's waste.

March is driving half-a-mile behind me in a parallel street. He must be feeling sick right now. Not just from the combined scents of smoke, gas, and rotting garbage suffusing the air and infiltrating our cars but also, I fear, from long-buried memories. He grew up on the edge of a township in Cape Town, a distant sister to this decaying hell. There, too, mangy dogs search the trash for their next meal, right next to children playing soccer in the dust.

A reddish blot cuts across the road. I slam the brakes, barely avoiding a pair of kids riding together on a sputtering moped. We're almost there: the buildings are getting sparse as I near the soaring side of the hill. Sunset outline the dark bones of a half-collapsed building with fiery strokes and gold and copper. Saint-Simon is over there, past the ever-smoking recycling plants, tucked under thousands of tons of sun-washed sandstone.

I slow down and park at the foot of the hill. "I'm here. I don't see anything, just garbage trucks and locals," I whisper for the benefit of the miniature earpiece and microphone I'm wearing. "I'm going in."

March's voice echoes in my ear like a warm, reassuring current. "I'm near the bell towers, I see you."

I glance left, just long enough to glimpse his tall silhouette before he disappears around the side of a round building. Good. My hurried footsteps raise clouds of dust as I cross the deserted square sprawling in front of the church. On the other side, a slope leads up to the top of the amphitheater, where up to twenty thousand churchgoers can sit during mass. Dozens and dozens of rows of bleachers plunge down into the belly of the cave, cramming around an altar only a few yards wide. From a gaping wound, the inhabitants of Zabbaleen have built the largest church in the Middle East. Stone saints watch me venture down the stone steps. Where the hell is Ramirez?

"I don't see him," I hiss softly.

The church is almost empty at this hour, save for a few old men in djellabas gathered together near the altar. Opting for a sitting duck strategy, I lower myself on a bleacher halfway down the amphitheater, where I'll be visible from all sides of the cave.

I don't see Ramirez coming. I *smell* him. A whiff of smoky, pungent cologne reaches my nostrils before a big shape sits down at my side on the stone-and-wood bench, too close for comfort. He leans back and flings an arm behind me. I go rigid, balling my fists as the black leather of his coat squeaks. "Perfectly on time, Miss Chaptal," he drawls as the sun disappears behind the horizon, leaving us alone in this darkened pit.

"Where's she?" I hiss.

He gives an infuriating chuckle and strokes his goatee. "Straight to the point, I see."

As he says this, the clatter of heels echoes in the cavernous vault of the church. I twist on the bench in the direction of the sound: two rows above us, a pair of Lions in civilian clothes are bringing Joy. Relief rushes in my veins, as if a dam had just broken in my chest. She's still wearing last night's black high-heel sandals, but someone gave her inconspicuous khaki coveralls at some point of her detention. Her eyes widen when she sees me before she combs back a heap of blonde curls from her eyes, revealing a necklace she wasn't wearing yesterday. The black plastic band cinching her throat blinks red in the penumbra. She's wearing a bomb collar.

My first impulse is to shoot up and run to her, but Ramirez's large hand clasps over my bare thigh, right below the hem of my shorts. "Not so fast, Island."

"Don't touch me," I spit.

"You didn't play fair, Miss Chaptal," he goes on, his nails slowly digging into my flesh. "But that's all right: I didn't either. You had six hours to get ready for our game. So did I."

Braving her captors, Joy attempts to leap forward, only to be hauled back by a beefy Lion. "Jaime called him! He's a fucking snitch."

I force my eyes to widen to keep up the act and flash my most convincing glare at Ramirez. March and I have suspected so since the attack on Franz's villa. Ramirez knew Franz had found Cornellà's hide at least a day before Franz shared his discovery with his producers. He knew Vince had seen—and possibly photographed—it, even when Cachemire claimed to have barely gotten a glimpse of it before Franz jealously closed the casket. Someone has been keeping Ramirez up to date with our every move, someone Franz trusted enough to share every detail of his research with. I release a slow breath to calm the tremors in my legs. That means we're going ahead with plan B.

"So, how's Jaime?" I ask Ramirez, mustering a cool tone even as one of his Lions frisks me—just like March predicted. "I guess he's not filming with Franz in Ain Sokhna after all."

Ramirez shakes his head, a predatory grin stretching his horrible goatee when his goon nods to him that I'm clear. "It seems you're always a move behind, Miss Chaptal."

"You think so? I didn't write down the coordinates; I even erased them from my computer. They're in here," I tap my forehead. "If I die, they disappear with me, and I won't give them to you until that collar is off and Joy is sitting in a car driving away from here."

The sight of Joy's middle fingers flipping up at Ramirez bolsters my courage. Who's a step behind now?

"Ah . . ." he snorts, extending his legs to rest them on the bleacher in front of us. "But what good are they to me now that I know you're capable of lying? No, that won't do. I think we're going to change the terms of our arrangement, Island. You and your exquisite friend are going to come with me on a little excursion. Once—and only once—I've ascertained that the first brothers rest in the place you're going to lead us to, I'll release the both of you. Or perhaps my men will be digging two graves in the desert come dawn: that depends on you."

"You think you can leave this place alive?" I grit out.

"I think, and I will."

The half-dozen red dots that appear all over my chest as he states this suggest he might, in fact, be right. Joy and I exchange a tense look as outside the cave, a low hum stirs the cloudy night: a rotor is approaching.

"Our ride is here," Ramirez croons. His voice turns flinty as he adds, louder, "If you care about their health, you'll kindly stay where you are hidden, Mr. November. If a single gunshot echoes in this holy place, I'm going to smear these ladies at god's feet."

In my ear, March simply says, "Island?"

All the trust in the world is contained in that single word. After we realized Jaime had to be our mole, we considered the possibility of this particular outcome. We're ready. At least I hope so, and there's no time to choose anyway: as long as Joy is wearing that collar, we need to play along. "Don't come out," I say tightly.

"Smart girl." Ramirez's hand jumps from my knee to my arm, gripping it tightly as a long black helicopter gracefully enters the cave's gigantic mouth—that's a military transport model: Ramirez brought his friends with him, or at least the ones March hasn't killed yet. The old men who were praying and chatting near the altar get to their feet, staring up in terror. Shouts in Arabic ricochet against the jagged walls as they run away. Ramirez hauls me up at the same time that his Lions shove Joy forward and up the amphitheater's stairs, toward the aircraft now hovering a few feet above our heads and raising a dust storm in the open-air church.

I manage to briefly grasp Joy's hand and squeeze it before a ladder is being tossed down to us.

"Do lead the way, my Bathsheba," Ramirez orders her.

Unmoved by the compliment, she struggles in panic when her captors force her hands on the helicopter ladder. "I can't do this! Let me go!"

"It's gonna be okay!" I shout over the storm of the rotor. "I'm going with you!"

She gives a shaky nod and hoists herself up, helped by two Lions who hold onto the lower rung to keep the ladder more or less straight while she climbs. When my turn comes, I remember that this is the second time I find myself climbing into a helicopter full of Lions. The previous one flew me straight to Stiles and his Roomba cats. Ironically, I now find myself praying, for Joy's sake, that the same experiment will yield the same results, nine months apart.

THIRTY-ONE
THE NUMBERS

Rica's sublime bosom heaved in anger and despair: Adolfo Judas
had been working for Ramirez all along!

– Kerry-Lee Storm, *Cost of Rica #5: Blaze of the Phoenix*

Two people I haven't really missed await in the seat opposite ours in the rising chopper. Jaime and Logan, Ramirez's pets, watch us being tossed and buckled up while the aircraft gains speed, leaving behind the desolation of the garbage city—as well as March and Angel. Jaime's gaze won't meet my accusing one. He's huddled in the corner of the seat, staring at the indigo horizon slashing the night sky.

"Are you okay?" I shout at Joy once I've managed to find my bearings. "Did he hurt you?"

"Not really. Burning Man last year was worse!" She manages a smile that becomes a wince when Logan leaves Ramirez's lap to crawl onto hers, resting a proprietary golden claw on her breast. The mere sight of him sparks a shudder in my belly. He's wearing his tiny black tactical vest again, and I'd almost find it cute if I didn't know what this sloth is capable of.

Meanwhile, the treacherous Lions flanking us on the seat have the decency to give us noise-canceling headsets. "Where are we going, Miss Chaptal?" Ramirez asks in the speaker, a sardonic smile perched atop his goatee.

I recite the latitude and longitude coordinates I've learned by heart and watch the horizon line shift as the pilot adjusts his cap. At an average 160 miles per hour, it should take us twenty-five minutes to get to the ruins. Depending on what kind of trick Angel has up his sleeves—and in his online catalog—it could take anywhere between thirty minutes and an hour for them to catch up with us. That's plenty of time for Logan to flay us if Stiles's Lions don't step in, but Ramirez won't get to that part of his program until he's been able to inspect the ruins. I swallow quietly. No point in losing myself in macabre calculations until we've touched the ground.

"So, you're actually a traitor?" Joy asks Jaime conversationally while crossing her arms and legs like she's the one in charge here. Angel and her kind of deserve each other—and I mean that in the best way possible.

"You don't understand . . . this is bigger than all of us," he whines in our headset.

"Oh no, we get it," I supply. "You're a fricking traitor."

Ramirez hacks a laugh. "No need to insult our friend, Miss Chaptal. You've quite simply met your match. Jaime here quickly understood that instead of wasting his time fighting the Collegium with Gualtiero Franz, he should simply join our ranks."

I level a disdainful glare at this new cub, who's hiding under a curtain of greasy hair because he can't even look at me. "Do you even realize who these guys are? Do you seriously think you're one of them?" I roar, motioning to the guy next to me, a thirty-something with cold tip-tilted eyes and shoulders almost as big as March. He's the real deal, a fanatic who not only got carved but betrayed his brothers to follow his guru.

Jaime unfolds and meets my eyes at last. "How can anyone live knowing that all the secrets are here, all around us, and we don't *know?*"

For all my dislike of this slimy little snitch, I get his point, and I can see what led him to the edge of the cliff he's standing on. Didn't I use to feel the same? I risked my life because I just needed to know: March and Dries's secrets, Anies's identity, the truth behind my mother's death. As Jaime aptly puts it—and I remember once telling March—I simply couldn't go on like before once I knew this whole underground world existed around me, that any man or woman walking by me on the street might be killing people for a living . . . and now Joy's life has been similarly altered— by my fault, I remind myself as her anxious gaze seeks mine.

"He has no answers for you," I tell Jaime, jerking my chin at a smirking Ramirez. "He ditched his brothers, and when they find him, they're gonna kill him, and they're gonna kill you too because that's what they do. There's your big secret. There's nothing in that tomb that will change the world."

Jaime's lips press together angrily, but before he can reply, Joy says: "Don't bother. They think they're gonna find coneheads or something."

I raise a dubious look at Ramirez. "Like . . . really?"

He gives me an avuncular look—by that, I mean the look of an uncle who ends up doing life without parole for touching the kids. "My poor girl, I have roamed this Earth for fifty-three years, and if you had only seen the things I've seen . . . there would be no doubt in your shriveled mind as to what Cornellà meant when he said our first brothers were no men." His eyes take on a mad glint as he motions to the barren immensity stretching below. "There's something sleeping in that desert that didn't come from earth, something we can barely comprehend with the limited reach of our science." Then, changing gears so fast it's giving me whiplash, he asks. "How did you find the tomb?"

Joy observes me with attentive eyes as I reply, "There's a sky map on the hide. A stellar alignment with Jupiter at opposition with the sun, above mount Ataqah."

Ramirez slicks his mustache in a way that makes me uncomfortable. "Fascinating. I found the Leo, but Jupiter totally eluded me."

I almost want to tell him Angel identified it, just so he knows that a guy who studied classics well over a decade ago and who's been selling fantasy print body bags since is a better archeologist than he is, but I swallow back the diss. Let's keep his mind busy rather than angry for now. "I used a NASA ephemeris to find the precise date and time Cornellà observed his stellar alignment, then I coded a script to calculate the point of observation."

He blinks a couple times, shakes his head. "What's a girl like you doing with a philistine like March?"

"He beats me at level 6 crosswords," I reply earnestly.

"And he's a god at Uno," Joy adds, grimacing as Logan sniffs her neck with his wet little nose.

Ramirez doesn't dignify her claim with a reply. His attention shifts to the jagged terrain below: the Ataqah chain. The helicopter veers right through a blanket of low clouds like black mist and dips toward the gorge where the ruins are nested. I swallow the lump in my throat, feeling my pulse pick up. This is it.

The gorge looks deserted as we slowly descend toward the cluster of collapsed brick structures of the Coptic chapels. Dust shimmers like a snowstorm in the beam of the LED torches Ramirez's men swipe at steep, rocky slopes. With a final sigh, the helicopter's blades come to a stop. The Lions help us out of the chopper, but this brief act of chivalry can't detract me from the collar still blinking around

Joy's neck. We need to humor Ramirez long enough for help to reach us. Ice trickles down my spine at the thought of what might happen if Ramirez is disappointed by his big find and decides to take it out on us . . .

At my side, Joy rubs her arms briskly. Night's cold has settled on the desert, and she's only wearing those coveralls Ramirez gave her. Scratch that: one of the Lions hands her Logan once more, who wraps his long, furry arms around her neck like the scarf she didn't ask for.

"I think he likes you," I whisper.

"It's Lima syndrome," she buzzes back.

"Island."

I jerk at Ramirez's commanding tone.

"Show us the way."

I look around at the gorge's walls, feeling my pulse pick up as the situation threatens to escape what little control I have over it. Where are Stiles's men? And how long will it take for March and Angel to be here? We had a chopper ready to take off seven hundred feet east of the Cave Church, but they must have waited long enough for Ramirez's pilot not to detect them. "We're here. I mean, that's the location Cornellà's coordinates led to. I don't know what else you want." I point to Joy. "But we had a deal. Take the collar off."

Before I can say any more, a flash of blinding pain cuts my breathing. Ramirez's hand has shot to my neck and grabbed it in a crushing hold.

"What sort of game are you playing, Island?" He growls, drops of his saliva spraying my face. I'm gonna be sick.

"I'm . . . not playing."

"Let her go, dickhead!" Joy shrieks, only to be stopped by the tightening of Logan's golden claws against her nape, then a Lion's rough grip on her arm.

Ramirez releases my throat, only to grab my hair instead, fisting it so tight I'm terrified my scalp is going to rip off. I go limp in his grasp, desperate to escape the agonizing burn at the back of my skull.

With his free hand, he produces a tiny remote from the front pocket of his coat and waves it in front of me. "We will be done when I've been able to verify your claim, little girl. And don't think for a second I won't kill you because you're Dries's daughter."

The idea never crossed my mind, but I'm glad it did his. I jolt my head in the semblance of a nod and release a shuddering breath when he lets go.

"So how do we find the tomb, Island?" Ramirez asks.

I wrench my hands, scanning the area. I don't know. I don't know, and I need to come up with something—anything—to humor his psychosis until Stiles's goddamn Lions make a move or March gets here. "It could be like the tombs in the Valley of the Kings," I babble to the surrounding darkness. "The entrance might be buried somewhere, under centuries' worth of scree."

Jaime emerges from Ramirez's shadow, his limbs jittery from fear and nascent excitement. "Yes . . . yes! Could Cornellà have been facing the tomb's entrance when he witnessed the alignment?"

Mentally picturing the satellite map I studied earlier, I point to the wall of rock in front of us. "He was facing west, so he must have been looking that way." I hop to the shattered Coptic brick dome. "And the exact center of the coordinates is basically here, near the dome. So, he was looking straight at . . . that." Rocks. Just rocks, and nothing else. "You're going to need an excavator," I say—and they're also going to need time we don't have, I remind myself with a shudder.

"Excellent. Bandile, get the RPG," Ramirez barks.

Hang on. *RPG*, as in *Rocket-Propelled Grenade*? I search Jaime's eyes for confirmation that this has nothing to do with proper archeology, but all I get in return is a sullen shrug as a dark-skinned guy in black fatigues goes to fetch a bazooka from the helicopter's hull.

Watching another Lion help his teammate by loading a rocket inside the steel tube, Joy rolls frightened eyes at me. I can hear her question as clearly as if she'd shouted it: *Are they seriously going to?*

They are: Bandile is already stepping in position, thirty yards away from the ancient gate. He aims the bazooka at the center of his target. Ramirez flicks his wrist for Joy and me to step back.

I raise my hands to protect my ears, encouraging Joy to do the same with a quick nod.

Bandile widens his stance, steadies his grip on the massive launcher propped on his shoulder. Muscles coil in his forearm as he prepares to press the trigger. The sound of his boots crushing gravel sounds thunderous in the quiet desert night. We all stand frozen, waiting for the shot.

I grit my teeth, my eyes glued to Bandile's finger on the trigger. Weirdly enough, a blazing trail lights up the sky before he's pressed it. First comes the detonation, booming directly under my ribs, then the deafening rush of air as the rocket rips over our heads to go smash into the wall of rocks and scree Ramirez meant to blow up.

The shock wave reaches me before I can fully process the fact that Bandile did *not* take that shot. My body feels like it's being pressed directly to a giant gong that's just been hit while a flurry of gravel hails on our heads. Joy staggers back and uses Logan as a shield. A protesting squeak alerts us to the fact that he's been hit. Ramirez lunges to tear him off Joy and gathers him in his arms. She screams in surprise, loses her balance, and tumbles on me as the ground under our feet rattles from a deep quake rumbling our way; my arms automatically clamp around her waist in a vain bid to catch her. If nothing else, I cushion her fall and grunt in pain as my back hits the rocky ground.

I blow a heap of blonde curls from my face, my jaw going slack the moment I take in our surroundings. The torrent of scree pouring down the gorge's slope has revealed a rectangular cavity. I roll us out of the way just in time, suffocating from the dust saturating the air. I refuse to believe this: Ramirez's sketchy brand of archeology actually paid off.

"We're under attack!" Ramirez shouts. He's already running to the newly formed rectangular entrance, flanked by Jaime and a tight commando of four men: I'm not even sure he cares if the rest of his Lions die here fighting. Apparently, the secrets of the first Lions are just for him and Logan.

I raise my head at the mayhem around us. I can't pinpoint where the rockets came from, but there's now gunfire rattling from the top of the cliffs, and Ramirez's Lions have taken cover. Bandile raises his bazooka, aims, and the earth trembles once more as he shoots—for real this time.

When a rock explodes barely two feet from our heads, I scramble up and help Joy to do the same. "We need to get away from here! I don't think it's March and Angel; they wouldn't shoot at us like that!"

"The tomb!" Joy screams, her head whipping in the direction Ramirez just disappeared.

On the one hand, it's a terrible idea to go after him. On the other hand, people are shooting at us and no one here is going to save us. So, I tug at Joy's hand, and we start our ascent up the slope's unsteady terrain. When she lets go of me, I experience a millisecond of panic thinking she's been shot, but I realize she's snapping off her heels to climb faster. "Shit. I thought he'd bang me in his pool, and that would be my weekend," she groans as we stumble in the dark toward the menacing maw of the cavity.

I bite back a scream of pain when I feel a sharp piece of rock cutting my palm. "Same!"

"Happy birthday!" She coughs, halfway between a sob and a chuckle when we reach the flat ledge leading through the gate.

We creep inside and huddle against the remnants of a stone pillar, just out of the line of fire. There's a tunnel ahead whose sculpted walls are lost to pure darkness. "We can't go any further." I pant. "He's in there."

Joy lets herself slide against the time-worn sandstone while bullets crackle from all directions outside. "So, we just wait and try to stay alive until March and Angel show up?"

"I don't know," I hiss, holding my bleeding hand.

The sound of fabric ripping echoes down the bowel of the ruin. "Here," Joy say, wrapping a piece of her sleeve tight around my palm.

"Thanks." My eyes snap open in realization as I feel a weight in my pocket. "I still have my phone."

Joy watches me take it out. "Do we have any network in the cursed tomb of Pokémon the First, though?"

I glare at the grayed-out icon on my phone screen. "No, dammit."

A soft clatter outside the tomb's entrance cuts through our debate. Joy and I look at each other. Then back at the dark canister fizzling a few feet away from us.

Her eyebrows quiver closer together. "Is that . . . ?"

It is. Adrenaline blasts through my system, pulses through my muscles as I leap to my feet. "It's an incendiary!"

We scramble away from the grenade just in time before the tunnel's entrance turns into a blazing inferno. A cloud of acrid smoke swells on our heels as we race along unseen walls, burrowing into pure darkness and silence. My throat and my lungs burning with each intake of air, I register Joy's erratic footsteps and whistling cough somewhere to my right. Blinking blindly, I fumble to turn on my phone's flashlight. Joy's features flicker out of the dark, her eyes wide with terror, half-curtained by a mess of dust-coated golden curls.

"Oh God . . . oh shit." She gasps over and over until her breath progressively slows down. "What do we do now?"

"I'm not sure," I admit, swiping my makeshift torch at the tunnel ahead, until its glare outlines a round object lodged in the wall, like a dusty, brown bowling pin with two holes.

Joy's hands fly to her mouth to bravely stifle a shriek. I stagger back, only to realize there are more skulls behind me, all around us, in fact. My heart ramming against my ribcage, I raise the phone, guiding it along rectangular alveolae carved in sandstone. In each one, a skeleton rests. Some still clutch a sword in their mummified hands, others lay wrapped in the frayed remnants of mortuary shrouds. Under each tomb, there's no name, only a few characters etched in a combination of Latin and cuneiform: the same I've seen in the lower portion of the lion scarification on March's back. Their code number.

"They're Lions," I murmur. "They're all Lions . . ."

Joy risks a trembling fingertip at the engraved characters. "You can't be serious. Franz and Ramirez were right. They were, like, their founders?"

My eyes narrow at one of the numbers. "No. Look, this one reads S259. Clearly, he wasn't the first. Not even close."

"So, it's more of a Necropolis," Joy concurs, hugging herself. The light licks her forearms, revealing the goosebumps peppering them. Her head snaps up all of a sudden. "Did you hear that?" she whispers.

A wave of panic rushes through my body that I can feel from the tip of my toes to that of my nipples. Yes, nipple-tightening fear is real, and it's bad. "Are you trying to creep me out?"

"No! Listen!"

We both go perfectly still and silent, every pore of our skins attuned to the dusty silence of the tomb, until a low growl echoes along the walls, rising from the unseen depths of the tunnel, followed by a familiar whine. Ramirez's and Jaime's voices.

THIRTY-TWO
THE PEN

"Ha ha ha ha ha ha ha!"

— Tales From The Crypt, *HBO, 1999–1996*

I shouldn't. I know I shouldn't, but I'm already taking quiet footsteps toward the shivering shadows gliding along the tunnel's wall.

"What are you doing?" Joy whispers.

"Wait for me here," I say, lowering my phone to conceal its glaring light.

"In the crypt keeper's Airbnb? Fuck, no!" Her now heelless sandals scrape the uneven ground as she scuttles after me.

With every step we take, the voices grow louder; I can now distinctly pick up Ramirez's flustered bickering with his treacherous goon.

"There has to be a circular structure! This can't be the only chamber."

Jaime's softer pitch answers him. "The tomb's layout is inspired by Egyptian tombs, with a primary, ascending gallery leading here. If there's a second chamber, it's probably been walled . . ."

We're now less than thirty feet from the bend, and the light paints hulking shadows that stretch across the tunnel's walls and the Lions forever sleeping there, as if in death they were once again children in their cot.

Entirely focused on Jaime's and Ramirez's bickering, I don't realize one of the shadows on the wall is growing, moving, until Joy emits a yelp that resonates deep into the tomb and reverberates back at me . . . too late. I smell sweat, Axe soap, and by the time I turn around, a big gloved paw has landed on my shoulder. Pain screams in my elbow as it gets viciously twisted behind my back. Joy's head snaps back as a Lion with angular cheeks covered in freckles fists her tangled mane and grabs her in a chokehold.

My legs kick the sand in a vain attempt to break free and rescue Joy, but there's no point in fighting a pair of trained soldiers twice as big as we are: Axe-man and Evil-Conan drag us in the dark toward the bend in the tunnel, where the dim bowel opens to a tall and narrow rectangular chamber. Lying in the dust, a few LED torches illuminate six stone sarcophagi. The chamber's soaring walls are engraved with winged lions and battle scenes: there, Nergal watches over his first warriors for all eternity.

In addition to the two assholes who jujutsued us in the tunnel, two Lions stand near the ajar lid of a sarcophagus. One of them looks like he could win a bodybuilding competition—he's likely the one who pushed that massive stone lid open. The skull I glimpse underneath looks entirely too human: Ramirez must be beyond disappointed. Swathed in darkness, the side of his face hewn by the glare of a flashlight in Jaime's hands, he's never looked more like a specter. Logan rests in his left arm, three golden claws splayed across the front of his master's leather coat.

Ramirez strokes his goatee with his free hand, a demented gleam in his eyes. "I did mean to spare you, Island. You should have never followed us here." His feverish bass seems to crawl and vibrate directly under my skin as he produces the remote to Joy's bomb collar from his pocket.

Her hands fly to the blinking device; she shakes her head in growing panic. "No! Please!"

All guns swivel to aim at my head when I step forward, but I ignore the threatening glint of their barrels and the emerald flare of their infrared scopes. All the courage I have left is condensed into a single goal: gain time. Just a little more time, another second, maybe two, ticking in tune with the sweat rolling down my temples. "You'll never push that button in here," I say, forcing my voice steady. "You'll never risk destroying the tomb."

I didn't expect the evil cackle that rises next, echoing up to the ceiling of this claustrophobic chamber. "What tomb?" He carefully deposits Logan atop the lid of the half-open sarcophagus and reaches for the skull of the mummified body inside, crushing it in his fist with a sickening crack. "*This* is not what I came here for." Tossing the shattered fragments of the skull to the ground and wiping his hands off one of the first Lions, he growls. "A mere decoy! The real chamber is somewhere . . . close."

Part of me is tempted to appeal to his men's sanity, but I remind myself that they've followed him until now: his discovering this tomb in spite of Stiles's skepticism has probably fueled their blind faith in him. I lock eyes with him. "You can always return with a microwave imager to check what's on the other side of those walls, but we both know that won't happen, right? There's a welcome committee for you outside, ready to kill you. And if you trigger a bomb in here, you'll risk everything you've worked for. Maybe it's time to negotiate with Stiles, don't you think?"

He launches into another round of sinister chuckling. "Negotiate?

Miss Chaptal wants to negotiate with Stiles!" he says like it's the funniest thing he's heard today and he's expecting his men to join in the laughter, but there's not even the slightest quivering of their lips. They probably know better than to take him up on the offer.

He shakes off the last of his amusement and jerks his chin at Jaime. "Which wall?"

Our self-appointed alien expert scurries across the room and flattens his palm to the rugged surface of a low relief of a pride of lions tearing apart a group of enemy soldiers. "If there's a second chamber, it should be facing the south. That's the most logical layout."

"Excellent. Come, come here, my beautiful Bathsheba. Against the wall." He flicks his fingers at Joy, who recoils in response, only to be hauled forward by Evil-Conan.

"What are you doing?" I scream, struggling in the grip of my own captor.

Ramirez bares his incisors at me in the parody of a smile. "We're about to open up a new chamber."

Joy and I realize at the same time that he means to use her as a human bomb. Her eyes search mine, wide with terror, and I'm out of fricking ideas, even as Ramirez's thumb rests on the remote's button. I don't have a plan: spurred by pure instinct, I writhe to sink my teeth in Axe-man's exposed forearm. He gives a roar of agony as I taste salt, then blood. He bats me away like a pesky fly, and I see stars as my back slams against a sarcophagus.

Joy redoubles her struggle against the beefy Lion dragging her toward the wall. He easily blocks her wrist and backhands her when she flings her arm to claw at his face. Her head lolls in shock as he tosses her in place. Her knees buckle before she slides against the rough plane, gripping the collar around her neck. "You're fucking insane! Island!"

The room is spinning fast. I'm seeing double as Ramirez tightens his hold on the remote. Blood and dust seem to cloud my vision in a brown haze, but my ears work fine: they can tell the crack that echoes next in the chamber is not the click of a button . . . but the sound of a bullet tearing through a suppressor.

Ramirez drops the remote with a shout and raises his bleeding hand. My stomach knots when I glimpse a glistening red stump where his forefinger was barely a second ago. His commando reacts instantly and whirls to face the chamber's entrance, but it's already too late for Axe-man: March skidded between two sarcophagi for cover at the same moment he shot off Ramirez's finger to create a diversion. Oh, thank you, Raptor Jesus, who sits in the firmament and loves the taste of blood: he made it. By the time Axe-man aims his Desert Eagle at the now-empty doorway, two bullets explode through his neck, severing his carotids in a cloud of blood.

As the chamber disintegrates into complete chaos and gunshots rattle in all directions, my gaze focuses on the remote that went spinning near the remnants of the first Lion's crushed skull. Joy is huddled in a corner of the room, curled into a shivering ball. Bracing myself against the fear pounding in my temples, I start to crawl toward her, but a flash of dark camo fatigues swipes her away from the line of fire before I can reach her. Angel covers her body with his and raises his gun, sniping Evil-Conan between the eyes in the same fluid movement.

Knowing that he's got Joy gives me the strength I need to act: I roll out of my hiding spot while March is busy trading bullets with the two remaining Lions, who have taken cover between the fifth and sixth sarcophagi. Ramirez and Jaime are nowhere in sight. They might have managed to escape, but the remote is still here, inches away from my fingertips. I claw at the dusty ground, flinching when a bullet smashes into one of the torches and plunges half of the chamber in obscurity.

"I've got it!" I shriek when my fingertips meet the cool plastic fob. "I've got the remote."

Stabbing pain shoots up my leg the moment I've spoken these

fateful words. Certain I've been hit, I look down, searching for the source of the wound. Two vicious black beads stare back at me in the dark. *Logan.*

I grab his furry arms in a desperate effort to pry him off me, even as his metal-coated claws sink deeper into my calf, drawing blood. He tightens his hold with a threatening squeak, and I shift my grip to his head to gouge out his eyes like The Mountain did to Oberyn in Game of Thrones.

Except I don't, because Logan gets latched off me with an inhuman roar by an irate Angel, who rolls away with him. I glimpse golden claws slowly reaching for Angel's jugular before he tosses Logan across the chamber like a football. Relief balloons in my chest as I snatch the remote to Joy's collar at last. I pocket it and look up to see a Lion flying over my head, only to land heavily on one of the sarcophagi.

He was the last man standing, and his career ends when he attempts to recover and fire his last bullets at March. Two of them shatter the martial frieze running along the walls, one hisses past March's hip, tearing his bulletproof jacket in the back. The fourth bullet is March's, a tungsten hollow point that shreds through the Lion's Kevlar and pierces his chest.

March leaps over the half-open sarcophagus and lands at my side. He tucks his guns back in their respective holsters and gingerly probes my calf, where Logan's claw left three bleeding punctures. "Let me look at this, biscuit."

"Is Joy okay?" I croak, turning to see her kneeling by Angel's side. She's breathing, unharmed. All is right once more within my world.

My gaze drifts to the darkened tunnel where the dust is now settling. "Ramirez got away."

"He won't get far: we made it as fast as we could, but Stiles's unit was faster. They've surrounded the perimeter," March says, quickly wiping fresh blood from my skin with one of the mini antibacterial wet wipes that never leave him.

"Those assholes started shooting all over the place," I mutter. "Joy and I nearly didn't make it."

Having stated this, I free myself from March's gentle ministrations with the intent to go hug Joy, who's still hunched over Angel's prone body.

"Island, something is wrong with him," she says, her voice thick with renewed panic.

I get up on my feet, the steady drum under my ribs revving up. She's right. Angel wasn't seriously injured: he should have gotten up by now. March glances in his direction too. His eyes widen in realization.

"Joy!" he shouts, jumping to his feet. "The EpiPen!"

Her eyes widen in realization as Angel's throat bobs from the struggle to draw a whistling breath. His right hand is shaking, too weak to reach the leg pocket of his black cargo pants. Joy rips the pocket open before March has even closed the distance between them, and stabs Angel's thigh without hesitation.

He groans from the sudden pain, but the shot of epinephrine starts working almost immediately after entering his bloodstream. After a minute or so, he's able to draw a full breath. Sweet Raptor Jesus, Logan nearly killed him: Angel is allergic to sloths. I didn't even know that was a medical condition you could have.

Joy stays at his side, stroking his sweat-soaked forehead while he recovers, and March holds out a hand for him. "Can you get up?"

A vein pulses angrily in Angel's neck. I suspect he'd have wanted March to mind his own business while Joy petted him and cooed soft thanks for saving her, but he takes the proffered hand nonetheless and allows March to haul him to a standing position.

"Are you sure you're okay?" Joy asks, watching him with a wrinkle between her eyebrows. I hate to say this, but knowing her, I think that discovering he had a weakness has only served to make him more attractive in her eyes.

"Yes." His charcoal gaze swipes around the chamber, alight with the flames of revenge. "The sloth got away."

"Maybe you can find him and kill him later," Joy says softly, resting her hand on his forearm. "I'd really like for someone to take this off me."

"I believe that can be arranged on short notice," March says, eyeing the tunnel, where a flurry of laser pointers are now swiping the walls.

Moments after, a squad of a dozen Lions in full tactical gear barges in, taking in the devastation inside the chamber. My first impulse is to reach out to shove Joy out of the way, but March stops me with a hand on my shoulder. A single squeeze and a slight shake of his head are all the reassurance I need: these aren't part of Ramirez's commando. Their leader, a black guy in his forties, lifts his infrared goggles and locks eyes with March. "Come with us," he simply says.

But Joy, who has every reason to be cautious considering how bad her weekend has been going so far, clings to Angel's arm and remains bolted in place. "Is this going to be another bloodbath with people firing missiles all over the place?"

Before the team leader can reply, a gravelly voice cheers from the back of the formation. "Are you Joy Richards?"

Joy's face bunches in wary curiosity. "Uhm, yeah?"

"We love your Instagram!"

This enthusiastic review, backed by a few understated nods among the rest of the squad, comes from a guy with a graying buzz-cut, whose deep crow's feet and open expression seem familiar. I squint my eyes at him. "Louis, is that you?"

For Joy and Angel's benefit, I say, "I've met him before: he works directly for Stiles."

March shakes his head. "I never knew you had such a broad following base."

"Neither did I," she replies as those legit, card-carrying Lions escort us out of the tomb.

March was right: the first thing I see when I step out is Ramirez, held at gunpoint by three Lions, while Jaime cowers between two others. Several armored trucks have made their appearance in the gorge while we were fighting for our lives. In front of one of them stands a "friend."

All baby-blue eyes and candid geniality in his bland, gray three-piece suit, Stiles came in person to clean up his mess.

THIRTY-THREE
THE BAKE SALE

"Well, we branch in a variety of sectors. As I always tell Ron: gotta make sure not to keep all your aliens in the same spaceship."

– Anonymous interview with Mr. S, *Aliens in Our Past: The Truth Revealed*, season 19, episode 13. SciFi Unlimited.

Stiles's features light up the moment he sees us. I keep my expression carefully blank in return. Ignoring him as he walks to us, I perform a quick scan of the players. Stiles showed up with a small army—I think Ramirez pissed him off more than he lets on. A dozen of Angel's men are here too, engaged in a stare-off with the Lions. Anies used to encroach on Angel's territory between the Ecuadorian and Colombian borders: the Lions did a number on Angel's troops at the time, and the enmity isn't going to wane anytime soon. Everyone has their forefinger poised on the trigger, waiting for the slightest hint that the other party cannot be trusted.

I spot Stiles's second favorite standing near the trucks, a blond bearded killing machine who insists on wearing sunglasses even at night, but Stiles's cats are nowhere in sight: that means he's dead serious and shit is about to go down.

Stiles meets us at the foot of the slope leading down the tomb's entrance. His first words are for Angel, who's glaring at him as if that might be enough to reduce him to dust. "We owe you, Mr. Somoza. I think that fruitful collaboration will seal a lasting peace between our families, right?"

Angel's fingers twitch—probably itching to reach for his gun in its holster. "I didn't do it for you. If I ever see one of your men on my territory again, it's *his* skin I'll send you."

Stiles gives a boyish wince. "I can work with that."

When he turns his attention to me, opening his arms wide, I leap back behind March's solid frame. "I'm not hugging you."

March's eyes narrow dangerously. "Indeed."

"But I came to rescue you," Stiles contends.

"Your men didn't give a damn about Joy and me when they raided the ruins: they nearly killed us. I bet you told them we were expendable as long as they managed to catch Ramirez."

He tilts his head, his mouth curving down in a sad pout. "Island, I think you're reading too much into this."

"Sure . . ."

March tips his chin to Ramirez. "I believe you have what you want. The tombs are inside. This is undeniably one of the brotherhood's early temples."

Ramirez chooses this moment to turn to us. Raising his bleeding fist defiantly, he roars for all his former brothers to hear, "If I must die tonight, let it be remembered that I died after having found the tomb of the hallowed first brothers, and that I was murdered by a usurper!"

March's jaw clenches a little tighter as he draws, I suppose, the same conclusions I just did: Ramirez's mania doesn't just feed on ancient aliens conspiracy theories. He's obviously part of a minority that didn't approve of Stiles's takeover last year. I wonder if he knows Stiles poisoned Anies to steal his throne faster . . .

Stiles levels a look of pure benevolence at his wayward brother and tells us, "Give me a second, will you?"

All eyes follow him as he approaches Ramirez, his features relaxing into a cold, absent mask. The strings holding his act together have snapped; that much becomes obvious when he reaches out a hand for Ramirez to shake.

Ramirez carefully lowers his left, intact hand, but Stiles gives a shake of his head. Nausea pushes at the back of my throat when Ramirez understands and offers his bleeding hand instead. Stiles takes it, looking him straight in the eye as he crushes his fingers in his strong grasp, his thumb digging into the protruding broken bone where March's bullet tore Ramirez's forefinger off. And the handshake lasts, unbearable to watch, and Stiles never breaks eye contact as blood oozes between their joined hands and Ramirez shudders in agony.

Stiles's lips move; I can't hear what he's telling Ramirez, but I can imagine. He's the commander, Ramirez betrayed him, and now he's called him a usurper in front of his men: I don't even think Stiles derives any pleasure from this gruesome display. To him, it's just another workday, and he needs to discipline an employee to make a statement to the rest of the company.

When he finally lets go, Joy has turned a pasty white. "So, that's their boss? The one who kidnapped you?"

I answer with a tight nod while her hand reaches to take mine, warm and comforting.

The sickening handshake being over, Ramirez staggers back, heedless of the guns pointed at him. His left hand dives to take something inside his coat; the Lion closest to him presses the trigger without hesitation, shattering his kneecaps. Blood splashes the sandstone, black as ink under the blueish hue of the trucks' headlights. The automatic rifle's brief rattle seems to echo endlessly in the silent gorge, in tune with Ramirez's howl of pain as he collapses like a disarticulated doll. Joy's hand leaves mine to clasp over her mouth. I look away. I don't know if he deserved it; I don't want to see.

Stiles shakes his head and turns around. "Lead the way, please. I want to see the tomb," he tells Louis, back to his affable self.

"Stiles!" Ramirez shouts, the sound like broken glass ripping out of his throat. "This truth will never be yours!" With this, he reaches inside his coat once more, and this time succeeds.

A ball of flames paints the night gold and red before I glimpse a flash of Stiles and several Lions flying backward. The deep-seated vibrations of a sudden shock wave wash over us as Ramirez self-detonates in a deafening boom. March and I lunge to the ground for cover, imitated by Angel, who all but tackles a bewildered Joy, even as a second deflagration thunders from deep inside the tomb.

In a split second, I see again that half-open sarcophagus in the chamber. Did he place something in it in case he'd fail? My question is answered by a threatening rumble coming from the heart of the hill before the tomb's entrance starts vomiting rocks. I'm reeling from the vertiginous realization that Ramirez blew it all up. This is a classic case of "if I can't have it, no one will," and he's going to kill us all over a failed venture that cost him his life in the first place.

"We need to get out of here," March grits out, helping me up.

Joy scrambles to her feet with Angel's help, and her eyes pop wide, set at a point past my shoulder. "The cars!"

That was half-a-second before a sizeable chunk of the hill's wall collapses and barrels down the slope. Boulders the size of a dishwasher roll down and smash into the half-dozen trucks crammed in the gorge, bending their steel armor like it's a sheet of aluminum. The Lions make a run for the trucks that remain intact, but one of them gets crushed under a renewed torrent of rubble before the engine can even start.

"Ramirez was right. There must be another larger cavity inside the hill; it's collapsing on itself!" I tell March, trying—and failing—to filter the panic out of my voice.

"Island!"

Our heads whip around at the sound of Stiles's cheerful yet urgent call. He points to Ramirez's helicopter further down the gorge that's been spared by the first volley of boulders. New cracks snake up the hill's side on each side of the tomb's entrance; it won't hold for very long.

"I vote Joe Exotic," Joy decrees in the face of March and Angel's hesitation.

That seals our fate: the four of us race toward the chopper as the ground shakes under our feet, announcing an imminent cataclysm. The blades start spinning, raising a sandstorm that nearly blinds me. Particles swirl and shimmer in the helicopter beam light, and I'm so sure I won't make it until I feel March's hands lifting me from the ground like a potato bag before he tosses me inside the cabin.

I blink and see Joy's and Angel's faces above me. She's trying to smile, and I register Stiles's voice coming from the front passenger seat as we prepare to rise above what's left of the first brothers' tomb. After I've managed to hoist myself to a sitting position and buckle up in my seat, I realize that Louis and four other Lions have joined in on the ride. I cast a frantic look around, my heart beating painfully in my ears as I search for March. Across from me, Joy yells something over the din of the rotor, pointing at the pilot seat. He's in there, holding the yoke. Thank you for always being on top of things, Raptor Jesus.

My muscles loosen from an incipient sense of relief until a shrill, desperate scream rises up from the rumbling rocks and the dark clouds of sands. Jaime emerges from the chaos, running toward the helicopter while behind him, the slopes of the gorge are shuddering and merging together like a riptide.

Even a crap historian with dubious work ethics doesn't deserve this. "The ladder! Toss him the ladder!" I yell.

True to his unforgiving self, Angel doesn't move an eyelash to help. Neither do the Lions, except for Louis, who nods at me and hooks the ladder in place while I unroll the nylon ropes holding together sturdy metal rungs. Twenty feet below, Jaime stumbles, catches himself up, and claws at the air until a sharp tug tells us he's got the first rung. We're gaining altitude, but March isn't speeding up yet: he's giving Jaime a fighting chance as he starts a life-or-death climb.

"We need to move," Angel tells March in the headset.

"I'm well aware," March shoots back. But we remain stationary.

Joy leans over Angel to catch a glimpse of Jaime's life-or-death stunt, and I chew on my nails watching him grip another rung. Just when I think he might make it, one of his hands lets go of the rung, and he slips downward with a chilling scream. I lean out the open door as much as my seat will allow. He's still holding on, but there's a shadow . . .

"Holy fucking shit, Logan's got him!" Joy shrieks, sparking some new level of interest in Jaime's fate amid our companions.

"Really?" Stiles asks in our headset. He can't see what's happening from the front.

"Yeah! Give me something, a gun, anything! We need to unlatch him!" I don't really want to have to kill a sloth—even that one—but my stomach twists at the sight of Jaime gripping the rung desperately with one hand while Logan has sunk his golden claws in his back— possibly in a misguided attempt to avenge his master's death. I mean, it's not like Jaime had anything to do with that part.

I'm starting to think I'm gonna have to go down there myself, when a dusty, black object flies my way. Joy just tossed me one of her sandals. Our eyes meet in understanding before I snipe Logan with a throw worthy of Tom Brady. Jaime screams again, louder. I clasp my hands over my mouth when I realize I missed and hit him with Joy's shoe. As if he wasn't in enough trouble as it is.

Joy is removing her remaining sandal when, at last, Angel moves. He draws out his semi-automatic. "I'll end this."

The part of me that's been sensitized by PETA campaigns and cute memes wants to stop him, but Jaime is still howling, pleading for help down there while Logan lacerates his back. We can't risk hovering in that unstable gorge any longer. We need to do something.

Angel braces his left arm against the helicopter's doorway and aims at Logan, who looks up. Their eyes meet in darkness. Logan's beatific smile never wavers as Angel's finger tightens around the trigger and prepares to take out his greatest foe, the sum of all his weaknesses. A squeak echoes in the night. Before Angel has a chance to shoot, Logan stabs his claws deeper in Jaime's shoulder, making him drop the ladder.

I watch in horror as they tumble together, swallowed by the cloud of dust raised by the hill's collapse. Angel releases a husky breath as he holsters back his gun. "He chose to die like a man," he says, a touch of reluctant admiration in his voice.

"No one liked Logan except Ramirez," Louis blurts out in our headsets. A fitting epitaph, I guess.

"It's always been a problem," Stiles concurs. "It's just not the sort of image we want to project."

I shake my head at their cold-blooded assessment and raise tired eyes at Joy, who smiles back. "We made it," I say. "And you were totally awesome back there."

She flashes Angel a playful side-eye. "Well, I don't want to toot my own horn, but yeah, I was awesome."

"Wonderful." Louis bobs his head in earnest agreement, imitated by Stiles and his stoic right-hand man.

Pricked, Angel rolls his shoulders threateningly, incinerating Louis with the Stare. "You're going to delete Instagram from your phone."

"No, he's not." Joy's face pinches defiantly. "Don't threaten my followers."

My lips purse to suppress a smile while they quietly fuss about Joy's social media presence and eventually engage in a staring contest. He won't get her off Instagram. Not with all the glaring in the world.

"It's a considerable loss." March's voice echoes in my headset as I, too, look out the window at the now-distant outline of the ruins we left behind. One half of the gorge caved in completely. The Coptic chapels were miraculously spared, but that's pretty all that's left in the aftermath of the destruction of the first Lions' tomb.

"Yeah . . . what a waste," I sigh in return.

The exhaustion I've kept at bay until now takes over my limbs, along with a sudden sense of failure. Ramirez's rebels died for nothing since the tomb has probably been destroyed beyond repair. All the anonymous Lions who rested there are lost to history for good, in spite of Cornellà's commendable—if not psychotic—efforts to carry their memory through time. Ramirez and Jaime died stupidly, and Logan died kind of heroically but doing the wrong thing, so I'm not sure it's any better.

"Damn, that's a lot of rubble to clean up for us, gentlemen," Stiles comments, as if he could read my thoughts.

Joy leans over Angel's lap to take a look, and I wish he'd look less comfortable with her half-straddling his lap. "Good luck with that . . ."

"Now, don't underestimate us," Stiles chides. But there's gravity in his gaze as he beholds the ruins. This is perhaps the first and only peek I'll ever get at the man under the many masks. "The Collegium is gonna be busy for a decade, and it's gonna take a hell of a bake sale to pay for it."

My head jerks up. "You guys do bake sales?"

"We've been experimenting with the concept," Stiles replies evasively.

In what must be a rare display of insubordination, blondie-sunglasses speaks up, the words wrought in his South African accent.

"It was a disaster. The kids were crying. Let's not do that again."

I shake my head. This, indeed, has Stiles written all over it. "Here's another idea," I say. "Why don't you co-produce a groundbreaking documentary about ancient astronauts and share the profits?"

"Share them with whom?" Stiles asks.

"Ecuapasión," Angel replies, his features set in his villain face #1.

Stiles turns around in his seat, his brow pinched in curiosity. "Go on."

THIRTY-FOUR
THE TSAR'S STONE

*"If he had just asked, I would have gladly become his bitch
for all eternity."*

— *Manila Clonk,* Clean Shot: A Hitman Romance

We landed on the tarmac of Cairo International airport, at the edge of the desert, where the sand never ceases to try to conquer the runway. Stiles is off doing his dark bidding—which includes taking over Angel's investment in Franz's documentary. He says he has great ideas for the script, so Angel agreed to sell him the contract. Franz will probably have an aneurysm when he learns that his new co-producer is the actual Collegium.

The night breeze plays in my hair as I watch the helicopter rise once more. Stiles and I didn't exactly make peace: I'm still pretty sure his Lions had orders to shoot Joy to get to Ramirez if necessary—Instagram fans or not. Yet, seeing him in the flesh had an unexpected cathartic effect on me. I can honestly say I'm no longer afraid of him. He'll never change, but I can deal with his personal brand of sociopathy. Speaking of which, he exchanged a few words with Joy under Angel's seething gaze before leaving. I think he was trying to get her number, but she dodged his attempt. She says he's cute but he's serial killer material: she's learning the ropes fast.

Angel's goddamn Concorde awaits on the tarmac: he said he'd fly Joy back to New York. They should be taking off soon, but first, March went on an errand to get a new passport for her, from a Jordanian guy who used to be in the military, but now shuttles back and forth across the Suez canal to deliver "things" to "people." What a resume.

For now, Mr. Somoza and Joy are studying each other from a distance. Him, at the top of the airstair, waiting. Her, barefoot in her dusty coveralls, twirling a blonde curl between her fingers as she contemplates all he can offer . . . and what he cannot. She eventually breaks that odd spell between them and turns to me, her eyes bright, exhausted. "I think I'm actually still in shock."

"You are," I confirm. "You're holding on for now because things keep moving fast and you're not really given any time to process any of it. Once it's over and you sit down . . . It's gonna be really weird."

"After Tokyo, you cried in bed for a week," she recounts. "I thought all that ice cream would fuck up your system. I started feeding you sugar-free cartons on the third day; I don't think you noticed."

"I did. But I didn't even have the courage to go to the store to get my fix."

A sigh breezes past her lips, stirring a stray curl on her cheek. "It was different for you. March had just dumped you, so you were dealing with twice the trauma."

"True."

"I'm not getting any trauma over Angel."

A bold lie has been spoken. I stare ahead, studying the incriminated party. "At first, I was super pissed when I realized he was coming on to you," I admit. "I was borderline paranoid he'd rape you or something."

She coughs an exaggerated chuckle. "Oh, wow. No. He has a host of issues, but honestly, I don't frame him as the rapey type. He's kind of . . ." Her mouth twists as she searches for the best description. "I know I'm gonna sound like a judgmental bitch, but here goes: half of him is basically every single ultra-conservative Christian nerd I wouldn't have touched with a ten-foot pole back in college. And the other half is everything that turns me on now that I've got some mileage, red flags included. All fused together so you can't get one without the other." She frowns. "I'm not sure why I like that so much."

"Because you're in that phase where you want a rebound who's Vince's polar opposite," I venture.

"Nah, he's not a rebound. When I want a rebound, I just go for the lowest hanging fruit, like, the gym bro who sends me a chest selfie and a shitty one-liner."

"I know." I don't dare to tell her that we're literally talking about Vince right now, and that she met him right after her Pilates teacher dumped her—and even he was, in fact, the last in a series of heated trysts all meant to wipe the unholy memory of David-the-clown-dick-accountant.

She hugs herself, her fingers worrying the fabric of her coveralls. "I'm not jumping from rebound to rebound and fucking up what's left of my twenties, am I?" Her gaze drifts back to the Concorde's ethereal hull line. "I mean, I still have my job, at least until I open my mailbox and I deal with what's inside. Also, I need to terminate my lease and move out of our old place now that I'm on my own." Her throat bobs once, twice. Her eyes grow glassy; she blinks the moisture back.

I pull her into a loose hug, rubbing her back. "Do you know what I'd do if I were in your place?"

"Tell me."

"I wouldn't take my advice, because you are not me, and Angel isn't March."

Her mouth cracks into a nervous grin. "That really helped, thanks."

"You're welcome. Jiminy cricket is always sitting on your shoulder."

"No one ever seems to notice that he must have made some shitty life decisions to be so broke at the start of the movie, by the way. I say drugs were involved."

I purse my lips in approval. "Right?"

While we debate the many failings of Disney's oldest offerings, March comes through the doors of the jet terminal and walks to us, his shirtsleeves impeccably rolled up and a brand-new passport in hand. He places it in Joy's upturned palm. "You are now free to go home, Miss Richards."

She flashes him a coy grin. "Thank you, Mr. November."

Her eyes dart to the Concorde's airstair once more. Angel seeks her gaze but makes no move to invite her. The choice is hers, and hers alone—something I should have figured out much sooner. Her head lolls slightly as she ponders her decision, then she whirls around without warning and pulls me into a tight hug. I return the embrace, patting her back awkwardly.

"I'll send you hourly reports," she whispers.

"I don't need all the details."

"You're getting them anyway," she assures me before walking away toward the airstair.

March and I watch her go together, kinda like we're sending off our first kid to college. Except our kid is twenty-eight, and we just gave our blessing for her to start an explosive affair with a temperamental arms dealer.

"He's not flying her back to New York, is he?" I muse as Joy climbs the airstair.

"Probably not. He knows what he wants and goes for it."

I rise on tiptoes to kiss his jaw. "Do I detect a trace of admiration in this statement?"

March looks away from Joy and Angel as they enter the plane. "Back when we were together in Tokyo . . . if I had been a different man, more like him, I suppose, I would have taken you somewhere without any regard for the consequences. I wanted to, but it didn't seem reasonable at the time."

"Maybe it was better this way," I rationalize. "I needed to grow up a little, to know I wanted you for you and not just because you were some Prince Charming who had come out of nowhere and swept me off my feet. You gave me time and space when I didn't realize I needed those, and looking back on it, I'm grateful for that."

He raises an incredulous eyebrow. "Really?"

"Nah. All those days I spent crying, I would have hurled my tub of chocolate ice cream at you if you'd suddenly entered the room."

He nods to himself. "I thought so. Island."

"Yes?"

"I love you. You're . . . everything to me."

I'm taken aback. March is rarely—if ever—that direct. "You know I love you too."

"And there's something I've been meaning to talk to you about, but there's been the gerbil, then Joy, Franz and Ramirez, Stiles and his bake sales, and I haven't had a second to . . ."

He sighs and fishes for something in his jeans pocket. I understand before I've even identified the sober black velvet of a small ring box. I bite down on my lower lip, my face scrunching as I try in vain not to cry. As March's left reaches to wipe the salty trails on my cheeks, I know I've lost the fight.

"Biscuit, please don't cry," he murmurs.

An ecstatic shriek reverberates across the tarmac. Joy was about to walk into the Concorde's cabin, but she spotted the box—girls apparently have a sixth sense designed just for those. "Oh my God, he's doing it! Angel, give me your phone!"

March endures her antics stoically, but I think he really wants her to get on that plane and let him finish. No such luck.

Joy squeals, "I'm filming everything! Island Chaptal And The Ancient Aliens' Treasure, take one! Show us that bling!"

Angel runs a hand over his beard—to conceal a smile, I suspect. "Why do I get dragged in your mess again, South African? Get on one knee so I can get my phone back and erase that video."

March narrows his eyes at him, a tense smile tugging at his lips. And against all odds—and all rules regarding public displays of affection—he gets on one knee on the tarmac of Cairo international, under Joy's cheers. He clears his throat. "Island. I haven't yet asked your father for your hand in marriage because there's little doubt he'll refuse and possibly file a restraining order against me."

I shake my head frantically, mouthing the words, "It's okay" as he opens the ring box, revealing a sober and dainty solitaire. Mounted on a gold band is a small emerald cushion, shimmering with blueish undertones.

We're looking in each other's eyes. Like when we fight, when we make love. March's lips part, hesitate.

I can't take another second of this suspense. "You know it's yes," I sob. "Of course, it's yes!"

His dimples appear as he cradles my fingers in his and slips the solitaire around my left ring finger. "For the sake of proper form: Island Chaptal, will you do me the honor of becoming my wife?"

"Yes, dammit!" I squeak, flinging my arms around his neck.

March leans to nuzzle my nose in the guise of an approval. I know I'm not getting a proper French kiss with Joy filming everything, but I go for the next best thing and run my fingers in his hair, soft there, bristly on his nape. And it all feels so right. Especially the fuzz on his ears. That's one of the first things I noticed about this man: he has top-grade fuzz.

I indulge in some ogling of my newly adorned ring finger. As it catches the glare from the headlights of a passing luggage truck, the stone turns purple, some of its facets flaring a crimson red.

"Oh my God . . . It's an alexandrite!"

March's blissful smile grows impish—apparently, the surprise played out as he expected. "Indeed. It changes colors depending on the light you expose it to. Beautiful, unpredictable and, according to modern lore . . . capable of bringing joy to people with too much self-discipline."

"You can't be serious."

He stifles a laugh. "My decision was made the moment I read that particular detail."

"This is even cooler than a mood ring," I decree, swirling my hand in all directions to catch what little light I can. Once the sun is up, I'm gonna play with it all day long.

Meanwhile, a low hum alerts me to the fact that Joy finally has consented to enter the Concorde, which is now getting ready to take off. As if a final thread tethering me to her just snapped, I suddenly feel a little empty. "She's taking off," I murmur, watching the jet glide toward the dusty runway. "What do we do if they actually get serious?"

March crosses his arms and tilts his head at the departing Concorde. "Well, I suppose Angel will have to sharpen his Uno skills." His eyes darken with the promise of agony. "Our battle will be legendary."

My answering giggle dies in my throat as I notice a deep line between his eyebrows. He's exhausted. There's not enough light in the blue of his eyes, and it tugs at my heart when he pushes himself beyond his limits like this. I reach for his hand and give it a squeeze. "You know what? Let's spend the rest of the week in bed."

"The suggestion has appeal," he admits, running a hand over the five o'clock shadow on his jaw. "But Mr. Franz called Phyllis with a reminder that he expects you on set tomorrow at dawn."

I stroke his forearm tentatively. "Is that okay with you, or do you prefer to return to Cairo? I understand if you want to ditch the whole documentary thing altogether."

His lips stir knowingly. "Do *you* want to go?"

"Well . . ." Twelve hours ago, when Gualtiero Franz's quest was little more than an obstacle, then an accessory to Joy's rescue, I'd have given anything to be rid of him and his aliens. But now that Joy is safe—or rather at Angel's mercy—and that my adrenaline levels have crashed, it's starting to hit me that I've been offered a role in *Aliens. In. Our. Goddamn. Past.* Me, against a classy desert background—or maybe a nice shot of the Milky Way—telling my truth, sharing my thoughts on extraterrestrial life with millions of avid viewers!

My lips part to answer March's question, but he already knows what I'm going to say. His features set in a mock-severe expression. "I'm afraid there's no way out of this contract, Miss Chaptal."

I look up at the star-studded sky, where veils of dark clouds are slowly stirring. "I know. If I flake out, mankind will never know the truth."

THIRTY-FIVE
ARRIVAL

"I can't go into any specifics, but yes, a few fine gentlemen from the Collegium were there to greet them when they landed."

– Anonymous interview with Mr. S, *Aliens in Our Past: The Truth Revealed*, season 19, episode 13. SciFi Unlimited.

It was all worth it. Flying halfway around the world twice in less than forty-eight hours, sacrificing my best friend to a crime lord, meeting Gualtiero Franz and battling Ramirez, watching his sloth commit suicide, skipping dinner and eating Snickers from the minibar instead. It all led me right here and now, watching the glowing outline of the third-quarter moon veiled in clouds behind the pyramids.

We found a hotel standing at the very edge of the desert, whose windows and balconies face the Giza complex. The receptionist was a little surprised to see us show up past midnight, but there was a good Turkish soap playing on the TV behind his desk, so he expedited our check-in to get back to it—he nearly missed the torrid kiss between the hunky businessman and the beautiful redhead.

It was so worth it, I think for the thousandth time as I study the alexandrite on my ring finger. In the garden below, a warm breeze ruffles the fronds of a few palm trees and wrinkles the oily surface of a deserted swimming pool. I feel it on my cheeks, in my hair, playing with the light cotton of a shirt I stole from March's suitcase—as is my God-given girlfriend right.

I could stay on that balcony all night long, but when I turn around and see him lying in bed, the moonlight playing with every slope and hill of this body I know and love so much, I can't resist padding back inside. He's not asleep; he's typing a message on his phone, but he sets it aside on the nightstand as soon as I step onto the room's cool tiled floor.

"Still working?" I ask, joining him under the sheets and molding my body to his.

He sighs, but no words come out. Instead, he draws me close and presses his lips to my hair.

I inhale the scent of soap and male skin and close my eyes, attuned to the warmth and the silence between us. There's something he won't tell me—can't tell me. I know it from the way he's holding me, the way he strokes my arm, over and over. "You know," I begin. "When I need to tell you something important and big words won't come, I usually try with small ones first."

March's lips slowly drift to my ear shell, then my temple. His voice is a little rough as he replies, "I texted him to tell him we're engaged. I have no idea why I did that."

I shift to look up at him, confused. The first face that painted itself in my mind when March said "him" was Dries's, but Dries is gone. *Him.* A man March can't even bring himself to name.

My chest grows tight as I search his gaze. His irises are the same color as the night, mottled with the lighter blue of the milky way. "Did you text your dad?"

He gives the slightest nod.

I'm . . . stunned. I wasn't even sure March's father was alive. To the best of my knowledge, they haven't talked since March left the house at the age of fourteen. A small-time British drug dealer, March's dad fled Manchester for Cape Town in his twenties, after one too many business ventures gone wrong. That's where he met March's mom. Barely out of childhood, she had escaped the suffocating comfort of her father's farming estate in the north for a taste of freedom in Cape Town's underground clubs. In the dark, where no one enforced apartheid laws, it was easier to forget about the recession that would soon hit, about political prisoners, blood, and bombings.

There was music and drugs: she loved both.

I don't know if she and March's dad were ever truly happy. All I know is that she fell pregnant at the age of seventeen and gave birth to a little boy she called March because she liked that month of the year. She could have tried contacting her family, asked for help; she never did. She stayed with March's dad, in a dilapidated flat that stood not far from the township of Lavender Hill. Too young and too high, too often, March's mom was virtually incapable of taking care of him, so he took care of her instead, and cleaned their house because the filth they lived in drove his father crazy whenever he was home.

She overdosed before the age of thirty, on speedballs March's dad had given her. March never talks about him: I don't even know his first name.

I stroke his cheek, his hair, over and over, as if that could heal all those old, invisible scars. "Did he reply?"

"No."

There's a part of me that wants to tell March that South Africa is in the same time zone as Egypt, so it's pretty late there, and maybe his dad is asleep, or maybe he's somewhere else in the world and none of the above apply. I bite back the rant before it has a chance to escape me. That's not what March needs. He knows all this, and he's probably torturing his braincells with the same flowchart I'm mentally crafting right now.

I shift to nuzzle his cheek. "You took the first step, and that's what matters the most." His embrace tightens a fraction, but I sense I haven't found the words he needs yet. This isn't about getting a participation prize for reaching out to his father. It goes so much deeper than that, and he chose to do it tonight because . . .

Have you ever given serious thought to the subject?

We're looking into each other's eyes, like when we fight, when we make love, and I think I get it, now. I release a trembling breath and give it a second try. "You took the first step, because you won't be the same father that he was."

His chest heaves, and there it is again, that damn little wrinkle on his brow. "How can you know?"

"Because I know you; I trust you. And look at how well you're doing with Gerald!" That earns me the rise of a skeptical eyebrow, but I trudge on anyway. "He's a problem child. Like . . . Chucky, or Damian, but you're taking great care of him. Honestly, if you just do the same with our kids, they'll grow up perfectly fine."

A dimpled smile lights up his features. "Are you advising me to spray them with fertilizer?"

"We could also buy a scratch tower."

A quiet chuckle shakes his shoulders before he reaches to stroke my cheek with the back of his knuckles. "I didn't realize you were this prepared."

He says it like a question. Like he needs an answer, so I touch my lips to his and whisper, "I am."

The first kiss is a soft, tentative brush of our mouths. His best friend—and ex—told me a long time ago that March wasn't a volcano. I beg to differ: it's subtler than that. In truth, the fire never leaves him. It's a flame that continually consumes long-buried anger and regrets, anxious joy and desire . . . I feel it in the heat of his skin under my fingertips, right under the surface, and ever ready to consume him.

All it takes is a spark. Like a bite to his lower lip, just hard enough to rouse him, and the kiss becomes different, wetter, more aggressive. I can taste the lingering sweetness of toothpaste on his cupid's bow, the mineral flavor of saliva on our tongues. His fingers thread in my hair, massaging my scalp as he covers my body with his. His cheeks are a little rough when I cradle them. He needs a shave, but I won't ruin the moment and tell him that: I need him too much right now.

"*J'ai envie de toi*," I want you, I whimper, hooking clumsy fingers in his boxer briefs.

I could almost scream in frustration when he pulls my shirt over my head, but his hands pause on the hem of my panties. His throat bobs as he casts a sideways glance at his suitcase that's sitting on a luggage rack across the room.

He didn't take out the condoms.

I left the window open earlier. A cool draft invites itself into the room and stirs the curtains. Atop mine, March's body feels warm and a little heavy. There it is again, that silent question in his eyes, all the things he won't say because we don't put big words on our desire, on the way we wear it like a second skin and it suffuses our love even when we're apart.

It's a quiet storm ever raging between us, something most people never notice when they see us watering Gerald or soldiering through all of March's cleaning rituals like an old couple. A safe and loving routine where I always carry mini wipes, where he almost never loses his cool, and never forgets the condoms.

I wrap my arms around his neck to bring him closer. Because, of course, it's yes.

His breath is a little short as he asks, "Are you sure?"

Nuzzling his chin, I work his boxer shorts down his hips and discreetly toe them under the covers—I know that if March doesn't notice the dark patch of fabric glaring against white sheets, he won't be so tempted to pick them up and go fold them on a chair. I smile at him in the dark. "We have a contingency plan ready, right?"

He molds his naked body to mine, warm all over. He reaches to cradle my hand in his, delicately rubbing my ring with the pad of his forefinger. "You're wearing it. All fifty slides of it."

I hear myself giggle before my panties come off with a sharp tug; then we're skin to skin, and our embrace grows desperate, messy in the way March so rarely allows, even in bed. I stroke the silky bristles on his nape as he kisses my neck, my breasts. There's some nipping and sucking on his part that will leave secret love bites under my clothes, some clawing on mine that makes his spine bow as if for me to better score it.

I love when it's like this, when my curls fall in my eyes and his hands are all over me. I crave the rustling of cotton sheets as I grip them, the whisper of his palms against my skin. I love that when he hooks his arms under my thighs, I feel his strength, his biceps coiling as he locks my hips in place against his mouth. I writhe and shudder from that most intimate kiss, arch off the bed and grip his head. It's too much and never enough, his tongue circling a single incandescent spot with the same clockwork dedication he puts into everything he does. He won't stop until I'm in shambles, until I beg him to.

But I don't want to crash down just yet. I push his forehead with shaking hands, manage a gasping moan. "Stop . . . Please stop."

He raises his head from between my thighs with a devilish smile, licking his lips like a sated cat. "Already? I was under the impression we weren't quite done."

I give another nudge when he lowers his head for another decadent kiss. "Please, I want to touch you."

He lingers between my thighs, his damp chin brushing sensitive skin there. He doesn't always let me touch him. Often, he'll kiss me and gently hinder my hands or my lips. On the surface, it's a matter of being a gentleman, of putting me first, but under all his layers, and amid the tender skirmish of our fingers, I know it's always ultimately about control: even with me, even in the dark, March is still afraid to let go sometimes.

Trying to read his mood as he crawls back up to be at eye level with me, I risk a hand between our bodies. Pure delight fizzles up my spine when he rolls onto his back, defenseless. *Tonight, it's yes.* His eyes track my movements, watchful sapphires in the dark as I scoot closer and let my fingertips skitter across my kingdom. It's a changing landscape of muscles, veins, and scars. Dents where he was shot, and I thought I had lost him forever. Grooves left by knife cuts, the smooth feel of an old burn on his left arm, and, of course, fields of untamed, silky hair everywhere on his chest.

My hands linger there, reveling in the curls coiling around my fingers, in the need I can breathe in the air between us. I bend to nuzzle his lips, his chin. March raises his head to catch my mouth, steal a brief taste.

"You know . . ." I murmur, my fingers skimming along the trail of hair on his abs. "I'm still obsessed with it."

The hit man is but a man: for a fraction of a second his focus lowers to where he needs my touch the most. "And it's a passion I'll never try to discourage," he says, his stomach rippling in anticipation.

Still petting the holy rug, I bite back a giggle. The moment he gets it, he throws his head back with a husky laugh that becomes a gasp as I stroke him at last. Hot silk pulses in the cradle of my hand until he can no longer speak: he manages a quiet groan as his hips roll to the rhythm of my caresses. I kiss him, taste him a little too, and he lets me. That, too, we don't do often, and already his fingers twirl in my hair, graze my cheek in a silent plea to stop.

It's the same for him: too much, too close, too soon. When he props himself on his elbows with the obvious intent to roll atop me and bring this voluptuous game to its natural conclusion, I press a hand to his chest to stop him.

March leans back to gaze into my eyes and trails the back of his knuckles along my jaw with an expression of earnest wonder, as if he meant to pierce a mystery he still hasn't solved. I kiss his hands before they glide down to my breasts, my stomach. His palms eventually settle on the small of my back, guiding me to straddle him. I wish I were a sex goddess who just moves into place magically, but there's a little wiggling, a little fumbling. Until I feel him . . . completely, and my heart is beating so loud because this is the closest we'll ever be. I want to say something, but my lips move quietly, unable to produce a sound.

He kneads my flesh, his features taut from sudden bliss. "Island . . ."

"Yes," I gasp, even as I'm being quietly shattered by a barrage of emotions and sensations I can't name.

March can't find his words either. He sits up in one powerful motion and buries his face in the crook of my neck, kissing the fluttering pulse under my skin. A gust drifting through the curtains send shivers running up and down my spine, I jolt, and my body starts moving of its own volition, so intimately attuned to his. He draws a quiet groan and just holds on to me, breathless as I make love to him. He squeezes my waist a little too tight, as if I were a bird he needed to keep from flying away. I cover his hands with mine in response and press harder against him as his hips buck to meet mine. Over and over.

"Biscuit . . . I'm close." The words escape him in a strangled hiss, straining the tendons in his neck, and I want more of that urgent, messy, sticky connection between us. I need to feel my heart pounding against his. And God, I need more of that pressure slowly building inside me, right where our bodies meet. I collapse, rise again, in a trance. The curtains dance at the edge of my vision, but it's only him I see. Every line and angle of his face, each glistening bead of sweat on his brow.

I lap at his mouth like the last drop of water on earth clings there. "*Un petit peu plus . . . March, juste un tout petit peu plus.*" A little more . . . March, just a little more.

We're one breath, one groan as I claw at his lion and pant for more. There's a beautiful storm clouding my mind, a supernova hurling toward me. I can feel it electrifying my nerve endings like live wires. It's so good, so blindingly good, and so fast. I think I black out and hear myself scream his name. My entire body goes rigid against his, paralyzed by the rush of pleasure crackling in my veins.

March's arms clamp around my shoulders; he gathers me tight against his heart. Then it's a few hard, hurried thrusts that shake me like a rag doll, a mumbled, "Island... love you," and he's there, in the eye of the storm with me. He gives a single hiss as his eyes screw shut, and his jaw clenches so hard I can hear his molars grinding together. I can feel the pulse of him in me, and we're one. The room, the world, everything is alive, and bright, and shaking.

Like . . . *really* shaking. The hotel phone is rattling across my nightstand and the rest of the room is quaking ominously. Reality rips me from my post-orgasmic haze when a violent gust of wind blows into the room, strong enough to topple a small flower vase that was sitting on the desk.

March snaps out of his own sensual stupor and blinks around to assess the situation. Thankfully, the vibrations subside, replaced by the low rumble of distant thunder. Safe in the shelter of his arms, I push wayward curls from my eyes and look through the windows.

Dear Raptor Jesus who went extinct for our many sins: this is not just a storm, or even a minor earthquake. Spinning above the pyramids and whipping the palm trees outside with roaring winds is the mother of all supercells: a monster cloud stretching as far as the eye can see and flashing blue from the sheet lightning in its center.

THIRTY-SIX
AU REVOIR

"Betrayed by my own blood. *Twice.* Now, hush and walk. We will have this conversation again, young lady."

– Manila Clonk, *Clean Shot #3: The Crystal Terrorist*

"Miss Chaptal, are you seeing this?"

I barely had the time to run to the balcony before Franz called. I lean against the balcony railing and look up, the shirt I hastily shrugged on flapping in the wind.

"Yeah! That's insane! I've never seen anything like it, and the weather was just so clear an hour ago," I yell into the speaker.

Franz's reply is briefly covered by the roaring of an engine in the background. "I'm following it online! We're on our way. I hope we won't be too late. The pyramids: it can't be a coincidence. They're . . ."

his voice catches. "I think they're coming!"

I'm not sure about that part, but I stand on tiptoe to better gaze up at the supercell's majestic beauty. March's arm hooks around my waist just as fast to hold me back. "Careful, biscuit . . ." He's slipped into his jeans and came out to stare, too, at this mystery that puts his cautious and skeptical nature to the test.

"I think we're safe here," I lie, combing my hair back as the wind keeps whipping it in my eyes. In truth, if that monster moves our way there's gonna be at least a few broken windows, if not a lot worse.

"The railing," March warns, steering me back from the metal bars. He's right: the sensation is hard to pinpoint, but I can feel it, smell it in the air as it saturates with ozone and humidity. My senses feel sharper, on overload as they wait for rain and thunder to unleash over the desert.

In the speaker, Franz's voice is growing hysterical. "I think—I think I see an object on the ground! South of Menkaure! The resolution is too low on my screen—can you see it?"

Against March's safety rules, I lean again and contort to better scan the dark shape of the pyramids. Menkaure, the smallest of the three, is barely visible, shrouded in a cloud of sand lifted by the storm. "I don't know. There's too much sand . . ."

And it's getting worse: the supercell seems to be slowly lowering, swallowing Menkaure first, then Khafre as it turns into a monstrous sandstorm. March shakes his head. "It'll be here very soon; we'd better stay inside."

Indeed, the threatening wall of sand keeps growing and swelling while, above us, thunder cracks and booms as if some ancient deity meant to obliterate mankind for good. I manage to snatch a few seconds of video before March steers me back into the room and closes the window.

I can't take my eyes away. Minutes ticks by during which I stand in front of the window, gazing in fascination at the roaring clouds, until it hits. Night itself is devoured by the storm as the room turns pitch black. Sand rages and clatters against the windows, and when March turns on the light on his nightstand, it looks like the entire hotel has been plunged in deep, muddy waters.

Checking my phone, I see that Franz and I have been cut off. "I hope he's okay."

"Ain Sokhna is sixty miles away. Even if they were speeding, he's probably going to miss this 'landing,' which is for the best."

"He's going to be so pissed," I sigh, letting myself fall on the bed.

The mattress dips as March lies down at my side. He presses a kiss to my hair. "Do you want me to keep the lights on?"

"No. I kinda like this weird atmosphere. Reminds me of *The Mummy* or something."

I register the click of a switch, and the room goes so dark I can barely make out his body. Outside, the sandstorm is unleashing its fury on Cairo. Muted crashing sounds suggest that the garden and swimming pool will be a disaster zone by the time the night is over.

March's hand reaches for mine, stroking my fingers. "I still can't believe I did that," he murmurs. "I've never . . . done that."

Draped in the comfortable fog of mental and physical exhaustion, it takes me a couple seconds to process the meaning of his words. Then, I smile and squeeze his hand back. March turned thirty-four this spring, and tonight is the first time he ever made love without a condom.

I roll to my side to snuggle against him. "I'm happy," I say, the words coming muffled in his chest hair. It's no small victory that he trusted me enough to let go completely. Next thing I know, we'll be leaving our dirty dishes in the sink overnight.

Okay, maybe not.

"What's on your mind, biscuit?" March asks softly, his breath tickling my ear.

"Nothing important. What's on yours?"

His hand releases mine and creeps downward to caress my thigh. "Are you tired?"

I've already started unbuttoning my shirt by the time I reply, "I think I've just found my second wind."

It's been a very long time since my mother has held me like this. Almost twelve years. She was never a cuddler or a hugger: yet her arms now cradle me in a loose embrace as I rest on her lap, watching the turquoise sea lap at the fine sand. There's a warm breeze that doesn't stir it, as if it were only a picture.

My mother strokes my hair absently. Her light perfume surrounds me, like it used to when she was home and she'd get ready before going out. Acqua di Giò: I remember the pale green bottle with its round golden cap. Dries is sitting at their breakfast table under the shade of a palm tree. He's sipping a cup of coffee, looking pissed. For the first time since visiting them here, I notice there's nothing behind him. No road, no signs: just dunes and grass stretching forever until they bleed into the blue horizon.

"I've missed you," I tell her, rubbing my cheek against the muslin of her summer dress.

But she murmurs, "*Tu peux pas rester là éternellement.*" You can't stay here forever.

I roll to my side and smile, watching Bolino play with the tablecloth's pristine edge. "You literally took in an armadillo. And I'm your child."

She twirls her fingers in my curls with a bubbly laugh. "I never said I was a good mother."

Behind us, Dries slams his cup to the table and shoots up from his chair, his lips a grim line through his beard. "And look at the result! You brought up a hussy!"

Abandoning the comfort of mom's lap, I jump to my feet to face him. "Aw come on, really? Are we gonna fight even in my dreams?"

"For eternity!" Dries bellows. Bolino rolls away out of an abundance of caution.

"This is terrible parenting! And I would have never met March if it weren't for you! The whole thing was entirely your fault, and you get to eat Nutella on the beach!"

Behind me, mom gives a playful wince. "She's not wrong."

Dries falls back in his chair, grabs a cannolo from the table, and stuffs it in his mouth. "You're not getting my blessing."

Fighting an eye roll, I go sit across from him. "How long will I have to wait?"

"I have all the time in the world," he says between two mouthfuls.

My lips quirk in spite of my best efforts to remain stoic. "Okay, and now?"

He pours himself another cup of coffee. "Still not."

Mom pads over to him, ethereal as her pale arms wrap around his shoulders. "You're a stubborn asshole. Always been one," she coos in his ear.

He stiffens, his nostrils flaring in indignation. "*I'm* the problem? She can have any man, except that one." He points his forefinger at me. "I'd rather give you to Bolino!"

I lean back in my chair and cross my arms. "Are you done?"

My mother's face bunches in amusement as she nods and stage-whispers. "I think he is."

"What if—" My voice catches as I try to force the words past my lips. "What if I don't come back? Is that how it ends?"

His golden eyes narrow at me, kind and severe at once; my father's eyes. "Good point. Soon you'll be too busy to drop by."

My heart tightens from the diffuse dread that he might be right, that eventually I'll stop coming here and we'll have to say goodbye for good. "No . . . I didn't mean it."

Dries gets up from his chair and walks to me. He kneels by me in the sand, in a whiff of santal and cigar. "But it's true. You're going to move on, live your life. It's not good to stay stuck in the past."

My mother drifts to us and rests a cool hand on my shoulder. "You'll be fine. You know you don't need us anymore."

I want to say something, but when I look down, I realize that the table is gone. Now it's just the three of us on that beach. Night has fallen. The relentless murmur of the waves has stopped.

My gaze snaps to Dries. "Wait, wait . . . How can I move on when you won't even give me some sort of blessing? I have to stay a little longer," I plead, my voice breaking.

"Au revoir, ma chérie." *Goodbye, my dear.* My mother's hand trails in my hair one last time, then she's mist dissipating in the void.

I whirl around to catch her as she vanishes. "Mom!"

Under my feet, the sand now feels liquid, and I can feel myself start to sink, but Dries grabs my wrist and pulls me into a tight hug. I breathe him, dissect the sweet, smoky notes of the cigar and the spicy, woodsy ones of his cologne. The scent of my father. I wrap my arms around his torso and feel my entire body shake from a wave of devastating sadness, a certainty that I won't dream of him like this again. That I'll never feel my mother's touch again. I feel my face scrunch up and gasp a silent sob. My fingers dig into his jacket in a vain attempt to stop time, but it's slipping through my fingers too fast.

"I just want to stay a little longer," I beg him, blotting the tears streaming down my cheeks into his shirt.

I register a hoarse sigh and realize Dries's shoulders are shaking just like mine are, and when he replies, his voice cracks like it never has before. "You can't." He pulls away to stroke my face, but I can barely feel his touch, his warmth. He's fading away, and I can no longer make out his features. "This is goodbye, little Island," Dries murmurs. A shadow grazes my stomach, but I'm not sure it's his hand anymore. "You tell March I'll return to haunt him. Ek sal sy piel plastinate." *I will plastinate his cock.*

LEGOED TOGETHER IN ETERNITY

"Marry him."

– *Manila Clonk,* Clean Shot: A Hitman Romance

"Miss Chaptal, are you listening?"

"Uh . . . Yeah . . ." Sort of. I don't know. I've had less than four hours of a troubled sleep, and Franz's call woke me up. He's speaking too much, too fast, and I haven't had breakfast yet. I struggle to a sitting position in the empty bed, squinting blearily to locate March. There's light coming from the ajar bathroom door, and the shower is running. "Good morning," I croak.

"Good morning, biscuit," March calls from the bathroom. I hate him a little for sounding so peachy when I'm basically a crumpled, disheveled ghoul. God, mornings bring out the worst in me.

"Miss Chaptal, are you still here? I *need* you here!"

"Here . . . where?"

"At the pyramids! The landing has been confirmed!"

The room is still spinning a little as I take a sip from the glass of water on my nightstand, but when Franz's words finally hit home, my eyes pop open wide, and I jump out of bed. Holding the sheet around my body with one hand and the phone with the other, I lumber to the window. "There's a spaceship?"

"No, it's gone," Franz explains, his voice tight. He sounds like he's more tired of my bullshit than I am of his.

I shake my head as I open the window and squint against the golden glare of the sunset. "Okay, I get it. It flew away."

"I suspect the structure is a docking pod. They probably landed just long enough to refuel with some sort of . . . electric energy—possibly plasma. What we thought was a storm must have been the wind raised by their engines."

"What are you talking about?" I ask, leaning against the balcony railing. As I feared, the garden below has been devastated. The pool's water has turned brown from the sand that accumulated in it. Half of the palm trees have been felled, and tables and chairs lie scattered all the way to the strip of desert across the road.

"Do you see it?" Franz urges in the speaker.

"Um, no . . . What am I supposed to—"

"The docking pod, Miss Chaptal! The docking pod!"

As he yells this, my gaze swipes up to the pyramids, and my jaw comes unhooked. Sweet Raptor Jesus, there is . . . something at the foot of Menkaure's pyramid, a large hole in the dusty ground, almost as wide as the monument itself. "I think it's a sinkhole," I muse groggily. "The storm probably caused it."

On the other end of the line, Franz's voice has turned deadly quiet. I think it's the first time he sounds actually serious. "You can drop the act, Miss Chaptal. They contacted me an hour ago."

I keep blinking at the mysterious hole. "The aliens?"

"The Collegium! There's a lot I need to tell you, but the bottom line is this: when they realized I was getting too close to the truth, they reached out to me with an offer."

"Oh, that. Yeah, I know about it. It was Mr. Stiles, right?" I have to bite my lower lip hard not to burst out laughing.

"Yes. Do you know him? He confirmed to me that they landed last night, and he's willing to participate in an interview about the discovery of the docking pod."

A whiff of soap and citrus after-shave alerts me to March's presence. He's already dressed, his shirtsleeves carefully rolled up. His eyes light up with curiosity when he sees me on the phone, but he remains a silent spectator to our exchange as I reply to Franz. "Why do you keep calling it a docking pod? It's mostly a hole, right?"

This time, I've apparently stepped on Gualtiero Franz's last nerve. He detonates with a shout so loud I have to pull the phone away from my ear. "For God's sake, Miss Chaptal, come *here*!"

"Very funny."

My lips twitch involuntarily as March presses a button on the Mercedes's steering wheel and Billy Bragg's voice comes out of the speakers, moaning that he's waiting for the return of his flying saucer—the lyrics seem to imply that he's in a relationship with either the saucer or the alien inside it, which is all the weird I needed this morning. One of the many things March has taught me is that there is *always* a country song that fits your mood: you just need to look for it.

As the Giza complex's parking lot comes in sight, it becomes obvious that there is something to see here other than the pyramids. According to the clock on our dashboard, it's barely 6:37 am, but there's already a little crowd ambling around the site.

"Do you think it's because Franz posted stuff online?" I ask, watching a pair of young guys taking a selfie in front of the pyramid.

"Possible," March replies. "Let's see what he thinks he found this time."

I climb out of the car and follow him up a dusty trail that snakes around the complex, allowing tourists to capture the pyramids from all angles. I've been here before as a kid with my mother, but the magic still works. As March and I tread in the shadow of Cheops's pyramid, I'm reminded of Napoleon Bonaparte's famous comment that, "From the heights of these pyramids, forty centuries look down on us."

I feel like an ant, and these timeworn stones are a powerful reminder that my entire existence will be a blink in the grand scheme of things. Cheops, on the other hand, made sure mankind wouldn't forget him any time soon. Long-dead dictator: 1. Island: 0.

"The hole is over there, in front of Menkaure," I tell March as we hurry along the south side of the pyramid of Khafre, a soaring structure barely smaller than that of Cheops. The whole complex stands at the edge of the desert: the endless, flaming sky scorching a flat horizon line only serves to emphasize the dizzying immensity of the Giza plateau.

Ahead of us stands a much smaller pyramid: some researchers believe that builders ran out of space on the plateau to erect Menkaure's tomb. I say a base nearly 350 feet wide is still better than a paper casket with kittens and flowers printed on it.

"Franz is already there." March sighs as he takes in the crowd of backpacks gathered near the pyramid. A few selfie sticks are being waved around. *Aliens in Our Past*'s fans wasted no time. We stop less than fifty feet away from the buzzing throng and exchange a pained look.

"Do we elbow our way through?" I ask.

March's mouth twists in hesitation. "I'd like to think I remain above wrestling teenagers."

Just as he says this, a familiar face emerges from the crowd. Messy dark hair that sticks out in all directions, craggy beard, and weirdly intense eyes: Wilmer apparently stayed behind to help Franz. He's no longer carrying a gun, and his leather jacket has been replaced by an ΛΙΘΡ T-shirt. He motions for us to follow him.

"So, do you still work for Angel or what?" I probe, walking to him.

"No. I'm starting a new life," he grits out with his thick German accent.

March tips his head at him. "Congratulations."

I consider the news with round eyes. "And you're doing the lights, right?"

Wilmer starts shoving his way through a crowd that's 90% male and 50% under twenty. "No. I handle security."

"I think you've found your calling," March remarks when Wilmer grabs a pudgy teen who wouldn't clear the way and casually headbutts him.

I mouth an awkward "sorry" at the boy who staggers away clutching his bleeding nose.

Wilmer may have yet to entirely renounce violence, but his methods work: we made it through smoothly. My heart rate picks up as he guides us around the pyramid toward the giant sinkhole. Franz is here, commenting the phenomenon in front of a new cameraman— a young woman with a pink headscarf who seems more legit than Sonny. She trails after him as he gesticulates at the hole and rolls enthusiastic eyes at the camera on her shoulder.

When he sees us, Franz freezes and waves his arms. "Miss Chaptal! Over here, quick!" He turns to a new production assistant, a sinewy guy with cargo pants and sharp green eyes—that one has Lion written all over him. "Nick, give her the hat."

The guy kneels down to rummage in a pile of bags and cases. From one of them, he retrieves a brown fedora. He walks up to me and drops it on my head before I've had a chance to protest.

His angular features crack into an unexpected grin. "Make us look good, Miss Chaptal. A lot of us are gonna tune in for that special."

March's lips quirk in response. Nick may not be South African—I can't quite place his faint accent—but he's definitely a Lion.

"Come here. Come," Franz asks impatiently.

Sending one last glance at March over my shoulder, I trot to the hole before the eager eyes of Franz's audience. As I'm getting closer, I realize that it is deeper than it appeared from my balcony earlier this morning. The perimeter has already been secured with some haphazardly placed yellow tape. A pair of police officers watch the fuss from afar, looking indifferent to this surge of alien fever.

"It's beautiful," Franz says huskily.

I take a few more steps, as close as the tape will allow, and peek down the hole. I glimpse something dark and feel my stomach lurch as a brief spell of vertigo overtakes me. Seeing me wobble, March lunges toward me, and stops in his turn, his eyes wide.

It's not a docking pod, that much is certain. But Gualtiero found something big at last—I'd say at least 400 feet wide, maybe 500. Revealed by last night's sandstorm is one half of a gigantic disc of black granite, engraved in tight concentric circles with ancient symbols. It's still half-buried under a layer of gravel and dust, but if that thing is intact, it's actually larger than Menkaure's pyramid. As for its height: I dare not speculate. Judging by the emerging part, it's at the very least two feet thick.

"Is it Egyptian?" March asks, unable to conceal the amazement in his voice.

"Obviously not," Franz retorts as he joins us.

"Those aren't hieroglyphs," I concur, barely aware of the camera's eye on me. "It looks like . . . Phoenician, or Etruscan." I can't take my eyes off that disc, but the more I gaze at it, the more I feel queasy, as if the characters were spinning. Maybe I shouldn't have eaten so much Panda cheese for breakfast.

When my ears start buzzing, I step back, brushing a hand over my chest.

"Are you alright?" March asks, a wrinkle of concern between his eyebrows.

"Yeah, just a little dizzy."

"It must be the electromagnetic field," Franz says, patting his midriff. "I felt a little nauseous when I first arrived this morning. This type of alien equipment generally emits strong magnetic fields, which can affect electrosensitive individuals."

A camera flashes behind us; its owner doesn't seem to mind that a considerable amount of pseudo-science has just been recorded for posterity.

I brace myself for Franz's fury as I say, "I don't think . . . I mean there's no clear evidence yet that aliens used it to land a spaceship."

"The blast from the engines unearthed it! We all saw it!"

"It was a supercell," I counter.

"Let's not lie to ourselves, Miss Chaptal. Last night was a verified sighting. And this," he points to the granite disc, "matches a recent archeological find in Rome. A similar disc, much smaller in size, but bearing the *same* alphabet. Do you believe it's a coincidence that two of the most advanced ancient civilizations produced similar artifacts, both located in zones of intense electromagnetic activity?"

I cringe. "Um, it's just how granite works. It naturally emits low electromagnetic radiations."

"Which is why they used it to build their docking pods!" Franz exults.

I'm debating the merit of pursuing this line of conversation when I catch a flash of orange among the crowd. A cat's fur. "Excuse me for a minute, please," I tell Franz before slipping away with March on my heels.

My eyes didn't betray me. Leaning against an old wall of sun-bleached rocks, Stiles is pointing to the pyramid of Khafre, showing it to Ron, his favorite cat.

"I doubt he cares," March says coolly.

Stiles waves happily, flashing me the kind of innocent grin I fell for a long time ago. "You'd be surprised. He's very curious." He strokes the feline's fur while it studies us through changing turquoise eyes.

"Are you seriously doing Franz's documentary?" I ask, removing the fedora. I fear it's too big for me, in every sense of the term.

"Silhouette only. They're gonna give me a chipmunk voice," he confirms.

His lips a thin line, March looks almost offended by the notion that Stiles might spare some time in his life to have fun. I, on the other, find myself smiling at his antics. "You're hopeless."

There's a knowing glint in his eyes as he replies, "But I'm your hopeless friend."

I shake my head; he never gives up. "Not really. You don't get human feelings at all. You might as well be one of Franz's aliens."

He looks down at Ron, then smiles up at me. "We're willing to educate ourselves. Where do we start?"

I'm about to reply when March steps between us. He levels a hard gaze at Stiles, tempered by some new level of understanding. I think he gets it at last: Stiles is a total asswipe, but when he says it's not personal, he means it. There's a whole chunk of humanity he's missing, and I have no idea how—or if—he's ever going to catch up with the rest of us.

March crosses his arms, tilts his head at him, and asks: "Have you read Accidentally Married to the Billionaire Sheikh?"

"It's not gonna work," I predict as we return to our car. "Knowing Stiles, he's going to root for Djahkobh."

"I expect he will," March agrees. "But perhaps he'll learn something from Djahkobh's downfall."

I grimace. "That you should always make sure she drank the roofie?"

March's shoulders shake as he indulges in deep, rich laughter I wish I heard more often. "Among other things."

As March reaches for the driver's door, I hop at his side. "Can I? I've never driven in the desert. I kinda want to make my Indiana Jones moment last."

"Certainly." He winks at me before he goes around and climbs in the passenger seat.

"Have you ever been to Legoland?" I ask out of the blue, adjusting the seat. Dammit, he's tall.

Random as I may sometimes sound, there's always a (convoluted) thread to my thoughts. Because March knows this, he turns in his seat and considers me with curious blue eyes. "I haven't had that pleasure, but I'd be happy to take you for a belated birthday celebration."

"There's one in California," I note, my heart drumming steadily in my chest.

Two dimples appear in his cheeks. "I see you've investigated the matter already."

I relax my shoulders and draw a slow breath. "Their website says that if you have a license, you can book a wedding package and get married by a giant Lego."

There's a sapphire gleam in his eyes that I'll never get enough of. "Your father would kill me—or at the very least sever our LinkedIn connection."

He's right. That LinkedIn invite was the pinnacle of my dad's efforts to accept March in his life, a reluctant offering of peace after a particularly strained Christmas dinner. I ponder this, watching the sun rise over Cairo, and eventually hold out my upturned palm. "Can I borrow your sunglasses? Road safety first." Wouldn't want to hit a sloth on our way back . . .

The smile never leaves March's lips as he takes out his aviators from his breast pocket and gives them to me. They're a little too big for me, even after I push them higher on my nose: a quick check in the mirror confirms that I look like a bug.

My gaze cuts to the Alexandrite gleaming green and blue on my ring finger as sunlight plays with it. "Kalahari will have your head if you marry in secret, and Joy has been planning my bachelorette party for years. Plus, gram thinks we're eventually gonna marry in church, and she'll make Jell-O salads and bologna cake for the guests," I remark, my thumbs rapping on the wheel.

My grandma plays in Angel's league where our Lord is concerned—she erects a giant inflatable Jesus on her lawn for Christmas every year, despite the many complaints of her chic neighborhood. While I have no intention of walking down the proverbial aisle and listening to a religious sermon on the biggest day of my life, I didn't dare to pop her bubble when she shared her grandiose Jell-O plans with me and flipped out a yellowed recipe book.

March's shoulders jerk in the faintest shrug. "I can't say I look forward to being the center of so much attention, but we can always organize a small ceremony later, for the benefit of friends and family." His voice softens as he searches my gaze behind the aviators. "What do *you* want?"

I bite my lower lip, give up: there's no fighting the grin tugging at my cheeks. "I want to be with you. Just you." March's features light up with a rare grin of his own as I add, "And I want to be married by a giant Lego."

He gives a firm nod and fastens his seatbelt. "Very well, Miss Chaptal. California it is."

Later. Later, down this highway to hell, there'll be time to face my dad's meltdown, my gram's mini salmon aspics, and Joy's plans to take me to a male strip club. But for now, I turn on the ignition, hit the gas, and raise a victorious fist. "To Legoland and beyond!"

HAVE YOU READ THE PREVIOUS TITLES IN THE SPOTLESS SERIES?

Island Chaptal—nerdy IT engineer by day, romance novel junkie by night—just walked into her messy New York apartment to find Mr. Right waiting for her. No, wait...Mr. Clean.

In a fresh, witty series that blends fast-moving action with romantic suspense, a romance book–addicted computer engineer and a charming, cleaning-obsessed professional killer team up to take on the bad guys...and forge a highly unconventional working relationship. With a splash of James Bond's sophistication and a heaping helping of Stephanie Plum's spunkiness, Camilla Monk's *Spotless* series combines high stakes and plenty of humor with lushly exotic settings and a funny, relatable heroine readers can't help but cheer for.

ACKNOWLEDGMENTS

I owe a debt of gratitude to Tiffany Yates Martin for editing the Spotless series and making it what it is, and to B. who's always here for me. More thanks go to Regina Dowling and Mitzi Carroll for putting their eagle eye in the service of copy-editing and proofreading this book, and to Cindy du Plessis for correcting my broken Afrikaans.

But most of all, thank you, reader, for sticking with me for five books. You have filled my life with joy.

ABOUT THE AUTHOR

Camilla Monk is a French native who grew up in a Franco-American family. After studying business in Paris, she taught English and French in Tokyo before returning to France to work in digital advertising. A self-taught programmer, she spent ten years building rickety websites for financial companies, before publishing Spotless, her debut novel.

Camilla is now a full-time writer and lives in Montreal, where she keeps a close watch on the squirrels and complains on a daily basis about the egregious number of Tim Hortons.

For more (questionably useful) information, visit:

www.ingramcontent.com/pod-product-compliance
Lightning Source LLC
Chambersburg PA
CBHW021230060726
47590CB00005B/1704